VESSLE *swept gloriously along the waterfront* — Chapter II

# ULTIMATE
# VOYAGE

# ULTIMATE

## A Book of Five Mariners

SHAMBHALA
*Boston & London*
MCMXCVIII

# VOYAGE

*Written & illustrated by*

## WILLIAM GILKERSON

SHAMBHALA PUBLICATIONS, INC.
Horticultural Hall
300 Massachusetts Avenue
Boston, Massachusetts 02115
*http://www.shambhala.com*

9  8  7  6  5  4  3  2  1

FIRST EDITION
*Printed in the United States of America*
♾ This edition is printed on acid-free paper that meets the
American National Standards Institute z39.48 Standard.
Distributed in the United States by Random House, Inc.,
and in Canada by Random House of Canada Ltd.

LIBRARY OF CONGRESS CATALOGING-IN-PUBLICATION DATA

Gilkerson, William.
Ultimate voyage: a book of five mariners/William Gilkerson.–1st ed.
p.   cm.
ISBN 1-57062-364-3 (acid-free paper)
I. Title.
PS3557.I3672U45   1998        98-9959
813'.54–dc21              CIP

*Dedicated to my root teacher, Lord Mukpo—who assigned this project to me in 1975—and to the earlier mentors whose teachings enabled its fulfillment: Blandford Jennings and Paul Erling Johnson.*

# THE CHAPTERS

# ULTIMATE VOYAGE

# I  The Port

URING THE WEEKS of spring, an early morning breeze off the ocean could usually be relied upon to move the Port's water traffic about its business. When this pattern failed on the first day of May, the fishermen and wherrymen of the place spent the morning mending nets and sails, reckoning that the afternoon would bring the sea breeze. But it did not. Nor did it the following day, nor the one after that, and those boatmen who needed to go somewhere were forced to row under an unnaturally hot sun, sweating, whistling for a breeze, and cursing the gods. Ashore, the heat and smells of the town gathered in its narrow streets, and in the anchorage, the great ships that were full of cargo and ready for sea floated with slack anchor lines on the glassy water. After four days, a delegation of frustrated mariners went up the hill to consult with the wise man of the place, the ancient seer whose predictions could usually be counted on.

"What has happened to the wind?" they asked.

"It has stopped," he answered.

"When will it start?" they asked.

"When it rains red frogs," said the wise one, adding, " . . . if it is the beginning of the prophecy." Then he refused to say anything more about it, and the mariners went back down the hill with the feeling of knowing less than they had before.

The unnatural calm prevailed until, on the fifth day, a breath of air came from the south. First to feel it were the deepest-draft vessels, those anchored farthest out in the harbor. In the well-defined hierarchy of the Port's shipping, these were the aristocrats, the carved, gilded three-masted ships with round basket tops at their mast doublings, like coronets. The breeze was barely a movement of air at first, but accompanying it was a small swell that entered the approaches, making the gentry curtsy and dip politely to one another as they stretched their anchor lines.

The grateful boatmen plying the outer harbor in their small craft shipped their oars and hoisted sail to take advantage of the welcome movement of air that breathed next into the inner waters, meeting the bourgeoisie of the Port, the pudgy coastal craft. These were tied up in pairs, as though married. The workaday lot of these vessels was to ply back and forth between the Port and other nearby places, generally carrying the same things outbound that they had carried the trip before and the one before that–a respectable, hardworking group, with a minimum of decoration. Their place was along the shallow south end of the main wharf, where they could ground and snooze when the tide went out. The tide was out when the first swells rolled in.

Next to feel the air stir were the fishing smacks, plebeians with long bowsprits taken inboard as they clustered chaotically in the tenement north harbor (where there was never room for even one more of them, except when another one came and elbowed its way into the crowd). As first the breeze and then the swell entered the cluttered harbor, the little craft shouldered and rumped one another rudely, setting up a chat and fuss. The fishermen ceased their mending of nets, halted their arguments, and squinted into the sky.

On the breeze, the odors that had accumulated over the fish wharf for days were blown past the time-blackened castle and into the open windows of venerable stone buildings, the Port's mighty mercantile houses. Entering their chambers, the rank air lifted a few pieces of parchment, wrinkled a nose or two, and rearranged the dust of generations only slightly. Beyond, whispers of breeze played into the narrow streets leading off from the main wharf, quickening through the lanes and alleys of the quarter catering mostly to sailors. A whisk of breeze scattered a neat pile of floor sweepings in a tavern door just as the taverner's pregnant wife was preparing to broom them into the street. "Oh!" she said, having felt at that exact moment her first labor pain.

Behind the Old City were the neighborhoods of the fishing folk and watermen. Humble but tidy, all of these houses had entryways facing the street. Once each week (or more often in special circumstances), all of the wives of the neighborhood emerged with buckets, as by signal, and scrubbed their steps. During that scrubbing, much of the Port's information was exchanged from house to house. Such a ritual was in progress when the breeze played past, stirring the good wives' laundry hung to dry on lines between the houses. The streets in front of these houses were narrow and guttered on each side to carry away the rainwater–along with horse droppings, sewage, and garbage–into the fishing harbor, where whatever was left of it would float, swinging with the tides until it sank or drifted to sea. Looking up, some of the sea-wise women noticed a slight diffusion of light in the sky directly overhead.

Where the hill steepened away from the water, a market street scissored the fishermen from the next neighborhood up, that of the coastal seafarers, whose tall stone buildings had slate roofs and housed a number of families each. Here dwelt the warrant officers, coopers, carpenters, boatswains, sailmakers, gunners, and other specialists. Higher up the hill lived the mates and masters, as well as the naval officers, many of whom at that time of the long prevailing peace were leading lives of involuntary retirement. Feeling the air stir, an unemployed Captain looked up from his parchment, saw in the diffusion of light an unfamiliar phenomenon, and searched the sky for its cause. At that moment, however, he was distracted by a summons from his wife. As he left the window, the breath of wind made the laundry flap in back of the house.

The wind gained strength as it climbed, setting the treetops astir on the hill's upper slopes, where the streets were broader, the sewers were underground, and the houses sat back a distance from the street. Here dwelled the patriarch merchant Captains of the Port, men who had made their fortunes, bought ships of their own, and moved ashore to spend their autumn years nursing their gout and watching their gardens grow. The wind, puffing in over a garden wall, took the straw hat off one such septuagenarian as he was strolling with his daughter.

"Aha," he said, and then, as he squinted at the diffusing light overhead, "hmmmm."

"Ohhh," said his pregnant daughter, for quite a different reason.

"There, there," the old gentleman said, patting her hand. As he reached to pick up his hat, however, the wind took it again, this time whipping it right over the wall and away. Poised on the updraft, the hat soared higher, to the very crest of the hill, where it lodged among the branches of a pasture oak. Here were the farmlands of a feudal estate, with acreage following the crest of the hill in its long arc across the base of the peninsula embracing the harbor. Below, to the south, spread the city and the sea; beyond the wall to the north were the farmlands, fens, and forests of the inland valley. The hub of the estate was the original small fortress that had guarded the land approaches to the city in olden times. Now, the ancient structure was enclosed by the township that had grown up around it. Its squat towers were visible above the surrounding roofs, and from the top of its flagstaff–the highest man-made object within view–its pendant was blowing straight out from the pole, snapping in the freshening gale.

From an upper window of the Manor, the Master of the estate viewed first the horizon and then the general bustle that was breaking out below. He saw a darkening sky through which the sun was still visible, but only as a red orb in the thickening atmosphere. He heard windows being slammed closed. A kitchen door banged open, spewing out cooks and varlets in a billow of smoke from a backdrafting chimney. Ordinarily, the Master would have been instantly responsive to any threat to his estate, but he remained in the bedchamber, where a more important event was in progress. He judged what was happening outside to be a freak squall that would soon pass.

It did not. It did change its direction, however, going abruptly into the western quadrant, whence it blew with still more strength. Down in the harbor approaches, small craft scudded for shelter while crews of anchored vessels struggled to set second anchors. Within a turn of the glass, most of the small sailing boats had found protection and all of the larger craft had been secured, but before anyone had a chance to go below and take shelter from the gale, the wind stopped entirely for a few moments, then struck again with even greater vigor, this time directly out of the north.

The gale now roared down between the flanking hills as though poured from a scoop, everywhere returning laundry it had earlier taken away. Hanging shop signs swung wildly on their support chains. The heavy wooden sign of the taverner was torn from its rod and sent careening down the street, just one object among a general swirl of debris. Overhead, the darkness had deepened and expanded to swallow the horizon, making the day like night. The taverner chinked the spaces around the bedchamber door to keep the draft from blowing out the candles. Light was needed there for the midwife.

Aboard the ships, every aspect of the wind's wild behavior was gauged by all, and two things were plain to see: the force of the wind was still strengthening, and its eye was continuing to veer from north to east. Then everything was blotted out by the gathering gloom until—all later agreed—there came total darkness. At the time the wind touched east on its clock, a single lightning bolt split the sky, brilliantly illuminating the entire Port, both dazzling and deafening it with a thunderclap, like the salute from a thousand cannons. Even the wind seemed stunned by the blast, as though waiting with everybody else for the next bolt. But there was only one.

It was at once followed by rain in a solid deluge. Rivulets at the crest of the hill became rushing streams, feeding the creeks; all the sewers and gutters got the scouring of their lives; water poured through holes in wind-damaged roofs in streams, through blown-out windows, under doorjambs, around casings. Like the wind before it, there was simply too much to keep out. In falling, however, the rain bled the sky of its darkness. A milky light began to radiate; the roar of water eased to a murmur and then stopped entirely just as the sun emerged with an orbital rainbow. The wind had veered to south and diminished to the ordinary seasonal breeze. Water dripped and gutters still spouted, feeding puddles in which were found thousands of tiny red frogs.

Their portent, or the prophecy to which the ancient seer had referred, was never learned, for sometime during the storm, his heart stopped. Miraculously, there were no other fatalities or even serious injuries, although several vessels were found to have dragged their anchors, and there was a good deal of damage to roofs and fences. To everybody's amazement, there was no evidence at all as to where the terrific lightning bolt had struck. The taverner (whose sign was found four blocks away) thought his own establishment had been struck by the blast, but he had been unable to spare it further thought because in that instant the head of his infant son abruptly appeared, and a moment later the rest of the child followed, kicking, squirming, and roaring.

He was one of five infants who had been simultaneously launched by the same thunderbolt. The wife of the naval officer was attended by a physician, who removed the infant from the mother's womb surgically, in order to preserve both their lives. The father, acting as the surgeon's assistant, saw in the white glare of the lightning the startled, wide-open eyes of his new son emerging from the bloody womb. Up the hill, the retired gentleman who had lost his hat acquired a grandson, who came out in the normal fashion. The midwife and her attendants were all impressed with the great beauty of the little boy. In the Manor attached to the castle at the crest of the hill was born the seventh son of the Master and Mistress of the estate, a remarkably fat baby who emerged by the breech and with his mouth open, as though demanding the nourishment he instantly received.

And there was a fifth birth as well, although it was more mysterious. In the immediate aftermath of the storm, a newborn infant was found in the very middle of the city square. The square had been scoured of anything movable by wind and water, but there on the cobbles was a clean, dry fishbasket containing a boy-child whose umbilical cord had been tied and who had been washed and diapered and blanketed and somehow left in the most public and open place by somebody whom nobody saw, although all were looking out their windows. The infant was quite well and apparently content, for he cried not at all, then or later. His appearance was one of the great mysteries connected to the storm.

T HE SON BORN to the taverner and his wife immediately distin-
guished himself by his activity. When awake, the child grasped
for anything within reach, kicking his bedding and all else
around him into continual disarray. When he cried, his bellowings
were audible all through the tavern. As soon as he was able to crawl–
which was very soon–he wanted to be everywhere and was constantly
underfoot. In what seemed no time, he was standing and walking, to
the great delight of his proud father and to the dismay of his mother,
who found herself moving all breakable objects out of reach. Walking
was soon followed by climbing–a climbing so vigorous that a kind of
harness and leash arrangement had to be devised to keep him safely
grounded. Even this didn't restrain him for long. One morning, he was
found standing on the ledge of an upper window, holding onto nothing, leaning slightly outward to get a better view of the street traffic
three stories below. His horrified mother snatched him back inside
and collapsed in a chair.

He started work early on–carrying wood for the fires, running here
and there delivering everybody's messages, wiping tables, and making
himself available for whatever was needed. He soon became a small-
time but zealous entrepreneur. Nothing deflected him from his purpose, which actually was a lot of different purposes at any moment,
making his movements appear erratic. On a typical errand into the
streets with, for example, a simple message from the taverner to the
brewer, the lad would run along a route that took him past the cooper-

age, upon which he kept a constant eye because the cooper paid a penny to sweep his shop and hired whoever was at hand when the moment arrived for the job to be done. That happened, the boy observed, when the shavings were about ankle-deep, which was when he had to be there.

From there, he might check one or two other situations not necessarily on his direct path, but he would always fulfil his mission in good enough time to permit a detour to the riggers' wharf. If he was lucky, he might be given something to take aloft to somebody working up a mast. He loved to climb the rigging. He was lithe, muscular for his age, fast of foot, and fast of mind. He took life seriously and had advice for everybody, even the professionals for whom he worked, most of whom were amused by his presumptuous self-confidence and liked his ambition.

"That's good knotwork," he once told one of the Port's master riggers.

"It fair makes my afternoon to learn it meets your good approval, young sir," the veteran replied. The irony was lost on the boy, who was already on his way somewhere else. His ambition and activity seemed limitless; the wind upon which he had been born seemed to attend him.

UP THE HILL, the weanling son of the naval Captain was also a precocious crawler. Whereas the taverner's boy was inclined in the upward direction, however, the Captain's child had a focus that seemed to lead always down. When down was not available, sideways would do.

"If you take your eyes off that child for one moment, he just vanishes," his mother exclaimed, searching the house for her prodigal infant for what seemed the hundredth time that day. She finally located him at the very back of a seldom-used storage chamber, where he was trying to force his way through a pile of old boxes to find out what was behind them. "Do you have to get to the bottom of *everything*?"

After he learned to walk, this same curiosity fixed itself on the vast world outside the house. One day, he found he was able to drag his tiny stool to the front door, stand on it, and reach the door latch. Doing so, he opened the latch, opened the door, got down off the stool, and went out into the street, which went uphill in one direction and downhill in the other. Unhesitatingly, he toddled off down the hill. He came to the busy market street, crossed it, and proceeded ever downward, like water, through the neighborhood of the fishermen and into the narrow alleys of the Old City. It was later determined that he had navigated through the entire Street of Taverns, somehow avoiding stepping on any of the shards of broken glass that always littered that place; crossed the quay; and negotiated the obstacles and traffic on the long wharf all the way to its end, where he was at last spotted as he was starting down a perilous ladder toward the deck of a barge tied up below.

He soon revealed an academic turn of mind that was his father's delight. The Captain, an avid scholar, put simple arithmetic into him before the child was even able to talk. When he did talk, he said little, then as ever. By age five, he was master of the small magnetic compass that he had been given; by six, he had been initiated into the mysteries of the constellations; and at age seven, he was an experienced navigator who had with his father threaded, by small boat in fogs, through the narrow and dangerous off-lying sandbanks.

"There's always a riddle to the sands," his father told him, squinting into the binnacle, consulting wet charts, and turning the minuteglass. "You've got to see things as they are, son," he added, the fog condensation dripping from his beard and nose. "It's everything in this work."

At home, it was navigational tables, mathematics, and the physical sciences, all subjects in which the Captain had ample time to keep up with the latest discoveries because of his unemployment during those years. He easily could have obtained command of a merchant ship, but he was a navy man at root, knew it, and would have nothing else but a worthy warship. He had served gallantly in the last war, leading a squadron during an important fleet action. Ironically, the consequences of the victory had led to the long period of almost complete peacetime. He retained his contacts among his fellow officers—most of whom shared his situation—and patiently awaited his opportunities. While waiting, he occupied his time with a full schedule of navigational instruction rendered daily to the often deaf ears of youthful classes in the training, as the Port's unique system of schooling was called. Besides teaching, he was researching a detailed naval history of the Port. He worked on this for precisely four hours each day, and the remainder of his time he spent with family, his wife–a straight-backed lady with a quarterdeck authority of her own–and his son, to whom he taught not only philosophy and mathematics but also fencing.

"Handle the sword not too tightly, not too lightly; don't hack–give point. Straight thrusts. Follow form, keep your balance. Faster. Don't think about it, just *do* it."

If there was anything the boy found difficult, it was *not* thinking about things, for he brought his analytical powers to bear on everything, including even such mundane lessons as the basic service disciplines of neatness, punctuality, and respectfulness, as well as how to sew on one's own buttons.

His father's questions came like surprise shots from a swivel cannon: "What's an *offing*, lad? By the book, mind."

"Aye, sir. *Offing:* that is, fromward the shore, or out into the sea; as 'the ship stands for the offing'–that is, sails from the shore into the sea. When a ship keeps the middle of the channel, and comes not near the shore, she is said to keep in the *offing,* sir."

Or on a broader theme: "What's the most important thing always?"

"Sir. To see things as they are. The *truth* of it, sir."

"Well spoken, boy."

The boy had eyes as round as an owl's, eyes that first viewed the world as a stab of lightning. They seemed even bigger than they were because his face and all the rest of him were thin. He had pale, wispy hair and the particular kind of fair complexion that does not take the sun well. His fingers were long and bony, with conspicuous knuckles, which, when he was upset about anything, he would pull on until they popped. He was a seemingly shy child, seldom with much to say. When he did speak, he chose his words for economy and clarity. His natural reserve and cool eye made him an odd child, even an uncomfortable one. The lad was endlessly curious about everything, however, and by his eighth year, he had read nearly every book he could get his hands on.

THE LITTLE BOY born to the daughter of the retired shipowner was, from the first, an ornament unto the world, and he was worn by his mother as such. He was all she now had, having lost her husband to the sea at the same time her father had lost one of his ships. Her father was long a widower, so they now had only each other and this dazzling new sun around which all household systems and servants at once took orbit. The sun child's every need was catered to as if he were a god, and from his god realm, he obliged them not only with his sheer beauty but with a far less definable personal magnetism. He liked to sing and draw, and especially to tell stories, which he could act out. At an early age, the boy could invent narratives out of the merest cobweb of thought. One day when he had been prattling on and strutting before a select audience of his mother's friends, he was so swept away by himself he forgot the thread of the story he was inventing. "To be continued," he said at once, and then made his little bows, exiting to the enthusiastic applause of all, and returning to make more bows, quite a few of them.

"You are my life," his mother told him when her friends had left. Kneeling to bring her face level with his, she took his hands in hers and gazed at him with eyes that were wells of love. He could not look directly into them for fear of drowning.

For his seventh birthday he was presented with a boy's lute, which he loved, and he was made to take formal lessons on it, which he hated. He enjoyed strumming and improvising, but he would not have bothered with the tuning of it, or the learning of scales, had those disciplines not been imposed upon him. He especially loved to dress up. His favorite holidays were costumed events. His mother was always at his service as seamstress and wardrobe attendant. He spent so much time in front of the mirror that his grandfather took note of it, not unhumorously.

"Well, lad, and how do you look to yourself today?" the old man would ask. He judged that when the boy joined the training, any sissified notions he might have taken on would be dispelled. He saw his grandson as a fearless performer who would weather the world well enough without his mother when the time came. Or so he hoped.

THE NOBLE INFANT born to the Mistress of the Master's estate entered a house inhabited by a host of first and second cousins, aunts, uncles, grandparents, some dozens of ghosts, and six brothers, all descended from the same ancient dynasty that had once ruled the surrounding lands. Many generations before, the last of the family's ancestral kings had wearied of the ceaseless wars and disputes with which he had always to deal, and so, in a masterly diplomatic stroke, he had abdicated the throne, retaining by treaty this family estate with its lands and castle and titles. Like this well-remembered forebear, his descendant had amassed an immeasurable fortune, which he shared, in one way or another, with just about everybody. The secrets and techniques that he used to make his money were the subjects of endless speculation, although many times he had repeated truthfully the only thing he could think of to say on the subject, to his children and anybody else who cared to listen: "You get back what you give out."

He was called simply the Master, because that was less burdensome than any of his many other titles. His hilltop house and its adjoining buildings had long ago expanded beyond the original fortified Manor house they surrounded. They had been added onto until the appendages, too, had sprouted appendages, as the fertile family continued to enlarge, along with its corps of retainers and supernumeraries. Surrounding the meandering main house were cottages, barns, stables, carriage houses, a mews, poultry houses, granaries, a brewery—indeed, a town. Quartered throughout the corporation of structures that was modestly called the House were chambermaids, nannies, nurses, housemen, cooks, varlets, assistant cooks, scullery maids, two barbers, an herbal doctor who was also Pursuivant of Arms, two bagpipers, a drummer, the entire cleaning staff, a variety of personal family attendants, various stewards, a Major and Mrs. Domo, one resident astrologer, and a battery of accountants, scribes, valets, and secretaries to the Master. In addition, there was an itinerant population of visitors and guests, guests of guests, tradesmen, tutors, petitioners, supplicants, itinerant merchants, the entire membership of the Collectors' Guild, peddlers, and diverse others too numerous to list.

Such a general mingle existed that it was possible for a complete stranger to walk in, keeping company with others who had business there, then find his way to one kitchen or another as though he belonged, and eat and drink his fill. This happened not infrequently, and, indeed there were usually living in the complex a handful of people who had simply strolled in, found a niche for themselves somewhere, and stayed on. Some had managed to incorporate themselves permanently and usefully into the community.

Surveying his domain, the Master inhaled the bustle and humanity with infinite tolerance for the controlled chaos of it all, and he loved that it was all his. He took great pride not only in his own burgeoning family–especially his newest son–but in all his people, very much including the servants. To an outsider's eye, it was difficult to distinguish members of the family from the servants, except on ceremonial occasions when the Master and his family wore the Royal purple.

If the Master hosted an intimate supper only for kin and close friends (say, thirty or forty people), the family then dined in the main hall, where no servants supped. Otherwise, it was customary for all to dine at the great tables in the largest of the kitchens, a hall in itself, the common room for gentry and servants alike, as well as various dogs and puppies, cats and kittens, caged parakeets and canaries, a 350-year-old tortoise, a colony of silkworms in a jug, six gerbils, a chained monkey, a dozen colorful fish in a specially made aquarium (which had to be aerated constantly by means of a hand pump fabricated from wood and leather), a pet raccoon who regularly rifled everybody's pockets, and a blind raven who had been living in the rafters since anybody could remember. The new infant's first memory was of this kitchen.

All of the neighbors with adjacent properties had standing invitations to drop by anytime they wanted to and have a bit of roast and a tankard of ale or a goblet of hock, a beaker of hot buttered rum, an ewer of small beer made on the premises, or a tumbler of gin. There were all kinds of libations from jugs, firkins, runlets, costrels, pipes, hogsheads, ankers, butts, kilderkins, kegs, puncheons, barrels, and bottles, many with unreadable labels or no labels at all.

It was considered a harmless eccentricity on the part of the Master that, of all of the containers in their endless variety, he wanted at least two specimens of each to be saved when emptied, for he had a collector's interest in them. Toward that end, the old armory had been given to storage space, as had several dozen cellars filled with all manner of empty containers, from floor to ceiling and wall to wall, as well as a number of the garrets and attics, not to mention some closets and pantries. In response to a complaint from his wife that the place was running out of storage space for other things, the Master had an entire new structure built on the grounds to accommodate the collection, which pleased everybody except the spiders, silverfish, mice, stoats, shrews, cockroaches, squirrels, garden snakes, wasps, and feral cats that were displaced from their homes by the move.

The Master solved quarrels and adjudicated most family disputes. He took a hand in Port and provincial politics and commanded the movements of scores of individual ships with their men and cargoes, yet he could pop up anywhere. His interest in even trivial things going on around him kept him well in touch with his universe. Within a year of his son's birth, it became apparent that, of all the seven sons, the youngest bore the strongest resemblance to the father. So remarkable was the similarity, it acted to the confusion of the boy's paternal grandmother, an otherwise alert old lady who became addled in her head when she saw him, thinking he was the father somehow back to that age again. Alone among the brothers, he was a true companion to his father. From the moment he could toddle, he tried to follow the Master everywhere, and often enough he would be taken along on the big fellow's shoulder. Later, he followed on his own two feet, and by the time he was eight years old, on horseback; his company was never rejected by his father at any time. "Come along, son," he would say.

One of the places they went most often was the great kitchen, for the Master was a talented amateur chef who took a daily interest in the menus of the establishment. Sometimes, he would dally over the preparation of some dish; other times, he would merely pass through, stopping only long enough to taste the soup of the day. When this happened, the cook on duty stood by respectfully while the Master spooned up a bit and tasted it, making little smacking noises. Always he would then hand the spoon to the boy. "Here, taste this, and let's have your opinion on it." It was a test there was no getting out of, for the lad was then expected to make some intelligent comment.

The Master worked endlessly with his youngest son, seeing in him the same near-legendary qualities that had caused their revered ancestor to renounce all personal ambition, starting with his own crown, adopting as his family motto:

### IN NOTHINGNESS IS ALL

On his boy's seventh birthday, the Master gave him a gold ring inscribed with the seal bearing that legend, although he was unable to explain its meaning. The words were considered by all to be a great puzzle, although they were high-sounding enough to command everybody's respect.

As to the surprise child discovered in the basket in the space of the city square, he was cared for by the fisherfolk who had found him. For a time. When it became apparent there was nobody to attach him to, they discussed what to do with him. None of the good wives who had shared the duties of nurturing and tending him felt compelled to keep him.

"You're a good wee one," he was told by the first woman who gave him suck, "an' there's nowt wrong wi' your appetite, but luv, why can't ye cry?"

Besides their unease over the portent of a baby who never cried, they were poor enough without taking in another belly to feed and another body to tend. Nevertheless, they wanted to do their best to pass the foundling into the most favorable situation they could think of. Reasoning there was only one facility that could absorb and nourish him in a proper way, three fishwives took him up the hill to the kitchen door of the Master's house.

"Poor wee thing is an orphink," they explained to the gaping churl who opened the door. He immediately got a house carl to come over and talk to them, and that person fetched the head cook. The head cook sent a valet to call a steward, at the same time ushering in the wives. The steward immediately sent a chambermaid to fetch Mrs. Major Domo, who came at once, followed by the head housekeeper, by which time others had gathered to see the foundling in his sky-blue blanket. The source of all the fuss looked back at them with wide eyes. Eventually, a page was sent to the House Mistress with a message for Milady herself, whose arrival coincided with that of the Master, and the wives pleaded their case for the foundling yet again.

". . . An' 'e *never* cries," concluded a fishwife as she displayed the child, holding him high so all could see it was true.

The Master had only recently been puzzling over how to have fewer mouths to feed. His brow wrinkled as he contemplated the small reversal being offered.

"He could be sent to the priests," suggested a counselor.

"Nay, let's not wish that on him," said the Master. "Let him stay."

So the foundling was passed over to a clucking nicety of nurses, who carried him away. In truth, one child more or less was scarcely noticed in that place, and the new person was never troublesome. Whereas the other infants in the nursery had to be watched with a close eye, he was largely self-tending. When put in a place on the floor, he could generally be relied upon to stay there. If another child snatched his toy away, he never made complaint or provocation, the lack of which was his main contribution. He came in for his share of the outrages that his playmates zealously inflicted upon one another, but without a murmur he survived onslaughts that would have raised shrieks and screams from any of the others. His nurses and nannies, and later his teachers, praised his equanimity, which they held as an example to their rowdier wards.

He grew into a heavyset young fellow, with short, thick legs, solid as stumps; so large were his feet, he was given the grown-out-of shoes from boys years older than himself. His face was wide, and his hair was always tousled. He did not care what it looked like, nor indeed any other part of him, either. It would never have occurred to him as something to be concerned about. He was thought not to notice much, and even the head Nanny, who came to love him for other qualities, found him a generally dull but obedient child. Old Nan noticed that little escaped his attention, although that was often not apparent to others because his unvarying way of dealing with just about any troubling situation he noticed was to appear not to notice it at all. He was very stubborn about that.

He adored the Master's son. Being the same age, they were together from their earliest memory. It was hard to say whether the princeling found some common thread in their being or whether he was just more than usually tolerant of the lowborn foundling, but their friendship was undeniable. They seemed to have placed themselves at each other's service, always with the aristocrat choosing their play.

"We need more sticks," said the Master's son one day when they were both building a pen for a little pet pig.

"Where should I get them?" his companion asked at once.

"Get them from the kindling pile in the woodshed." Off the little fellow ran, and a few minutes later, he was caught stealing kindling and spanked briskly for it.

"I didn't get any sticks," he said, returning empty-handed.

"Why not?"

"They caught me taking some and spanked me," he explained, wriggling because his backside was still smarting.

"Oh. Well, you can probably get some from the house, from the boxes by the fireplaces. But don't get caught a second time, or we'll never get this thing built."

Off he went again, without hesitation. Later, he was the one to muck out the pigpen while his comrade was the one who fed their pet until it got too big for them to keep anymore and was sent to live and die with the rest of the pigs. On that sad day, the Master's son wept. His companion endured the ordeal with dry eyes, as usual. Nor did he ever laugh, although he did learn to make the same sounds and movements of others who were laughing for the sake of appearances.

When, in their eighth year, it came time for the training, both boys were entered into it together.

# II  The Training

T HE PORT WAS a place less of the land than of the ocean. The ocean joined it to all other lands; warmed it in the winter, cooled it in summer; and during all seasons yielded full holds of fish. The ocean bestowed its blessings to all citizens with impartiality and with equal impartiality received back into itself the consequences of its largesse, which was everybody's sewage. And so, in the ocean all citizens were joined at last, the meager with the mighty of the place. It was a vigorous, orderly, well-satisfied, and wizened matriarch of a city, who had been early attacked and wounded in her flirtations with the land and so had armored her back against it, embracing forever the sea. To it, she bared her breast and trained all her sons.

The process was simply called the training. The five boys were enrolled in it when they were eight years old. While their families spanned the scale of society, the training united them in an egalitarian form of apprenticeship that assured the Port of an ongoing source of skilled people to build and man the ships of the next generation. By tradition, boys were assigned into small, convenient groups to be taught the ways of the sea and ship. The training was conducted by a varied and rotating series of teachers, some of whom were relatives or friends. At the same time, a bit of useful work was got out of the lads.

The system quickly revealed the boys whose destiny was ashore, for whatever reasons, and these were withdrawn to make their livelihoods elsewhere. Within the training, the officers sorted themselves from the forecastle hands, as did ship handlers from sail handlers, and navigators from cooks. At the same time, everybody received a taste of what problems everybody else worked with, so all trainees were given the opportunity to see where their own service fitted into a broader world. Role was held more important than rank, and both were self-determining within an ancient process that had long produced renowned mariners. Everybody was well-satisfied with the training, except, of course, the trainees themselves, who had to learn a good deal more than they wanted to know about a great many things.

"Hey, boy, don't gouge that wood! Keep that scraper flat! Mind you get it all!" yelled the dock keeper. It was the first day of the training for the new group of boys. All five had eagerly reported to the fish wharf for what they expected to be a lesson in boat handling. Instead, they had no sooner met one another when they were issued long scrapers and set to scrape sun-browned offal from the dock by a fish-cleaning shed. The square-built little orphan boy had drawn a yell from their supervisor for accidentally digging the scraper blade through the reeking offal skin and into the wood of the dock, gouging it.

"Ughhh," said the sun child, who thought he had never had to do a more sickening, demeaning task, although he did not want to be seen as the first of their company to complain.

The Master's son did the work without enthusiasm, but if he thought it either disgusting or beneath him, he showed no indication of it. The Captain's son handled his scraper surgically, taking long, straight slices through the caked gurry, with each cut precisely overlapping the one next to it, so the planks he had worked were evenly cleaned. The taverner's boy went at it vigorously, scraping twice the area of anybody else, pointing out as he did so any holidays he saw left by any of the others (while not noticing a few of his own). He took quiet satisfaction at how much faster he was than any of his more highborn new associates. Largely because of his zeal, they finished the odious job before they were expected to, leaving time for them to shovel the scrapings into the hold of a sailing lighter that would take it elsewhere to be sold for fertilizer.

When they finished, the lads were allowed time to eat their noonday meal, which they took down to the beach. Loosely grouping themselves on the rocks, they eyed one another, perhaps sensing some portent to their situation. The work had aroused all their appetites, however, and they lost no time unwrapping their food and having at it. The event was carried by the Master's big boy, who had made up an extravagant hamper and assigned it to his friend to carry and finally open up. Out of it came several varieties of buns, breads, and cakes, some buttered, with a choice of cheese and meats, plus fruits and nuts for dessert and a small jug of weak beer to wash it down. All were invited to partake, and all did, even the Captain's pale son, who was not normally that interested in food. The taverner's boy was immediately attracted into the circle by the feast, and he ate and ate, even managing to conceal a bit for later. By the time they were summoned back to duty, they were all doubled over laughing at the prodigious farting of the Master's son.

They spent the afternoon aboard the sailing barge they had earlier loaded, first getting lectured on the ropes and parts of the craft, which most of them felt they knew well enough already. In this, they were mistaken. All but the Captain's boy proved to be awkward new sailors. The Master's son, enjoying the ride, turned in a laggardly performance, causing the boatman to bark at him, "Pay attention there, fatty, and jump to! D'ya think you're here to work or be a passenger?" He resented being called "fatty" because it was disrespectful, but he said nothing, for he had been well taught to absorb in silence the prattlings of servants.

His close companion also came in for some unwanted attention: "You there! Pick up your big feet an' keep 'em clear of the lines!" The boy had shuffled into a coil of a halliard flaked on deck, getting a turn around his foot in the process.

The shipowner's grandson fell into the open hatch on top of the gurry heap, and the taverner's son moved too fast. "Hey! Slow down! Move slow an' she comes easy."

The following day, they learned still more about scraping, spending most of the day removing all the barnacles from the hull of a beached bawley, and the day after that brought lessons in bailing and scrubbing. By the end of the week, they were inseparable companions, and when it was discovered that all shared the same birthday, they implored their parents for permission to spend it together. This was granted. They all met by the wharves and then larked together through the streets and over the cobbled docks; at the beach, they dined from the big hamper loaded in the Master's kitchen, and at day's end, they held a solemn meeting in council–their first–in which three things were clearly agreed upon: First, they would be friends for life, come what might. Second, they vowed they would one day have their own ship; it would be a ship capable of going anywhere in the world, and they would sail it to every place where nobody had sailed before. Third, they fixed upon their roles and from these derived the names by which they agreed they would always be called.

The taverner's son was to be called *Bosun,* which was short for *boatswain,* which was what he had already become–that important person whose responsibility is the care of the sails and the rigging. His interest had led him to experiment with improvised rigs in the rowboats with which his group was sometimes entrusted, and he was cleverer with ropework than any of the others.

The delight of the old shipowner's daughter would be called *Flags.* He had already designed various flags he thought they could fly from their ship when they got it. More practically, he had proved himself a very useful spokesman whenever something was needed from some adult. For any permissions, the sun child was the one for the job, being easily the most persuasive and the most skilled liar. It was a skill the Captain's boy (who had been taught to revere truth) found odious, but he accepted along with everybody else the benefits.

The Captain's boy became *Pilot.* He could hold a steady helm and navigate them safely through shoals. Along with an amazing ability to see through most things, Pilot had a cool dignity and a sometimes sharp tongue that commanded respect; he was the company's pilot by the common consent of all.

The nobleman's son was called *Steward,* a name that he easily condescended to accept in the same way he generously packed the hamper of plenty. If money was needed by the group, the Master's son could usually get some from one or another of his aunts, uncles, brothers, or grandmothers, so he became financial patron as well as general supplier. The name *Steward* amused him, son of kings. He thought it suitably modest for one who looked after his people so well.

His orphan companion was not so easily named. One by one, they had agreed to the roles and formal titles by which they would be known, but when his turn came, nobody had any ideas. He alone had no specialty or distinguishing talent, and his comrades were baffled as to what he should be called. There were some attempts at discussion, to which he made no contribution.

"What do you want to be called?" his friend Steward asked him, knowing he would have to be prodded.

"I don't care," he said.

"Well, what are you, then?" asked Pilot, piercing the essence of the question.

"Uh, maybe the crew?" the boy asked.

And there it was. To be sure, there was only one of him, but he was a willing hand with anything to be done. He seemed content to let his comrades plan things, never participating much in those discussions, except by being there and available. For instance, without him, the others would have had to work out some system of taking turns carrying the big hamper, but the orphan boy didn't mind. All chores he took on willingly, and so *Crew* he was.

When the darkest and coldest part of winter settled over the city and the waters of the inner harbor froze, many maritime activities were curtailed or slowed pending spring, the training among them. This was the time of year when the city's children received whatever schooling their families found for them at home. Having no project together in that time, the boys all yearned for one another and hoped they would be placed together again in the same group come spring. All pleaded with one plea to those who controlled their lives, but the issue was resolved in their favor by a birthday gift from the sea.

The fifth day of May was almost like the summer for its warmth. With one mind, the lads all pleaded to be allowed to play together. There was no restraining them. Moments after Bosun started up the hill to Pilot's house, he met Pilot coming down the hill to collect him, and they both went up to find Flags, who had gone to fetch Steward and Crew.

22

"Yay!" they all cheered, reunited, dancing and clapping each other on the back and shaking hands with their secret handshake. Then they all ran off to scour the water's edge for whatever accidental treasures the winter waves might have cast onto the beach. They were chasing one another through the rocks between the north castle and the river mouth, their bare feet making smacking sounds in the wet sand, when they raced around a cluster of rocks and almost collided with a skiff that had floated in on the tide and grounded among the foamy debris at the high-water line.

It was a weathered old thing of flaking paint, its bilge full of water and debris, some bits of line, a rusty anchor, a bailer, and one paintless, worn oar, which had survived the derelict's uncharted driftings. Crew was the last to see their find because he was the slowest runner and was further burdened with the hamper. As his mates stood admiringly examining the boat, he was still a long way back down the beach, puffing along, his short legs churning through the sand. When he finally came up, the rest had already made an appraisal of the situation.

"Let's get it bailed out," somebody said, and Crew unhesitatingly clambered into the boat, took up the bailer from the dirty bilgewater, and started emptying it. It was a lengthy job, but he performed it happily, while the rest of them discussed the possibilities. When the boat was clear of water, they dragged it–with difficulty, for it was heavy– back into the water. There it floated, awaiting the whim of the new owners, for as jetsam, it was the property of its finders.

The boat was immediately seen by their teachers as a useful training tool, and it was agreed to assign the boys exactly the task they had begged for–the rehabilitation of their great find. This was to happen in what spare time they had. All their work on it was to be under the strict supervision of their teachers, and whether or not they were allowed to keep the boat depended in the end upon their doing the work to the satisfaction of those to whom they had to answer. They readily agreed, vowing between themselves to have it ready in a month.

A month passed, and another, and many more. The first anniversary of the skiff's discovery fell on a chill, drizzly day of low clouds. There was no frisking on the beach on such a day, nor any skylarking, for the boys' project had absorbed all playtime for the year past. At the outset, every flake of cracking paint had to be meticulously scraped away inside and out. No process was begun before the previous one was finished to the satisfaction of supervisors who seemed to compete with one another in finding fault.

"No holidays!"

The rain and weather had got into the rabbet where the top two starboard planks joined the transom, and rot had started in the plank ends. Both planks had to be removed and replaced, their surgical detachment involving the use of unfamiliar tools with which the boys needed long practice before being allowed to apply them to the boat at all. Each fastening had to be drilled out whenever it was possible to preserve still-good frames and other planks. When at last all was off, the rot was found to have infected the transom head itself, so the whole top of it needed cutting away and replacing, meaning the two top portside planks had to be sprung. Over the course of the year, they had become far more familiar with every inch of their boat's hull than they had ever wanted to be.

Crew plugged along determinedly; his work was always sloppy, and he was slow. Pilot's work was so meticulous it was even slower, and it seemed to the rest of them that he spent all his time sharpening his chisels. Steward, phlegmatic but bored, had actually been found sleeping on the job. Steward had not only been unapologetic but had done it again on several subsequent occasions. Flags had often been more distracting than entertaining. Only Bosun had pursued the work with unremitting diligence, but his disdain for the rest of their efforts had been apparent even when he tried to keep it to himself—which had not been often. There had been sulks and squabbles.

"It seems like there's hardly anything left of it," said Flags gloomily, referring to the skeletal, starkly scraped hull. It was gray as the day itself, although the occasion should have marked a moment of celebration, of sorts, because the first phase of the work at last had been grudgingly pronounced complete.

"Well, lads," said their supervisor, "she came apart easy, but she'll go back together some slow."

All but Bosun felt like giving up. "Come on, let's get back to it." So spring became summer, and all the glorious days were swallowed by the training and the demands of the boat. The work had become more engaging, however, and warm fingers made for better progress.

On the autumn day that saw the last piece of the boat's hull in place, its restorers celebrated by admiring their handiwork and then clambering into it with Steward's hamper to take their noonday meal. While munching, they held an informal meeting in council. There was much to be discussed, for they had begun to regain their original enthusiasm for their project. Already, Flags had made a persuasive case to their teachers for letting them put a sailing rig into their boat.

So, though still high and dry, they were able to lay plans for their first voyage. This would be an expedition to Pirate's Cove, only a ten-hour round-trip sail with a fair wind, according to Pilot: "But we'll have to allow for a lot more if there's any tacking. And we'll need time to search for the treasure while we're there." The off-lying island where Pirate's Cove was situated was traditionally thought to have been a hiding place for pirate treasure in olden times. Many people had searched for this over the years, digging up large pieces of the island in the process.

"We'll be famous if we can find it," said Flags.

"And rich," added Steward.

"Rich enough to buy a bigger boat," said Bosun, "but we'll have to go armed, in case somebody tries to rob us. We'll need shovels and picks and–"

"Provisions," said Steward.

"And a map, if anybody can find one," put in Pilot.

They agreed that sacks would be needed because the treasure would most likely be found in chests too heavy to transport–unless it was diamonds, rubies, and pearls and such. These would be easier to carry than bullion but harder to spend, all agreed, leading to a discussion of how best to evaluate and sell very large quantities of precious gems. They were interrupted by the reappearance of their teacher of the moment, who put them back to work.

To accompany the sailing rig, a rudder was needed, and a tiller and a mast step. The forward thwart had to be modified for a socket, and various cleats and leads needed fashioning and mounting. They found making the mast an amazingly complex process for such a small, simple pole. "That's the way you do it when you do it right," said their teacher, and so that is the way they did it, and fall turned into winter. The other spars were easier, being untapered, but the boys were continually amazed at how long everything took, even simple things, if they were to be got right according to the standards they were forced to honor. During the cold months, there was the caulking and sealing to be done, tackle blocks and rigging to be made up, and the mysteries of sailmaking to learn, with Bosun taking the lead in all the work having to do with rigging and sails.

The second winter in the shed was more comfortable because Flags obtained permission to rig a hearth to keep fingers and paint from freezing. Several coats of paint were needed. Flags was able to get the colors he wanted and even some precious varnish for the spars. He also tended the fire, talked less, and put his mother to work making the various flags and buntings he hoped to see fly. Pilot shaped four good oars so the boat would not be solely reliant upon the wind. Steward made two new bailers and raided his father's container collection for a bucket and a water breaker. Flags talked his grandfather into contributing a fancy boat lantern that supposedly wouldn't blow out, and Pilot obtained a small binnacle with a good compass in it from his father, along with dividers. Also, he traced one of his father's charts, showing the harbor, its approaches, and the off-lying shoals and islands, including the island in which they had a special interest. It was surrounded with various dangers. These he carefully noted in ink.

TWO YEARS AFTER its discovery, the boat was launched on a spring day of alternating showers and brilliant sun, making rainbows. For once, there was plenty of help, and the boat was picked up bodily by everybody who could find a handhold on a gunwale and carried down into the water, where it floated jauntily. The taverner and Bosun's mum were on hand, as were the Captain and Pilot's mother and also Flags's mother and elderly grandfather, proud parents all. Down from the hill for the event came the Master, the Mistress, three of Steward's six brothers, a few favorite aunts and uncles, and several cousins. The Master's party was also accompanied by a tumbrel bearing condiments, breads, a baron of beef, and a barrel of scrumpy.

As the boat went into the water, all applauded and sang the "Launching Song," just as though a mighty ship were being cast upon the seas instead of a skiff. Though tiny, she was much admired. All of the hard work had paid off, and she was gemlike in her new paint. From the mast flew the jack made by Flags's mother to his design—five equal vertical bars, one for each of them. Flags had chosen red; Bosun took green; and Steward chose a deep yellow. There was some discussion as to whether Pilot or Crew should have white, the other option being blue. Crew didn't care, however, so Pilot took white and Crew blue. The flag fluttered brightly.

The boat had been named *Vessle,* the same name that had been discovered under the crusted paint on the transom, where it had been applied by hand unknown. The new owners had intended to change it, or at least to correct its spelling, but each had a different idea, and they had bickered interminably. In the end, their teachers had settled the issue, commanding them to restore the boat's original name and get on with the work. So *Vessle* she remained, and a worthy vessel she appeared to all who beheld her. Bosun cast off the gaskets; sheets and halliards were manned; up went the sails; off went the dock lines; and away from the wharf the boat bubbled with a brisk breeze abeam, to grins, cheers, and toasts, with Flags posed heroically and conspicuously in the bow. Pilot had the helm. *Vessle* swept gloriously along the waterfront with her flag and pendant snapping. During the next hour, the little boat was put through all the evolutions anybody could think of, and she did everything required of her. Although Bosun found some minor adjustments he felt he would have to make here and there, they were well pleased with their craft and its sailing trials. Also pleased were the Captain and the parents, who granted permission for the overnight trip to Pirate's Cove, with the understanding that the lads would turn back from fog or poor weather. They had the necessary experience, the Captain judged.

And so, with midsummer came the long-awaited moment of their great adventure. On the night before their departure, none was able to sleep, and their excitement was palpable in the morning as they attempted to stow aboard all of the things they judged they would need, which turned out to be more than the boat could hold. At last, the lines were cast off in a flurry of impatience, and away they sailed with a fair wind blowing them past the mole and beyond the approaches, with Pilot at the tiller. A watch schedule had been set to permit all of them the helm, and at the second turn of the glass, Bosun was ready to take over at the moment the last grain of sand departed from its upper chamber. Bosun had argued in vain that they should pick a captain for this voyage, thinking himself the logical choice.

"We're all in charge of our own departments," Pilot had responded, and all the others had agreed. Bosun had not brought up the matter again, but he was resolved to take command should the good of the ship ever depend upon their need of one master.

"Course is south southwest," said Pilot, moving out of the helmsman's seat and checking his chart.

"South sou'west," Bosun repeated. Behind them, the Port and coastal hills beyond were melting into an uneven purple line against the sky; on their beam was the arm of the peninsula. Here, they received the true wind.

"Now we're being headed," Pilot observed.

"Trim sheets," said Bosun. He had been aware of the shift as soon as Pilot had, and he found it irritating that his order sounded as if it had been prompted by Pilot. Off the headland was a choppier sea, and with *Vessle* pointing as close to the wind as she could trim, the little boat began to pound, jumping off one crest to smack her round bow into the next, sending up a sheet of spray to either side. On every wavelet, the spray to weather was whisked by the wind back over the forward part of the boat, soaking everyone there and driving all aft except Steward, who decided to crawl under the cuddy and lie down. He suddenly felt very tired, perhaps even a bit queasy. Their lack of rest the night before now began to make itself felt.

"We could put a reef in the mainsail," suggested Pilot, who also felt a bit leaden. "She pounds so."

Bosun had just been thinking the same thing, but to have Pilot call the situation for the second time was intolerable.

"She can carry what we've got up," Bosun retorted. Just as he said it, *Vessle* took a particularly ambitious leap, landing with both a pitch and a roll.

"Uhhhhhhh," said Crew, as his stomach repeated the evolution. He vomited without warning, trying to get to the lee rail as he did so but spewing over Flags in the process.

"Arghhh," said Flags.

"I think we should ease off to the southwest," Pilot said.

"I'm still laying the course you gave me," said Bosun.

"Aye, but now we're so close to the wind, we're losing in speed and to leeway what we gain by the compass," Pilot responded truthfully.

"I'm the helm. It's my choice," said Bosun, stretching his authority. "You laid the course, navigator; I'll steer it close."

"Now, I'm giving you a new course," said Pilot. "Steer south." Bosun made no response, steering close as before.

"South," Pilot repeated, a rage growing in him. Still, there was no reaction from Bosun. Pilot glanced at the glass. There were only a few minutes left of Bosun's watch; then, by previous decision, it would be somebody else's turn at the helm–Steward's. Pilot set his teeth. *Vessle* pounded and pounded, feeling pressures she had not yet experienced since her restoration. Deep in her fabric, new wood flexed against old; under this new stress slight bendings and repositionings occurred, re-opening a few seams just sufficiently to let in the rivulets of water in places that had been tight until then. This was unnoticed by Crew, with his head over the lee rail; or by Flags, who was trying to clean himself off as best he could.

Again the last grain of sand in the glass ran out, and this time it was Pilot who was watching for it. "Change the watch," he called. Getting no answer: "Steward, it's your watch!" Again, there was no answer.

Pilot moved forward to where Steward was curled up in the cuddy. "Your watch," said Pilot, tugging one of Steward's legs. Steward seemed not to notice him, and no amount of pulling, calling, or punching had any effect.

Finally, Pilot gave up and returned aft. "Well enough, then, I'll stand Steward's helm," he told Bosun.

"Unnecessary," Bosun responded, shortly. "I'll stand it myself."

"Then come to south."

"I'll hold our present course." Bosun's jaw was set.

So was Pilot's. "I'm navigator by common consent. I make the courses."

"Aye, and you've given me two courses. I take the first. We can hold it," said Bosun. *Vessle* took another hard plunge, and the spray raked her fore and aft.

"Because I give a course doesn't mean it's the course for the rest of our lives, you lout," said Pilot, his indignation getting the better of him.

"Piss in your hat," said Bosun. Pilot's icy anger ignited into something hotter, and he lunged for the sternsheets, seizing the tiller, trying to wrest it from Bosun.

"Hey," yelped Flags. "Give it to him, Bosun, he *is* Pilot!" But his words were spoken to the wind. In their struggle, Pilot tried to pull the tiller to windward, and Bosun tugged it in the opposite direction. Being the stronger of the two, he was winning when, while shifting to brace himself better, he put one foot on a slippery bilge board; the leg shot out from under him and Bosun fell, abruptly letting go his hold on the tiller. With the unexpected release of opposing pressure, Pilot fell backward, tiller in hand, and *Vessle* shot up into the wind's eye, hanging there and rolling violently while the sails flapped and snapped. In falling backward, Pilot struck his head on the thwart and was knocked unconscious. He could have fallen overboard, but Flags made a lunge, caught his leg, and pulled him down into the boat. Bosun recovered, lurched for the untended tiller, and slipped a second time, cruelly barking a shin.

"Back the jib," he roared, dazzled by the pain. If the jib could be backwinded, the head would pay off and control could be retained. Both Crew and Flags reached for the sheet at the same time, falling over each other and tumbling down on top of Steward, who was just emerging from the cuddy. The boat saved them from further catastrophe. Blown backward, *Vessle* gained sternway rapidly until the water pressure forced her rudder over and the boat into a turn. The wind caught the jib aback, pushing the bow off so that she fell easily onto her new tack, hove to, with her jib backwinded and her mainsail undulating and spilling, balanced, riding comfortably as a duck in the motherly sort of way boats have when they are properly hove to. A sloshing in the bilge took Bosun's attention.

"Bail for your lives," he called. Water was over the floorboards ankle-deep. So long as the boat was heeled, the water had accumulated unnoticed to leeward, but as soon as they came to an even keel, it had washed amidships in a flood. Pilot was lying in it, out cold. It had not been the squabble, but Steward's unpleasant discovery that he was suddenly lying in water that had shifted him. Grabbing the bailers, he and Crew started scooping it out as fast as they could; Bosun was already bailing with the bucket, which was bigger. Flags bent over Pilot, propping him up so his head would be out of the water.

The bailing quickly cleared the bilge. With the pounding and straining removed, *Vessle*'s leaking reduced itself to a trickle, so in a few moments, it was possible to lay Pilot down on floorboards that were no longer awash. His breathing was deep and regular.

"Let's just let him sleep," said Bosun. "I'll put us on an easier course, and we'll make a long tack out, then a short one into the cove."

"That's what Pilot wanted in the first place," said Flags, "and I want to go home."

"Home?" said Bosun. "Why home?"

"We'd best get Pilot back."

"Why? He's well enough. He just needs sleep."

"Well, I still want to go home," said Flags. "We're all wet, the chart's ruined, the glass is broken, your leg's bleeding, Crew's sick, we're not even halfway where we're going, and the day's half gone. I say to hell with it. Let's go home."

"Mummy's boy wants to go home."

"Well, the chart's ruined, and–"

"Who needs it? There's the islands. You can see 'em clear enough."

It was true. The purple outlines of their destination were clearly visible through the summer haze, a windward haul. "I say we go on." Bosun looked to Steward and Crew for support. Crew shrugged, and Steward yawned. With the excitement over, his need for sleep had returned.

"I don't care," Steward growled. "Do what you want. Wake me up when we get there." So saying, he crawled back into the cuddy.

"Crew, let go the weather jib sheet and trim to leeward," Bosun said crisply. Automatically, Crew did as he was told.

"Oh, have it your way," said Flags, helping Crew haul taut, "but we'd better wake up Pilot to navigate us."

"Let him sleep," said Bosun, "until we need him."

"Have it *all* your way, then," Flags snapped.

*Vessle* leaped forward again toward their original goal, making good time and with an easier motion on the new course. Crew lay down on the bilge boards next to Pilot and was soon outsnoring him. Flags sat in silence, looking glum, watching Bosun's continual small adjustments to the sheets until his own lack of sleep caught up with him, and he curled up in what little space was vacant in the bottom of the boat. Bosun settled himself for a long haul. He felt quite alert, and it was good to be the undisputed master of his ship. He could easily handle her alone, and he was happy to let them sleep the day away if they wanted to.

By midafternoon, the bearing of the boat from the island had changed appreciably, but their progress toward it seemed insufficient. Bosun began to think they might be fighting an adverse current. Not having had Pilot's special tutelage in all the quirks of coastal tidal currents, he did not quite know what to make of it and considered awakening his colleague for a consultation. Instructions more likely. He decided instead to come about and simply try the other tack for a while. Bosun took up the jib sheets and put the helm down. The breeze had slackened as the day had worn on, and the evolution went gently. With only a slight rattle of the blocks, *Vessle* luffed up, then paid off on her new course. Down on the floorboards, the boys all rolled a few inches to leeward, but nobody woke up. *Vessle* steadied on her new course.

Bosun hummed softly to himself and counted the waves, lulled by the easy motion and the warmth of the hazy sun. The pain in his shin had eased somewhat. How foolish it had been of Flags to want to go back. How foolish it had been of Pilot, actually, to have attempted to seize the tiller from him. It was like, well . . . almost like *mutiny*. Even if the mutineer *had* been right. He was forced to admit that, at least to himself. Of course, he'd known it at the time, but should he feel wrong about not jumping just because Pilot, son of the great Captain, had snapped his fingers? He did not think so. Only in the matter of navigation did he admit Pilot his equal in anything, and among the many goals Bosun had set for himself was becoming a better navigator than Pilot as soon as he could find the time to learn as much about the subject as Pilot knew. Bosun had no doubt of his ability to do that. "You can do anything you set your mind to," were the words his father had spoken to him many times. Feeling the boat and thinking his thoughts, he had watched the mainland growing ever hazier behind them. There was good progress on this tack, he thought, and cranked his head around to see how much closer they were to the island since last he'd looked. To his surprise, it was nowhere to be seen. Nor were any of the others.

"Where did they go?" he said aloud, jumping up abruptly and scanning the horizon for the missing islands.

"Where did what go?" Flags asked, waking up.

"I can't see the islands anymore," said Bosun, shading his eyes with his hand as he peered at the apparent emptiness before him. "Wake up Pilot and the others." In a minute, they were all up and searching– Pilot, too, with a headache.

"What happened? Where are we?" Pilot asked.

"You hit your head," said Bosun, "so we let you sleep. Everybody but me's been sleeping. We've been making good time ever since. We tacked. Then this haze came up suddenly, and now the islands are gone. They were right over there the last time I looked," he pointed, and looked back toward the mainland, but it had also vanished. "Now I can't even see anything at all," he said.

"Show me our position on the chart," said Pilot.

"The chart's ruined," said Crew, producing the soggy remnants. "The ink's run, and you can't hardly read it anymore." Only areas of land mass were still vaguely discernible. Pilot groaned.

"What course have you followed? And for how long?" he asked. "And what speed have we made through the water? What time is it by the glass?"

"The glass got broke," said Bosun.

"What about the courses, then?"

"I . . . can't be sure," Bosun answered.

"Fine," said Pilot, "just fine. How far was the island the last time you did see it?"

"Perhaps a league."

"Perhaps a league. Well done, Bosun. You've got us lost." Pilot did not easily give up, however, and after questioning Bosun on the details of how he had sailed since their last fixed positon, he felt able to draw on the remains of the chart a circle within which he reckoned they had to be.

"Our position's somewhere around in here," said Pilot, stabbing the point of his divider into the middle of it. "At least, it's where we must be if what Bosun tells me is true," he added. "I can only guess on a course to the cove, and there are obstacles starting a mile off its entrance."

"Obstacles?" asked Bosun.

"Rocks. Shoals. Banks. The worst of them I had marked, but as you see, it's no longer readable. Any course from here is a guess. I judge it imprudent for us to try it now."

"What?" asked Bosun, hearing their expedition endangered again.

"It would be stupid to try it even with a chart. That we have no more, nor time glass, nor position, nor clear sight of land."

"It's only a mist. Still, we can see a fair distance," Bosun argued.

Pilot spoke in greater detail, telling them of the crosscurrents that ran in and around the islands, currents that could sweep them over shoals. He reckoned also that the afternoon mist could be a sign of decreasing wind, and the tide-raked island would be a dangerous place to be caught becalmed. Also, there were rocks, many of them lurking just beneath the surface of the water. Tacking as they were, it would take them the rest of the day to get there anyhow. "And to be by darkness taken in those waters could be the death of us," he concluded, without realizing it having talked himself into the undertaking.

"Home, then, it is," said Flags.

"But yet," said Pilot, before even Bosun could get a word out, "we've come this far, and perhaps we could sail on for a bit. Perhaps the mist will clear by evening. There's no telling, but with this wind, we can turn for home when we choose. No need to sail in harm's way."

EVENING FOUND THEM almost completely becalmed somewhere close to the island, in thickening mist, unknown currents, and with night coming on. The prudent but belated decision to turn for home had been made two hours earlier, shortly before the breeze had failed, leaving them helplessly rolling in the swell.

"Only seven fathoms here," said Crew, bringing up a dripping length of line with the weight of the lead at its end. He handed it to Pilot, who made an examination of the bottom residue clinging in its tallow cup.

"Sand and broken shell," he pronounced. "Different from the last lot. We're being set by a current–perhaps a strong one, to judge from the bottom changes–and it's not taking us in the direction we want to go. We've plenty of water under us now, but we should perhaps–"

"Anchor," Bosun finished his sentence for him.

"Aye, anchor," said Pilot. With their present position hooked, they could simply wait until the turn of the tide and then get a bit more offing. In a moment, Bosun had brought out the anchor and tossed it over the bow. Its line began to uncoil rapidly, giving them for the first time an idea of the alarming velocity with which the current was running. There were twenty fathoms of anchor line.

"I'll let it all out," said Bosun. They had been well taught about the greater holding power of a long rode. As the last few flakes of line payed out, it occurred to Bosun to wonder why he did not recollect having tied it off. He moved forward to investigate, but at the same moment, the last of the line whispered out, taking with it the unsecured end. Abruptly, it was gone, with a plip, into the water.

"Who didn't tie off the anchor line?" asked Flags, amazed.

"It wasn't *my* responsibility," said Bosun automatically.

"Then whose?" Pilot wanted to know.

"Why, yours," said Bosun. "You're the navigator. The anchor line's not my rigging. I didn't bring the anchor aboard. I didn't stow it."

"I think we had better get out the oars," said Pilot, "and try to get out of here." The lashings holding the oars in a sheaf under the thwarts were cast off, and all began to pull but Pilot, who held the helm, sitting poised in the sternsheets, his eyes attempting to penetrate the surrounding gloom during the last twilight. He saw nothing. He did not like it that the swells seemed to have more lift than they had earlier. That accorded all too well with the diminishing soundings. Pilot could still just see the compass rose in its binnacle box. He decided to alter course the better to breast the stream, which was carrying them sideways. He reckoned their progress was probably sufficient to contradict whatever current had them. No doubt it was an eddy around the tip of the island. A quarter-hour passed, and Pilot could no longer see the compass.

"In oars," he called. "Flags, can you fire the binnacle lamp?" Flags was better at starting a fire than any of them, and he kept the tinder, flint, and steel. "Crew, another sounding?" Bosun and Steward furled the useless sails.

"An' a quarter four," said Crew, reeling in the dripping line.

"I think it's just sand now," said Pilot, scrutinizing the bottom sample in the small light that came from the binnacle.

"Shoaling and we're still being swept," said Bosun, making a hurried last lashing around the mainsail. "Let's get back to rowing. Pilot, are you steering to breast this current or cross it?"

"Both," Pilot said, "but it's pulling us backward, and I'll steer more into it. Pull." They pulled.

"And let's put our backs into it," said Bosun. They had no need to be told.

In the total blackness, Pilot could see nothing except the binnacle's minuscule light before his eyes, but the rhythmic thumping of the oars against their thole pins told him his mates were keeping a brisk pace. The only other sound in his inky universe was the occasional sigh from a swell passing beneath. Or was there something else?

"Avast pulling," he said. The thumping stopped abruptly.

"Want another sounding?" asked Crew's voice out of the darkness.

"Not yet. Shh." All was silent. No, there was something, a momentary impression only, as of thunder so distant as to be hardly audible, more felt.

"I heard it," said Bosun. "It's–"

"Shh," said Pilot, who was turning his head slowly this way and that with his hands cupped behind his ears to better pick up the direction of the sound when it came again.

"Breakers out there somewhere."

"Where?" asked Bosun.

"Where we're being taken," said Pilot. The others had already commenced plying their oars again, more briskly than before, with hands beginning to blister.

"How far away?" Flags wanted to know.

"I don't know," said Pilot. "Just row." Somewhere in the direction they were being swept was apparently a mass of troubled water, perhaps some bank too shallow to allow the swells to pass without breaking on the bottom; perhaps sea striking ledges, cliffs, or other masses of rock. Whatever the thunder's source, its discovery would likely be their final one. After a few minutes, Pilot switched places with a sweaty Flags, who took the tiller with relief. The booming became audible over the sound of their oars.

"That's closer," Bosun said.

"Maybe it was just a bigger wave than the others," said Steward. But it soon became apparent that was not the case. Also, the swells had begun to lump noticeably, an ominous sign.

"The tide—any notion when it might turn?" asked Bosun.

Pilot knew the tidal cycle but had lost track of their time. "Perhaps soon. Let's hope. And pull." There seemed nothing to be done other than what they were doing. He was sure they had been dragged into a bore or a tidal rip of some sort. It was simply faster than they were. And so they rowed and rowed, with the helmsman spelling the weariest oarsman until it was Pilot's turn again at the tiller. Looking over his shoulder, he was the first to see some visual sign of the thunder's source, an almost inperceptible green line directly over the stern. It was there for a moment only, suspended in the blackness, and then it was gone. Then it was there again, the unmistakable green of phosphor startled by breaking seas. Pilot altered course to starboard, but in a short while, he saw the line extending in that direction also. At the same time, the light of it was brighter, and he could see its undulations. It was fast approaching despite their best efforts.

"I . . . don't know . . . how much longer. . . I can pull," said Flags.

"Raise your eyes and look," said Pilot. All looked, and found new strength.

As Pilot gazed at the dancing green ribbon, he saw a curious phenomenon: a piece of it seemed to detach and move slowly toward them, as though chasing them. At first, he could not understand what he was seeing, but within two or three more minutes, the lone patch of dim light overtook them close to starboard, and as it passed ahead, he saw it was a curl of turbulence around the base of a dark object—a rock.

"What's ahead of us I can't say, but there's the first of it," said Pilot. The rock's foam slid into the darkness.

"No use pulling now," said Pilot. "Current's too much for us. Save your strength and stand by. We'll pull when we must to dodge the rocks. So long as they come one at a time and we can see 'em, we'll pull fromward." He didn't believe it would do them much good. Whatever was making the boil toward which they were headed was bigger than any patch of individual rocks.

"How do you dodge the rocks you can't see?" Bosun wanted to know. The answer to his question was dramatic. As he spoke, *Vessle* lifted on a wave and then fell into its trough; the trough was like a mouth with one tooth in it, a fang of rock that the boat brushed in passing. Although it struck only a glancing blow, the contact was as though a giant sledge had struck the hull from beneath, spinning *Vessle* half round, nearly swamping her, and tearing the portside oars from the hands of Bosun and Crew. The blow was accompanied by a cracking of wood from somewhere and shrieks of terror; simultaneously, the tiller removed itself from Pilot's grip. Having been struck, the boat was lifted again on the next wave, and as the descent began, all waited for the next terrible impact. But the rock was no longer under them. By some miracle, they still floated; for how long, none could say.

Bosun was the first to recover. "Crew! Bail!" he screamed, snatching the oar from Steward next to him. "You help bail," he said. "I'll pull."

"But with only two of us . . . ," said Flags, who held the other oar that had been spared.

"Pull!" shrieked Bosun, and so the two of them pulled with all their strength. Pilot thought the whole effort futile. If they had not been able to breast the stream with four fresh oarsmen, how could they be expected to do better with two who were spent in a boat now half full of water? Let them try, he thought, and groped for the tiller. Not finding it, he searched further and discovered that not only was the tiller missing but quite a lot more besides.

"The rudder's gone," he called, his voice sounding thin over the thunder of the approaching breakers.

"We can steer with the sweeps," said Bosun. "If it's the end, it's the end, but 'till then let's pull fromward. Pull, Flags! Puulll . . . and bail! Puulll . . . and bail," he began to chant. Pulling with him, Flags took the cue and began to sing:

> O we'll pull awaaay for home, me lads,
> We'll pull awaaay for home . . .

It was a well-known chantey, and Bosun joined in, half singing, half bellowing:

> An' when we've pulled to home, me lads,
> It's never more we'll roam.

Steward and Crew, kneeling in water admitted by damage un-known, bailed to the beat and joined in.

"Folly," said Pilot, choosing to meet his own death with chill re-serve. But after a few more waves had passed, leaving them still afloat, he joined in with the singing, too. The wall of breakers was no closer, so far as he could make out. In any case, at that moment they still lived.

> O we'll pull for all our sweethearts, lads,
> And when to home we've come,
> We'll pull away their petticoats
> And pat 'em on the bum.

Bosun and Flags had found a second wind. Watching the wall of breakers, Pilot was now quite sure its livid line was no closer. Thinking to look in the opposite direction, he saw again the luminous turbu-lence at the base of the rock they had previously passed, and now they were slowly passing it again, this time in reverse.

"Avast pulling," he said.

"We're pulling out of it," said Bosun, who had seen what Pilot had.

"Aye," said Pilot, "but it's the tide pulling us, not your oars." It was true. The tide had providentially turned, and its new set was carrying them away from the menace. Wearily, four small, blistered hands took up again the heavy pair of remaining oars. The rest handled the bail-ers. There was no more singing. The green ribbon faded into the night.

After midnight, a breeze cleared the mists, at the same time filling their grateful sails. With the old lighthouse twinkling their way, they limped and bailed home, not to a heros' welcome.

# III  Meanderings

THE BOAT WAS made shipshape again in due course, and the boys were again permitted to sail, albeit well inshore for the rest of that summer. As the terror and the wretchedness of their first voyage faded, its drama shone ever more vividly, and everybody's recollections were told and retold with embellishments, at least between themselves. They sensibly decided it would not be in their interest for *any* outsider to know the peril they had experienced. On their twelfth birthday, their freedom was reinstated, and they made another attempt at the island.

The second expedition went as well as the first had gone badly. On a perfectly clear day, they fetched the island on one tack, watching its profile grow on the horizon as they bubbled along with a fair westerly wind on their beam. Before noon, they reached the approaches and started into the tricky channel that threaded the shoals, with Pilot keeping them true in the middle of the fairway. On their starboard, they saw clearly the mile-long claw of rock ledge that had nearly claimed them, and they heard again the murmur of its surf. This time, however, they were on the other side of it with good offing, a good chart, and an anchor line well secured at its bitter end. Into the cove they stood. Off an inviting sand beach, they rounded to and grounded precisely in time for the noonday meal. The afternoon they spent exploring the sands and dune grasses and the tumbled, half-buried old stones that had once in some dim time stood here guarding . . . what?

Pilot could find no clue as to where to dig. Bosun went to the top of the hill with his father's huge old cutlass hanging from his belt, the tip of its scabbard dragging, making a little furrow in the sand behind him. While the rest of them searched, he stood lookout, periodically running down the hill to see how the search was progressing. It seemed to be going slowly.

About midafternoon, Steward stumbled upon a perfect place to take a nap, and Crew fell into a crevasse among the jumble of old stones, leading Pilot for one hopeful moment to think they had discovered an opening to an old tunnel, but it was not. Flags pretended to find a coin he had hidden when nobody was watching him, but the ruse was immediately seen through by Pilot, who spent the rest of the afternoon making a map of the island. Later, under the stars, they sat round their campfire in the dunes, and Flags told them stories. Their return the following afternoon was as serene as the passage out.

It was the summer of *Vessle.* By the end of it, the lads had investigated everything within their reach, and Pilot had annotated the existing charts with additional information as to the lines of soundings, seafloor composition, obstructions, conspicuous landmarks, and current. Flags wanted to decorate it with drawings and designs, but Pilot saw no purpose in mere embellishment. Steward just sat back vastly enjoying his comrades, their collection of quirks, the interplay, and the worlds through which they sailed. He astonished Flags by throwing open the Hall of Flags at the Manor, revealing in their majestic hundreds the pendants, wimples, streamers, standards, pencels, ensigns, jacks, banners, bannerets, burgees, and buntings comprising an assemblage of centuries. Pilot was given the run of the Master's library, a place he would later haunt, although he had little enough time for it that summer. Bosun kept everybody moving so that nobody stood still too long, and as Crew reflected on it many times in later years, there was never a time in their lives that had been more perfect.

When, in the waning days of autumn, they dragged *Vessle* up the skids and put blocks under her, they were full of plans for the following year. The only thing unresolved was whether they would go north up the coast, as Pilot proposed (backed by Bosun), or south, as Steward and Flags wanted. Crew's balance vote was stubbornly withheld or ignored, as always when there was an even split on any matter. There would be plenty of time to resolve that, they reckoned, as they lashed onto their boat the tarpaulin that would keep out the falling leaves, the rains, and the snows to come.

But the next trip was not to be. Just as their lives appeared to have joined into a single path, they were split apart by twin strokes of fate. The first blow was struck by their training, the initial phase of which they had now completed. Those who controlled their lives felt the time had come for each boy to be given over to the work for which he had shown the most aptitude, and so they were separated. Pilot's continuing education was taken over largely by his own father, who intended to navigate him through the advanced mathematics and sciences. Bosun was sent to toil among the riggers and sailmakers, which suited him well enough, and Flags—who was thought perhaps to have the makings of a good supercargo, or ship's ambassador and businessman—was sent to learn the ways of the trade, which suited him not at all. Steward was assigned to the Port's mercantile houses to learn about the complex inventories required by ships and their companies. Crew was given over to general ship's duties.

The second source of disruption was puberty. Everything that was happening seemed new. There were new people, new situations, new friends no longer shared in common. While the shipmates still sailed together on *Vessle,* one or two of them always seemed to have something more pressing elsewhere, as Crew in particular deplored. Within their company, his devotion and his alone found no distractions.

On their fourteenth birthday, Crew assumed that all five of them would be reunited for at least a sail around the harbor. As soon as he left his bed that morning, he went off looking for Steward so they could pack the food hamper and go to the docks. But Steward was gone; nobody knew where. Having searched for him everywhere without success, Crew made the trek all the way down the hill to the boat by himself, hoping the others had preceded him. But they had not. *Vessle* bobbed in her berth unattended.

Crew stood on the dock thinking about it, not knowing exactly what to do. Should he go back up the hill, stopping at the houses of the others on the way? What if, while he was doing that, he missed them because they were somewhere else? Where else would they be? He sat down on a piling to think about it some more. When an hour had come and gone with no sign of any of his comrades, he clambered aboard the boat and had a seat. At least Bosun should have been there, he thought after another hour or so had gone by. Bosun was usually there before anybody, ready to yell at him. Crew didn't mind being yelled at by Bosun for being slow. He knew he *was* slow. It never bothered him except when it bothered his friends—mostly, Bosun. Still, he liked Bosun a lot. He was grateful they liked him, although he couldn't think what he had to offer them. Their ability to envision, choose, plan, and decide was a great comfort to him. It left him free to concern himself with other matters. In the absence of any other matters with which to concern himself, he was unconcerned. Except he wished they would show up.

After a while, the warm sun and the friendly chuckle of the water lulled him from his lonesome thoughts. His head nodded down onto his chest, and he started to snore. Crew snored when his sleep was for any reason troubled, the volume depending upon the level of his discontent. On this occasion, his rumblings caught the attention of some passing children, who gathered on the dock to laugh at him. Eventually, one reached out and prodded him with a stick as though he were a sleeping walrus. Crew grinned at the kids, and they ran away. It was not that Crew was completely without a sense of humor and couldn't see a joke—on himself or anybody else, what difference?—it was just the matter of *laughing* that was so incomprehensible. How easily the children did it, he thought—seemingly without effort, like a burst of birdsong.

"Yay, Crew! What cheer?" Here was Bosun suddenly on the dock.

"Yay, Bosun! Where is everybody today?" asked Crew.

"Where, indeed?" said Bosun. "But if they're not here yet, they're probably not coming. It doesn't surprise me," he added, unburdening himself of a string of heavy tackle blocks he was carrying over his shoulder. "I see Flags still hasn't touched up the scrapes he got in the paint when he laid *Vessle* alongside the stone quay last week. And I see somebody forgot to coil down properly, and if you don't mind my pointing it out again, Crew, you've brought sand aboard from your shoes. Try to be more mindful next time. By the way, you're going to be here for a little while longer, are you not?"

Crew just blinked, not having thought about it.

"Well, if you don't mind, please keep an eye on these blocks for a few minutes. I have to deliver them down that way, but first, I have to go to the loft. I'll be right back." So saying, he was off at a fast trot. On his way again, Bosun reflected again on how badly things went aboard *Vessle* whenever he did not personally attend them. Suspecting he might be late, he broke into a run.

Noon came and went. Crew noticed he had become hungry and began to think about what, if anything, he could do about it, when he saw Flags approaching with a girl.

"Yay, Crew!" said Flags.

"Yay, Flags!" said Crew. "Bosun was just here, and he's coming right back, he said." Crew found himself staring at the girl, who was very pretty.

"Ah," said Flags, "Crew, this is Rose–"

"Rosemaryn," said the girl.

"Rosemaryn, yes," said Flags. "Crew, Rosemaryn and myself were thinking of taking out *Vessle* for a short sail. If none of the others has shown up, I doubt they're coming."

"Bosun's been here. Those're his blocks. I'm watching them."

"Then he's doing other things. Nobody else will mind if Rosemaryn and myself take out *Vessle*."

"All right," said Crew, "but we'll have to wait for Bosun."

"Well, Crew, Rosemaryn can only be away for a short time, so I wonder if I can persuade you to wait with Bosun's blocks up on the dock so we can go now, while we have time?"

Crew clambered up out of the boat, carrying the blocks. He helped Flags with the lines, watched the couple sail away, then sat down to wait some more. He wondered what would happen if the others showed up now while Flags was out sailing by himself. Well, not by himself because there was the girl, of course, but by himself in the sense that all the rest of them had been left behind.

"Yay, Crew!" It was Bosun again, loping toward him out of breath.

"Yay, Bosun!" said Crew. "Flags took the boat out. With a girl. I stayed here with your blocks."

"Sorry I took so long," panted Bosun. "They kept me forever, and now I'm *really* late. Thanks for watching these. Maybe I'll see you later," he said, grabbing up the blocks and starting off down the dock again. Crew sat back down on the same piling where he had begun the day. He watched *Vessle* tacking back and forth in the harbor, all her flags flying. Sometime later, her occupants steered past his vantage point and waved. He waved back, and they sailed across the harbor again. When *Vessle* ultimately returned to the dock, Flags was relieved to find Crew still there so he was able to hurry away with Rosemaryn, leaving his friend to rig the springs and warps, adjust the fend-offs, coil down, wash down, twiddle the tiller, stow the jib, run in the bowsprit, and harbor-furl the mainsail. That done, Crew was at last free to trot back up the hill to the Manor. He was very hungry and hoped to arrive in time for the supper sitting in the great hall.

Crew stayed in the hall after he had finished eating, mostly watching the 350-year-old tortoise making its way from one side of the vast room to the other. For reasons known only to itself, it had made the same journey without fail every evening at the same time since at least the previous century, returning with equal punctuality every morning, each transit taking from one to four hours, depending on distractions. The venerable creature would sometimes stop to investigate morsels it encountered. It would also stop–very respectfully, it seemed to Crew–if it found people sitting or standing in its accustomed path. Then, it would simply wait, until eventually they went away. It never went around them. The patience of the tortoise seemed infinite, and its purposes indefatigable. It moved by lifting one ponderous leg and then another, easily brushing aside any unattended chairs or benches left out of place.

The tortoise was not bothered if, as sometimes happened, it acquired a load of passengers. All the children had ridden it many times, as had some adults. Also, every person with a yen to play a drum had beaten upon its great, intricately patterned shell with spoons. Whether the beast was in progress or standing still or sleeping, it did not seem fazed by it, as far as Crew could tell.

There was some question in his mind as to whether the great animal ever slept at all. Many times, he had peered into the half-closed front flap of its shell when the tortoise was in repose and seen in the shadowy interior a pair of reptilian eyes, open and alive between the slits of their leathery lids. One year, the tortoise had surprised everybody by laying a round blue egg the size of a large cannonball, an event that appeared to substantiate the views of those who had always held it to be a female turtle. There remained some who thought it was a hermaphrodite turtle, however, which in fact it was. When the egg was eaten, it was found to be delicious.

"Yay, Crew! Good birthday!" It was Steward passing through the kitchen. Steward had made an early morning expedition out to the summer market because it was a Faire day, and he wanted to see a bit before joining his friends at the boat. So fascinating had he found it, however, that he had spent the whole day there. He told Crew about some of the wonders he had seen and promised to take him along next Faire day so he could see for himself.

An hour or so after the tortoise completed his and her transit across the hall, Crew retired also, feeling lonesome. Sometime during the night, he dreamed that he and all the others were together in *Vessle.* The wind falling calm, all of his companions jumped overboard, and to his horror, each swam off in a different direction, Bosun going north, Pilot east, Steward south, and Flags to the west. As he watched, they all swam swiftly out of sight, leaving him alone and adrift on an empty sea. The dream kept coming back to him the next day, although he could not remember how it ended.

I F CREW HAD TOLD Flags of his dream (which he did not, nor anybody), and if he had asked him the following day what he might have been swimming toward, and if Flags had answered honestly, he would have said "Rosemaryn," but only if the question had been asked before suppertime, when Flags noticed Clematis for the first time. He had known Clematis for years as the little girl with the big round head on the end of a long neck. But at the dinner between their families that evening, Flags was surprised to find the neck of Clematis curiously graceful, greatly enhanced by the black ribbon she wore round it, which led to a further examination that made him forget Rosemaryn entirely for the rest of the evening and almost entirely for the rest of the week. Until Fuchsia. Flags found his world fragranced not just by the opening of one or two flowers but by an entire garden with Camellia, Laurel, Forsythia, Lily, and even a mature, fast-climbing Begonia that went right up a trellis attached to the side of his house and into his open bedroom window in less than two minutes one night of no moon but many comets. Flags began to learn how much work was involved with tending a proper garden when he accidentally let two or three of the more fragile blossoms die of neglect while tending too busily to others. In time, he learned how to prune and tend more evenly, giving each plant just the nurture it needed to keep it robust, rearranging beds as necessary.

"I never see you anymore," said his mother wistfully, stitching one of his jackets to make it a better fit.

"Can't you do that any faster?" asked Flags. He was boiling with impatience to put on the jacket and be out the door.

"Not if you want a perfect fit," lied his mother, desperate for a bit of her sun child's company and sewing as slowly as she could to prolong his presence. "Besides, it gives us a bit of a chance to talk. I never see you anymore, except when you need a tailor. You used to talk to me," she gently accused, "and you used to play for *me.*"

"I'll get my lute now," said Flags, grateful for an escape. He was going to need it for his next rendezvous in any case, and he might as well tune it while waiting. He knew his mother would be content with that.

The music instruction that had once been painful was suddenly so

socially useful as to warrant actual practice, and he found himself playing frequently and well. He was also gifted with a good singing voice.
At first, he memorized the songs of others, but as he grew into his per-
forming, he found himself composing his own lyrics and often tailor-
ing them to one person. Later, these words could be readapted, although he soon learned caution. Having dedicated essentially the
same poem to two different girls, he was mightily embarrassed by
being found out. He had handled the situation with such charm that
neither girl ever suspected his embarrassment.

There were many other embarrassments: always his mother; often
an out-of-tune lute string; once a nimble and perfect leap over a twilight garden wall that landed him knee-deep in a reek of fertilizer;
eternally the embarrassment of unrequited love, the occasional embarrassment of rejection, overeagerness, undereagerness, awkward-
ness on the part of his partner; the embarrassment of falling out of
love with no graceful exit; finally, most profoundly, the embarrassment of embarrassment itself. Flags experienced it all in full measure–in fact, saw it as the main enemy and invented lush veneers with
which to cover its rawness. Also concealed was his almost total disin-
terest in his assigned work, although he did whatever was required of
him to stay on the good side of his instructors. Failure would have
been too embarrassing.

Bosun was by no means uninterested in girls, but he had little time
for anything that did not contribute in some way to whatever was his
task at hand. Having spent his childhood engaged to his ambition, the
moment he came of age, he wedded it and prepared to spawn a large
enough family by it to ensure generations of new ambitions, all his.
Understanding that perseverance and efficient work were the unfail-
ing instruments of ambition, he sacrificed himself to it in the manner
of a fine athlete, taking his reward from doing well whatever he did,
the greater reward being in doing it better than anybody else and the
greatest reward of all being the epiphany of self-sacrifice involved. Or
so his father had told him, urging him from earliest memory to create
the finest possible self, meaning self in the sense of a tool. "You can do
it, lad. Rise above your station. Take wing."

On the wharf, when he had charged Crew to watch over his string of tackle blocks, he was on a perfectly plotted circle of errands that included, among several other things, getting a lesson in seaming from a knowledgeable old sailmaker. The lesson had taken longer than he had planned to give it, making the boy edit out the least important of his remaining errands in order to get back on schedule. He planned to be outseaming everybody in his own loft by the following day. Having practiced what he had learned long into the small hours, working with needle and palm by candlelight, he was able the next day to accomplish the goal he had set himself. This impressed his master sailmaker–who didn't know how a junior apprentice had accomplished it–and made a permanent rift between himself and all the jealous senior apprentices, who were all the more aggravated when Bosun generously offered to show them what he had learned. He was mystified as to why they would reject his lesson. He noted well that his own position was advanced, and theirs was not. This he took as compensation for his rejection.

He did miss his four comrades a great deal, genuinely regretting their growing estrangement. He took on the self-appointed responsibility of tending *Vessle.* It was more work for him, but it would not have been done without him, at least not respectably. Although he grumbled always about being only one-fifth boat owner who did half the work–more than half–he was always down on *Vessle,* adjusting her dock lines and fend-offs, keeping her clean and shipshape and safe.

In Steward's view, girls were merely extra tidbits in a world that was already a feast. He could not become overly engrossed with any one ingredient any more than he would imbalance the flavor of a good recipe with too much onion, though he was fond enough of onions. Only recently had his life offered him the opportunity to taste the full flavors of the Port, but none of the city's offerings was half so succulent as those of the wondrous summer market. As good as his word, Steward took Crew to the summer market on the next Faire day, and his other comrades as well, bringing their complete company together for the only time that summer.

He accomplished this by decree. Finding them one by one, he simply informed them that everybody would be getting together to attend the Faire, and they would meet at the southwest gate at noon. It was fine with Pilot, though he thought the activity perhaps indulgent. Flags was delighted, immediately offering to bring girls, but Steward told him the event was his treat, and he wanted to see everybody leave his work behind. Bosun had a thousand things to do.

"No excuses. Just come," said Steward. "We hardly see each other anymore. We're all going. My treat. Southwest gate at noon. See you there."

The summer market was located outside the city wall. As implied by its name, the market was a seasonal place, renewing itself annually with the advent of the first warm weather. Most inhabitants arrived in the spring with their wagons. The wall's huge stones formed the back of the improvised stalls, offering crevasses and interstices to accept the poles and beams for the shelters constructed there by scores of craftsmen and traders. Later arrivals had to build away from the wall, making their booths self-standing. This haphazard collection of structures perched back-to-back with the city, like a rebellious child to its parent, looking out over the cool green countryside beyond. On Faire days, an entire metropolis of tents sprang up around the summer market, doubling its size, filling the whole space between the wall and the river. Altogether, the Faire was a city in its own right, but without the weight of permanence. Its stands, stalls, pavilions, and hutches were covered with bright canvas awnings and tops in all hues, cuts, and shapes, like the surrounding tents. As the comrades beheld it all, the afternoon breeze played in and out under the striped fabrics, making them swell and undulate and their flags flutter, so the whole of it resembled a living hedge of movement, color, and life.

"Ay, ye gods, I just love it!" expostulated Steward, and they plunged in among the craftsmen, artisans, entertainers, food sellers, and itinerant merchants. Every kind of goods were hung, stacked, spread, and piled under the awnings. Their progress was often impeded as they encountered small crowds gathered to watch a particularly impassioned bartering session, or raggedy buskers under the sign of a golden toad. The boys had been taken to the Faire in previous years by their parents, but this was the first time any but Steward had been there unchaperoned, free to browse. Flags had seen the fire-eaters before; he found them no less fascinating now. Pilot watched in astonishment the accuracy of a knife thrower who concluded his performance by running the length of a rapier's blade down his throat.

Everywhere were musicians, some playing a drum with one hand and a whistle with the other; others had lutes or lyres and sang. All kept as much distance as they could between themselves and the pestilent strolling bagpipers, who never seemed able to get their instruments quite in tune no matter how much they pinched and wet their reeds. Steward seemed to enjoy everything, for to any performers whose hats fell within his reach, he gave small coins from the cash reserve he had gathered for the event. Steward's treat to his own comrades was to buy them whatever they wanted to eat. Pilot found a brass astrolabe that he would like to have bought, but its price was too dear. Steward found and bought a runcible spoon, without dickering, and Flags bought a thin paper of powdered unicorn horn from a swarthy purveyor of medicines, elixirs, and aphrodisiacs. According to the salesman, anyone ingesting the powder in their soup or wine was guaranteed to be irresistibly stimulated. A very small quantity of it was extremely expensive, but Flags persuaded the salesman to let him have the little packet for three silver coins, all the money his mother had given him. (When he came back the following day indignantly to demand its return, the man was gone.) They watched mummers, mimes, and a magician who could change a perfectly ordinary walking staff into a live snake. But they never lingered too long anywhere before an impatient Bosun wanted to be moving along. Bosun, whose buy of the day was a new sailmaker's palm (his old one was nearly worn out), remained constantly on guard against pickpockets, and he kept a protective eye on his mates, all of whom he thought careless, especially Steward, who carried his bag of coins in a pouch slung round his neck by a lanyard.

"Somebody could cut that lanyard and be gone with your money before you knew what was happening," Bosun warned him several times. The Faire was a well-known hunting ground for cutpurses, muggers, scoundrels, and other ne'er-do-wells such as blind beggars who could see, cripples who were faster on their feet than one might suspect, and gamblers with games that promised much profit but somehow always cost dear.

"You can't be too careful in a place like this," said Bosun. The City Guard had no jurisdiction beyond the gates, which were well-manned with alert sentries whose job was to keep out or arrest known predators. There was no such protection at the summer market.

Among those not allowed to pass the gates of the city were the Gypsies, who were alleged to steal babies. Romantic stories were told of them. It was said they could seep anywhere, like water, no matter what cautions were taken against them, and among them were *brujos,* or sorcerers, who could sour milk and do nobody knew what else. Indeed, on the very site where the Gypsy camp was now attached to the Faire, a number of their forebears had been burned alive as sorcerers a century before. Sorcery was still a dangerous profession; supposedly, the real ones carefully hid themselves under different labels.

Bosun was alert in every fiber as they approached the place of the Gypsies, but even to Bosun, the reality of the place seemed less threatening than some of the other parts of the Faire.

"What's an O-R-A-C-L-E?" asked Crew, reading a sign on a Gypsy tent.

"An oracle? It's a seer," said Pilot, "an individual who has–claims to have–the ability to see the future and tell people what their fortune may be. My father says it's all a lot of nonsense. Why do you ask?"

"Because there's one," said Crew, pointing to the sign. They all looked. In smaller letters underneath the title, the sign read: "Your future told by the Pythoness–families and groups at reduced rates."

"We're a group," said Crew, pleased at the opportunity to say so again.

"My treat," said Steward, walking toward the tent, leaving the others to follow along.

"Ahoy the tent," said Steward, but there was no immediate response. The only person nearby was a nondescript old woman who was splitting wood and apparently had a cold, to judge from her sniffles.

"Where's the Oracle?" Steward asked. "And what's a Pythoness?"

"A moment," said the old woman, gathering an armload of wood and going with it into the tent through a rear flap. A minute later, she appeared at the front flap and beckoned. "*Oracle es,*" she said with an unknown foreign accent. "What is your question?"

"We would like you to tell us our fortunes," said Steward.

"We're a group," put in Crew.

"I see," said the Oracle. "Well, come in, then."

Flags, who was already disappointed in the costuming of this old actress, resigned himself to an amateur performance the moment he saw the interior of the tent. It had no dramatic trappings at all, containing only a chair and a small table with a candle on it and, conveniently, five stools. A curtain divided off the tent, making a back room, but this backdrop bore none of the astrological or cabalistic symbols it could well have used, thought Flags. A skull on the table would also have helped, he reflected, and an owl would have been a good touch. The Oracle motioned for them to be seated and sat down herself, brandishing a handkerchief.

"Since coming to this climate, I've had a cold," she noted, "and when you've left, I'm going back where I came from."

"Where's that?" asked Pilot.

"It's unimportant. Let's get on with it. My fee will be one piece of silver from each of you."

"We are a group," said the parsimonious Bosun.

"Yes, as noted," said the Oracle with her hand open. And a rather stiff fee it was, Flags thought as he watched Steward pay it over. That done, the Oracle took up a handful of sticks that were painted in different colors. "Now, watch. You hold them like this, and you let them fall. See?" Gathering up the sticks, she handed them to Bosun, who cast them. The Oracle became absorbed in a silent examination of their pattern, a process unrelieved by any of the dramatic devices Flags felt would have made for a better piece of showmanship. When she picked up the sticks and handed them to Pilot to cast, his turn took as long as the first, and then the diviner spent twice as long in her study of Crew's cast. Crew's! Flags could not help yawning repeatedly. The old ham—well, not a ham; quite the opposite—was sadly overplaying an already extended act, he thought, beyond tedium. How could she make any money if she took this long with everybody? Next, it was Steward's turn, and finally, his own. To Flags's irritation, the examination of his cast took less than half the time of anybody else's.

"Sorry," said the Oracle to Flags, leaving him wondering why she had said it anyway. The Oracle leaned back in her chair and took up her handkerchief again. "First a couplet, for all of you, which you may take as your situation." She paused, not for dramatic effect, but for a sneeze, which took a while coming and was followed by a lengthy blowing of the nose. Finally, she closed her eyes and recited:

> One is five, and five are one,
> Land and sea, sky, wind, and sun.

"What does that mean?" asked Bosun.

"That's not for me to say," the Oracle responded, "but there's more, a quatrain for each of you individually. I'll start with you," she said to Bosun.

> When wind at sea blows properly,
> It fills the well-trimmed sails,
> But when with Force and Jealousy,
> Mind hurricanes and gales.

Next, the Oracle turned to Pilot:

> When ice is here and ice is there,
> And ice is all around,
> Within its glare find something fair,
> Or hell will find no bound.

"Now you," she said to Crew:

> When spaciousness is vast and wide,
> Its wisdom knows no doubt,
> But emptiness solidified
> Makes space turned inside out.

Then to Steward:

> When overloaded is thy plate
> And poisoned is thy cup,

> Before the hour grows too late,
> Make sure thou do'st throw up.

Finally, to Flags:

> The hearth blaze heats both house and fold,
> The candle lights the night.
> The chimney fire, taking hold,
> Burns everything in sight.

At once, they were full of questions, but the Oracle held up her hand for silence. "Those are your cautions, but there is a last part; for all of you equally again":

> Five are one, and one is five.
> Close the circle to arrive.

"Arrive where?" Pilot wanted to know, but no amount of questioning elicited any further information, and another round of sneezing ended the interview.

"Have a good voyage," she said, bustling them out.

"What did it all mean?" asked Crew as they emerged from the tent.

Bosun shrugged. "A waste of money."

"I think the point," sniffed Pilot, "is the absurdity of trying to learn anything at all except by an examination of facts in a scientific way that has nothing to do with little sticks or any other superstitious stuff."

"But what did it mean, what she said?" asked Crew.

None of them could remember more than a few fragments of what the Oracle had said, everything having been so easily forgettable. Flags noted she didn't even look like a Gypsy.

"Well, she did say something about the voyage we're going to make together, didn't she?" persisted Crew. The rest had turned their attention back to the Faire. Getting no response, Crew tried again. There was one valuable thing he saw in it, and he wanted to underscore the point. "Didn't she talk about our voyage?" Still, they didn't seem to hear, and so he let it go.

Soon, they were distracted by a female tightrope walker making amazing body contortions on her high perch, and after that, they saw a dancing bear, the fattest lady in the world, ten pipers piping, nine drummers drumming, an unplanned dogfight, a tattooed weight lifter, a pair of dwarf twins with a trained seal, a three-headed pig, and a berzerker who came running through the crowd with an ax in his hand, chasing in a very determined way somebody they never saw. On the whole, they agreed it was a very successful afternoon, the disappointment of the Oracle notwithstanding.

T HE SUBSEQUENT Faire days that found Steward wandering among the sunlit stalls and canopied compounds clinging to the base of the wall found Pilot somewhere within the wall itself, or under it, probing its secrets; in them, he had found a challenge to which he was inexorably drawn.

With somber and massive majesty, the Old City wall brooded, a thick serpent of chiseled gray rock following the hill's arc across the neck of the peninsula occupied by the Port. Its ends terminated in fortresses footed on rock cliffs descending into the sea. Between the two castles were towers, bastions, and ravelins spaced at half-furlong intervals. Barbicans enfolded the gates. The body of the wall itself was nearly two hundred chains in length and fully four rods thick at the place where its base was thinnest, which was also the measure of its average height. Nobody knew how old the wall was. It had been built in time before memory. The wall viewed by the lads' generation appeared much as it had for the previous few hundred years, although it had undergone countless minor modifications.

Not always had it appeared thus. It was well known that before the present wall, there had existed at least one much older. Some sections of this more ancient presence had been incorporated into the later one. There were also foundations of ancient forts and other anomalous structures that had once attached to the wall, like parasites. So many of them were there, and of such antiquity, nobody could make any sense or pattern of the ruins. In its most recent incarnation, the wall had withstood armed assaults many times, as well as formal siege. It had been breached only once, and that had been due to treachery from within. Even then, the enemy penetration had been blunted by swiftly moving reinforcements through the passages built within the wall, and the attackers were trapped and annihilated. In the time of the long peace, the Port had experienced no serious threat of invasion by land for two generations, and so, inevitably, the wall had fallen increasingly into disrepair. Ironically, the wall guards now patrolled the time-eaten battlements, not against any exterior enemy, but to keep the Port's own citizens off its walks and out of its crumbling interior, protecting them from the massive entity that had for so long been their protector. It was not a good place for children to play or adults to stroll. Long ago, the wooden doors into the towers had been spiked closed, and all the other, less obvious entrances had been permanently sealed off.

There were a few routes by which the wall could be scaled, where old mortar had crumbled out of the masonry, providing toeholds for those daring enough to climb, but there were also a few easier routes onto the wall that were known to most of the Port's boys. These included a tower door that looked solid to the adult eye but contained a removable plank. Pilot had early found this entrance to lead no farther than the tower's interior, which was filled with old rubble that had fallen when the roof caved in many years earlier. For that reason, it was well illuminated, but it was also a dead end. Pilot was one of the few boys who returned to the wall more than once. For one thing, being caught on the wall meant serious trouble for the offender, from the authorities and from parents. For another, the wall had many genuinely forbidding aspects, and it was for good reason that the whole thing had been made rigidly off bounds to everybody. Its towers and fortresses were full of decrepit stairs. Many of the long, winding wooden casements were rotten, and some of the masonry steps had stones so loose they needed only the tread of a single foot to send them crashing and bouncing down onto anyone following. Such accidents had taken ample toll of the heedless over the decades.

Also, and most frightening of all, through and beneath the wall and its structures wove a vast, cancerous labyrinth of caverns and passageways. In former times, colonies of bandits and homeless men turned brigands had camped there. From their secret lairs, they had raided out into the city, until a systematic sweep by soldiers had cleansed the entire structure of its human vermin. With the soldiers had gone masons, to seal off those narrow passageways where not even the soldiers cared to go, and it was assumed that many of the undesirables were encrypted alive at that time, to haunt their dark tombs for all eternity.

Pilot had been fascinated from the first by the tales of the deep labyrinth. His own parents had unwittingly pricked his interest with their warnings regarding the wall and its dangers. His curiosity aroused, he had learned the known ways into the wall and systematically investigated all of them. All had led into upper areas, and in none did he find any opening into the supposed tunnel system within. There were plenty of walled-up portals. Having no way of breaking through these, he took his investigation to the outside.

Steward's family estate backed up to a section of the wall containing archaic ruins and the foundations of once-attached structures. These foundations were now home to a small woods in a place visited only by children. Searching there along the surface of the wall, Pilot located several patched areas where doors had once been, high up, but he could find none near the level of the ground. One day, he went there during a rain, which permitted him to follow a small stream of runoff water to a point where it seemed to vanish into the bushes. He pushed into the shrubbery and almost at once found that the water ran into a shallow concavity filled with dead leaves. Under these, he found some rotten wooden boards, which came away in pieces, revealing a rectangular opening carved between the massive foundation stones of the wall just beneath the surface of the ground. It was a tunnel entrance.

Without hesitation, he entered it. He found himself within a vaulted corridor of perspiring masonry, dimly illuminated for only a short distance by light filtering in through the thick foliage outside. A few feet beyond, all was darkness and silence, but for a distant dripping of water from somewhere in the blackness. Pilot hardly breathed.

"Black as the pit," he thought, pleased, peering into the dank depth of it. Much later, he would remember that whisper of thought and be haunted by it.

Over the course of the following week, he found time to plan and equip his first exploratory expedition, anticipating all the things he would need. These included three light sources. The first was a fire-pot, a cylindrical canister made of thin brass perforated with scores of holes punched in patterns around it. It had a removable cap so that a fire of small, dry twigs could be started in it. When the fire was going and the top replaced, the firepot was carried dangling by a bridle at the end of a piece of line, like a censer, and it could be swung around in circles so the air whistling in through the holes would fan the fire within, making it blaze. The device gave only a dim light even when its tinder was burning brightly. It was, however, difficult to extinguish by accident and so provided a nearly indestructible source of fire, which could be used to ignite Pilot's other light sources.

One of these was a torch, which had been made by tightly binding and sewing rags around the end of a short staff. When saturated with oil and ignited, it gave a bright light, but only for a short time. When its fuel was consumed, it had to be smothered and recharged with oil before it could be relit. He had also devised a leather skullcap with a socket on top for a candle. It gave good light and was handy because it did not shine in his eyes, but it was vulnerable to drafts. He had also equipped himself with a walking staff heavy enough to be a weapon but light enough to be used as a probe. In his pocket was a small compass, marking chalk, and a notebook and pencil. Lighting the firepot and a candle, he entered the hole and started forward into the tunnel.

He found he could see very well in the candlelight, and he made fast progress for seventy-two paces, at which point a low point in the overhead vaulting knocked the candle off his cap. Up to that place, the tunnel had been a featureless throat of moist stone, tending slightly downward. He realized almost at once that he would have to invent a bubble level of some kind with an angle measure attached so that he could record his rate of descent or ascent, enabling him to calculate his depth or elevation. Counting paces gave him distance, and his compass gave him direction. The compass told him the passage had curved a full three points to the north. He whirled the firepot until it blazed, being careful not to strike a wall. Finding it provided just enough illumination, he marked a conspicuous chalk mark "1" on the biggest stone, made a notation in his book, and moved on, tapping the shadows ahead with the staff, feeling with it for obstructions or holes. Soon, his owl's eyes made another adjustment, and he found he could see almost as well as before the candle had been extinguished. *Whooosh, whooosh, whooosh* went the firepot as he swung it; *tap, tap, tap* went the stick, probing, antennalike into the darkness.

Without warning, there was a wall directly in his path, detected simultaneously by the dim glow from the firepot and the tip of the stick. His tunnel had abruptly run at right angles into a second tunnel, which led off upward on his right, and downward on his left. "Better and better," he said, pausing just long enough to take the new bearing and record it. He marked the wall "two" and turned left. Nine paces later, his probe found a step, and then another–seventeen of them in all, all duly recorded, along with the new bearings and number of paces. *Whooosh, whooosh, whooosh* went the censer, and he found his tunnel joined at that spot with two other tunnels, both somewhat broader, but apparently level. Having made the notations and his chalk mark, he entered the right-hand passage, which went straight, then angled left two points, and returned to its original course, where he sensed some kind of change. Unable to define it, he stopped, listening, staring at the dim reflection from the firepot onto the stone, trying to receive whatever subtle signal he had just intuited. But there was nothing.

*Whooosh, whooosh, whooosh; tap, tap, tap-tap.* Now, he identified what he had noticed: the sound of the taps had changed, subtly: they were slightly more hollow sounding, which he assumed must mean the tunnel was approaching a larger space of some kind. *Whooosh,*

*whooosh, whooosh* went the firepot, trailing sparks, but the small glare it made found no surface except the stones of the floor.

With no warning, the blackness in front of him rushed into his face on dry wings; the staff clattered from his hand, but then the black rush was past and vanishing down the passage behind him. It had startled him, but his study had led him to expect bats in the tunnels. He hoped to learn something of their ability to fly in total darkness without crashing into things. He relit the candle. Still, there were no walls. He lit the torch. At once, everything was bathed in yellow light–a high, vaulted ceiling supported by columns whose black shadows danced against distant walls. Pilot found himself standing in a large, oval chamber, with many other tunnels of various sizes entering it. Turning slowly, he counted a dozen tunnel mouths, some of them accessible by steps leading up, others containing steps leading down. The thin corners of his mouth twitched into a smile. A rusty brazier clung to one of the columns; Pilot stuck his torch into it, seated himself on a stone that had at some time fallen out of the ceiling, and began diagramming the complexities of that dark honeycomb world.

N O MAN WAS EVER to learn all the secrets of the labyrinth. None of its many builders ever knew more than the small parts of it that they had excavated, and the same was true of its designers. Over the centuries, fresh tunnelers had stumbled on former tunnels of which they had been unaware, and so passages were blocked up or incorporated, depending upon the purpose of the later work. There were dungeons aplenty, as well as subterranean meeting and even dwelling places and secret storage chambers, but for the most part, the purposes of the various sections of the labyrinth were secrets that had died with their makers. Not even the talented Pilot could chart all its innermost mysteries, although in time he came as close as any man had ever come.

At the outset Pilot obtained permission for what he termed his study by simply telling his father what it was about and showing to him the schematic diagram he was constructing. The Captain was dubious but in the end decided it was a test the lad had chosen for himself, and it would be best to let him run his passion through. The Captain had no doubt of the boy's ability, and he considered the more ominous stories about the wall to be superstitious.

With the Captain's sanction, and the freedom of his spare time, Pilot vanished from the world of his comrades to follow the riddle of the labyrinth. In his prowlings, he learned very nearly to see in the dark, discerning, correlating every pale particle of distant reflection on sweaty stone. He learned to walk comfortably through many of the tunnels with no light at all, though he only did that in sections he had come to know well, where there were no sudden holes in the floor or unexpected steps. He had found the tunnels within the main mass of the walls mostly predictable in their linkages to the towers and old forts, where certain patterns repeated themselves. But most of the system—especially the deep system—had no apparent reason or logic. Some tunnels terminated enigmatically in cave-ins, where rotten vaulting had given way; others had been walled off; others wound in baffling tracery, apparently leading nowhere, sometimes branching off, sometimes turning back on themselves. Some passages, like the one by which he had originally entered, led to points outside the wall into the foundations of forgotten structures. Most of these had been sealed with mortar and stone, but he found some that had not, including one that ran nearly half a league down the hill, to a point he reckoned to be under the Old City, where it terminated in a door that was bolted from the opposite side, but which (he noticed) had well-oiled hinges.

During the nearly three years it took Pilot to map the labyrinth, he found most of its forgotten passages and all of the straight, broad corridors that ran within the wall for its whole length, connecting the towers. These were patrolled. The main corridors had been built as concealed avenues of retreat or reinforcement if and when the wall was breached. The guards on their patrol duty were no match for Pilot, whose presence they never suspected. They carried lanterns and could be heard approaching from a great distance. Sound carried far in the tunnels, and Pilot found the patrols easy to avoid. Indeed, he sometimes followed them, until he had learned their habits and patterns. He was aware of occasional beings other than himself and the soldiers. Several times, he had avoided men passing through the upper tunnels with shaded lanterns on dubious errands. Pilot wore soft leather shoes; he had padded the tip of his staff so that it tapped no more; he always listened as he proceeded, and he moved with the silence of the rats.

Once, he encountered a group of older boys blundering through the passages on an adventure. From their voices, he recognized them as a well-known pack of bullies. He crept close to them in the darkness and then shattered their universe with a demented shriek. Wetted with the sudden hot wine of terror, they ran, careening into walls, driven by a panic beyond panic, and with a snarling ink-black fiend in dark pursuit.

Nevertheless, it was a dangerous business he had undertaken, and he had reminders of that. Under a section of the south wall, deep underground, he stumbled into a bear's den reeking with decaying offal, and he fled for his life, fearing the beast was nearby. Another time, exiting from the labyrinth by the same passages he had explored earlier in the day, he found his chalk marks rubbed out, by what hand he never knew. He did not like it that someone as darkling as himself had been behind him on his route. He tightened his cautions after that.

After more than two years of Pilot's preoccupation, it became clear to his mother and his four comrades that it was consuming him. He had once taken the other four members of his company–he had no other friends of his age–with him into the maze of tunnels. They had been interested enough in the mysterious place for the space of a morning, but by lunchtime, all wanted to get out into the sunshine again. None had any interest in returning, although they all wanted Pilot back into their company. The Captain might have tried to curb

Pilot's obsession, but he had departed the year before to command a convoy into distant seas. In his absence, the Captain's permission still held, and his wife's remonstrances with Pilot had no sway. The boy's normal reserve deepened, and while he maintained a tolerant interest in his worldly life, some part of him abided in dark corridors.

Flags tried to deflect his interest, bringing a particularly vivacious and attractive girl, one Syringia, to meet Pilot. Although she brought into play all of her considerable inventory of resources, she made no impression on him. This was a first experience for her and a painful one for Pilot, who fidgeted. Even in normal circumstances, he was shy with girls. He finally responded by lecturing to her at length on the extraordinary night vision of bats.

The other lads also tried to interest him in their pursuits, but they had no more success. Pilot considered Steward's fixation with entertainment to be indulgent; he did not share Bosun's soaring ambition; and Flags's campaign to seduce what seemed like the entire female population of the city seemed to Pilot little better than the frenzied ramblings of a blind dog in a meat house. During Crew's one experience in the labyrinth, he had moved like a stampede of cattle, crashing into walls, tripping on steps, and finally complaining of claustrophobia. So Pilot pursued his dark quest alone, and that suited him well enough, until at last the labyrinth itself did for him what his friends and family had been unable to accomplish.

Having mapped all those parts of his subterranean world that he could discover without excavation, Pilot turned his investigations back to certain puzzling areas that, in passing, he had marked for further study. One of these was a deep vault that was featureless except for a rubble of stones and a small drainage gutter carrying away into a hole in the masonry the runoff from a dripping, vaulted ceiling. He was interested in where the water could be running to, because the vault was deeper–far deeper–underground than any other place he had found. Eventually, he found concealed under a cairn of loose stones a small trapdoor, whose wood was sound but whose hinges and hasp had rusted entirely away. When he pried it up, there emerged from the aperture a long exhalation of cool air as his fluttering candle revealed an even deeper chamber directly beneath the vault, with steep, narrow steps descending into it. He lit his torch and went down.

It was a crypt. The high walls were featureless but for their vaulting and had no apparent exits save the one by which he had entered. There was an expanse of bare, stone floor with a cistern or well casing in its center. The cistern was covered by a heavy, round cap resembling a millstone. Propping his torch in a brazier, he heaved against the stone with all of his weight. It moved and then slid aside and crashed to the floor, revealing what seemed indeed to be an open well. With his torch, Pilot could peer deeply into it. It was a straight, vertical shaft with no visible end.

"Well," he said aloud, "let's get to the bottom of you." So saying, he picked up from the floor a fragment of fallen mortar, held it suspended over the middle of the well, and leaned over so that he could watch and listen into its depths. Releasing the rock, he started an even count: "One a-thousand, two a-thousand, three a-thousand. . . ." He stopped counting at sixty, having heard or seen nothing. He repeated the experiment, straining for any distant message, but with no better result. Finally, he dropped into the hole a rock so large he had difficulty lifting it to the middle of the pit. He was sure its crash would be audible no matter how deep the hole. Yet again, there was nothing, no distant click or scrape to indicate the stone had been deflected in its fall, even though, in the awesome silence of that sounding tube, any slightest noise should have been transmitted a vast distance.

"Perhaps some light on the subject," said Pilot, dropping his torch into the hole. In its flaming descent, it cast flickering patterns on the walls of the well, but within a few seconds, its reflections were too dim to see; another moment its blaze was only a prick of light; then, it was gone. Pilot contemplated the pit, and the complete mystery of it, with irritation. After a while, he lit his cap candle and made his way up out of the crypt.

For his next visit, Pilot equipped himself with a skein containing a quarter mile of light line. He made his way again down into the crypt; this time, he lit no torch to illuminate the chamber, for his interest was in only one light–that of a lantern that he attached to the end of the long line. To its bottom, he attached a small lead, as on a sounding line, with a smear of tallow on it. It was his idea to pay out whatever length of the line was required to reach the bottom of the well. He had decided that the bottom must be soft; possibly, it was covered with such a thickness of fungus or mosses as to absorb dropped objects, deadening sound and smothering light. He reckoned a fragment would come up with the tallow.

Arranging the skein of line so its coils would pay out properly, he began to lower the light. Its unflickering descent illuminated an unchanging bore perfectly round and cased neatly in a shiny, dark rock, like slate. Down and down went the light, the line snaking slowly out until there was no line left. Amazingly, irritatingly, the weight of its illuminated plumb bob still tugged at his hands. There was nothing to do but haul it back up again. Pilot reviewed for the hundredth time all of the possibilities. It was not a well, nor could it be. He reckoned a bucket at the end of a mile of rope would find no water. Nor was it a cistern; cisterns had less need for depth than wells, and besides, there was no water running into it from inside or out, nor any indication that any ever had. It was not a vertical tunnel, for its sides were smooth, with no kind of ladder or arrangement for handholds. Overhead, there was no ringbolt for a pulley or winch, nor any place for such an apparatus. What purpose, then?

He had another scheme, postponed until last because it required a grenado. This was a hollow cast-iron sphere loaded with gunpowder and fused, a dangerous munition not readily available to anybody not in the military. Pilot finally obtained one from a favorite uncle who was also a naval officer. The boy got it by simply explaining exactly what he wanted to do with the weapon. His uncle, knowing him to be a prudent and scientific lad, saw no harm in taking one grenado from his ship's supply. He even helped Pilot arrange a long and sure-burning sheathed fuse that would detonate the bomb three minutes after it was lit. To prevent the grenado's landing on its fuse or sinking in water, it was contained in a large, hard gourd. If the contact was with water, it would float with its burning fuse contained; if with rock, the gourd could shatter, the grenado would not. When Pilot descended with it to the crypt on his final attempt, he was sure he had in hand the means with which to get to the bottom of the thing.

"Now, we'll see about you," he said to the pit as he prepared the grenado. He reckoned, that, whatever its terminus, no matter how far distant, the brilliant blast of the bomb should be reflected visibly even in a curved shaft, and if not, its tremendous explosion should carry in that sounding tube for miles. Pilot lit the fuse, assured himself that it was burning correctly, and capped the gourd over it, sealing it home. Within, there was air to feed the fuse's fire for more than the time of its burning. Pilot held it over the hole and then let it slip from his fingers.

"Have this," he said.

There was nothing to be learned by counting except when to expect the blast. When two minutes had passed, he reflected that the bomb was at that moment either lying or floating on whatever surface had stopped it. Three minutes came and went, however, and then five, and then fifteen. Pilot remained fixed, straining his eyes and ears into the blackness. Perhaps the fuse–so reliable during testing–was burning longer than anticipated. It was the only explanation he could think of. Nothing else made sense. But then again, nothing about the whole situation made any sense at all.

Pilot relaxed his vigil, straightened his body, rose, and lit a torch. For a long time, he stood, peering into the pit with no more idea where it stopped than he'd had at the beginning. Obviously, there was that point down there somewhere, awaiting discovery. Perhaps someday, but not now, he decided. At last, he mounted the steps to the chamber above, pausing at the top. In the dancing light of his torch, he contemplated again the vaulted chamber and its eldritch secret. Pilot regretted his inability to cover over the pit again, but he could not lift the heavy stone lid back onto the casing. Why had it been covered in the first place? "So stay open," he said, then climbed into the chamber above, replaced the wooden trapdoor in the floor over the crypt, and distributed over it the same rocks that had hidden its presence since unknown antiquity. Emerging from the labyrinth, he found himself completely resealing and rehiding his secret entryway. Then, he walked in sunlight down the hill toward the sea.

IN THEIR SEVENTEENTH YEAR, each of the lads was required to make a working voyage on one or another of the Port's ships. Bosun was the first to receive his assignment, as sailmaker's assistant aboard a galleon bound on a voyage of nearly two years. His departure was in the summer, and he was given a festive send-off by all. Steward sailed in the autumn on a yearlong voyage aboard one of his father's ships (as steward, appropriately enough), and Pilot departed in the winter, signing articles as a volunteer junior officer in the navy as navigator aboard a warship accompanying a convoy to the east. Of their company, only Crew was left to send off Flags, sailing as supercargo in the spring, and when Crew left soon thereafter, before the mast on a trading galleon bound for far places, he waved good-bye to a dock that was empty of any person who was there to wave back to him.

# IV  *Alembic*

STEWARD ESCAPED from the meeting with his father's financial
counselors. He did not sneak, but he did manage to withdraw
without being noticed, and he headed for the rear gate by the
most direct route. This took him to the great hall, where he heard his
name being paged before he had even entered the busy place. Realizing there could easily be a dozen people there looking for him, he
abruptly turned into a side corridor by which he could circumnavigate
the hall and avoid it entirely. Walking quickly, he made his way
through the scullery and the laundry room, then up past the arbore-
tum and the mews, around the cooperage, and out a little-used back
door near the stable, where he roused a groom to saddle his horse.
Mounted, he spurred from the yard, reining his steed hard to starboard into an alleyway between the brewery and the bakery. This took
him a direct line to the south gate, through which he clattered with a
friendly wave to the startled sentry. Only when he had cantered far
enough from the Manor to be sure he wasn't being followed did he rein
his mount to a walk.

"Free!" he bellowed to the sky. The horse, who had been enjoying
the run, broke hopefully into a canter again, but Steward put him back
to a walk at once.

"Horse," he said, "if I must flee like a felon from my own house in order to get a few moments to myself on my twenty-sixth birthday, let us stretch those moments and savor them." He reflected on those precious years of his youth when he had once had lots of spare time and the run of the city and its delights. It seemed so long ago.

He took a deep breath, inhaling the fragrance of spring. Below him spread the Port with the late afternoon sunlight vividly reflecting from the roofs of the buildings, turning them into gold. Beyond spread the sea. The breeze on his cheek was gentle and from the southwest. If it veered at all, he thought, it would be fair for the departure of the small convoy of his father's ships assembled in the outer harbor. He could see them quite clearly in the anchorage, and he wished they were gone. Their sailing was still delayed, however, by the discovery of contaminated casks of salt beef among the provisions and a possible pox case aboard the flag vessel. This ship had now been shifted to the quarantine anchorage, he noticed. To add to his troubles–for the sailing of the squadron depended in great measure upon himself–he had just received the news of an apparently mutinous assault on the master of the brigantine. He would have to learn more about it tomorrow morning. Then, the afternoon would be occupied with the adjudication of a disagreement between the estate's farmers and the keeper of the granary, a tenured retainer who was better at his job than anyone else but chronically unable to get along with anybody. It was a matter that was really the responsibility of sons number three and five, but as usual, those two of his brothers were off hunting.

As the youngest of the Master's brood, Steward wondered how so many responsibilities had devolved upon him, although when he considered his brothers, there was no mystery in it. Brothers two and four stayed closer to home, but their squabbling was interminable; number six, his immediate elder, had become the curator of the container collection, many of which he had also helped empty. Number one, the heir apparent, was useless for anything but officiating at ceremonial occasions, and not totally reliable even for those, Steward–everybody's surrogate stand-in these days–knew better than anybody. As his family had inevitably come to rely more and more upon him, Steward had come to feel more and more the weight of it all.

"Whew!" With a sudden exhalation, Steward cleaned his mind and lungs at the same time, blowing out his thoughts like a cloud of gnats, returning his attention to the moment. Inevitably, the gnats gathered again at once, but this time more invitingly, as thoughts about this splendid day–a meeting again with his four oldest and best friends, all together again for the first time in years.

At the same moment, Flags was making his way toward the same destination thinking similar thoughts. They had all been seventeen when they had been sent off to sea, which was the last time their whole company had assembled. Then, they had all sailed over the horizon. He had not seen Crew since, although he was aware of his stolid friend's several voyages. Crew had returned to the Port only briefly between trips before shipping out again. He had been well liked in his ships as a treasured listener in a sailors' community of talkers and a rock of stability in any chaos. Crew. Flags smiled. How he missed his old friend. How he missed them all.

Even though the other three had been in the city since he returned, he had seen them only from time to time. On the one occasion the four of them had met together, they had dined at the Manor, but Steward had been so continually interrupted throughout the evening, he had hardly been able to be with them. In truth, Steward seemed as busy as Bosun, and Bosun was busier than he had ever been. Bosun was a great success, having begun a sail loft that had quickly become very profitable. He now also owned a part interest in a coastal trading vessel, and he had organized some of the city's urchins into a group of errand runners for hire. In fact, one of them had delivered the message (in Pilot's handwriting) assigning the rendezvous toward which Flags was headed at that moment. Pilot. Reclusive Pilot, off on ships or buried in his books. Pilot had also gained local success–as a cartographer and writer of navigational instructions for various waters.

Flags sighed. He alone of his company of childhood companions had not made his mark. He had finally returned to the Port and his mother's house after his lengthy stay in the classical land on the Middle Sea, the sea of the world's renascent civilization and its seat of culture as far as Flags was concerned. Missing it for the ten-thousandth time, Flags let his mind linger in his memories–select memories–of that fantastic, sunlit culture with its galleries, palaces, and theaters. He had fallen in love with the place at first sight, which had happened on his second voyage as supercargo. His employers had been sorry to lose him, but Flags had claimed his freedom without a backward glance, shedding his career like a sweaty costume. He had then submerged himself in the great civilization's arts and culture–as well as its Jasmine, Rhododendra, Honeysuckle, and other flora, replacing the garden he had left behind with a semitropical counterpart. Its very lushness had been directly responsible for his abrupt departure. Since coming home, Flags had made every effort to bring a whisper of that distant warm land to the Port, with drama and song, even opening a theater with funds provided by his mother. She had been overjoyed to do something to keep him at home and had suggested the investment herself. His theatrical presentations had made him aware–embarrassingly aware–that one charming performer does not a whole theater make. Too, there was his obligation to his mother, whose need of him since his return had seemed even more intense than he remembered it. His grandfather had passed from the world, leaving her his ample estate but nobody to fix her love upon but her son. Feeling the weight of it in full measure, Flags had taken on the chore of providing her with more of his company since his return, which was preferable to his guilty feelings when he did not. He turned a corner of the lane and encountered a breeze carrying with it a fresh breath of the sea.

Bosun was determined not to be late to the great birthday meeting, not by a minute, and he had finished all he had to do in time to be there punctually. Now, standing on the threshold of the street door, he consulted the checklist he had made of everything that needed doing before he could leave the loft in the hands of his chief assistant, a good enough journeyman at his work, Bosun felt, but nobody to be trusted with full responsibility.

Bosun strode forth at a brisk pace, using the time to review other matters on his agenda, modifying some as he thought of them, rearranging others, planning their sequences, at the same time noticing the wind direction and the set of the sky, in which the late afternoon clouds had swallowed the sun. Pilot's message had made *Vessle* the point of rendezvous, for whatever reason. Bosun had kept her ship-shape over the years. That was unchanged. He had been appalled by her condition when he had returned from his first voyage. After that, he had made arrangements for her to be professionally tended during his absences, and now, she was looked after by his retainers. He still intended to do some of her work himself, if he could ever get to it. Meanwhile, his four comrades would find their boat in good order. He had long ago given up the notion of getting help with the upkeep from any of the others, even when they were there.

It was a marvel to him how their lives had changed. In looking back over the years, he reckoned Steward, Flags, Crew, and Pilot had been the best friends he had ever had—even with their quirks and even if they always had stuck him with most of the work. He corrected himself; they were his *only* real friends, though he hardly saw them anymore. Not his fault. Crew had been gone, Flags had his theatricals, and Steward was as busy as Bosun himself. Pilot had been ashore the six months past, mostly sequestered, writing a tract on navigation. It would be good to see him. All of them. Bosun quickened his pace.

Pilot himself was descending the hill from the east, heading for the place he had carefully chosen. Wearing a black cloak with hood that made him look more like a monk than a sailor, he walked close to the sides of the building, blending with the gray streets so well that his passage appeared as the passing of a shadow. Anyone whose eyes were quick enough to notice him and who looked closely enough would have seen that he was carrying a small parcel and something else half hidden under the flap of his cape. Rounding the last bend on his route to the harbor, he saw the docks, and there was *Vessle,* with somebody sitting in her. Crew? Pilot smiled.

It was indeed Crew. Well before the appointed time, he had been there, and it felt good to him to be awaiting, again, all of his comrades. He had first sat for some time on the same good old piling he had parked his bottom on in former years, just to see if it felt the same, and it did. He had then gone aboard *Vessle* and sat there, marveling how well Bosun had kept her up. And here he was. And suddenly, here was everybody else—all grown up, all different but all the same. Here Pilot, here Flags, here Bosun, and Steward on a horse—all arriving together from different directions with the precision of clockwork figures.

They met with a cheer: "Yay!!!"

"C'mon aboard," said Crew, beckoning to them from the diminutive boat of their childhood. They grinned at each other. *Vessle* had never looked smaller, nor had their company ever looked bigger. Steward seemed a giant.

"C'mon," said Crew, holding up the bailer. "I can still bail." So they cautiously stepped aboard, Steward first, seating himself on one side, making the boat tip crazily and forcing all the rest to position themselves to balance. For one moment, it seemed *Vessle* would capsize, but they all got themselves situated, with Pilot sitting at the helm. And so they sat there laughing and jostling one another, with everybody talking at once. Then they trooped off to the old tavern run by Bosun's parents. Sturdy Crew trudged, his feet planted wide at each step; Steward ambled, leading his horse; Flags strolled elegantly, turning heads of passersby; Pilot was catlike; Bosun strode out ahead, repeatedly having to wait until the others came up, then outpaced them again. At the tavern, they were the guests of honor, welcomed by Bosun's mum and dad with a round of drinks on the house. An outline of Crew's travels was prodded out of him, but it was hard going because he had been so many places he couldn't remember them all. He could hardly pronounce the names of those he did.

"I'm just glad to be back here with you," he said again and again, wishing he could think of something more eloquent. He alone among their company looked every inch the sailor, wearing the long, belted wool tunic (much patched) and knit stockings common to sailors just about everywhere in that time. The stockings came up above his knees and were full of irregularities. He had knitted them himself. "I learned how to knit," he said to Bosun, thinking it would please him. An examination of Crew's haphazard handiwork brought on new hilarity. He couldn't remember when he had ever had so much attention from them. Bosun wanted to know what his plans were next, thinking he would make a place for him somewhere in one of his enterprises.

"I don't have any plans," shrugged Crew. "What are your own

plans?" Bosun realized he had so many plans he didn't even know where to begin answering that question.

But Steward did. "Bosun's done very well for himself," he said, telling of Bosun's many successes. Bosun listened uneasily, not from modesty, but because he knew each of his accomplishments had brought with it some new frustration. Yes, his work had surpassed that of all his peers and teachers alike, but he had no friends among the many competitors he had embarrassed and the revered authorities he had dethroned. His modest shipping investment had paid off, yes, but what none of his comrades knew—and what he had learned only the day before—was that his partners were cheating him. Yes, there was his successful cadre of messengers for hire, but in employing a group of waifs who were as much like himself as he could find, he had given himself a lot more to deal with than he had anticipated, and he had already decided to dissolve that troublesome venture. In short, it seemed to him that all of his winning enterprises had soured in some way. Now, he found himself trapped like a pocket of dead air, sheared from the wind by a configuration of the land. As he listened to Steward's generous recitation of his accomplishments, Bosun found himself growing more and more envious of Crew's carefree life, such a marked contrast with his own. He was spared having to listen to any more by the announcement of supper.

During this, Flags regaled them with stories of the rich land where he had dwelled for so long, weaving wondrous descriptions of everything but its flora.

"Why did you leave?" asked Crew.

"Ah," said Flags with a wave. "So much . . . so rich . . . after a while one wants a rest, eh? Also, my mum needs me," he added.

Steward made note of Flags's theatrical endeavors (a recital Flags found as ironic as Bosun had found his); the memory of his grandfather was toasted, starting a succession of toasts to their various parents, including Bosun's parents several times because they were there and hosting the event. Then Crew proposed a toast: "To my parents too, whoever they are." And there was a clanking of tankards and the echo "Whoever they are . . ." This was followed by a toast to Pilot's parents, especially their early mentor the Captain, now Admiral, and to

Pilot's book, which was a sensitive topic. They all knew of his epic *Seaman's Pocket Primer of Navigation,* written over a period of eight years as an instruction by which anybody who could read it could navigate a ship. Its publication created a furor, however, and the entire printing had been called in by the Port authorities and burned. No reason was officially given, but there was little doubt that the admiralty wanted no such text in the hands of ordinary sailors. In fact, his father had cautioned him early in his project that there would be many who would regard such an "instruction" as an invitation to would-be mutineers.

"Only officers know navigation. With an instruction such as yours, any clever group of ambitious scum could take over their ship and go off on their own account. Even in the training, the navigators are separated early. You should know." Pilot did know that, but he had reckoned his work would be of such self-evident value as to overwhelm any objections. He had taken the responsibility for the misjudgment.

"But that's behind me," he shrugged, and then brightened: "In any case, I have a much more interesting thing to show you." He produced a roll of vellum. An area of the table was cleared of its clutter, and Pilot spread before them a carefully scaled line drawing showing the hull profile and sail plan of an unusual small craft, eight fathoms long on her deck and with a fathom's draft. It was of yawl rig, with one tall mast just forward of the midship line and a small steering mast aft. A long bowsprit extended by more than half the length of the boat overall. On another sheet, the hull was drawn as seen from below and from bow and stern. Bosun wanted to know what vessel they were looking at.

"It's a boat of my design," said Pilot, "incorporating the most efficient features of several kinds of small craft, with some innovations of my own. Its efficiency should appeal to you, Bosun."

"I could see it better in a model," said Bosun, "but it might be benefited by a bit more sail. What's its purpose?"

Pilot treated them to one of his occasional slight smiles. "It is a vessel I propose to build and sail on a voyage of exploration. I believe it's of adequate size to be sailed by a small crew over any distance."

"To where?" Bosun wanted to know.

"To the Southern Continent and the Western Isles," said Pilot.

Bosun whistled. "Do they exist?"

From childhood, they had all heard legends of a great Southern Continent, a place rich and fertile beyond the dreams of men, and of the seductive Western Isles, fair and beautiful, from whence supposedly no man ever returned once he had seen them. They had also heard of the vast oceans that separated those places and of the inconceivable difficulties in reaching them. It was a well-known fact that oceans did exist beyond the charted seas, but they were so vast and formidable, few men had ever attempted them. Indeed, none of their company had met any single mariner who could lay credible claim to having crossed them. In the absence of any reliable witnesses, charts, or evidence other than the persistent stories, most learned people now regarded the tales as mythical, especially since the loss of an exploratory expedition that had set out from the Port in the previous generation. It had sailed with high hopes of profit, but only one vessel had returned. Three years later, it had come drifting into the Port's approaches, a perfect wreck that had sunk as soon as its lone surviving crewman was carried ashore. Whatever had happened, he had been driven crazy by it, and nobody had been able to make any sense from his fantastic ravings where he had been or how the ship had managed to return to the Port at all or anything else. The investors had lost everything. After that, nobody had been eager to again take up the dangers and expense of any exploratory voyages.

"I'll bet everything I've got that *this* boat is capable of the ultimate voyage," said Pilot, stabbing the drawing. "Bosun thinks it could use more sail, and I welcome your further critique." And before they knew it, they were into a heated technical discussion. Steward thought the vessel Pilot had designed was too small, unable to carry enough provisions for a protracted voyage and still have room for cargo. Bosun also felt Pilot's boat wanted more size, with deck space for guns. Flags suggested a ducktail lift to its after end, improving the boat's look. Bosun thought Flags's concern with the boat's appearance to be frivolous, but Flags insisted that vessels that looked right sailed right, for whatever reasons, and an attractive vessel always made a good impression. Flags wanted to see some decoration. Pilot's design had no embellishments at all.

"How much can you afford to spend on this boat?" asked Bosun, ever practical.

"I can pay for perhaps half the hull," said Pilot, "but that's all."

"Then, how can you proceed?" asked Bosun.

"Only with partners. I was hoping I might interest the present company. After all, have we not vowed under solemn oath to do this very thing? Was it not prophesied by an Oracle? Pooling our resources, I believe we can do it. Think: all of us are well enough established to return to our occupations if need be, but if we find what we set out to find and return, there'll be profit by it. None of us has wife or family–yet. We've our good health and knowledge and resources. What better to go for than a goal that has defeated so many others?"

"I'll come," said Crew. "I always knew we were going to do it. I've saved all my wages, and they're yours."

"That makes two," said Pilot.

"I'll go," said Bosun. In an instant, Bosun had reviewed his entire life and veered like a sudden shift of wind. "If I sell what I've got, I'll be able to pay my share." Having said it, he had immediate doubts, but he did not take it back. In one breath, he had blown away his troubles like a dandelion puff and taken on a new goal.

"I'm in," Flags heard himself say. "With a loan from my mother . . ." The thought of asking for it made him wince with guilt, but there was no other way.

Then Steward spoke. "Pilot, you've given us a lot to digest. I for one can*not* come, whatever my own wishes. I can't say how my family would fare without me now. They need me more than you do. I'll gather a fifth share somehow, and you shall have it." He wondered how he was going to do that, for, with all he had done in his family's behalf, as its junior member he saw little enough wealth trickle down to him.

"I'll get the money somehow," he affirmed, "and I'll pay the wage of whomever you pick to fill my berth." Beyond that, he could not be budged.

And so it began, like *Vessle* all over again, it seemed, but with layers of added complexity. Nearly a fathom was added to the length of the new vessel, and her lines changed accordingly, including a bit of decoration to suit Flags. Bosun argued for and got his larger sails by simply being a bully about it.

"The sail and rig are my authority," he said, with a set to his jaw that got him his way. Bosun wanted four deck cannons each throwing a four-pound ball, but this was reduced by common consent to two three-pounder cannons. (It was agreed to cut an extra gunport on either side so both guns could be brought to bear from port or starboard.)

The work was begun on schedule in the early spring. When the boat's keel had been blocked into position, finished, and griped, her stem, sternpost, and deadwood were raised, followed by the sawn frames of her rib cage, and then the keelson was positioned. Bosun took over the work–scheduling for the various craftsmen who were hired or who came to help. There was also assistance from groups of training boys, whose help was dubious at best, as Bosun kept pointing out while he drove them.

"It's not like the old training," he would say, shaking his head in amazement at the ineptitude and laziness that had overtaken boys since the time of his own service. Bosun worked from first light until long after dark, doing more than anybody, as usual, driving the project. Steward procured all necessary supplies, getting bargain prices. He told his father of his commitment to purchase a one-fifth interest in the voyage and to provide a good sailor to serve as cook and steward in his own absence, for all of which he would need money.

The Master assented at once. "You've more than earned it," he said. "But why do ye not ask my permission to go with them? I've been expecting it."

"Father, you know well," said Steward. The old Master said nothing, and that seemed the end of it.

Stringers, clamps, shelves, and beams were fitted to the hull, bringing it to that tricky point where the sheer lines had to be perfectly matched on both sides. For the faering, the first six planks were marked off so the dubbing ax could follow the guiding twist of the batten. The covering boards were installed, the sheer strakes were fastened, and then the skeletal timbers were planked, edge to edge, down to just beneath the turn of the bilge. From the keel, the rest of the planks progressed upward, until there was only one more needed to shut the boat on both sides. When the second of those was put in, Steward arrived with a cask of ale, and everybody took an unaccustomed break in the work. Their boat had begun to come alive–in the way a boat is alive. Before anybody else, the old men knew it. They could hear it by their hammers' beginning to ring with a sharper ting, vibrating in the vessel's whole fabric.

Decks were laid down in the fall, and the caulking followed. By the time of the first snow, the hatches and scuttles were in place, so the boat was closed to the weather, permitting inside work to proceed by lantern light. Under a low quarterdeck, the sleeping cabin was installed aft, with its five berths and chart table. The cabin had two windows in the stern and another on each quarter, so it would be an airy chamber, full of light. Forward of it was the hold, where a bulkhead divided the cargo space from a commodious galley with a fiddled table for dining. Forwardmost was a cable and gear locker under the peak, where Bosun built a small workbench and bins to accommodate his rigger's inventory of bits and pieces.

Bosun spent most of the winter in the spar and rigging shed, where he worked long into every night. The shed grew heavy with the woodsy perfume of pine tar as the walls became festooned with new rigging. On their chocks, all the spars took shape. Still, Bosun found time to poke his nose everywhere, always checking everybody else's work, even Steward's, whose lists had begat other lists and finally even lists of lists. So expensive was it all, Crew's savings turned out to be short of his fifth share, but Steward quietly made up the deficit. Flags settled his own share by pointing out to his mother that he would be leaving with his comrades in any case, but her investment in the enterprise would assure them of what they would need for a safe and prosperous voyage.

This brought the sigh and the tear he expected, and the expected assent. "You know I can't refuse you anything. Since you're bound to go, you'd best have what you need to be safe." And so she became an investor in the tiny boat that would take her golden boy into unknown peril. Flags designed the carved wreaths surrounding the gunports and a blazing, golden sun on the transom.

When it came to the painting of the ship's name below it, there was no argument this time. Pilot had initiated the vessel and the whole new direction of their lives, and this choice was his. "Her name," he told his comrades, "will be *Alembic*."

"What does it mean?" asked Crew, putting the question for all.

"It is the chemist's container in which matter is mixed and changed," Pilot answered.

Bosun was puzzled. "How does that suit for the name of our boat?" he wanted to know.

"It is also the crucible of purification in which the alchemist is said to convert lead into gold," Pilot added. Among the many astonishing books in the Master's library, Pilot had found a few on alchemy and the philosopher's arts. They had intrigued him. He understood little of what they had to say because they were partially in a language of puzzling symbols, but Pilot planned to pursue the mystery further, in the meantime choosing for the vessel's name the word for the alchemist's vessel.

"Lead into gold? Sounds good," said Steward, who had just dispensed enough money for the boat's lead ballast to make it seem more like gold. "If it works, we'll have golden ingots to replace the lead and the finest ballast ever to fill a bilge." So *Alembic* was the name the little ship wore in gold leaf on her transom on the day of her launch. Their old friend *Vessle* went onto chocks fitted over the hatch, now to serve them again, as their tender.

On a day of offshore breeze, *Alembic* was given her harbor trials. Her sails were stretched, she was freed from the dock, and she moved through her element, feeling the smooth flow of it under her belly, with its gurgling exit making little tumults around the rudder blade. She dipped to the breeze, picked up her heels, and surged past the lighthouse out into the approaches, where she was put through every evolution successfully. Finally, she awaited only her cargo and perishable stores. Much thought had been given to the cargo, for nothing was known of the peoples to whom it would be offered or their needs. There was no room for anything bulky, so an eclectic array of small trade goods had been chosen.

As the date of departure drew nearer, Steward became more and more brusque. When at last it came time to amass the provisions, he took personal charge of the casking of the meat (which had to be completely covered in brine so saline that a potato would float in it) and the dipping of hundreds of eggs, one by one, into boiling water, after which their shells were greased. Packed carefully in straw, they would keep for many months. There were barrels, casks, kegs, and crates, two coops full of indignant chickens, and all manner of other things to be stowed. Looking at it all, Bosun could not help thinking Steward had put more food into them than they could ever need or conveniently carry.

"You've victualled for a crew of ten, not five," he told Steward, who was checking items from one of his lists.

"You'll use it," Steward told him.

"I doubt it, with you not along," said Bosun.

While Steward made no response, the look on his face made Bosun want to bite his tongue off. The matter of the surrogate fifth crew member had been postponed and then repostponed. None of the partners wanted to confirm Steward's decision not to go. Finally, the day arrived when the matter could be put off no longer. Their company needed a fifth member. There were any number of candidates eager to go, and a selection had to be made. In discussing it, the partners all pleaded with Steward to change his mind. Their probes struck bedrock, and they resigned themselves to offering the position to somebody else, an experienced sailor and a good sea cook as well. He would be paid a wage for his services. That settled, the meeting turned to other pressing matters. Steward no longer felt entitled to vote on general issues, having only his money invested in the enterprise, whereas his partners were staking their lives. He sat in silence for a while, listening, until, growing sadder by the minute, he excused himself, pleading other business.

As usual, a messenger was awaiting him at the Manor with an assortment of requests, notes, and petitions. At the top was a request from his father for a word with him. Steward went at once. The audience was not a long one, but he remembered it always. His father's hair, once a rich red-brown, was now white and manelike around his face. The old lion stood in front of a window through which the late afternoon sunlight illuminated his mane from behind, making it incandescent.

"When do our friends depart on the voyage?" he asked. Steward said *Alembic* would sail in a week, the gods willing, and there would be a send-off to which he hoped his father would come.

"Wouldn't be anywhere else in the world," said the Master, "and I trust ye've alerted the kitchen we'll send down refreshment?"

"Yes, sire. Everything."

"Tell me the destination. I've not asked, and if ye've told me, I heard not your reply." Steward had previously given vague answer to his father's question on this subject but now he explained the exploration aims of the voyage in detail, the quest for the Southern Continent and the Western Isles.

"And what true chance of success do you see for it?" asked the Master. Steward responded honestly that he did not know, but he knew no better sailors, and Pilot had a genius. So did they all in their own ways. He gave them good odds.

"And who's to be *you*, then?" his father asked. Steward explained about the surrogate who had been chosen, whom all knew and a good sailor and sea cook. He began listing the man's merits, but the Master stopped him.

"I've not said it. It's been your decision, but I think you should go with them. Honestly, now, d'ye not want to go?"

Steward admitted he did, but that had nothing to do with it. He had made his commitment to his family. The old man sighed and sat down.

The movement took his head from the shaft of sunlight into the shadows. Thus dimmed, his father seemed a tired old man, drained by his years.

"I'd hoped," said the Master, "ye would have come to it yourself, but since not, I order it. Attend your comrades. Go with them."

At that moment, Steward loved the Master better than he ever had. What other father would make such a gesture? Indeed, it seemed to him that his father's sacrifice in letting him go was equal to his own sacrifice in staying. For that, he now felt new resolve. Even the Master had struck bedrock.

The son knelt before him, taking his hand between his own. "Nay, sire, that I cannot do."

"Cannot do?" asked the Master, blinking.

"Nay, sire."

"Why not?" His father seemed not to comprehend.

Steward sighed, patting his hand and speaking softly and plainly to him as to a child. "Because I'm too much needed here, sire, as you know. That's why for the first time I will not obey."

"Will not obey," the Master repeated. Steward again patted his hand, but the hand had been abruptly withdrawn, leaving him to pat thin air. The old man was standing up, bringing his head again into the light. Steward hastily stood up also and at the same time took two steps back. "Will not *obey*?" said the Master in a voice Steward had rarely heard from his father, and never directed at himself. "Will not obey me? You will not obey me because *you* are too much *needed* here?" The voice gained in volume, and at the same time, the old lion's body appeared to swell to twice its size and vibrate. His backlit hair seemed to burn. Suddenly, Steward was aware he was no longer facing his father but an apocalyptic force ringing havoc into a sin-laden world populated solely by himself. Steward discovered a profoundly different assessment of his root worth than he had ever known. In this surprising new view, Steward's best efforts on his family's behalf had created no end of trouble. He, Steward, who had the least hereditary authority of any of them, had collected the greatest power of all through his accumulation of functions. He had started a stew of resentments. And there were questions: had he thought a family dynasty that had managed to exist for some hundreds of years was now in imminent danger of collapse without *him*? Did *he* presume *his* insignificant presence indispensable to the Master or anybody else? He heard new definitions of arrogance, overweening pride, and *now* disobedience, until he found himself standing several more steps to the rear. After a minute or two the Master seemed to return to his normal size.

And so had his voice when he spoke again.

"Now, let's try the point a second time without also trying my patience any further, lest you make me cross. When your friends sail, you will sail with 'em, d'ye hear?"

"Aye, sire."

"Eh?"

"Aye, sire. Yes."

"Good lad," the Master said pleasantly. "I trust you'll dine with your mother and myself tomorrow at supper? Good. And I trust you will find time to attend your cousin's wedding in the afternoon? It'll be a good chance to make your good-byes to all. There'll be a family dinner before you go and the send-off, of course. You'll have many personal preparations to make. I've made arrangements to lift your duties from you, so don't trouble anymore about those. Thank you for the visit."

"Aye, sire. Thank you." Steward hesitated.

"Something else?"

"I . . . had better speak to those who will now be responsible for the things I've been working on. There's much they should know about the tax matters, the wedding arrangements, the ship being greaved, the–"

"Is it not odd," asked the voice from the shadows, "how difficult a thing to let go of is a collection, even when unwanted?"

"Sire?"

"Say whatever ye have to say to whomever. Have finished with it by the time of the wedding feast. Savor the emptiness as best you can, and be careful what you fill it with. I'll not detain you longer."

When a subdued Steward presented himself on the dock the following morning, there was great joy among all the comrades. "Now we are complete," said Pilot, speaking for all of them.

With departure imminent, there was no time for celebration. They had to get away by spring and be well along their chosen northern route–chosen by Pilot–by summer's thaw in the far north. Their objectives were accessible from only two approaches. The first (and most inviting) course was to the south, but previous explorers (those who had been lucky enough to return) had reported an impenetrable barrier there made up of every kind of navigational hazard, reefs, shoals, and midocean shallows that had never been breached. The alternate route was an eastward passage around the unexplored northern reaches of their continent. It was Pilot's hope to make this north passage around, find their objectives, then make a return by breaching the barrier from its *opposite* side, sailing again north. It was a bold plan. When Pilot presented it, he found himself opposed by Flags and Steward, who did not like the cold, and by Bosun, who simply favored the most direct route.

"Remember the last expedition to try the ice," said Bosun. "One ship returned, a wreck, with one man alive, and him crazed." But Pilot invoked his navigational authority (in the way Bosun had with the sails and Flags had with the paint and Steward had with the victualing), and he was not to be budged. In the end, they let him have his way, with the stipulation that they would turn back if they could not obtain assurance of a clear passage through the ice from the natives there.

Pilot had attempted to find the only man alive thought to have actual knowledge of their possible route–namely, the crackpot Ancient Mariner. Few questioned that the old man had seen those distant seas, but whatever hardships he had encountered had so deranged him, nobody could believe the fantastic story he told and retold. As boys, they had all heard him emote, as had most of the children in the Port at one time or another, and their parents, too, who gave him pennies for food. Pilot wanted at least to attempt getting something useful out of him. He thought that might be possible if the mariner could be questioned, but the old man had vanished from the Port again or perhaps died.

With only four days left to departure, Pilot had resigned himself to doing without whatever information the addled old eyewitness might have provided. It was the last thing on his mind when a mounted messenger from the estate came clopping over the cobbles of the wharf with a note for him from Steward: "Ancient Mariner at wedding. Is it your wish we question him, or should we detain him pending your arrival?" His comrades had gone to the wedding of Steward's cousin, but as usual, Pilot had avoided a social event.

He arrived at the Manor within the hour and was met by the others. Steward, back to his jovial self, was hugely amused because the Ancient Mariner had cornered a particularly odious in-law who was a wedding guest. The old man had detained him, first by actually seizing him, then by holding him with his glittering eye. Despite the guest's protests, he had apparently become hypnotized by the fierce and melancholy tones of the old storyteller, for he had been there the past hour, seated on a rock, listening to the whole interminable recitation. It was accompanied by the merry din of minstrelsy from the feast within.

By the time Pilot arrived, both events were just ending; the old mariner urging the guest to accompany him somewhere to pray, but the guest escaped into the hall as he was being admonished to love all sentient beings. The mariner started to follow him, hoping for some reward, but Steward stepped before him offering a flagon of ale, suggesting he must be very thirsty after having spoken for so long. The old man nodded his thanks, took the ale, and drank it down in long gulps. Flags stepped forward, offering another flagon, congratulating him on his performance. The old man had a long, frazzled white beard and hair that stood out as though something had exploded inside his head. He wore an ankle-length robe of sackcloth that gave him the look of a penitent. Steward went inside and reappeared almost immediately with a platter of meat pies. The mariner's skinny hand darted out with amazing speed and seized three of them.

"Thankee, good sir," he said. All waited until the hungry old storyteller's eating had slowed to permit him to talk between bites.

"There was a ship," quoth he, unhesitatingly starting his story again, but he was interrupted by Pilot.

"Sir, we've heard your rhymes more than once, and we hope you might answer a question or two as to the navigational details of your voyage." Pilot paused, but the mariner merely munched and regarded him with eyes of cracked glass. "For instance," Pilot went on, "we are most particularly interested in the ice fields you passed through–"

"The ice was here, the ice was there, the ice was all around," said the old man.

"So I recollect your having said, and noisy, too. Let us begin at the beginning. On the first leg of your journey–"

"The sun came up upon the left, out of the sea came he! And he shone bright, and on the right went down into the sea."

"Aha. So you say, but that implies a southerly course, whereas you have established within your own narrative that you were headed into ice, which is, of course, north. Do you think you might have got that direction reversed, possibly in favor of making a better verse?"

"All poets do it," Flags assured him, "and with good license, but here accuracy is required."

The old mariner seemed confused at what Flags had said, so Pilot tried a different tack. "Very well, let us take it the other way around. When you finally cleared the ice fields, what bearing did you then lay?"

"The sun now rose upon the right: out of the sea came he, still hid in mist, and on the left went down into the sea."

"Excuse me, but again, that seems backward," said Pilot. "What did you find beyond the ice?"

"We were the first that ever burst into that Silent Sea."

"Good. Now, before entering the Silent Sea, you were in the ice. Ice?" he repeated, wondering if anything at all he was asking was finding a lodging in the old fellow's comprehension.

"Then it grew wondrous cold: and ice, mast-high, came floating by—"

"Yes," said Pilot, "but I beg you abandon the written line and regard my questions separately. We've truly heard your composition and all about your unfortunate incident having to do with the bird . . ."

"I shot the albatross," said the mariner. Pilot immediately regretted having reminded him, because the old fellow's face took on a melancholy so profound it seemed to reflect all the sorrows of mankind. "It ate the food it ne'er had eat, and—" he interrupted himself with a little gasp, having inhaled a spray of crumbs.

Pilot pressed ahead: "When you cleared the ice, you must presumably have steered south—for several weeks, unless I miss my guess—until you found doldrums? Flat calms?"

"So passed a weary time. Each throat was parched, and glazed each eye. A weary time! A weary time!" Pilot reflected that he was having a weary time of his own; Steward was going to sleep on his feet; Bosun had begun to pace, and Flags had moved toward a window to see if he could catch a glimpse of the bride, whom he had known for many years.

Pilot made one last sortie: "I'm well aware these things happened a long time ago, but we hope you might refresh your memory on our account, for we plan to sail those same waters soon. By what course did you steer to return here?"

"We drifted o'er the harbor-bar, and I with sobs did pray . . ."

Finally, Pilot gave up, thanking the poor old fellow and giving him some silver for his trouble. As they departed, they looked back and saw him clutching with his talonlike hand at another hapless passerby.

"Aren't you glad you came?" Steward twigged Pilot.

"To find the truth of it?" Bosun added.

"And how do *you* sort false from true?" challenged Pilot.

"That's a good question," said Crew, making his only comment of the day.

"In truth," said Pilot, "who can tell what the old man knows? It must be something, but it seems forgotten or sunk in madness. In any case, we now know we've no help from anywhere. We're on our own."

Three days later, when the wind came fair to the southwest, *Alembic* was ready, and her departure was given more fanfare than any galleon's. Families and friends were all alerted, and almost all showed up, along with a legion of well-wishers, doomsayers, and gawkers. Steward's family–led by his parents, wearing ceremonial purple–comprised a small army, and with them came a wagon filled with every manner of refreshments. Bosun's mum and dad added a cask of the tavern's best beer, and the Captain, now Admiral of the fleet, arrived in a smartly handled navy cutter with Pilot's mother and a brass six-pounder to give the lads a rousing send-off.

Flags's mother was there, teary-eyed but making a brave thing of it, centered in the drama of departure. She was closely attended by Flags, assisted by Magnolia and Begonia and others, many of whom had brought handkerchiefs to blow their noses on and scarves to wave when the ship sailed away. Dutifully, Flags made his good-byes to one and all, trying to give to each some indication of the special importance she held for him. Meanwhile, two bagpipers honked in rotation so one was playing all the time while the other drank the Master's scrumpy. In the middle of it all, the Lord Mayor of the Port arrived, wearing his chain of office and making a few congratulatory remarks. He noted how proud of the Port everybody should be for its having produced such sailors as these with the initiative to build such a fine, small ship. In the middle of his remarks, the Mayor realized he did not know their destination, and Steward was the only one of their company he knew by name, so he addressed instead their collective spirit of adventure. He, for one, saw it as further proof of the ascendancy and prosperity of the Port. Bosun twitched with impatience to be off.

At last, all the farewells were said, and all the visitors were cleared from the ship, including two would-be stowaway boys. The lines were cast off, the sails were loosed, and *Alembic* gathered way to the sound of the pipes, cheers, and a mighty blast from the naval cutter's brass cannon. Bosun, *Alembic's* gunner, returned the salute, and then the ship's company was busy with sheets and halliards. Under sail, the boat fairly flew; the crowd on the dock became smaller and its cheers fainter until *Alembic* cleared the harbor, and the farewell wishers were blotted from view by the seawall. Making the final adjustment to a jib sheet, Flags struck a pose and quoted:

> The ship was cheer'd, the harbor clear'd
> Merrily did we drop
> Below the kirk, below the hill,
> Below the lighthouse top.

As *Alembic* rounded the lighthouse, her course was set for the open sea. She plunged into the long swells. Ahead, a rainbow arced across the morning sky, and her bowsprit pointed like a javelin at its middle.

# V  The Passage North

THE WIND THRUMMED in the ship's rigging, stretching the new sails and hurrying the little ship northward. It was a summer wind, fair from the southwest, just strong enough to fleck the sea with playful whitecaps and make *Alembic* pick up her skirts and fly. Bosun, at the helm, felt the easy surge of her as she drove powerfully along, with every sail drawing to perfection. Not quite perfection, he noted, for there was just the hint of . . . not exactly a wrinkle, but a slight deformation in the set of the mizzen. It was only one of many minor problems and adjustments aloft awaiting Bosun's attention. Only he noticed them, but that was his job. He glanced at the half-hour glass by the binnacle. Its sand had nearly run out, but not quite.

"It's almost noon," he called, loudly enough to awaken Crew, who was having a snooze on the foredeck. He knew Flags was similarly occupied down below, in his bunk. This was their fourth day at sea, and the first day that had seen a general relaxation–for all but himself. Since the departure, *Alembic*'s crew had worked continuously to finish the various small tasks that had been left for the passage north. Most of these things had now been done to the satisfaction of everybody but Bosun. Bosun had never made friends with satisfaction, a seductress who invariably had lulled him off form whenever he had flirted with her, misdirecting his attention from some underlying problem. While it was true that all seemed well enough on this glorious sailing day, with the leagues boiling away in the ship's wake, Bosun had no intention of being lulled in the manner of some of his shipmates. *Alembic* was in dangerous waters. At the moment, even Pilot seemed a bit off guard. He was seated on the crosstrees rather than at the masthead, where more of the horizon was visible. Impatiently, Bosun again looked at the glass. It had another five minutes to run.

On *Alembic*'s watch bill, all but Steward stood watch-and-watch, four hours on and four hours off, so a helmsman and a lookout were always on duty. As cook, Steward was exempt from the tyranny of the watch, although he lent a hand as needed. Not even he was exempt from being called up at any time of the day or night if some emergency arose or if more than the deck watch were needed for sail handling. Even in normal circumstances, it was a rigorous life, demanding a high level of performance and the alert attention of all. Greater than any enemy around them was the enemy of exhaustion. Feeling a taste of it, Bosun rubbed first his eyes, then his ears in a futile attempt to stop the ringing in them. He had hardly slept for weeks, having worked ever more frantically on the ship as their sailing date had approached. There had been not only his own responsibilities to attend, but as usual, he'd had to keep an eye on everybody else's as well. If he had not checked on them, who else would have done it? There were thousands of details, and their lives could hang on any one of them. These demands upon him had multiplied when they had put to sea, and now their ship was sailing in waters where there could be pirates.

He looked again at the glass. There were only three or four minutes of sand left to run, he reckoned, and that was close enough. Locking the tiller with its relieving tackle, he stepped to the bell and rang it sharply eight times in four groupings of two rings each, one for every half-hour in the four-hour watch.

Then he turned the not-quite-empty glass, took the tiller against his hip again, and called out: "Flags!" A moment later Flags emerged from the companionway yawning. "Course nor'west and a half north," said Bosun, turning over the helm.

"Nor'west and a half north, aye," said Flags, barely awake and squinting in the bright sunlight. Forward, Crew had gotten to his feet and was stretching. It would probably take Crew a good while to climb to the crosstrees, Bosun reckoned as he went up the weather ratlines at a run.

Seeing him coming, Pilot started down. "Nothing in sight," he said as they passed.

"I want to see from the masthead," said Bosun.

"I was there ten minutes ago," Pilot told him, but his listener was already at the peak, standing on the topgallant yard, holding the mast with one hand, shading his eyes with the other as he swept the horizon.

There was nothing to seaward. To starboard, distant three or four leagues, were the pine-clad rocks of the Northern Archipelago, a jumbled complexity of hundreds of islands giving shelter to many craft. In ancient times, the peoples of this coast had been famous sea raiders. Now, their descendants were mostly fishermen and farmers, but it was known there were still some among them whose catch was not always limited to fish. The local craft could be sailed or rowed by large crews of armed men noted for their ferocity with swords and axes. In the present wind, fast *Alembic* would have the heels of the Norse vessels, but an even more dangerous breed of pirate was sometimes to be found here–the large, fast corsair barks from the south. Those raided their own waters in the winter months but had been known to probe this far north in the summer in search of stray prizes.

Piracy had been stamped out in the waters adjacent to the Port in the previous century, but the sea-robbers had been more difficult to exterminate in remoter areas. The corsairs had been like cockroaches in their ability to survive even the most vigorous fumigations, and Bosun was determined not to be caught off guard. The southern pi-

rates were known for their whimsical cruelty and for leaving no sur-
vivors to speak later of their bloody deeds.

Satisfied that no other sail was in view, Bosun seated himself on the
yard with his arm around the mast and made a more leisurely search
for other perils. He searched the water ahead for deadheads–trees that
had been uprooted and washed down the northern rivers to sea. They
could float for years, becoming ever more waterlogged and dangerous.
None was in sight, however, allowing him to examine yet again the details of his new rigging for any trouble signs, primarily chafe. Chafe
was the mortal enemy to the rigging's fabric in the same way personal
exhaustion was to her crew. It could start anywhere. While a slight
deflection to a stretched line might appear inconsequential, the inces-
sant rubbing of it in one spot hour after hour, day after day, wore away
its fibers in that place. Then, when the line came under the unfair
strains of a surprise squall, it could part, with possibly disastrous
results. In the same way, the sails were vulnerable. Any line that was
allowed to crease or rub against a stretched sail would insidiously gall
not only the flaxen fibers of its material but also the rows of stitching
that held its panels together. Bosun saw no trouble spots now, although he would continue to be alert for any that might develop.

"Anything in sight from up there?" Crew's voice came up to him
from the crosstrees, where he had at last taken up his station.

"Nothing now, but stay alert."

"I will. You should get some sleep," called Crew, a piece of advice
that Bosun ignored. His head felt clearer at this high station. From
this height, the boat below looked like a model, surging along with a
white bone in her teeth and swirls of foam in her wake. With each
wave, her movement carried the masthead in a wide, sweeping circle
through the sky. Most sailors found this rhythmic rushing through
space an uncomfortable thing, but to Bosun it was curiously restful,
even enjoyable. He seated himself on the yard. Against his legs swelled
the topgallant sail. In order to rig that high sail, Bosun had given
*Alembic* a prodigiously tall topmast–dangerously so in the eyes of
some, but now the upper sail was giving the ship tremendous drive. To
be sure, it would be the first sail taken in if the wind increased; then
they could proceed comfortably under the press of other canvas, espe-

cially the huge mainsail, his masterpiece. Like the topmast, it had been a point of contention. All of the others, even Crew, had objected to the length of the half-spirit, or gaff, that carried it. Bosun had no regrets about overruling them in defense of it. Indeed, in the present breeze, the press of *Alembic*'s combined canvas was giving her a speed she could never have attained under any less lofty rig. As he had pointed out frequently, there was nothing to be gained in undersparring a boat, and there was a good deal to be lost in the way of speed. Their small vessel's speed and weatherlines were her best protection.

He closed his eyes for a moment, turning his ear to the sounds of the ship. Below, at the doubling, the gaff jaws worked hard, with the dull rubbing sound of leather against leather; each of the running lines drawing tight over a sheave made its own small, high *errrrk;* the heavier, standing rigging made an *uuuukkk* as it stretched in baritone; and the mast and spars groaned in basso. When there came a slight snap to the boat's roll, everybody would sing in unison as the blocks squeaked. Bosun had the ear of an orchestra conductor for each detail of his rigging's song. If any player had begun some small disharmony, he would have noted it at once. But all was as tuneful as a lullaby at the moment, and he went abruptly to sleep.

His arm kept its hold on the mast; his body retained its superb balance, still swaying instinctively to the roll and pitch of the ship, but his head nodded sideways to rest on his shoulder. Thus did Bosun sleep, only when it took him by surprise. He had ever been an insomniac, but for the fortnight past, that condition had become chronic, as had the ringing in his ears. His few moments of impromptu slumber brought him momentary relief from it, until he was awakened by a burst of laughter from the deck. He turned his attention there without being aware he had been asleep at all.

He saw that Flags, who had the helm, had lashed the big tiller, fixing it so he could lounge against it while chatting with Steward, who was seated on the chicken coop peeling potatoes. From Bosun's high perch, the ship's wake was clearly seen as a snakelike line astern, far from straight to his eye. Bosun frowned. Traditionally, the helmsman's first duty was to keep a straight course. It was the equal responsibility of all others not to distract him. As Bosun watched them, Crew was at his station, but not looking around particularly, as far as he could tell; Pilot was nowhere to be seen. He was probably below, asleep. Bosun considered it a marvel that everybody could be so relaxed while their ship sailed a crooked course through waters where pirates could be. He shook his head, feeling the full burden of his responsibilities. There were many things that he intended to change, and soon. Very soon. While his shipmates were dear friends and–in their own ways– most useful in their individual roles, he found them amazingly feck-less, childlike even, in their blatant disregard for even the most funda-mental principles of shipboard comportment. More laughter from the quarterdeck.

Not only had Flags and Steward abandoned all vigilance as far as Bosun could tell, but they were obviously having an exchange that was entirely frivolous. He thought they could at least have used their time to discuss something important–most particularly, the vital issue he had raised for their urgent consideration. In the meantime, Flags's carelessness was adding distance to their course in waters they wanted to clear as quickly as possible. There was so much to be done. With a last sweep of the horizon, he slid down a halliard past where Crew was paring his toenails with his sheath knife.

"I hold it important you keep a sharp eye open, mind?" he told Crew. Crew nodded. Bosun slid the rest of the way down to the deck and came aft. Apparently, another joke was in progress.

He interrupted it: "Flags, you'll steer a straighter course if you free the tackle from the tiller and watch the compass."

"She's steering herself better than I can," said Flags. "Whatever the variations are, they're no greater than normal, Bosun."

Steward agreed, adding a thought of his own: "We've been working with no rest for weeks, and it's the first chance we've had to take our ease and enjoy our lives. Be easy, Bosun. Get some sleep. I've not seen you sleep since we left, and before that, who knows? Your eyes are at half-mast and red. Have a tot of rum and turn in."

Bosun shook his head. "Not yet. Too much to do."

"Then at least enjoy the day," Flags urged. "It's surely a fair one; and we're sailing free and easy. Look at the beauty of *Alembic,* of your rig. Feel the ease of her. Have a dram and join us here."

But Bosun was unseduceable. "Things are fair enough at the moment, but things also turn. Which reminds me: there'll be small-arms drill at midwatch." This got a groan from Steward. "We've all agreed to it," Bosun reminded him. "We've a proper inventory of arms, but we've not drilled with them. Our lives could depend upon them at any time, and if–"

Steward held up his hand. "Yes, yes, yes. No need to go over it again. Small-arms drill at midwatch."

"We'll start with the cutlasses," said Bosun; then he ducked down into the aftercabin on his next errand. At least, Pilot was to be relied upon for a good position, although it occurred to him Pilot might have gone to sleep. But he had not. Pilot was completing an entry in his journal, a document of dry reading for anybody not interested in water coloration, soundings, sightings, distance run, and other such observations. "You're awake," said Bosun.

"As are you, no surprise," said Pilot, closing the book. He replaced it in the precise vacancy it had previously occupied in his small book rack.

Bosun asked the same question he had put to Pilot every few hours since the outset of the voyage: "What progress d'you reckon we've made?"

If Pilot was irritated by it, he gave no sign. "We're now about here," he said, tapping a point on the line he had made on the chart. It marked an equal distance as to the previous point, and the one before that. "Conditions haven't changed much."

"Mmmm. We'll make worse progress for the half-watch, because Flags is on the helm. You'll want to take his crooked course into consideration when you make your next calculation."

Pilot nodded. "Aye. I know Flags's foibles, and I compensate. He favors the port by a degree or so."

"He steers a bloody crooked course is what he does," said Bosun.

Pilot shrugged. "A bit more than most."

"Would you steer so wide?"

"Nay, nor would you, but it's Flags," said Pilot.

"Does it not trouble you?"

"To what avail? It's only a factor, a known variation, and consistent," Pilot answered. Bosun thought over this response, wondering how Pilot could be so untroubled by something so inefficient, so unuseful. Bosun's mind automatically sorted all phenomena into the categories of useful and not useful. For instance, Crew's or anyone's truancy on lookout was very unuseful indeed, whereas Steward's preoccupation with the flavoring of food was only mildly unuseful, on the scale of things. Flags's lackluster performance at the helm was something Bosun weighed as definitely unuseful, and Pilot's tolerance of it was therefore also unuseful to the like degree. Didn't Pilot know better? Apparently not. And yet Pilot was a wizard in his own way, a navigator without parallel. Which was useful. Very useful. On the other hand, he had stood on that authority when he had induced them to attack their destination by the most roundabout course imaginable, which was not only not useful but deadly dangerous as well. Bosun was not troubled by the danger particularly. He even liked the challenge of it, but he questioned Pilot's efficiency in the process of sensibly getting where they were going. It was possible they would be turned back by the ice and be forced to retrace this entire leg of their voyage, which could hardly be considered useful. On measure, Bosun judged Pilot lacking in the overall qualities required of a true Captain.

Pilot had replaced all of his implements in their slots. Last, he folded the chart along its seams and opened the door to his locker with its chart drawer. Bosun noticed the hilt of Pilot's rapier protruding from the slot that had been built for it. The rapier presented another mystery about Pilot, for Bosun saw the slender weapon as useless in the real rough-and-tumble of any antiboarding actions.

"Why did you bring that?" Bosun asked, pointing to it.

"It is the weapon of my choice," said Pilot.

"We've cutlasses for the ship."

"Yes. For you."

"A hard blow from a good cutlass will snap the blade of that thing," said Bosun. "The blade's too light; it will not cut, but only penetrate."

"A hard blow from a cutlass will never touch it because a cutlass is too heavy and slow. Also, a puncture is deadlier than a slash."

"Aha," said Bosun. "A point of competition. A challenge, in fact."

"You would fence with me?" asked Pilot, regarding Bosun in mild surprise.

"Rapier against cutlass at singlesticks," said Bosun, referring to the wooden cutlasses commonly used for shipboard fencing practice. "Let's make it a demonstration when the half-watch rings, to start the small-arms drill." Pilot pointed out that there were no singlesticks aboard, but Bosun had an answer: "I can make one by four bells, and you don't need one if you have a button for the tip of your blade."

"I do, but we've no protection masks. Also, you're too tired for this. You need to get some sleep."

"Masks?" A grin. "I'm not so tired that you're going to lay a blade on me, and the strokes I lay on you will be gentle."

"That's very considerate of you," Pilot said with his slight smile. "In that case, I'll accept your challenge."

"A wager on it?" teased Bosun.

"Wager what?"

"The captaincy."

"What?" Pilot looked puzzled, then began to comprehend what Bosun was suggesting. "Ah, you make that issue between you and me? Truthfully, I hadn't considered it because I don't want it, and I'd feel more restful if you didn't."

"Who, then?" asked Bosun.

Pilot deflected the question. "If it's a wager you want, let it be for something within our power to bet. Make it a penny."

"Too little. Let the loser stand the winner's watch, then," said Bosun. Pilot pointed out that Bosun was already standing everybody's watch, but Bosun insisted and prevailed, and so the match was set.

Bosun headed for the forepeak, where he had a serviceable piece of ash in his work locker as well as a saw and a drawknife with which to cut and shape it into a singlestick. On his way below, he paused only long enough to make sure that Crew looked alert at the crosstrees and that Flags was not too badly off course. Then he dived into the forward scuttle and went to work.

As he shaped the wood, he had much to consider—primarily, Pilot's remark that he didn't even want the position of Captain. If true, it seemed to Bosun to remove the last possible obstruction to what he considered the most pressing issue facing them, the question of who was to be in ultimate command. In Bosun's view, the voyage they had undertaken could not be safely carried out under their old anarchistic children's rules. It was not child's play out here. Every ship needed a Captain in any greater or lesser emergency, lest everybody start insisting on his own way. The dangers of it were so obvious to Bosun that he could not understand how the others could pay it so little heed. They were lucky to have weathered their childhood experiences in *Vessle,* as he had pointed out to them repeatedly, but somehow the matter had always got shunted forward until here they were, four days at sea, still with no central commander. They had been lucky that the wind and weather had been smiling upon them, but every sailor knew that never lasted. And what when difficulties came? How could any external chaos be confronted if there was chaos within their own company? For this and other well-proven reasons, ships had Captains. What ship had ever *not* had a Captain? It was time to settle it. Past time. He had therefore called a meeting in council, invoking one of their childhood traditions that he considered to be still useful.

He put down the drawknife and examined his work, hefting the singlestick, then hefting his cutlass. The comparison made him decide to shave the stick a bit more, taking the wood from its edges to give it a more oval cross-section. He considered this fencing match with Pilot a lucky thing, useful in both direct and indirect ways. Most directly, it would make a good beginning to the arms drill he had pressed for. His demonstration of expert swordsmanship would set a useful example and should also stimulate interest. Indirectly it would provide a timely example of his prowess and leadership.

Finishing, he again hefted the stick, and it felt good in his hand. He put it down on the bench, then went on deck again, making his observations of horizon, helm, lookout, weather, and trim. All looked good, except he noticed Steward was spelling Flags at the helm. They were still chatting. Had the wind veered slightly west? Were they a bit off course?

"How's our course?" he called to Steward.

Steward glanced at the binnacle and made a slight correction on the tiller. "I had her a bit high at that moment," said Steward, still with his eyes on the compass, "But she's on the mark . . . now."

"Steer small," said Bosun, turning to go back below.

"Aye aye, sir," said Steward.

"What?" asked Bosun, turning around again.

"I said, 'Aye, aye, sir,' sir," said Steward, grinning.

"You called me 'sir'?" asked Bosun.

Steward laughed. "Sir, I sometimes do," he responded, at the same time giving Bosun a broad wink. Flags was all grins, too. Bosun had the feeling of having missed something. "Very respectful," he said, and abruptly went back up the mast for another look around the horizon.

When four bells rang, all the ship's company gathered on the foredeck, the only area on little *Alembic* that afforded enough space for swordplay. In consideration for the special event, the tiller had been lashed so the helmsman could attend, and the lookout had been called down for a few minutes. Bosun convened the lesson with a few introductory words on the importance of the cutlass in any boarding action.

"Now, we'll begin with a demonstration of cutlass against rapier, which should demonstrate why the cutlass is the best ship's sword." Pilot was chalking his rapier's button with a piece of terra-cotta. "It'll go fast," the instructor continued, "so watch close. I'll demonstrate both backhand and forehand cuts, moves you'll all be practicing. Ready?" He took the chalk from Pilot and rubbed it along the whole length of his singlestick's edge to make a mark wherever he scored a slash. It was agreed the match would begin at a word from Steward, the judge, and would be stopped by him when he saw a score. The first to place two marks deemed mortal would be declared the winner. Both fencers took their stance. Pilot looked gangly; he had removed his stockings, and his limbs seemed sticklike compared to superbly muscled Bosun.

"Ready then? Commence!" said Steward.

Neither fencer made any immediate move, each waiting to see what the other would do. The point of Pilot's rapier made quick little circles; Bosun watched the sword point, saw Pilot's rear foot move backward, and the front one follow it; a step back. He was getting more distance, but Bosun, with the slightly shorter weapon, wanted to stay close, so he followed. If Pilot repeated the move, he now knew what to do. Sure enough, the rear foot moved backward again; at the moment he anticipated the front would follow it, Bosun lunged, slashing at the side of Pilot's head, finding it not there. Bosun whirled sideways with the grace of a dancer, delivering a lightning-fast backstroke that found only air. How had Pilot managed to avoid those blows? Bosun continued his turn to face him again, still perfectly balanced. Pilot, however, stepped back and lowered his sword so its tip pointed to the deck, regarding him cooly.

"Halt," said Steward.

"We've just begun," Bosun protested.

"I think you've just finished," said Flags, amused.

"What?"

"Regard your front," said Steward, pointing. Looking down at himself, Bosun saw a chalk dot marking the front of his green tunic, just below the level of his breastbone. Amazing! He'd felt nothing.

"The first match to Pilot," proclaimed Steward.

"An accidental brush of the point in passing." said Bosun. "I never felt it!"

"Fencers to the mark," said Steward, smiling. "Ready?"

Bosun gathered himself, with full focus. The accident must not happen again.

"Commence."

As before, Pilot was poised before him, the rapier tip licking like the tongue of a serpent, awaiting any movement for its lightning riposte. Very well, thought Bosun, he knew the same game. Let the serpent come to him; he would hew off its head. For an instant, he gazed at the eyes of his opponent; then, curiously, Pilot was gone–simply not there. He was somehow lower, at an oddly foreshortened angle, with a straight line between the heel of his rear foot, past his shoulders up the length of his arm, and thence up the blade of the rapier, which made a small curve only at Bosun's breast, on which the button rested politely.

"Match!" called Steward.

"Well done, Pilot!" said Flags, applauding along with Steward and Crew. Pilot had withdrawn to the salute position, reminding Bosun to respond in kind. Everyone admired Pilot's feat, for they knew Bosun's well-deserved reputation with the cutlass.

"How was it done, Pilot?" asked Steward.

"It was a simple lunge," said Pilot. "The rapier's light blade allows great speed in its thrust. The same stroke can be delivered with a cutlass, but not so quickly, so Bosun was at a disadvantage in that respect, but he's right in telling you the cutlass is a better shipboard weapon on the whole, and he's also quite right to encourage our practice with it."

"I don't need to be humored," growled Bosun. "I want another match."

"We're here for a practice," said Steward, "not an ongoing contest. Pilot, let's see how you did that." Pilot obliged with a demonstration of a lunge to full extension and then repeated it more slowly. Crew had questions regarding proper foot placement, and Flags asked Bosun if he could borrow his singlestick so he could try the thing himself. Bosun handed it to him, trying to conceal his exasperation. Things could not have gone more badly, he thought, although he tried to take some consolation from the enthusiasm with which Pilot's fencing lesson was being received. Steward had located a short batten to use for a singlestick, and Flags was making extravagant lunges at points in space. "Now, what's the proper parry?" he asked.

Bosun watched them for a minute or two more, then abruptly ran up the ratlines to the masthead, where he remained longer than necessary to discover that no sail had hove into sight during the recent proceedings. Without question, he thought, he would have made a better showing if he had been better rested, and he resolved to make a real effort to sleep. At all cost, he must be fresh for the meeting in council he had called for the following day, something more important than any singlestick lesson. However, there were several things he had to do yet before he could turn in to his bunk, and he supposed he had better support the drill he had imposed by rejoining it, even though he was no longer the teacher. He would have plenty of chance to sleep on the twelve-to-four watch. He returned to the deck, aloofly watched the lesson until it was over, and then spent the rest of the daylight hours shifting a few of the ballast blocks from the bow to the stern, working up a good sweat.

"She's head-heavy, so I'm trimming to compensate," he explained. When suppertime came and went without Bosun's appearance in the galley, Steward went looking for him with a bowl of stew. He found him in the aftercabin with his head under the floorboards, wrestling one of the heavy lead pigs into position. Bosun mumbled a thanks, more drinking than eating the bowl's contents. Handing the empty bowl back to Steward, he wiped his mouth with the back of his hand and returned to his task. Steward shook his head, wondering how Bosun could consume food thus, in the same manner as a dog, urgently bolting every morsel with no taste of it. Steward viewed it as an inexplicable thing, possibly some hereditary defect. He had never given up trying to find some treat to awaken Bosun's palate.

Before dark, the mizzen sail and jib were struck; at the same time, the bonnet was removed from the mainsail and the topgallant sail was brought down on deck with its yard, so *Alembic* was snugged down for the night. This greatly reduced her speed, but it reduced also the chances of their being caught wearing too much canvas by any surprise squall during the hours of darkness. Again, Bosun was urged to turn in, with Steward offering to stand his helm, but the offer was curtly declined. Bosun took his own trick at the tiller and did not get into his bunk until after midnight.

Any other person in Bosun's state of exhaustion would have passed out the moment his body was horizontal, but with nothing now to watch or listen to, Bosun heard only the ringing in his ears, high-pitched and unremitting. It was a phenomenon that had been with him all his life, although never with such intensity as now. Ordinarily, the ringing was a low-keyed thing, hardly noticeable, a background noise so muted and familiar as to be easily disregarded, like buzzing insects. Now, however, it was like a wire stretched through his head. He rubbed his ears and tried to will himself to sleep, but there were other distractions. His mind automatically wove and rewove his strategies regarding the matter of command, the most pressing issue of all, to be resolved on the morrow.

After a while, Bosun did doze, but even then, his body twitched and jerked. He was beset by unsettling dreams, and he awoke well before the watch change, again with the disquieting intuition that there was real danger nearby. Unable to remain in his bunk, he went out on deck, peering into the darkness, seeing only a pale glow in the eastern sky. Pilot was on the tiller, his face reflected in the small light of the binnacle. Flags, on deck watch, was sleeping in the lee of the weather rail.

"You let him sleep?" Bosun immediately confronted Pilot.

"At night? Why not? What's to be seen but darkness, and I can see that as well as anybody," said Pilot.

Bosun ran up the ratlines to the masthead to see what there was to be seen. The day dawned gray under torn clouds. Bosun thought it likely there would be a change in the weather, although the wind still blew fair from the southwest. The ship could stand more sail now. The waters ahead were visible, and the continent emerged from the mists to starboard. Bosun remained aloft only until he could plainly see the horizon's vacancy, then he climbed down. Somehow, he was no less uneasy. Passing Flags, now on station at the crosstrees, Bosun warned, "I smell danger in the air today, and I hold it important ye keep a sharp eye open, mind?"

"Aye aye, sir," said Flags. Again the "sir," and it was no less suspicious hearing it from Flags than from Steward. What were they saying of him when he was not there to listen? He speculated on this as he reset the jib and then the mizzen and then commenced relacing the big bonnet to the foot of the mainsail.

"Bosun, do you reckon we'll need that extra sail today?" asked Pilot. "The sky looks to have more wind in it than we've yet felt."

"If more wind comes, we'll shorten down when it arrives," said Bosun, not looking up from his task. "It's best to be clear of these waters."

During the forenoon watch, the wind veered, so all hands mustered to trim sheets. By the end of the afternoon watch, the wind was heading them, and by suppertime, it had come right around to the north, forcing a tack to seaward. Throughout the day, Bosun was haunted by his strange foreboding. It drove him to a redoubled diligence and gave urgency to the meeting that would be held after supper. There could be only one outcome to it–and the sooner the better. Bosun's thoughts on the matter were intricate and ever changing, but the simplicity of it was that the ship must have a Captain, and he was that person. It was not that he *wanted* to be (and that would have to be made clear), it was that he *was,* and that, too, would have to be made clear. His credentials were persuasive, he being the only one among them who was ship handler, sailing master, and master-of-arms all in one, by their own admission. If not him, who? Steward had the presence of command, and then some, but he was no ship handler; Pilot did not want the role, and wisely so; Flags was no Captain, nor was Crew. In fact, he, Bosun, was already doing the job. Couldn't they see? All he demanded was the acknowledgment due him from those for whom he would lay down his life. He would still be called Bosun, not Captain, and nothing would change at all, except he would hold authority in situations of danger or other great need, when "Aye aye, sir" would be the form in earnest.

He had hoped to be able to convene the council immediately after supper, but Pilot wanted to do a round of navigation, meaning Crew had to make soundings with the lead, during which Steward was occupied with the cleaning of his galley. By the time he managed to gather them all aft, where Flags was on the helm, the second dogwatch had come and gone. It was a gray evening with a chill to it. The wind had increased, so the ship was driving, taking the occasional wash over the weather bow. Bosun came right to the point: "Our greatest peril is that there's none among us–"

"who is Captain," Pilot finished his sentence for him.

"Yes. It's past time for that," said Bosun. "What thought have you given it?" Nobody made any response. Although he watched them sharply, he could read nothing in their faces to give any indication of their politics. The silence stretched on, and when it was broken, it was by a rumbling fart from Steward. Flags made a nimble leap upwind. All but Bosun laughed.

"I insist ye take this as serious!" he growled.

"We've heard it all," said Pilot. "And there's no dispute that all you say is true in ordinary circumstances, but we have a partnership all but you are happy with. In truth, nobody but you seems to want to be Captain."

"*Want* to be Captain?" asked Bosun. "That I do not. But Captain I am, through no choice, and I'll have your recognition of it!" It was a surprise gust and a fierce one. "There *must* be authority!" he roared.

"There *is*," said Pilot soothingly. "We're all Captain in our own areas, as you well know. For instance, as the ship's physician, I recommend a drop of laudanum for you; it will let you sleep." All agreed, and Steward moved for adjournment. "The wind's chill, and the point's resolved," he said.

"The point is not resolved!" Bosun insisted, but Steward and Flags were already on their way to the galley, and Pilot was repeating his offer of a sleeping potion.

Bosun shook his head. "I'm still on watch," he said, "and the point is not resolved. You can tell the others from me it is *not* resolved, but it *will* be when I come down." Furious, he went aloft. They had bent before him like reeds, but they had not yet experienced the storm force he was going to use next to blow them away. Nursing these thoughts, Bosun settled himself again onto his high perch. Watching out over everybody, as usual, he reflected. There was Flags's wake winding its way astern. As usual.

"Flags!" Bosun barked. "If you keep your eyes to the front and mind the compass, you can steer straighter. You can rely on me to keep an eye out."

"Aye aye," called Flags, with no "sir" this time. Well, they had some things to learn, Bosun reckoned, and if they chose not to learn easily, their next lesson would be a hard one. By a trick of the light, Bosun's huddled form looked like that of a predatory animal waiting to pounce. Although his body was still, his mind remained active until it was kidnapped again without warning by sleep.

So he did not see the fleck of white that appeared on the horizon behind them. It remained stationary for a few minutes, but then its aspect changed into three flecks, indicating the sails of a full-rigged ship that had seen them and changed course toward them. As the ship settled into its new heading, its sails again seemed as one sail, but larger, as more canvas was broken out. Bosun slept throughout the rest of the watch, lulled by the swooping of the mast and the rigging's song, until his slumber was interrupted by a sudden yell from the deck.

"What?" said Bosun.

Flags was roaring, "Sail astern! Sail astern!" gesticulating wildly. And there, no more than a league off their lee quarter, he saw a warship surging toward them, hull up, with the muzzles of its cannon visible. It was a black frigate. Steward, Crew, and Pilot erupted from the galley all at once. Sliding down a backstay, Bosun tried to sort out his stunned brains. This was not just a catastrophe, it was *his* catastrophe entirely. He must have somehow fallen asleep, with the worst possible consequences. How could he have been more useless?

"What have I done? What have I done?" he asked himself, feeling the burning of the rope, which he was descending too fast. Then his feet touched the deck, and he was helping to harden the jib. The rest of them had already sheeted in the mainsail; now, Flags let *Alembic* luff up just enough to ease the straining headsail, allowing it to be sheeted home close-hauled. The ship surged ahead. Bosun couldn't help but notice the wordless efficiency with which they had responded. No Captain's orders had been necessary. There had been only one thing to do, and they had all done it with one mind.

Cut off from flight toward the archipelago, their best hope–their only hope–was to work gradually upwind of the big warship, for it could not lay so close to the wind's eye as *Alembic*. Except for that, the frigate had every advantage, especially the greater speed of larger vessels over smaller ones in a stiff breeze and a seaway.

"He came up so fast . . . I didn't see him . . . ," said Bosun.

"Never mind. You're our best helmsman for this work," said Pilot, so Bosun took the tiller and in it found refuge, sailing the ship as finely as she could be sailed, using every lift of the wind to gain into it. Flags stood by the relieving tackles; the wind was still increasing, and there were real pressures on the helm. If there was any question as to the nature of the pursuing ship, it was settled by the hoist of a black flag to his main truck.

"If we can evade him for two hours, we'll have darkness," said Steward. Pilot shook his head. It was apparent to him they would be under the powerful guns of the frigate long before then. Granted, *Alembic* was forereaching as hoped, but she was slowed by bucking the sea. In Pilot's cool judgment, the pirate would catch them in perhaps an hour at the longest.

"We can tack better than he can," said Steward, "and perhaps evade him longer."

"Yes," said Pilot, "but when we tack, we'll be under his guns."

It was true. Whereas *Alembic* could cross and recross the wind's eye more nimbly than the frigate, the turn would make them vulnerable to the pirate's whole broadside. Any one of his cannonballs could sink or dismast them. "We're better to carry on and use our time to arm ourselves and see what develops." The cutlasses and half-pikes were laid out ready, and the pair of three-pounder guns were loaded, but all knew what forlorn odds they faced. The black-hulled frigate relentlessly advanced, the water creaming and frothing under his round bows, the lift of every crest bringing him closer. His decks swarmed with men. The big ship nodded and dipped easily in the still-freshening breeze, liking the wind that was beginning to make *Alembic* labor. Bosun saw and heard the strains on his new rigging.

"Bosun," called Pilot, "would your rigging bear the press of the topsail in this wind, if we were running rather than beating?"

"Yes," said Bosun. The strain aloft would be greatly eased if they sailed from rather than into the wind.

"Good," said Pilot, "because we'll need that sail for the only plan I can think of." Pointing out that the frigate would be prepared for their last-moment attempt to tack away, the pirate Captain might be caught off guard if they did just the opposite thing. Pilot proposed that when the frigate's guns started to come into bearing, *Alembic* be turned downwind, right toward their pursuer. If it was done fast enough, they could avoid his guns and cross his bows at right angles. *Alembic* would then be at point-blank range to his leeward battery, but Pilot reckoned they would be past before those guns could be manned, pointed, and fired. It would take many precious minutes for the big square-rigger to turn and retrim his many sails to the new point of sailing; meanwhile, if it worked, *Alembic* would be shooting away from him, driven by the press of the topsail, which would have to be broken out at precisely the right moment. All agreed, and the preparations were made. A few minutes later, a momentary blossom of white smoke appeared at the frigate's bow; it was whipped away by the wind, and an instant later, there was the *boom* of the report and a sound overhead like paper being ripped, a cannonball tearing the air.

"Now?" asked Flags of Pilot. "We'll have a broadside from him if he yaws off. We're nearly in musket range." The ship was closing quickly on their quarter.

"Stand by," called Pilot.

*Boom* came the next cannon report; *twang* went the gaff vang, cut by the cannonball.

"That found us," remarked Steward, taking up the mainsheet.

*"Down helm!"* said Pilot to Bosun. As *Alembic* rounded into her turn, Pilot took the helm, and Bosun ran up the ratlines to the topsail yard, riding it, loosing its sail as its yard was raised by heaving arms below. In an instant, the sail was sheeted home and drawing. Bosun saw the spars below him bend like wands, but they took the strain, and *Alembic* bounded on her new course, now with the wind behind.

At the first moment Bosun could take his eyes from what he was doing, he did not have far to look for the black frigate. *Alembic* was right under his bows. Like the horn of a charging bull, his bowsprit reached for their taut rigging, but it raked air. The terrier had evaded the rush of the bull and was bounding away to leeward before the great beast could check his momentum, turn, and start a new charge. At the moment the two ships were nearest, Bosun clearly saw the surprised confusion on the pirate's deck below. Pilot had been right: the leeward guns there were lashed, barrels pointed to the sea; before they could be cast free and brought to bear, the two ships were past each other. One pirate sprang into the frigate's mizzen shrouds and fired off a pistol at them, but then the big ship had surged past, out of bearing. Bosun saw the pirates' frantic efforts to free bowlines and readjust the whole ponderous rig while the terrier widened the distance between them with every bound.

*Alembic* was capable of no greater speed than she gave them then, and even that speed she exceeded on the crests, when she rode the seas at their own velocity for whole seconds, rudder vibrating. A few moments later, they saw the black ship turn and his yards come around to square. Now on their same course, the frigate wallowed, his best drawing sails blanketed by the ones behind.

Bosun joined in congratulating Pilot, but Pilot was grim. "He'll be on us again soon enough," he said, turning the helm back to Bosun. As they watched, they saw the frigate come into proper trim, beginning again his inexorable approach. The long northern day was at last drawing to a close, but it would be a near-run thing.

"We'll not evade him even with darkness unless we can keep some distance," Pilot said, "and that will only be with luck." He was also concerned their speed might be the death of them, for *Alembic*'s helm went dead during the seconds while she rode a crest, a situation that could broach her sideways on the wave's forward slope and capsize her. Bosun had never sailed her planing but soon had the feel of it. And so they fled toward the darkening horizon, watching the spars bend aloft under the unfair pressures of the still-rising wind. Astern, the black frigate crept toward them. But nothing parted aloft on *Alembic*, and Bosun somehow managed to control her mad rushes on the crests. The twilight gloom around them thickened into night, swallowing their pursuer even though he was now close astern. Bosun could no longer see *Alembic*'s sails. He felt them, however, and their groaning yards. He feared that if nothing else gave way, the whole mainmast might go. There was no way of getting in the huge mainsail without rounding-to, but the topsail might be struck.

"Pilot, take the helm," he said, yelling to make himself heard over the wind. "The topsail must come in!" Pilot appeared out of the darkness at his side, taking the tiller. "Topsail halliards," he called. Bosun leaped toward the shrouds, but it was too late. As he reached for the ratlines, a backstay parted, and he felt from aloft the splintering surrender of his topmast. It was disaster. It was also the last thing Bosun remembered, for at that moment, he was struck a crushing blow on the back of his skull by an unleashed block.

*Bosun whirled and whirled, blown in the gale like a fragment; careening, slowly turning over and over, no longer feeling the wind because he was borne by it, helpless, whipped along by its force. He struggled, but there was nowhere to struggle to and nothing to struggle against. He was being blown through an endless emptiness, opaque with the wind, of which he was part, so that there was nothing to be done except stop struggling and blow and blow and blow . . . and he surrendered and became the wind, and there was no Bosun. Only the wind, whirling.*

Then stillness. Darkness.

*The wind was a whisper, playing, lifting him, and it was a warm wind, in clear space, rising from the cool green earth far below, and he rested on it as on a cushion, among the clouds, in perfect equilibrium. He found that by moving his arms with breaststrokes, he could propel his body in any direction he wished, swimming as though in water, but powerfully, through the air. He could soar. He could fly, and he flew, and he had never known a more pleasurable sensation, too delicious to question. Down and down he dove, spreading his arms to end his dive in a swoop toward the sun. Effortlessly, he rolled in circles, and it was more delightful than there were words to describe. Below him, there was the Port. He spiraled down, trod the air, hovering for a moment over the lighthouse, then coasted in the breezes, lifting, floating over the city's streets and roofs, and over the harbor. Below, all of the people were emerging, waving and waving to him excitedly, and he laughed and gamboled on the winds of morning.*

Darkness again.

*He flew over the sea, but he was trapped between the water and lowering gray clouds, their bellies torn by the wind. Below was* Alembic, *dismasted, rolling drunkenly in the breaking seas, with shredded rigging dragging alongside, under the guns of the black frigate. The pirates had boarded his ship. He struggled to get closer. He screamed to them, but the scream emerged tiny, such a small sound, and was swal-*

*lowed by the wind. He saw four pirates pinion Steward against the stump of the mast, and he watched as a fifth inserted a long knife into Steward's belly and sliced quickly sideways, ripping, so that Steward's poor, pink entrails emerged from him and spilled on the deck. Bosun struggled furiously but was blown back. He watched them skin Flags alive and dismember Crew in his bright blood and put their dagger points into Pilot's eyes, and Bosun screamed and wept for his helplessness, and he had done this to them. His were the lookout's eyes that had failed them; his was the oversize topmast that had carried away; his was the rigging that had failed when they needed it most. His tears were blown in streams from his face by the wind.*

Again, darkness.

When the wind reached him again, it was a brush of aromatic air across his face. Steward had just opened the galley scuttle to let out some of the steamy atmosphere from his cooking, letting in a cooling draft at the same time. Bosun was somehow in the galley. There were Steward's hundreds of dried fruit slices, strung in festoons everywhere; there was the brass hanging lamp, swinging over the table; there were the pots and spoons making clickings on the bulkhead as the ship surged easily through long, gentle seas, the rigging creaking happily. So peaceful. Bosun's hands discovered his own head, with nose and other features, including a turban. How oddly Oriental, he thought. Aha. Not a turban . . . a bandage. And there was Steward, fussing over him, twitching at his blankets. Bosun seemed to be in a bunk where a storage rack had been, and there they all were, the lot of them, alive, alive all, looking down at him.

"Bosun? Bosun?"

"Who's at the helm?" he wondered weakly.

"The helm's lashed. She's steering herself," said Flags, smiling at him. "You've been unconscious for a week, and we're too far north for pirates here."

While Steward spooned a bit of broth into him, he learned that the topmast had snapped at the cap and then dragged alongside, bringing *Alembic* helplessly up into the wind. In that position, they had got in all their other sail moments before the pirate ship had frothed past, an evil loom in the darkness, seeking their sails and therefore not seeing them. They had been able to retrieve most of the gear from the topmast, later to be rerigged, but he was not permitted even to think of fixing it until he had mended himself. *Alembic*'s working, lower rigging was intact, and she was sailing under it nicely, he was assured. Meanwhile, he was to rest in the berth that had been improvised for him in the galley, where it was warm and where he could be better tended. Bosun was amazed nobody blamed him for anything.

"You were right about the rig," he said. "It's too tall."

"Perhaps," said Pilot, "but without its press of sail, that ship would have had us. And none of your rigging gave way; all held. Your topmast went because the iron strap of the backstay chain broke at a fault. We owe our lives to your good work, mate." Bosun didn't know what to say.

They all found moments during his recovery to spend a bit of time with him. Crew just sat, having commiserated with him about going to sleep on watch. "Believe me," he said, "I know how easy that is to do." Steward made curried stew too delicious to be ignored even by Bosun, and Flags brought out his lute. Pilot provided constant navigational details and reports on progress north. That had brought them at last to the latitude of the continent's northernmost point, where they could turn east. The first leg of the voyage was behind them.

And Bosun was glad to be Bosun.

# VI  East into the Unknown

THERE WAS A brittle clarity to the Arctic light quite unlike any other Pilot had ever observed; it was a light that made all form and color naked. Sighting over his cross-staff, he viewed the northwest shoulder of the continent, measuring the elevations where its rampart mountains rose from the sea. In primordial time, the mountains had burst from the earth's crust and into the clouds, fists of treeless rock, their northern backs entirely bound in cerulean snow, their south-facing sides showing bare scars of black basalt, where the summer sun had reached. Their peaks dwelled in eternal winter, and the morning light reflecting from their snowfields and glaciers blazed with cold fire. Pilot finished with his bearings and angles and replaced the instrument in its thin case.

"Come east southeast," he said to Flags, on the tiller. He would have to correlate his various morning observations below, over the chart, but his intuition led him to anticipate that slight course correction. There was southing in it here because they were heading in toward the land, approaching the only port of call they would see before sailing off the chart and into the unknown seas of the far north.

"East southeast she is," said Flags.

Here came Crew, up from the galley, bearing mugs that steamed in the crisp air.

"What's this?" asked Pilot.

"Hot cider. From Steward. He says it'll warm you up."

"Mmm," said Pilot, taking a sip, then handing the mug back to Crew. "Steward put a fair quantity of rum into the mulled cider."

"But it's good, though," said Crew. "Go ahead and have some. I had some, and it really will warm you up."

"Crew, you are assuming that I wish to be *warmed up,* as you put it. I'm quite comfortable. Give it to Flags. I believe it's your turn to cast the lead."

"Aye," said Crew.

"Flags, would you mind marking the chip?"

"Aye," said Flags, lashing the tiller in place and stepping to the quarter where he could look down over the rail. Pilot went forward, took aim, and threw a chip of wood into the water. It lit clear of the bow wash at a point even with the stem. At its splash, Pilot began an even, silent count.

"Mark!" called Flags at the precise moment the line of the taffrail passed the floating chip.

"Mmm," said Pilot, returning aft to make a notation of the speed. As the air and light of the north had sharpened, so had Pilot's mind, increasingly, as though honed by the chill and luminous clarity of the environment. He felt like a sharp blade, slicing and dissecting his phenomenal world with dispassionate precision, and he did not want to dull his edge with any of Steward's rum.

For the present, they sailed in waters free of obstructions—if his charts and sailing directions were accurate, which was by no means a reliable assumption. For the last century and more, whaling ships from the temperate lands had sailed here, where the fishing was rich. They had charted the continent's northern coast for some scores of leagues, with diminishing accuracy, until coming to the mouth of a narrow channel, or lead, that opened every summer between the northern shore of the continent and the ice pack. Only whaling ships had ever entered that lead, but they had not gone far into it. These waters were simply designated as "Lands of Ice and Snow," words that had fascinated Pilot from the boyhood moment when he had first read them on one of his father's charts. He did not know why he had been always magnetized to this place, but now that he was here, he felt somehow as though he had come home.

*Splash* went the deep sea lead, Pilot's probe. Crew leaned outboard from the chain plate channel, letting the line run through his hands as it was dragged downward by the plunging lead weight attached to it.

"Fifty-two fathoms here."

"Aha," said Pilot. The sounding more or less correlated with their assumed position on the chart. Crew hauled in the long length of dripping line. By the time it was all up and coiled, he looked as if he had been through a rainstorm.

"Thank you, gentlemen," said Pilot, gathering up his tools and going below into the cabin. There, he leaned over the chart table, laid off the bearings he had taken, and made a fresh tick mark on the chart. Comparing it with the previous tick, he found they had indeed been set somewhat off course by a crosscurrent (as he had suspected, judging from the peculiar prance to the waves, among other indicators). He found the new course he had given Flags to have been accurate. Again his eye proved correct. Pilot's eye seemed to miss nothing, so finely sensitized was it to the tiniest nuances of elemental change. Everything conveyed some message to him. The coloration of water, its surface, clouds, weed, waves reflected from shores or gales too distant to be seen, lines of current marked by flotsam, the different behavior patterns of various species of seabirds–all manifest phenomena were duly noted and correlated.

Concluding his navigation for the time being, Pilot made a last entry in his book, closed it, and replaced it in its slot between the ephemeris and the almanac. Most of the other books in his library were mathematical in character, although there was a tract on human anatomy and simple surgical procedures, and another on chemistry and medicines. Pilot was the ship's physician and medical authority, having learned whatever he could from the naval surgeons. He found the human mechanism a fascinating study beset by mysteries. Also on the shelf was an alchemical treatise, a manuscript liberally sprinkled with symbols and patterns that were meaningless to him until he could read the associated text. Unfortunately, that was in a classical language he had not learned, so there was also a grammar and dictionary of that language should he ever have time to begin the investigation. He had almost left these books behind for the space they took, but in the end he had brought them as his one indulgence.

Above the books, Pilot slid the cased cross-staff into its slot. His entire locker was intricately compartmentalized. Each bit of his paraphernalia had its own niche. The cross-staff lived in a section given to navigational gear, just over the alidade, astrolabe, and quadrant, which he used only in the calmest conditions. Next to them in the locker was a rack of sand glasses, graduating from a tiny quarter-minute glass all the way up to the huge twelve-hour glass, which was always kept running and turned. Next to them was a loud, complicated, but not very accurate clock (which was miraculous but had to be constantly reset), and rules and dividers, everything arranged like instruments in a surgeon's chest. Indeed, there was just such a chest, in the cavity over the rack of wax-sealed bottles full of powders and herbs or liquids, each neatly labeled. There was also a mortar and pestle. In the central section, by the chart drawer, lived Pilot's rapier, regularly oiled though not used since the match with Bosun. The locker was cleverly constructed so that its hinged doors had depth; when opened, they extended the cabinet like wings, each with its own row of compartments.

The only other tidy locker in the aftercabin was Bosun's. His was also compartmentalized, although much more loosely. Bosun often changed the order of his possessions, whereas Pilot never changed any detail. While Flags's area always appeared superficially tidy, and was the only one that was decorated (with pictures and a curtained bunk), the inside of his locker was unorganized. Steward had more belongings than would fit into his space, so many of his things were simply rolled and piled on his bunk, where he slept among them. Crew's plain locker was a rumpled mess.

Pilot closed his cabinet and went forward to the galley, where he hoped Steward would have some warm water for shaving. If his calculations were correct, they would be dropping anchor in the Port of Dogs shortly after suppertime. The business they had to conduct was important, and Pilot wanted to be trim.

T HE PORT OF DOGS was the final place on earth. It was a port only by virtue of providing a sheltered, deepwater anchorage and being inhabited by two or three hundred of the caribou people, together with their caribou and the barking, yammering, yapping multitude of dogs for which the place had been named by the crews of the whaling ships. Under the mountainous backdrop, the village occupied a long shelf of land, a vista of gray-green moss interrupted only by outcroppings of lonely rock.

Far warmer than the land were its inhabitants. *Alembic*'s approach had been seen from a great distance, and she was greeted by an impromptu flotilla of canoes. Pilot knew these natives by reputation as skilled mariners who had sailed and paddled their hide boats over astonishing distances. If there was navigational knowledge of a northeast passage to be had, it would be here. Pilot was relying on it. If not, he would be forced to agree to turn back and retrace *Alembic*'s course, making the alternative attempt by the southerly route. Either way, there was need for fresh water, provisions, and firewood. There was also the broken topmast to repair.

Bosun's apprehension about the aboriginals was immediately put to rest by their friendly manner. They did not attach themselves to the ship but hovered at a respectful distance, chattering among themselves. By signs, they guided *Alembic* to an anchorage handy to the beach. When the ship was secured and no official canoe of any kind had approached, *Vessle* was swung out and manned by a shore party of Flags, Pilot, and Steward, with Bosun and Crew remaining aboard to watch the ship and work on the topmast. Ashore, willing hands helped them beach their boat. One helper, named Uyurak, greeted them in their own tongue, having once been employed aboard a whaling ship. He told them that whatever business they had would have to begin with the village Elder. So through the village they trooped with Uyurak, following the main path between a hodgepodge of log structures that were part above ground and part dug in, with roofs of sod-covered animal skins sewn to driftwood beams.

The Elder's lodge was the largest. Entering it through a kind of tunnel, they stepped up into a windowless chamber dimly illuminated by oil lamps. The walls were surrounded with sleeping shelves, and every surface was covered with furs. The fetid density of the atmosphere made Pilot feel so nauseous he had to fight not to show it as he was introduced by Uyurak. They were seated facing the Elder, a cheerful man of leathery face and indeterminate age who was flanked by a number of women and girls. Flags formally presented three strings of glass beads to the Elder. The caribou people were known to favor these beads, so *Alembic* had been stocked with a good supply of them, and they were well received. All of the lads were then brought bone cups filled with fermented caribou milk, which they were expected to drink with the Elder. Even though Pilot was prepared for the worst, the stuff almost made him gag.

The Elder wanted to know all about them and what had brought them there, for they obviously were not whalers, the only other southerners these people had known. Flags answered through the interpreter, telling of their voyage of discovery. As he spoke, Flags realized his audience was one of the most appreciative he had ever known, so he expanded his answers into narratives. Within a few minutes, the chamber was completely filled by as many of the Elder's family and friends as could squeeze into it, including the rest of his several wives, two of whom fell instantly in love with Flags. Nor did they hesitate to show it, giggling and making eyes at him shamelessly. Pilot felt crushed by the close press of bodies in the windowless chamber as he pretended to sip the vile contents of his cup. Steward drank the rest of his liquor, apparently enjoying it. Flags talked on, telling everybody about their escape from the pirates. That had to be explained in great detail, as it turned out, for pirates and piracy were unknown concepts to these people.

Pilot listened to Flags's narrative as patiently as possible, but when he judged Flags was indulging in mere dramatics, he speared the first pause. "Gentlemen, please excuse me," he said. And then to the interpreter, "May we ask our gracious host some questions about these waters?" The change of subject was easily accepted by the Elder, who told them there was indeed a navigable lead between the ice pack and the shore at this time of year. It had just opened and would normally be some seven to twenty leagues in width.

"How far does it go?" was Pilot's urgent question. The Elder shrugged.

"He does not know how to answer your question," said Uyurak. "The lead has many parts."

"Does it go through to another ocean?" asked Pilot. When the question was put to him, the Elder spoke for some time before the translator was able to turn to them with what he had said.

"It is known that the lead is very long. It goes beyond these mountains, then passes land where everything is flat for a great distance, and then there are more mountains. Yet farther to the east are floating mountains of ice, and beyond is a sea stretching to the south." He pointed out that these things were common knowledge among his people. While no one person that he or anybody knew had made the entire journey, many related tribes inhabited the whole length of the northern coast even beyond the distant sea, and all of it had been navigated.

"Aha," said Pilot, wanting to punctuate that point to Steward and Flags. "How long a journey is it to the far sea?" he asked. Again, the Elder spoke. This time, his words were all cautionary. He did not know the length of the entire voyage, but he knew that not even the largest of their own boats could make the passage within one season, and he doubted that any craft could do it. Everything depended upon the ice. The wind would favor them, but if it blew from the southwest for a few days, the ice pack would drift in against the shore, crushing any unprotected ship. In colder summers, the lead did not open along its whole length, and when the young ice formed in the autumn, there was no more movement by water until the following season. In the event of their being caught by the ice, their ship would be lost.

"When will the new ice form?" asked Pilot. According to the Elder, that varied from year to year by as much as a month on this side of the continent, and he assumed it was so on the other, although he could not say. He suggested they consult about that with the Matriarch, who was a seer. The Elder was very dubious about their ability to make the trip safely. He said there were, in the lead, many other dangers that Uyurak could tell them about. Uyurak, they learned, had penetrated the lead farther than anybody else in the village.

"Aha," said Pilot, cracking his knuckles. He did not wish to dwell on difficulties until he could speak to their translator privately, so he asked the Elder about water, wood, and provisions. All could be attended to in exchange for the precious glass beads. Last, Uyurak turned to Flags, telling him he had been requested by the Elder to linger ashore as his guest until the following day. Flags started to demur, but Uyurak explained he had little choice but to accept the hospitality because his company had been requested by the Elder's two youngest wives. At that moment, the two wives were buried in their furs, giggling. The Elder was smiling broadly, and the whole audience seemed amused by the situation. For once, Flags was caught flat-footed.

"Really," said Uyurak, "things will be so much easier if you simply accept." He assured Flags that he would like the wives and that they were very pretty and would make him laugh. Steward kept a straight face as he reminded Flags that duty was duty and that it was harder at some times than at others, but a good entry was called for here. Seeing his own opportunity to make a withdrawal, Pilot said his hasty thanks and good-byes, arranged to meet with Uyurak the following morning, and fled the place. Steward followed, first admonishing Flags to make a good impression on behalf of the ship. Outside, he found Pilot gratefully inhaling the cool, pure air.

"According to them, the passage goes through," said Steward as they made their way back to *Vessle*, "but it sounds risky. Very risky, in fact."

"That it goes through is the main thing, and it confirms all we've heard. If we hold east, we will come to the old mariner's Silent Sea. It is what we needed confirmed in order to continue," said Pilot. Steward was unconvinced. He said he would like to know what the translator had to tell them about the hazards and also what the Matriarch would have to say about the ice. Pilot promised a full discussion of everything, then deflected Steward's attention to the question of what victuals might be available in this place. As they rowed back to the ship to lend a hand with the work on the topmast, the conversation was of dried meats and the preservative qualities of smoking it.

On the following morning, the interpreter came paddling out in his canoe with the tidings that Flags was still preoccupied ashore and that the Matriarch would speak with Pilot if he wanted to go and see her. Pilot was not so concerned about what the seer had to say as he was about Uyurak's firsthand knowledge of the passage. Wanting to talk to him alone, Pilot slipped away with him while Bosun and Crew were occupied in stepping the topmast and Steward was below going over the list of supplies expended.

On the way to the lodge of the Matriarch, Pilot learned from Uyurak that some of the obstacles with which they would have to deal included shallows, currents, floating ice chunks, calms followed by sudden gales, and fogs. Again, there was the caution about the ice pack moving into the land. By the time they arrived at their destination, Pilot had heard nothing he wanted to hear, and the Matriarch was no more cheerful. She was witchlike, with thick, greasy black hair. She sat on a bare floor, surrounded by bones. Arranging the bones into a pattern, she then entered a trance. When she opened her eyes, she pronounced that the ice would form in the eastern end of the lead three lunar cycles hence.

"Is it enough time to navigate the passage?" Pilot asked.

"She says that, with good luck, the time is perhaps just enough," said Uyurak, "but she also says that, if you go, your ship will be frozen in the ice." Pilot was startled. He asked how she could know such a thing. "Because when she closed her eyes, she saw your ship locked in the ice, among the floating mountains, with snow falling from a cloudless sky."

It was all she had to say. Pilot gave her a few glass beads, thinking it a waste. On the way back to the ship, Uyurak asked Pilot if he was not troubled by the vision. Pilot said he was not.

Uyurak's response was surprising. "Her magic is held in high regard by our people, but whether it works for others beyond our tribe, who can say? Between now and winter, there is still summer, and if you go, you will need a guide. I will guide you for one string of your beads each day." As part of his service, he would forage for them and continue as translator as well as helping with shipboard chores and teaching them about the Arctic. Anybody would be free to cancel the arrangement for any or no reason at any moment.

"Done," said Pilot, "if my comrades agree. I expect they will, but you'll not help your case if you say anything of the old woman's dream." Uyurak replied that it was Pilot's prophesy to speak of or not.

Pilot did not. Instead, he told his companions that circumstances were favorable. When Flags eventually returned to the ship around noon, Pilot convened an immediate council. He wanted to put to rest any remaining doubts as to their route, treating it as a settled matter. In light of what they had learned confirming the continuity of the passage ahead, he judged their greatest question answered. He further told them of Uyurak's offer to accompany them as guide. But still, there were questions. Steward brought up the pessimistic advice of the Elder regarding the hazards of the voyage, and Flags wanted to know what the Matriarch had said.

"She said the journey takes three lunar cycles," Pilot answered.

"Is it enough time before the ice forms on the other side?" asked Bosun.

"She said the time is perhaps just sufficient," Pilot told them, and he saw them swayed by the words of someone they had never met, an old woman who greased her hair and lived among bones. He said nothing of her ominous vision.

"Do you believe her?" asked Flags.

"I believe in nothing whatever," said Pilot. "But the only people who know this water have confirmed the actuality of our route; we have one of them as a guide; they have told us there are risks to it, but we came here prepared to take risks." At last, he overrode their remaining doubts, and all agreed to proceed into the ice, accompanied by Uyurak as the sixth member of their company.

Later, Steward had a last question regarding something Pilot had said. "Do you really believe in nothing? Nothing whatever?" he asked.

"Nothing at all," Pilot confirmed.

"How can you live without beliefs?"

"How can you live with them?" asked Pilot. "By definition, any belief is something that somebody hopes is true; conversely, a disbelief is a hope that something is not true. Neither has anything whatever to do with the real truth, except to obscure it," said he who had just obscured it in his own way.

By the end of the third day in the Port of Dogs, *Alembic* had wooded, watered, and provisioned, thanks in large measure to the favor of the Elder. Bosun's new topmast was in place, now of more prudent length, and planks had been fastened to the hull at the waterline to protect it from the sharp edges of drifting ice. Uyurak came aboard, a berth having been prepared for him among the cargo, and his skin canoe was lashed on the foredeck. Hours being precious, sail was made at dawn on the following morning. Most of the canoes of the village put out to see them off. One large craft contained the Elder and some of his family, including his two playful wives, who seemed even more smitten with Flags at the end of his visit than they had been at the outset. All beat the sides of their canoes with their paddles in a drumming intended to distract the attention of evil spirits so none would cling to the ship. To the sound of the drumming, *Alembic* sailed into the Arctic mists.

THE ENTRANCE TO the lead was but a half day's sail. Pilot stood his watch, fixed their position on the sketchy chart he had drawn with the help of their guide, then pulled off his boots and climbed into his bunk to get an hour's sleep during the afternoon watch. He wanted to be well rested when *Alembic* entered the lead. Pilot slept for five hours out of each day, twice for two hours each and once for an hour. Normally, he went immediately to sleep upon lying down and automatically awoke at precisely the correct moment, but in this instance, it was not so. Possibly, the same forces of the north that created wild deviations in the ship's magnetic compass had interfered with the mechanisms in Pilot's head, for as *Alembic* approached the lead, he remained awake, watching the odd play of the light coming in through the stern windows, making grotesque shadows that moved to the roll of the ship. After a while, he slept, but well before the turn of the watch, his slumber was riven by an unsettling dream about the bottomless, black pit.

He had never revisited the labyrinth with its weird crypt. He would have liked to forget it entirely, but again and again, his thoughts had returned to it over the years. Especially now. Perhaps it had something to do with the proximity of the ice, but whatever from that eldritch well of darkness had lingered with Pilot now made itself felt again. In his dream, he was leaning over the pit, looking down into it, when he lost his balance and fell in. He was gripped by terror. The falling was endless. Down and down he fell, turning and turning, as though the space in the well were a vortex. He awoke believing he was doomed to fall forever. Moments later, there came a hard thumping on the deck overhead, a signal from the helmsman summoning all up from below. It was an emergency signal, and it brought Pilot out of his bunk at once. Snatching up his boots, he was on deck within seconds.

"We are in a whirlpool," said Uyurak, pointing.

"She answers the helm," said Crew, on the tiller, "but we're being turned in a big circle. Look." It was true. They were on the outer edge of a huge vortex, caught in its grip.

"Stand by sheets and braces!" called Bosun. Their only chance to escape was to try to sail out of it crosswise to its current. Sail was adjusted and readjusted, again and again, as the helpless vessel was swung farther in her wide arc to the point where she was swept in reverse to her original course. As the course changed, so did their bearing to the stream; the sails were gybed and retrimmed, but to no avail. Pilot could think of no solution to their predicament. No doubt it was a tidal occurrence, a maelstrom, but there was as yet no way to tell if it was increasing or diminishing in strength or what force was in the middle of its vortex. As *Alembic* completed a full circle, Pilot began a count in order to time the next one.

Suddenly: "We are free!" exclaimed Uyurak. And it was true. They had been released by the whirlpool after one rotation of its wheel and had been set back on their original course. "It is an omen for you," said Uyurak, but when he was asked what he meant, he could not say. "I know only that it is an omen, because I recognize it as such, and I am sure it is your omen, not mine. I do not know the meaning of the message. As you leave the waters marked on your sea map, you have been turned in a circle. That is all."

On the following watch, the soundings showed shallowing water, and their guide announced that the ship had entered the lead. The somber shoreline loomed to the south as before, but now visible from the masthead was the prickly white line of the eternal Arctic ice pack limning the northern horizon. Down the middle of the broad avenue of water, *Alembic* sailed with miles of offing to either hand and a fair quartering wind. Their guide seemed exhilarated at the little ship's speed. Thanks to his knowledge, they were safely piloted past unseen shoals, and Pilot, seeing Uyurak's reliability, was freed to chart the coastline with its obstructions, islands, and elevations. He found their guide to be an endless font of information, and the chart and sailing directions he recorded relied heavily upon what Uyurak had to say.

After they had traveled in the lead for five days, Uyurak pointed out the gray bones of two whaling ships marking the point beyond which no person other than the caribou people had been known to go, and he told them in detail about the fate of the whalemen. Caught by a movement of the ice pack onto the shore, the crews had abandoned their stranded ships and tried to march overland to the west. Having no local guide in their party, they experienced terrible privations, eventually turning to cannibalism. The frozen corpse of the party's last survivor was found only yards from the edge of a village and salvation. In his pockets were fragments of human flesh and bone. The whole dismal story of their doomed trek was later reconstructed by the hunters who found the remains of the whalemen and their ships. Pilot thought their guide's descriptions were unnecessarily vivid, and when he launched into further stories of Arctic horror, Pilot irritably asked him to desist.

"But you have no worry of such disaster," said Uyurak, surprised at Pilot's edge, "for if this ship is caught by the ice, I will guide us as well on land as I do in this lead, and with the help of my people, you will survive."

Pilot realized only too well how much their safe progress depended upon their guide, and it nourished his anger. Anger in its various forms had been a companion to him all his life, and he saw it with great clarity. He also saw the absurdity of being angry with their indispensable benefactor, who was also a cheerful, energetic adventurer much like themselves. So Pilot's anger was reflected back at himself, absorbed, and added to the deepening pool of orphaned angers that were percolating in him. At that time, he experienced an inexplicable impulse to turn the ship around and sail back, before they sailed so far into the lead as to preclude any return against the prevailing wind. Nor could he put from his mind the irrational vision of the old witch.

He did not speak of his doubts, although he did ask Uyurak how long he intended to remain with the ship. Having found the ship and its crew friendly, Uyurak was enjoying the voyage. He said he would remain with them at least until the point beyond which he had not traveled, where he thought they could engage a further pilot. He told them honestly that the beads they were paying him represented great wealth, wealth that increased with the distance from the last trading port. Their guide was also interested in finding how far to the east his tribal relatives had settled. The entire journey was a grand adventure to him. And so the point was left open.

During the second and third weeks into the ice, the days were mostly veiled by overcast, but it was the season of no night in their high latitude. Hence, they could sail continuously, and they made fine progress. On the morning of the twenty-first day into the lead, the sky cleared, the wind went calm, and Uyurak pronounced warning of an impending gale. Sail was therefore shortened, although Pilot neither saw nor sensed anything untoward on the horizon. Then, two hours later, they were struck by a sudden blast of wind strong enough to lay *Alembic* onto her beam ends. Uyurak anticipated the rush of lathered water toward them, and he shouted the alarm just in time for the sheets to be freed. Almost certainly they would have been capsized had it not been for the intuition of their guide. It took both anchors to hold the ship against the solid force of the storm.

The gale passed within an hour, and then they were on their way again. Leaving the mountains behind, they sailed along a low shore for day after day, and then week after week, sometimes threading their way between islands, sometimes halting to wait out a fog. They encountered other caribou people, hunting and fishing parties with whom they traded and from whom Uyurak learned of his tribal relatives here. When they reached the limit of Uyurak's own travels, he easily found a cousin who helped guide them for another fortnight beyond, until finding a cousin of his own to carry on a fortnight further, and so there was always at least one other camper on deck, with Uyurak remaining as translator.

Pilot's work was ongoing and difficult, complicated not only by his unfamiliarity with their surroundings but by the frequent fogs and the erratic behavior of the compass. They had also encountered areas of floating ice fragments that had detached from the edge of the pack and then drifted into the lead. The pack itself remained a comfortable distance offshore until, during their eighth week, they skirted a great cape of land that took them farther north than they had yet been. There, the pack was close into the land, leaving only a narrow lead between itself and the graveled shoreline. As *Alembic* approached the tip of the cape, the wind went into the southwest and blew fresh for two days, which alarmed Uyurak and his most recent pilot-cousin.

"The pack has begun to move," he announced.

"Nonsense," said Pilot, who had measured with his alidade the angles between the ice and the shore and had found no change. He also pointed out that it was illogical to think of the ice moving against the wind.

"But it does," said Uyurak. He warned that, in another day, the pack would close the lead entirely, and they could only save their ship by anchoring behind a small island in sight ahead of them. Pilot thought their best chance was to try to clear the tip of the peninsula, but he was overruled by their guides, and hence by all. It was a good thing, for the ice pack did move south–and quickly–grinding onto the barrier island's northern shoreline in great, broken slabs that shouldered their way up in a hideous jumble. *Alembic* floated safely in the clear water on the sheltered side of the island, but she was trapped. Neither of the guides would guess when or if the ice would retreat.

"It is one of the things you were warned about," noted Uyurak. "Now that it has happened, it is very difficult to predict what the ice will do. Perhaps it will be gone in a few days. Perhaps it will remain longer. At the worst, the ice will stay until the winter, and then your ship will be lost." He was unconcerned about their personal prospects should the ship be icebound here, for in that event, they would all travel overland to find the people of his cousin. "In their hands, we will be safe. With all of your beads, we will be very wealthy and can trade for dogs and sleds when the thaw comes." He reckoned it would take two whole summers to trek back across the tundra, taiga, mountains, and rivers they had passed by so quickly. "Then, when you are back where you started, you can wait for a whaling ship to come and pick you up. They come usually every other year." Having spoken those reassurances, Uyurak announced that he and his cousin were going off in their canoes to do some hunting and would return to *Alembic* within a week. Cautioning the comrades again about landing if there were white bears about, the two departed.

With nothing to be done about their predicament, *Alembic*'s crew found themselves with nothing to do at all for the first time anybody could remember. They gathered in Steward's galley. Always the ship's social center, the galley with its big table was a cozy cubicle of warmth in an otherwise desolate landscape. Steward made a batch of hot rum with butter and dark sugar. It eased much of their apprehension. Their fates were cast in the wind, but their lives seemed safe. They had plenty of fuel for Steward's hearth, for driftwood was carried plentifully by the many rivers that emptied into these coastal waters. Flags built up the fire, then took up his lute to tune again its strings. Bosun, who prior to his accident might have been driven crazy by such enforced inactivity, began macraméing a bottle, something he had always wanted to do. Steward and Crew were happy to be doing nothing. Pilot sat with them for a time, but he drank none of the rum. After a while, he went above, sliding the hatch closed behind him.

"He's been a sour mood since we came north," Steward noted. "And in truth, time is not improving it."

"He feels keenly his responsibility to us, having led us here, and it weighs on him," said Bosun, adding that he knew how Pilot felt. Bosun's diagnosis was partially correct, but if Bosun had actually experienced Pilot's mind for one moment, and if his sanity had survived the revelation, he would have noticed how awesomely far past simple responsibility Pilot's mind had probed. On deck, Pilot was one with the darkened landscape. They had passed through the summer, and now there were nights again, although the horizon still glowed with the retreating sun.

After three days, Uyurak returned with a canoeload of fresh caribou meat, fish, and–to Steward's delight–a dozen fat eider ducks. He also brought a new cousin to guide them farther through the lead and the news that a shaman whom he had consulted had seen the ice clearing away from the shore by the end of the following day. These tidings raised a cheer among all except Pilot, who marveled again at how easily his companions believed whatever they heard, just as long as it was what they wanted to hear.

But the ice did indeed part company with the land, allowing them to make sail and follow again the barren lead, dodging the drifting cakes of ice. According to the latest of the cousins, they had half again as far to sail as they had already sailed in the lead. He even drew a rough chart that brought little cheer to Pilot's heart. By his calculations, clearing the lead before the winter freeze would be possible only with luck and no more delays. It would be a very near thing. Their latest native pilot was about to confirm that, but Pilot turned away.

"That man has a blackness in him," commented the cousin to Uyurak as Pilot vanished into the aftercabin.

"Yes," said their guide.

"Do you know what it is?" asked the cousin.

"Yes, I think so," said Uyurak, explaining about the seer's vision of the ship captured by the ice.

"Why, then, did he come here?" asked the cousin.

"That I cannot say. He seems driven."

"What does he seek?"

"It is a puzzle. I do not know that he knows what he seeks."

"Then, he is crazy. Why do the others follow him?"

"He is their navigator."

"Then, they are crazy, too."

"Yes," said Uyurak sadly.

As the long days grew shorter, the endless flat shoreline went by until a height of land began to rise to the southeast, and in their eleventh week in the lead, they again approached mountains, all wearing new snow on their peaks. The sudden winds gusting down from the valleys brought winter's first breath. At last, their guide had run out of cousins, or even cousins of cousins, until he could barely understand the tongue of these distant peoples. Nevertheless, he obtained navigational instructions as well as provisions, and he remained with the ship until the last place on the continent from which he could take a safe departure.

Uyurak was very confident of his ability to find his way back eventually, although he wanted to see if along the way there might be another place he preferred to live. Perhaps he would take one or more wives. He did not know nor seem to care. As the only man of all the tribes to have navigated nearly the whole length of the northeast passage, he would have great prestige wherever he traveled, and with his bulging sackful of glass beads (he had been paid double the agreed wages), he thought it possible he was the wealthiest man in the Arctic. He admonished *Alembic*'s crew not to worry about him but about themselves and to find out from the people here when the freeze was expected. He reminded them that their remaining Arctic journey would take them away from any help, so their next move would be irrevocable. But his suggestion was brushed aside by Pilot, who saw no reason to expend precious time visiting another witch doctor.

When they reached the cluster of sod roofs marking the last village they would see, they made their good-byes to Uyurak. *Alembic* was hove-to only long enough to launch his hide canoe. "I will ask the gods for your safety," he told them. As the ship was sheeted to the wind and put back on course, Uyurak beat upon the side of his boat with his paddle, and it was a small, lonely sound.

ITH WINTER AT her heels, the ship sailed eastward, into the gray sea where ice floated in all fantastic shapes. Some pieces seemed to rival in size the edge of the continent from which they had crumbled. *Alembic*'s world was one of brilliance and shadow. Sometimes, she was driven at speed by wind whistling through the icy corridors, and at other times, the sails hung slack and the stillness was violated only by the voices of the ice itself.

*Craaa-aa-ack,* said the nearest ice.

"Brrrrrrr," said Flags, at the tiller, shivering for the dozent time in the hour. It was heavy mittens and warmest clothes on deck, with shortened watches at night when the chill was greatest. Flags felt the cold more keenly than any of them, although he was the best suited against it, wearing the warm, new caribou parka that had been given to him by one of the Elder's young wives and the leggings and boots he had received from the other.

"I think this is the coldest it's been," said Crew, on deck watch. A gibbous moon clearly illuminated the waters before them, permitting *Alembic* to ghost along safely, threading between the looming forms to either hand. Before nightfall, they had clearly beheld the frozen body of a gigantic monster suspended within one of the ice pinnacles, outlined by a refraction of the light.

"The ice was here, the ice was there, the ice was all around," quoth Flags. His recitation was interrupted by the ice's emitting a loud, eerie groan, like something in agony. According to Uyurak, the sounds were those of dead spirits trapped inside the ice, unable to go to the place of the dead.

"It's like a growling noise sometimes," observed Crew, "and sometimes more like a roaring and howling."

"Like noises in a swound," quoth Flags.

"What is a swound?" asked Crew, just as Pilot appeared on deck.

"I'm not sure," said Flags. "I'm not sure I like the swound of it. Let's ask Pilot." For most of their company, Flags's quips, songs, and outrageous puns added a welcome warmth to their frozen world, but they did not reach Pilot.

"A swound is a loss of consciousness," said Pilot tersely, terminating further conversation. He looked like a gray ghost, hardly there except for the two needles of condensed lightning that were his eyes.

"Crew," he said.

"Aye?" said Crew, at the alert.

"I need a mark."

"Aye." Crew stepped to the rail. Pilot cast the chip; its passage astern was marked by Crew, and then Pilot left the deck as silently as he had appeared, with no word of cheer. His departure was punctuated by another dismal groan from the ice.

Below, in the unheated aftercabin, Pilot made his notations of speed and course, pinched out the candle, went into his bunk, and rolled himself into his cloak without removing his boots. He lay with his eyes open, watching the black shadows. These moved around the geometrical patterns of moonlight coming in through the cabin windows. Perhaps he could have slept had he wished, but sleep was another form of darkness. Whatever darkness Pilot had manifested outwardly was only a ghost of what he carried within. Having no wish to contaminate his companions with it, he had simply withdrawn from them, but in sleep, he was defenseless against the darkness leaching into him.

The disturbing dream of the bottomless pit had recurred more frequently with winter's approach, and that nightmare had been sometimes accompanied by others no more welcome. During the days when *Alembic* was blocked by the ice, Pilot had dreams in which he saw the old witch-woman's vision of their vessel finally trapped. He had awakened with a very sharp view of how coldly he had manipulated his comrades into this place and perhaps to their deaths. He could find no pity in him, however, for his misled comrades or most particularly himself. Altogether they seemed like snowflakes–fragments of snowflakes–floating briefly through a world where any notion of permanence was the greatest illusion of all.

Even worse was a more recent dream that had shown Pilot not only hell's living presence but its machinery as well, vividly demonstrated from his own experiences. In his dream, Pilot stood atop the highest of the Arctic peaks, looking south at the entire panorama of the world with its geographies and inhabitants. People were revealed in great detail wherever his eye fell, and he saw with stark reality their eternal, tortured struggles toward gain. Monetary or spiritual gain made no difference, for in a world so demonstrably made up of lust, aggression, and ignorance, what was to be gained but more of the same? From his mountaintop, Pilot had seen everywhere man's frenzied pursuit of pleasure, his terror of pain, his cannibalism, with everybody hungry for whatever nourishment there was to be got from his fellow sufferers. He saw the right honorable Lords fueling their fires with not just his book but thousands of others; he saw nobly costumed priests uttering the prescribed prayers of decadent hierarchies that had learned how to feed well on hopes and fears by creating gods in man's own image. He watched also the futile graspings of those who fed on human despair in the name of fighting it, and he saw their utopian dreams absorbed into the same immutable neurotic patterns from which the seductive dreams had sprung in the first place, insidious and hope-giving jokes. To what avail science? Pilot saw man's accumulation of scientific knowledge expanded to fill huge archives, while his mind remained the same size. Had man become in any way better equipped by the repeated trials? In a sweep of history, he saw that it was not so. Worse yet was a glimpse of the future revealing the whole earth swarming with antlike men and machines devouring everything that could be torn from the planet–and poisoning everything that could not. He saw every attempted alteration by science of the natural world to contain an inevitable hidden price, terrible in proportion to the alteration.

The horror of the dream had been in the cold truth of it, and seeing no further, Pilot had awakened with the feeling of having been irrevocably impaled, as though on an icicle, upon the very truth to which he had devoted himself. In reflecting on his long pursuit of truth, he realized too late the chill consequences of its discovery. Now, with no target for his anger but himself, there was nothing to be said. There was only the ship to be navigated, and that he did automatically, with little remaining interest. Dispassionately, he wondered whether they would clear this sea before it froze. Dispassionately, he found he hardly cared.

On the following afternoon, Bosun's cry from the crosstrees informed all below of clear water beyond the ice mountains, opening to the south. With the end of the long passage in sight at last, a cheer was raised, but within an hour, the breeze diminished to a whisper and then died entirely. With the calm came the hardest cold yet, and so *Alembic*'s four sweeps were brought into play, and the long row began. They put their backs into the job, for the steely air that froze the sweat on their faces could also freeze the sea. The water's surface was still agitated by residual small waves, but aprons of ice were growing on the last of the floating mountains through which they slowly passed.

Throughout the rest of the day they rowed, until *Alembic* crept to a point separated from open ocean by two last mountains of ice with a clear corridor between them. As a rising moon revealed them nearly through, there came a snapping sound like the bone of a bird breaking, and the still water within the passage froze; in an instant, the two ice giants were joined together by a paper-thin sheet of young ice, and in it was *Alembic*. The sweeps broke through it easily enough at first, and with Bosun churning the crust from beneath their bows with the boat hook, some further progress was made, but it became harder as the ice thickened. At last, they could make no further way through it. Their best efforts were futile.

"I predict the wind will raise enough of a sea tomorrow to break it up," said Bosun as they panted clouds of steam in the moonlight, through frosted beards.

"On that, we can take a drink of rum," said Steward, ducking below into the warmth of the galley.

"And perhaps put a stick or two on the hearth," said Flags. He was followed along by all but Pilot, who remained on deck, watching a fall of snow that had begun from the clear, starlit sky. In it, he saw the vision of the old woman of the bones, and he knew they were doomed, for the formed ice would not be broken by waves as the others hoped. The ice now thickening around them would not depart until a sunless winter had passed. There was no help for them on the wintry shore even if they could reach it when the ice could support their weight. *Alembic* carried firewood in every place it could be stowed, but it would last no longer than a few weeks. Their provisions would outlast the wood, but when the fire was gone, they would no longer be able to melt their frozen water for drinking, nor thaw their victuals to eat, and then they would die.

Pilot went below. The rum was already having its effect on the others. He expected to be questioned regarding his views on their predicament, and he was prepared to tell them candidly, but he was not asked. Instead, the conversation concerned the palatability of walrus meat and led into one of Steward's detailed recollections of memorable meals eaten in other times and places. To this, Flags associated a meal story of his own, drawn from his memories of that warm and classical land where he had so happily dwelled. Soon, he was into other nostalgic stories of that place. Pilot sat through it all until well after supper, when Crew and Steward went to sleep with their heads on the table and Flags and Bosun seemed bent on drinking themselves into the same condition. Finally, he took his darkness on deck.

Nourished by the night and the snow, Pilot's anger overflowed. At first, it generated a feeling of warmth, then heat, then burning, as he allowed his universe to ignite; he floated in a sea turned to molten lava; the towering ice burned, and the deck under his feet felt like scalding iron. At that moment, Pilot went quite mad. He vanished into the aftercabin, reappeared a moment later with his rapier, and slashed at the air, trying to cut his way through the flames. Before his eyes, he saw the bottomless pit and lunged at it, putting his sword's point into the middle of its eye of blackness. The blade struck not bottomless space but the frozen oak of the stem head. Against it, the surprised steel shattered. As Pilot stood with the broken sword in his hand, the fires went out, starved for any fuel of logic. Again there was only the vast reality of a frozen universe. He heard a burst of laughter from below, and it was from another world altogether.

As Pilot had fought his hot hell, so now he surrendered to its opposite, the cold hell, the god-killing hell of Fimblewinter—winter eternal with no flicker of flame or warmth or light. He sat down on the forward bitts. The hilt of the broken sword fell from his fingers, the hand vanished into the folds of his cloak, and Pilot's figure was still. In big flakes, the snow fell on him, building up on the surfaces of his cloak and on the top of his hood with tiny drifts forming in the folds. He welcomed the cold and the dreamless sleep it offered.

The snow stopped when the morning sun appeared in the east between the snowy peaks, illuminating Pilot's still form like an ice sculpture. The brilliance stabbed through his frosted eye slits into the consciousness still flickering beneath, teasing it. The eyelids opened. Unobscured by truths or thoughts, Pilot examined the fascinating details of the wintry world around him. Close on either side, the twin ice mountains were thickly blanketed with the new snow. He saw its textures and watched a playful cascade of it run sparkling down a gully, creating a small slide where snow had piled itself too precariously upon other snow. In the absence of any Pilot to obstruct its functions, Pilot's mind was as sharp as his eye. The ice statue moved. After some difficulty standing, it went stiffly to the galley scuttle, opened it, and called hoarsely down to where the forlorn revelers slept in the dissipating warmth below.

"The cannons," he croaked. "Up, Bosun, you're gunner. Load the cannons. Use double charges." Bosun's head ached, and he thought Pilot had gone insane. He looked insane. So Bosun humored him, breaking out the gunner's stores and loading the guns with double charges. "Now, fire them off together on command. Ready?" The shock and thunder of their simultaneous detonations impacted on the ice slopes above them, startling into existence innumerable snow slides. These converged and gathered strength until masses of snow came crashing down in an avalanche onto the young ice, shattering it.

*Alembic* pitched and rolled in the wash of the waves, again afloat, all her company pushing and thrusting with the sweeps against the bobbing shards of ice, poling their craft toward the clear water beyond. Before long, the eastern sun brought a morning breeze, the sails filled, and they gained freedom. The crew crowded around Pilot, slapping him on the back and hugging him, congratulating him on his inspired idea. Steward spoke for all of them when he said, "Whatever you got us into, Pilot, you got us out of it, too."

"Will that get me a drink of your hot rum?" asked Pilot. Steward was delighted to oblige, so the off-watch trooped below. Sipping his rum while warming his feet by the hearth, Pilot was so communicative as to lecture on the physics of avalanches, explaining how any vibrations could trigger the fall of unstable snow masses.

"Yes," said Bosun, "but what made you think of it?"

"In point of fact," Pilot answered, "I was not thinking."

"Wherever your mind was," said Flags, "the sound of that snow cracking the ice was music to the ear."

"You could call it the swound of music," suggested Pilot, regarding Flags down the length of his thin nose.

"Pun my word!" said Flags, "I do believe you've come back to us, Pilot." But Pilot had begun to nod off. Just before letting himself sleep, he thought with pleasure of the recent surprise discoveries awaiting his examination when he awoke, including the parallel existence of contradictory truths and the fascinating potentialities of non-thought. He would have to think more about it later, he thought, allowing the warmth to steal into him.

# VII  The Silent Sea

THE SLOW SLOSH of the ship's movement through the lazy sea was the only sound in a silent universe. Ocean and sky were relentlessly blue, a blue that deepened upward and downward into the profundity of both depths. Above was the sun, a dot in space; below the ship's keel was the space of the ocean's whole mass. Both voids met at the plane where ship and horizon were the only reference points in an otherwise empty universe. To a bird, *Alembic* would have seemed like a gnat on a vast blue platter. But there were no birds.

The brassy clangor of the noon bell broke the still air. In the greater silence, its sound was tiny and, although it signaled the watch change, it caused no stir on *Alembic*'s deck. Flags was helmsman, but the tiller was lashed, and he was seated in the shade of the small awning Bosun had rigged to protect part of the quarterdeck from the sun. Flags was composing verse while the ship steered itself. The breeze was consistent, and on an orderly sea of measureless depth, there was little for the helmsman to do. It was the same for the navigator. Having finished his noon sight, Pilot turned the hourglass. Without a chart or any known landmark, his only reference was the sun's angle from the horizon by day and the moon and stars by night.

"What progress since midday last?" asked Bosun. Bosun was in the rigging, finishing the job of dressing a weather shroud with a protective mixture of black paint and pine tar. Crew worked just beneath him.

"By my best reckoning, we've made a good twenty-eight leagues since yesterday," said Pilot.

"Not so good as the day before, eh, Pilot?" asked Steward, throwing another soft potato overboard. He was sorting through a crate of them next to the galley scuttle, finding few still edible.

"No," said Pilot, "not so good as the day before. Nor was the day before quite so good as the day before that." He sighed. "Still, we've made good progress, taken on average. We're on the line between north and south."

Crew listened as he brushed the thick, hot blacking onto the rigging. The ship's progress meant far more to his comrades than it did to him, except . . . because of its importance to them, it mattered to him accordingly. His comrades were his touchstone to the universe. They were his family, his all. He had in his life no personal destination other than to be with them, and his only ambition was to assist in making everything go well, as defined through their eyes, not his. So far, all had been well since Pilot's recovery during their escape from the ice. Due south they had sailed, seeing no land and seeking none in favor of a straight course toward their next destination, the southern ocean with its legendary continent. The first fortnight of this leg had gone very well indeed. After clearing the ice, everybody had been exhilarated by the fresh, favorable wind and the leagues boiling away behind them.

"The furrow follows free," Flags had laughed.

Subsequently, the wind had eased, but it had remained more or less consistent on their quarter, and still they had made good progress. Exhilaration had settled into well-being. Day after day had passed with no new danger, and then week after week. The wind had continued to diminish, and well-being had faded into the current humdrum, workaday existence. Bosun and Pilot, for whom things had not always been well, were quite well now, Crew reflected. Between his ordinary duties, Bosun was finishing another macraméd bottle, and Pilot was submerged in his studies, back to normal. He was learning an ancient language so he could read an alchemy book. All was well elsewhere, with Flags composing a long poem about their adventures so far, and Steward was responding creatively to the challenges posed by a diminishing inventory of provisions. All that seemed well, but Crew knew Pilot well enough to have caught in his sigh the first indication of some problem, having to do with their slowing progress. It was only a slight leakage of space, but Crew was drawn into its vacuum.

Pilot had said their overall progress was good, so Crew thought that was the part best talked about. "Well, it's good we're getting there," Crew offered.

"There? Well, that's optimistic, Crew. It assumes there is a *there* somewhere in front of us. If there isn't, then I suppose it's good we're getting on to the extent we're able."

Crew studied the remark. "Where are we now?" he asked.

"My dear Crew," said Pilot, removing the conical canvas hat he had made to protect his sun-sensitive skin, "I promise you I will tell you the very moment I find out." He wiped the sweat from his forehead and replaced the hat, wondering how it was possible for Crew to have avoided learning the most elementary principles of navigation.

"I mean, you said we've made good progress on average," said Crew, stubbornly determined to pursue whatever the good of it was.

"I can measure our latitude, Crew, but not our longitude–not without a timepiece more accurate than anything yet invented. I can tell you that we are on the equator and that our average progress has diminished daily. Beyond that, all I can tell you is that the eastern part of our continent is over there to starboard somewhere too distant for birds to fly, judging by the lack of them, and to port is a lot more ocean, as you see. Behind us are a lot of miles, and in front of us, who knows? We've come to nothing yet, but I judge we'll come to something eventually, unless the world really is flat and we sail over its edge."

Crew paused in his tarring. As he considered whether or not he should make any further response, the tar in his poised brush puddled into its tip, slowly sagged into a thick string, detached from the loaded bristles, and then separated into falling droplets, pattering down around Steward and onto his head.

"Dammit!" said Steward, looking up just in time to catch another splash in the eye, which brought him to his feet.

"Mind your tar!" he yelled at Crew.

"Oh, sorry," said Crew, hastily plying his brush to stop the black rain.

"Crew, you are incorrigible," said Bosun, descending. "Go down and clean up that mess on deck."

"Aye, sorry." Crew hastened down and set about fetching rags and a scraper. When he had cleaned the tar spots as best he could, it was time to wet down the decks with buckets of salt water, an ongoing process that kept the planks swollen and tight. It had to be repeated often. That done, he scrubbed the soup cauldron for Steward, greased the windlass at its pall and bearings, and dressed its wooden barrel with oil. By the time he was finished with all the jobs nobody else wanted to do, his trusty old work tunic had acquired a few fresh stains among the mosaic of splotches from former times, and he had worked up a sweat. He gave the decks another sloshing and then went aft.

Flags was still there, musing over his iambic pentameter under the awning. Pilot sat listing conjugations of irregular verbs in the language he was studying. Bosun had put aside his macramé work for the moment in favor of some socks that needed darning. He did this using a cannonball for a darning egg, a three-pounder being just the right size. Crew nudged in next to them in the small shade spot, causing all to shift their seats slightly away from his rich smell of sweat and turpentine. They sat in a silence broken only by the precise clicking noises of Bosun's needle, the scratching of quills, and the small gurglings of ship and sea. Crew hoped somebody would start a conversation, if only to fill some of the space. There seemed too much of it. The silence seemed to make it press in.

Gazing at the perfect, unbroken circle of the horizon, Crew thought this vast ocean was somehow more like a desert than like the sea. "It *looks* flat," he said after a while, causing them to look up.

"I beg your pardon?" asked Pilot.

"You said before, if the earth wasn't a ball, we would sail over the edge. Well, I know it really is a ball, but it certainly does *look* flat."

"Oh? How do you know it *is* a ball?"

"Because you said it is. You've always said so."

"What if I'm wrong?"

"You wouldn't be wrong about something like that."

"How do you know that?"

"Well . . . ," Crew considered, "because I trust you."

"Aha. Never trust anybody. Trust yourself. How do *you*, Crew, know you are on the surface of a sphere?"

Crew's wide brow wrinkled. As usual, something he had said had gone wrong. Crew knew himself to be no scientist, but he also knew that Pilot was not going to let him off without an answer, so he considered the matter. "Because if it was flat, nothing would keep the water from just spilling off the edge . . . ?"

"Ah . . ." Pilot nodded, "but what if the earth is flat with a *rim* around it to keep the water in, like a big pie plate? How can you tell it's not like that?"

Again, Crew's forehead creased, but no new inspiration came to him.

*Scratch scratch* went the quills, *click click* went the needles. After some minutes had passed with no response, Pilot glanced up and saw that Crew's mind was adrift. He was staring glassily at the monotonous horizon, his fingers toying idly with one of the fishing lines. When their ship had first entered this sea, these lines had yielded an occasional fish, but during the past fortnight, no bait had drawn any nibble, and now the lines trailed largely forgotten. The water seemed as lifeless beneath its surface as the sky above them. Crew appeared to have forgotten Pilot's question entirely, and Pilot troubled him no further. He had learned long ago that not even his rapier mind could penetrate Crew's outer thickness. He could always demand Crew's attention and fix him to the spot, but only his husk. Crew would nod and agree, cowlike, while his actual consciousness wandered and grazed in distant pastures. At other times, however, Pilot had observed Crew to be a person of amazing perception. He had no explanation for the contradiction, nor for his particular obtuseness in the few days past.

"Dammit," said Bosun, having accidentally allowed his cannonball to roll out of the stocking and onto his bare toe.

The expletive jerked Crew awake. Thinking it directed at himself, he said the first thing that occurred to him, hoping to appear as though he had been pondering Pilot's question all along: "If the world was flat, wouldn't it be awfully thin?"

Pilot gave Crew a baleful look, then gathered his work and carried it below to the aftercabin.

"Well," said Crew to Flags, "I'm no scholard, but I know it's round."

Flags made no response. He was struggling to finish a final stanza before the watch change. Not that there was any hurry, but four bells would be attended by another small interruption, and he almost had his rhyme.

"Well, it is round, isn't it?" Crew asked.

"Yes, Crew," sighed Flags, "as round as your head would be if it wasn't so square." Flags glanced at the hourglass just as the last few grains of fine, white sand from its upper section splashed the tip of the perfect small cone formed by their predecessor into the bottom. Pilot reappeared to turn the glass and ring the bell. Flags tried to recapture the thread of his former thought. "Can anybody think of a word that rhymes with *silent*?" he asked.

"*Violent,*" suggested Pilot.

"Aha, that's it," said Flags.

*Ding-ding ding-ding*, said the bell.

An eventless week was followed by another and yet another, and as the wind slackened, each day *Alembic* made slightly less progress than the day before. For a week or so, the whole company helped Bosun, who designed and then fabricated a large square foresail to hang from the main yard and then a set of studding sails with all their gear. Their booms were fashioned from two sweeps. When rigged, they set to either side of the square topsail like wings, catching more of the light breeze. Bosun would have also made a pair of lower studding sails, but there was not sufficient spare canvas remaining, so he had to be content. As it was, *Alembic* ghosted under a towering assemblage of sails. With no strains or chafe aloft, there was little maintenance.

Crew had nothing to do but slosh the decks. Bosun had returned to his macramé, and Pilot to his books. Steward did little cooking. Because of the heat and their dwindling supply of firewood, the galley hearth was fired only every other day and then only for the mandatory boiling of their salt meat. Creative cuisine had become impossible from Steward's ravaged pantry, so he mostly slept. Flags brought his long verse to the point where there was nothing else to be written until something else happened, then entertained everybody with a reading. Although it was pleasantly received, it was not an entire success, either, and even its author perceived that something was flat. In rereading it to himself, he could find nothing wrong with the writing, so he decided the flaw had been in its delivery. It seemed to him that all spoken words here were made lonesome by the silence into which they fell. This effect was pervasive.

Earlier, social intercourse had yielded its normal flow of episodic conversations, some of them dating back to their boyhood. Hence, the nature of sea monsters was reargued for the hundredth time, as was the existence or nonexistence of mermaids and the comparative qualities of the women of many lands. The phenomenon of the whirlpool was the subject of some speculation, along with Uyurak's opinion that it was an omen. There had been some attempt also to recollect the words of the Oracle who had once predicted their present voyage, but her prophecies had been badly remembered even at the time they had been uttered a dozen years before, and only a few words of them remained. Steward recalled having been cautioned not to eat poisoned food, and Bosun remembered a warning about windstorms. Flags wanted to know if anybody could remember anything about his prophesy other than its having a fire in it. Nobody could. Bosun remembered Pilot's as containing a lot of ice, but if Pilot remembered more, he held his peace. Of Crew's, nobody could recollect anything whatever, although Crew said he remembered very well that the Oracle had cautioned them to stick together whatever happened.

"Where are we going to go?" Bosun asked.

As the breeze diminished, so did the flow of words, until few were spoken and those that were gave emphasis to monotony.

"Let's try to remember to be watchful," Bosun admonished repeatedly. "The danger always comes when you're not watching." Although all knew his cautions to be prudent, the words had become repetitive sounds, mechanically delivered. Bosun would have welcomed a whiff of danger to relieve the tedium. But there was nothing. In the complete absence of any elemental events, the tiny occurrences of shipboard life were magnified easily, like punctuation marks in the silences, intensified by boredom and galvanized by the heat. Noting this, Crew became more and more concerned that all was not going well, and so he redoubled his efforts to be as helpful as possible. In the absence of anything with which to help, and no special interest of his own to occupy him, Crew attacked the silence he felt enshrouding them, becoming the most garrulous member of their company rather than the most taciturn.

"What is that book about?" he asked Pilot, insisting on explanations for things Pilot knew held no interest for him. "Where did you learn to draw?" he asked Flags, who had taken to making illustrations for his verses. Moments later, Crew spilled Flags's inkwell. "I'll clean it up," he said. He told Bosun how beautiful his sails were just as Bosun was glumly viewing their sag, and he warmly congratulated Steward on barely palatable meals. When Crew slept, which was often, he snored loudly, the sure signal that all was not well, in his mind. The immeasurable solitude of the Silent Sea had seeped into all of them, but to Crew it was a near-mortal intensification of the same quality within himself. Mistaking the reserve of his comrades for a fragmentation of their unity, Crew worked ever harder toward their cohesion, giving form to his fears, conjuring them by accident from space.

Conditions for the conjuration were fertile. *Alembic*'s deck was the sun's anvil. The rare shade spot from any migrant cloud was so merciful and fleeting as to make the sun's intensity seem worse after the cloud had passed. By day, all the cabin spaces were ovenlike. Only night brought any relief. Then all could go below and sleep in their comfortable berths.

THE FIRST NIGHT of their ninth week in the Silent Sea was moonless. The ship's serene presence was a black shadow against the stars. The stars and the ship would have floated together in perfect silence but for an anomalous roaring that came and went, a resonant, inhuman, irregular sound that seemed to issue forth from a different world, so abrasive was it against the tranquillity of this one. For periods, the sound achieved the steadiness and strength of a fog signal, then changed to an uneven burbling, gurgling, hawking, rumbling, remarkable for its combination of phlegm and grit. At irregular intervals, it ceased . . . as if some inconceivable, slow strangulation had finally terminated in the sweet mercy of death, but then, hideously, it would be reborn, commencing a new cycle–sometimes a grinding, as of cannon barrels dragged in clusters across textured rock–sometimes as the liquescent escape of gases bubbling from the bloated corpse of a beached whale. It vibrated from keel to masthead. The whole boat trembled with it, but it was at its most unspeakably formidable at the open cabin companionway, whence Bosun emerged reeling on a fresh wave of sound.

"Ah, God, how he snores," he gasped.

"It is unbelievable," acknowledged Pilot, who had the watch with Flags. They had both gone to the foreward bitts, as far from the sound source as it was possible to get without climbing into the rigging.

"It's been bad lately, but this is the worst I've ever heard it," said Flags. The rest of them had learned to put plugs in their ears and sleep through it more or less. Usually, it terminated of its own accord after a while, but on this night, there was no silence, nor surcease, nor succor from its pervasive reverberation.

"It's intolerable," declared Bosun.

"Steward is still down there in it," Pilot noted.

"Steward's amazing," said Flags. "He can put up with anything." The words were hardly out before Steward emerged, hands to his ears.

"Welcome to the great out-of-doors," said Flags.

"I tried to wake him up," said Steward. "I tried everything. I tried stuffing a shirt in his mouth, and he just blew it out."

"There's no sleep in the daytime for the heat," observed Flags,

"and now there's no sleep at night, either. Something has to be done."
All agreed.

The following morning, Crew appeared at breakfast, well-rested and hungry. He perceived from the demeanor of his comrades that all was not well. "G'morning," he nodded at them, making his best grin. Finding it stonily received, he gave his entire attention to a bowl of six-day-old porridge that had to be cut with a knife. He tried to show that all was well by making appreciative eating noises.

At last, Pilot spoke. "Crew, nobody could sleep in their bunks last night for your snoring."

"I'm sorry," said Crew.

"Not as sorry as we are. In fact, it's intolerable. It means either you have to vacate the cabin or the rest of us must."

"Where else should I sleep?"

"In the forepeak. Bosun's agreed to clear a space among his gear there for your bunk." They all glanced at Bosun. He had not wanted to yield any of his work room to Crew but had reluctantly agreed. There was simply no bunk space below decks other than the part of the galley Bosun had occupied during his recovery, and nobody wanted Crew there. The forepeak was as far from the aftercabin as possible, and they reckoned that with the hatch closed, Crew's catastrophic snores would be muffled. Crew nodded, examining the backs of his hands, with their patterns and deposits of dried tar.

"It's only for sleeping, mind," said Bosun, "and only nights; I'll need my work space during daylight."

"All right," said Crew. "I'm sorry for snoring. I can't help it."

"There's something you *can* help, Crew," said Steward, "and that is how you present yourself at the table in my galley. Look at you, man. You're wearing everything you ever spilled. Also, you reek of sweat, and it's enough to ruin what appetite's left for the food we're forced to eat."

"And, by all the gods, throw away that tunic, Crew," said Flags.

Again, Crew nodded as he continued to stare at his hands–hands that were suddenly an embarrassment to him. Abruptly, he put them out of sight under the table. Knowing the others were all looking at him, he did not raise his eyes, but then he began to feel silly, staring at the table in front of him. He started to brush some crumbs into a neat pile, then realized he had again placed the grimy, offending hands into view.

"I'll go wash, then," he said, and went up on deck, where he stood numbly. He should have gotten soap from Steward before coming up. He thought of going back down and asking for some. He sighed. The sun had started its climb, and the heat of the day was beginning. There was the deck to be wetted. Taking the bucket with the lanyard, he dropped it over the side, gave the line a twitch to fill it, brought it back up, and sloshed the water onto the dry planks. He repeated the process the two dozen times it took to wet the whole deck. When it was done, all but Steward had dispersed from the galley.

Crew tapped at the hatch coaming. "Soap?" he requested. It was passed up. He drew another bucket of seawater, removed the offending tunic, poured the water over his head, and began to wash his square, thick body and his big feet. Crew ignored anguish with the same stolidity he accorded all adversity. He knew the others had much more creative ways of dealing with life's vicissitudes. Long ago, he had realized himself devoid of their colorful qualities, which he so admired: Pilot's brilliance, Bosun's efficiency, Flags's charm, Steward's solid authority. His own offering, such as it was, he saw as his faithful, dogged reliability. It had always seemed sufficient. Now, he found he had given such offense that even the supremely tolerant Steward was unable to accept him. He found no argument with their criticisms, although he was puzzled by them. He could not experience his own snoring. He had heard others snore, plenty of times, and hadn't found it troublesome, any more than the smell of work clothes. Shipboard life was not fancy. Oh, well. He could accept his exile. He could sleep in the forecastle, or on the deck for that matter, unless it rained. There had been no rain at all. He didn't care where he slept, so long as it kept everybody happy. Having finished washing, he toweled himself with his old tunic, which he found not very absorbent. He stood looking at it and had to concede it was a mess.

"Overboard!" It was Flags shouting at him. "Throw the damned thing overboard!" Crew shrugged, threw the faithful garment over the side, and watched it settle as the boat crept slowly past it. Except for the wet place around him, the deck had nearly dried again, so he took up the bucket. He comforted himself with the thought that all would be better when they got more wind.

But instead of more wind, they received even less, and then less yet, until finally what was left of it toyed with them maddeningly, sending minuscule cat's-paws to riffle patches of the sea's still surface; sometimes distantly, sometimes playing close aboard, putting out occasional small fingers of breeze to stir a slothful movement from the sails. The helm would be put in this direction or that, and the bows would be sluggishly nudged back on course; then the whisper of air would depart, leaving *Alembic* to drift in lazy circles. At last, there was no further movement of air whatever. The surface of the ocean was a perfect mirror, and the rigging's song was still.

A SAILING VESSEL, even a small sailing vessel such as *Alembic,* is capable of keeping the sea nearly indefinitely, provided she is not damaged by shoal or storm. When sailing, her greatest enemy is chafe aloft to lines, sails, tackles, everything that moves and rubs in a seaway, insidiously depleting fiber, creating weaknesses to be discovered by hard strain. More limiting to the endurance of a vessel than her own vulnerabilities are her crew's, whose needs are greater than their ship's in a variety of ways. As it was Bosun's duty to point out (and as well he knew), the greatest dangers result from inattention, exhaustion, panic, and the many other manifestations of human frailty that have cost more ships and lives than all other causes. The antidotes are embodied in the traditional shipboard disciplines as well as the normal ingredients of a sailor's life: hard work, challenges, sometimes dangers, followed by periods of relaxation. If deprived of these things, a ship becomes like a prison.

At the beginning of her twelfth week in the Silent Sea, *Alembic*'s gear had been subject to no chafe whatever for near a month, and for a fortnight she had floated totally becalmed. Now chafe's immutable law, deprived of its normal exit through the fabric of the ship, found expression through her crew. Bosun had enlarged the awning to shade as much of the quarterdeck as possible. There they sat or lay, each enduring in his own way and in his own solitude. Quoth Flags:

> Day after day, day after day, we stuck, nor breath nor
> motion;
> As idle as a painted ship upon a painted ocean.

Flags had intended his recitation as a small contribution of good cheer, but it did not have the desired effect. It had no discernible effect at all. Until as recently as the week before, he had provided a bit of entertainment by playing his lute each evening, until its sounding board had cracked open from the dry heat, collapsing the instrument's bridge and making it unplayable. Subsequently, he had made drawings to amuse himself. He considered going below to fetch a sheet of parchment from his almost depleted supply, but the thought of the cabin's heat made him decide not to.

"Water, water, everywhere, and all the boards did shrink–"

"Belay it," Bosun interrupted him. "Spare us any more. You've said it enough." Having run out of bottles to decorate, Bosun had begun to macramé the tiller and was running out of twine.

"Well, the old mariner was certainly right in his description of where we are," said Flags, shifting position to rest his eyes from the surrounding glare. "The very deep did rot, ye gods! That ever this should be–"

"I said belay it," said Bosun. "We've heard it."

"Oho," said Flags. "It's Captain Bosun come to visit again, perhaps with an offering from his own repertoire of perennial favorites. Perhaps we'll be treated again to the immortal recitation on how we should always be alert for squalls just when we're least expecting them? We haven't heard that in some time. Or possibly we could have a stanza or two of the old 'There's Always Danger' aria."

Bosun made no response, but Flags's "Captain Bosun" reference found scar tissue. Since the pirates' chase, Bosun had been content with his role. Now, when a stirring of old aggressions reappeared in him, he recognized them and was determined to keep them well blocked.

"Does the new rule against poetry apply to just the quarterdeck," asked Flags, "or is there an area where it is permitted? Is there a schedule to it . . . Captain?"

"Don't try me too hard, Flags. Bosun will do. Just Bosun."

Pilot waited to see if it would go further. His study had been interrupted by the petulant exchange. It was as though an ember had been whipped into a blaze by a passing williwaw of wind; the fire's updraft had intensified the wind, which had in turn intensified the fire. But the williwaw passed, and the flame died. Pilot judged it was about noon from the mast's shadow. Somebody had forgotten to turn the glass. To find the approximate time, he would have to go below. He considered fetching the astrolabe and taking a sight, but he knew it would give him the same angle he had measured for the past fortnight, so he returned to his book. He was now reading the volume on alchemy and making slow progress.

"Isn't it about noon?" asked Steward. Steward had made pillows by rolling up bundles of clothing, and he lounged among them.

"Yes," said Pilot.

"Are you not taking your sight?" asked Steward.

"No," said Pilot.

"Have you given up navigating?"

By way of reply, Pilot threw a chip of wood into the water. It whirred past Crew (who was propped against a stanchion gazing over the side) and splashed down, spreading concentric wavelets.

"Tell me when the ship moves any distance from that mark," said Pilot, "and I'll navigate. Since you raise the subject of duty, what do you have in mind for our noon meal?" Getting no response, Pilot went back to his study. He was finding the book's contents a confusing mixture of chemistry, astronomy, and other ingredients that were more obscure. His mind felt sluggish.

After a while, Steward hauled himself to his feet, braced for the impact of the direct sun, and stepped out from under the awning. Going forward, he descended into his galley. Once the center of all sociality and cheer, Steward's kingdom was now a hot box smelling of old grease and new fungus. It was unlivable, unvisited, and unyielding of culinary delight. Through Steward's foresight, there still remained stores adequate to prevent starvation, but none with any savor—except to the flour bugs, weevils, ants, worms, and cockroaches, which had proliferated beyond reason in the heat.

Each day for weeks, he had thrown rotting food over the side until there remained only dried stores or those that required cooking. There was the salt meat, some flour, rice, peas. There remained ship's biscuit—hard, dry, and full of weevils; stone crocks of desiccated cheese; soured molasses; pemmican; strips of smoked jerky obtained from the Eskimo, like the dried caribou meat from which the mold had to be scraped; a few loaves of sugar whose grains had so welded themselves together that they had to be broken like bricks, with a chisel; and the rationed supply of dried fruit slices, which were like leather but provided their only protection against scurvy. Drinking water had thickened in the casks until its living organisms could be clearly seen wriggling and the nose had to be held when drinking it. Mercifully, there was still some rum. Steward uncorked a bottle and drank deeply. He drew a biscuit from the bag, tapped it sharply against the table until its inhabitants emerged—three fat, white weevils with black heads—and then munched the rest of it, softening its hardness with another swig of the rum. Much of Steward's girth had melted away from him, so for the first time in his life, he looked gaunt. Reemerging from the galley, he returned to the afterdeck.

"Your noon meal," he announced, dropping the sack of biscuits into Pilot's lap. Startled, Pilot half rose, then resettled himself with a frosty look at Steward. He pushed the biscuits to the middle of the deck, brushed the flour dust from his book, and said nothing.

Flags was not so reticent. "We feast again!" he said." And to delight our palates, we find biscuits! Mouthwatering, munchy, and filled with delectable, fat, white worms! Oh, well done, cook! Plaudits! Accolades!"

Throughout, Crew had been motionless but for the occasional unconscious movement of his hand to his ears, as though brushing away buzzing insects. He had been gazing into the water. It was perfectly transparent to a great depth and by no means as lifeless as it seemed from its surface. A garden of weeds had begun to grow from the ship's hull at the waterline, and it was alive with diminutive crustacea and fish. The whole body of the water was flecked with tiny organisms. At a casual glance, the smallest of them seemed like mere specks, but on closer inspection, he saw they were living beings, propelling themselves through their watery world with great vigor, their efforts rewarded by progress measured in hairbreadths. Also, below the keel were countless thousands of jellyfish in all sizes, layer upon layer, into the depths. Peering closely, he saw that each one consisted of a translucent, pulsing diaphragm with long tentacles extending far beneath it, like pale mandarin beards. These were grazed by silvery fish. Every now and again, one of the fish would browse in among the threads and remain there. After some time, Crew realized they had in some way been trapped. Looking even more closely, he saw that most of the larger jellyfish held a fish, which they were absorbing by some extraordinarily gradual process. The meal was not seized, or even eaten, but passively incorporated into its captor. All of the jellyfish, large and small, propelled themselves in the same direction, together making a directional drift with their corporate mass. Where were they going? He beheld a small, lone jellyfish traveling for some unexplainable reason in a direction opposite to the general movement. Why? He marveled. Mystery upon mystery. It was as though the whole space of the water were thick with life and consciousness and puzzling purpose.

Suddenly, the glass through which he peered was shattered. Pilot's chip of wood had described its trajectory past his head and splashed down, fragmenting his vision with wavelets, forcibly returning him to the world of the boat–his own fragmenting world. Again, bickering assaulted his ears; again, the isolation came crashing home. Had *he* invoked the whole malaise with his stupid snoring and dirty tunic? His personal pain of exile was tolerable, and could be ignored, if only the others were united. It was intolerable that now, monstrously, the whole fundamental structure of his family was dissolving. For weeks, he had watched helplessly as his comrades had withdrawn, manifesting petty irritations more and more freely, damagingly, each time opening a further distance. And what else besides them was there? Without them, what sanctuary? And was he, Crew, not like the jellyfish–passively pulsing, initiating nothing, doing nothing, a mere mechanism waiting to absorb another meal?

It was time to slosh the decks. He rose, went forward, and took up the bucket, his thoughts persisting: was this the best contribution he could make, sloshing the decks as his world crumbled? Crew held these questions. He had nothing else. Uncharacteristically, there came an answer–a plan. In fact, his agitated mind gave birth to two plans. One being too drastic to think about, he concentrated on the other, which was extreme enough.

Crew entered the forward scuttle and made his way through the galley to Bosun's area in the peak. There he found the tarpot. Plunging his fingers into it, he drew forth a glob of the black goo and daubed it onto his clean tunic, smearing it around, then rubbing the excess into his hands and onto his forearms. Before putting the lid back onto the pot, he poured a puddle of it into the middle of Bosun's workbench.

Turning back into the galley, he rummaged among Steward's stores until he found a crock of molasses. This he dropped onto the floorboards, where it broke, yielding a slow, sticky flow. Crew climbed back out onto the deck, where he planned to complete an inventory of actions intended to so upset all of them that they would again unite. It would be against him, to be sure, but their wrath would be an insignificant thing to bear if he could but see them again conjoined.

After standing unnoticed for some time, he spoke: "Ahem," he said. "I have something to say you're not going to like." Here and there, an eye blinked open perfunctorily, and he made the plunge.

"Bosun, I've spilled tar on your workbench, and I'm afraid I've messed up my other tunic, too, Flags, and then I dropped the molasses in the galley," he said, adding, "and I don't care." To drive home the point, he made a careless gesture with his arm that knocked Pilot's hourglass off the binnacle box. It fell to the deck and shattered. All their eyes were on him, and he braced for their united onslaught.

When the reactions came, they were far from what he had imagined. Bosun simply shook his head and turned his eyes back to his macramé. Steward wordlessly buried his face in a pillow.

"Well done, Crew," said Flags. "Plaudits. Accolades." He closed his eyes again.

"Well, you'd better clean it up," Pilot sighed, "and get yourself out of the sun. You've had too much of it."

After a while, Crew squatted and began gathering up the pieces of the broken hourglass, determining his next move. Having set himself on a course, he would follow through in the manner of a rolling boulder dislodged from a mountainside. He would persevere in his purpose with all the stubbornness in him, which was quite a lot, and would deliver a more telling stroke. He would do the unimaginable. But he would have to await his night watch on the helm, when the others would be asleep.

T IS UNLIKELY Crew would have done the thing he later did if he had heard the exchange taking place far over his head at sunset. At that time, Pilot was seated on the starboard crosstrees. He had climbed there for a loftier view of the world as soon as the sun had sunk sufficiently to free him from the awning. Just at dusk, Bosun made his customary climb aloft for a last look around the horizon before darkness fell. Seating himself on the port crosstrees, he made a futile sweep of their empty universe, then gazed at the drooping sails.

After a while, Bosun interrupted the solitude with a question to Pilot: "What's your candid view of our situation?" he asked.

"Dire," said Pilot. "Our victuals, such as they are, may last two or three weeks, according to Steward; the water's perhaps good for longer, though it gets no thinner or sweeter with time. When we do get wind, if we do, we've yet to find land somewhere in this ocean, for which reason we'd best get wind soon. If we do not, our enterprise may end badly."

"In truth, it seems none too good as it is," said Bosun. "Crew's going mad, Steward's soured, and I fear I'll put Flags over the rail if he goes on as he has."

"To what avail?" asked Pilot. "Because his insanity is greater than yours or mine? His prattlings are born of desperation. We're all oppressed nearly beyond endurance. A clear perception of our painful situation doesn't lessen the pain, but it is helpful in preventing our adding self-created suffering on top of it."

Bosun pondered this, finding something in it that led him into a long, hesitant question that emerged in badly organized form. As best Pilot could understand, during the encounter with the pirates, Bosun had experienced a revelation of himself that had shocked him, and he had thereafter put behind him those things he had not liked. That accorded with Pilot's observations of his friend and bore similarities to his own recent experiences. Bosun was troubled by an unwanted clinging of thoughts and feelings he thought he had dispelled. "If I was so blind before and did not know it, what is to prevent my still being blind, not knowing it as blindness?" Using an analogy to fit Bosun, Pilot likened the situation to seeing the mind tied in knots that had to be somehow untied once seen.

"I thought my knots had untied themselves," said Bosun.

"So did I with my own," said Pilot. At that moment, the last sliver of the red sun slipped below the horizon, making an amazing bright green flash seen only by the two lookouts.

Crew had the midnight watch. There was nothing for the helmsman to do except remain awake and watchful for any change, and it was one of the few rigid disciplines that had not been relaxed under the prolonged siege of silence. No bell was rung, nor did Flags have to awaken Crew, for he was right there.

"Steer a straight course," said Flags, going below and into his bunk.

Giving Flags time to fall asleep, Crew paced the foredeck in the moonlight, seeing the whole luminous sky twinned by its undisturbed reflection on the Silent Sea. After a while, he moved aft to the companionway. By the breathing of his comrades, they were asleep. Steeling himself to the deed that would not–could not–be ignored, he entered the cabin, went to his old bunk, climbed into it, and with great deliberation, prepared to snore. Of all his failings, of all the things he had done to offend his shipmates, he knew his snoring to have been the worst. Intolerable, Pilot had called it, and they had been concerted in their anger. It was in his power now to use it again, and the new outrage would be doubly compounded by his dereliction of duty and uninvited return from exile. In their rage, they would be reunited.

Closing his eyes and arranging himself as though sleeping, Crew pulled air in, creating a hollow, vibrating snore. He had secretly practiced in the forepeak, doing it quietly, and it was easy enough. Now, he gave it full volume, resolved to continue the sound until the last moment, when he expected to be thrown out bodily. He did not know what they would do. It would be bad, but whatever the sacrifice, it had to be made. After a dozen or so of his best snores, however, he could hear only breathing. He redoubled his efforts.

Although he had no way of knowing it, Crew's conscious efforts produced only a feeble imitation of the inconceivable eruptions that had come so naturally from his unconscious, unhindered being. His counterfeit snoring was as a kitten's mew to a lion's roar. Nevertheless, he persisted even after his throat started to hurt from it until at last he thought he heard some other sound nearby. He delayed his next snore to listen. Among his pillows, Steward had begun to snore, and Bosun started to emit a sound like the ratchet of a battle rattle. Within moments, a whistling noise began to issue from Pilot, and from Flags came a cadenced, descending glissando. The night had come alive with snoring. Knowing defeat, Crew got up and went back on deck.

He did not usually feel handicapped by his inability to cry, any more than he would have by, say, colorblindness, tone deafness, perhaps a missing finger, or any other minor impediment. At various times, he had wondered which he would choose, laughter or crying, if he could be somehow miraculously gifted with one or the other. Ordinarily, he had thought laughter the more desirable choice, but at this moment, he would have given anything for the anesthesia of tears. When his watch was up, he woke up Bosun to relieve him and then went forward to lie down by the bitts. Eventually, he slept, his body curling into the attitude of an unborn infant under the brilliant luminosity of moon and stars. He did not snore, but later he dreamed.

Crew dreamed he was under the sun's eye at midday. He sat alone on the deck, feeling a fear that would not permit him to gaze into the vastness of the surrounding space, although he somehow knew he would have to do so eventually. Postponing the moment, he examined the features of the deck and began to see clearly the spaces between the individual fibers of the planks, so the wood became transparent before his eyes. Wherever his gaze fell, upon whatever object, that object began to separate into its individual component particles, until nothing was solid. He stole a glance at the sky; its intense light did not hurt his eyes, but terrifyingly, he knew that if he looked directly into it, he would be able to see into infinity, and he could not look. The fear of it was overpowering. Trying to close his eyes, he found they would not close, and when he put his hands over them, the flesh and bones of his fingers turned translucent, and then his whole body dissolved, evaporating, until he was quite gone, leaving a perfectly formed Crew-shaped hole in a mould of solidified space like poured glass. All that was left of him was an articulated cavity.

Crew was awakened from the dream's horror by the first rays of the sun, mercifully finding his body real and restored. He was delighted to move freely, stretching his arms, dispelling the vivid claustrophobia of his nightmare. Here came Bosun, down from aloft, where he had seen nothing, obviously.

"G'morning," said Crew, wriggling his toes and fingers in an exaggerated way.

"G'morning," said Bosun, making his customary rounds of inspection. One by one, the others emerged into the light and solitude of another windless morning. Pilot came up, viewed the day, and then bathed under the bucket, noticing the chip of wood he had thrown overside yesterday still floating in the exact space where it had landed. A half-hour later, Flags appeared. The first thing he saw as he stepped from the companionway was Crew, arms akimbo, standing on one leg, with the other stretched out to the side, like a dancer. Ordinarily, it would have been the most comical sight, but in the circumstances, Flags took it as a further and alarming symptom of Crew's deterioration. As he watched, Crew went into an exaggerated kind of prance, like a trained horse. Flags's customary spot on the quarterdeck seemed uncomfortably close to Crew's range of operations, so Flags went all the way aft and sat down where he could keep an eye on things from the vantage of the place where Steward usually sat. Although Pilot and Bosun showed no sign that they noticed Crew's bizarre behavior, Flags knew they were aware of it; he thought it possible they might all have to restrain him in the event he became violent. After another few leaps followed by a rotation or two and some arm flapping, Crew desisted and came aft. Flags watched him warily.

"G'morning," Crew said to him pleasantly, seating himself in his accustomed place and gazing down into the water.

Steward emerged soon after the first prickle of the day's heat made itself felt. It being past time for the morning meal, Steward went to the galley and breakfasted in solitude on ship's bread washed down with rum. He then took the biscuit bag and hard cheese back to the binnacle box and left it there for anybody who wanted any. He found Flags occupying his spot.

"You're in my place, Flags," he said.

"Oh?" said Flags, not moving. "Is your name written on it?" It was true there had been no agreed division of the deck area under the awning, or of anything else on *Alembic*.

"Trifle with the others as you will," growled Steward, "but never, never make that mistake with me. You have not known me cross, and you would not like it." Steward loomed over the trespasser. Flags remained motionless long enough to raise questions as to the outcome before he at last got up and went to the biscuit bag, then to his customary place. The exchange was followed by a silence in which menace still marinated. Nor did it lessen. With no movement of air to waft it away, the malaise hung like a poisoned mist, causing Crew to rise and flail his arms, as though dispersing invisible smoke. He walked back and forth doing this, watched by all, before seating himself again. Nobody made comment, and the silence deepened.

"Well, what would everybody like to do today?" asked Flags. After a lengthy search, he had found some kernel of amusement in their situation. "Perhaps we could all have a group sing."

"Forbear starting your provocations again," said Bosun.

"Oh, ye gods," said Flags. "Has everybody lost every stitch of cheer? In the immortal words of our ancient and esteemed old colleague, the mariner: 'The many men, so beautiful, and they all dead did lie, and a thousand slimy things lived on, and so did I–'"

Bosun was on his feet in an instant, standing before Flags. "No more, d'ye hear?"

"Another warning? We seem to be having a warning morning," said Flags, rising to his feet to meet his threat squarely.

"We seem to be," said Steward, feeling the rum on his empty stomach. "And I have another for you. If you fight, I'll put you both over the side to cool you off."

Pilot let go of his solitude in the way a mountaineer feels his fingers slipping from a handhold on a cliff face. "Absurd," he said. "You're all quite absurd. If we are dying out here, and so it seems, have the grace to suffer in–"

"*Silence!*" Pilot was interrupted by a voice nobody there had ever heard before–awesome in its volume and sheer authority, transfixing them with its message.

"*We must be together!*" Again, the bell-like tones rang out. To Crew's amazement, the voice was coming from himself. There they all were, all looking at him with openmouthed astonishment, waiting for the voice to speak again. He, too, waited, but it said nothing further. How absolutely extraordinary, thought Crew. Where did it come from?

*Nowhere,* the answer came to him, and abruptly, *he laughed.*

Having been impervious for his whole life to the smaller jokes, Crew had perceived at that moment the larger one; his sides constricted, tears rolled from his eyes, and he was stricken by a convulsion of laughter that made him sit down. It was just more funny than . . . than . . . why, the very outrageousness of it . . . , and yet there it was, and it had to be accepted, with all of its implications . . . , and even its acceptance was accepted, and all without anybody to perform the acceptance! A new wave of laughter so wrenched him that he rolled on the deck, drumming his heels, wracked by it.

The others looked at one another in amazement to see if any one of them had an answer for the extraordinary event. Then a slow rumble began somewhere within Steward, infected by Crew's laugh; then laughter caught them all, starting a new surge in Crew, whose sides hurt unbearably from it; he wanted to stop but couldn't, which, in turn, regenerated the others, until all were roaring. They did not know the joke, but it was a good one.

Seeing them all laughing, Crew's relief mixed with his laughter, changing it to–wonder upon wonders–*crying,* and he found it was somehow exactly the same as laughing, which became another facet of the joke, so the crying changed back to laughing again. At last, they all lay gasping and weak, still experiencing seismic aftershocks of laughter.

Abruptly, Crew sat up. "Look," he said, pointing, putting his hands into the air. "D'you feel it?" A breeze had sprung up, caressing them, starting to fill the sails. Crew reached to slip the lashing from the tiller and felt the boat's rudder begin to bite.

"Sheets and braces!" said Bosun, leaping up to trim to the new breeze. Again, they heard the rigging's song and the bubbling of the wake, and another sound came to their ears, tiny but unusual: the twitching of one of the long-slack fishing lines now with something on it, something that turned out to be a fine, fat fish. Steward immediately took it to the galley. With the wind scoops again effective and a line of cool rain clouds moving across the sun, he lit the galley fire in preparation for a feast of fresh food.

Pilot went below to fetch the half-hour glass, which would have to be turned twice as often as their broken hourglass but would do. He would reestablish ship's time with a noon sight. He noted from the watch schedule that it was Flags's helm and set himself to the reestablishment of the routine.

"Flags, I believe our course is south," he said, still chuckling.

"South, aye. I think Crew laughed us up a wind."

Crew thought it a good moment to clean up the mess he had made on Bosun's workbench, but when he arrived in the forepeak, he found that Bosun had beat him to the job, so he went back up on deck and stood enjoying the morning, with its pattering of raindrops into the tarpaulin rigged to catch them, and the ship's good motion, and much else.

Later, as they sipped fresh water and devoured fillets fried deliciously with a batter of bread crumbs, Pilot turned to Crew with a question: "Crew, what started you laughing this morning?"

"Nothing," said Crew, munching. "Absolutely nothing."

# VIII   At the Southern Continent

"LAND HO!" The cry was expected: all had smelled the land since the previous day, and the ship was in soundings. The dark blue of the deep ocean had given way to a sea made emerald by the sun's reflection on the golden sands of the bottom. Everywhere was life. On the surface floated patches of weed that were home to soft-shell crabs, and *Alembic*'s company had had all the fresh fish they could eat since the day they had gotten wind. Flocks of seabirds rode the waves, and brightly colored land birds flashed overhead.

Steward particularly was amused by the fishing techniques of the yellow-orange pelicans, who fell from the sky like stones on their prey, crashing into the water with an impact so dramatic as to appear more damaging to the pelican than to its target. But when the splash subsided, the bird would be seen floating unharmed, swallowing the fish it had scooped up. Some birds caught more than they could eat, storing the surplus in the pouches under their beaks. The pouch could hold a weight of food that–added to that already in the pelican's stomach–prevented it from taking off. At the time Bosun's cry of "Land!" was heard from the masthead, *Alembic* was passing through a drifting flock of these birds. The sudden cheer rising from the ship startled them, and there was a great flapping as they took to the air, leaving a few of the most gluttonous beating the water with helpless wings.

Soon thereafter, some outrigger fishing canoes were sighted, hailed, and questioned in sign language as to the direction of the nearest port. The sienna-skinned fishermen pointed off to starboard, where the coast trended southwest. The sails were trimmed accordingly, and by evening, the ship was sliding along the land closely enough to permit its crew a clear view of a shoreline dense with tropical trees. Beyond stretched forests and hills. Here and there could be seen the smoke from villages, and during the night watch, an offshore breeze carried with it the unmistakable smell of cooking.

"I'll swear that's pork roasting," said Steward, sniffing. "By all the gods, I'm ready for a meal that comes not from the sea."

Morning found them rounding a point of land that turned out to be the northern arm of a vast bay ringed by civilization. Flying full sail and all colors, *Alembic* stood up the bay, slowly approaching the outer edges of a great, sprawling city, aglow in the noonday sun. It was many times larger than their own home Port, and far different, with vast outlying regions of grass-roofed, ramshackle structures. In some places, these extended out into the shallows on stilts, where the waters around were covered by an epidermal layer of offal and filth. The central bay was somewhat cleaner, scoured by the flow of a river emerging through canals and channels, staining the water with brown soil for many miles to seaward. An inner bay was protected on either hand by two low forts. When *Alembic* approached to within a mile of the nearest of these, a puff of smoke was seen from its ramparts, followed a few seconds later by the boom of a cannon.

"That's a signal gun, likely having to do with us," said Pilot.

"Aye," agreed Bosun, "but who knows what it portends?"

"I think we're about to find out," said Steward. Sliding out from behind the fort was the low, dark red profile of a war galley, its banks of oars looking like wings as they caught the reflection of the sun. From its bows protruded the grotesquely styled muzzles of several large bronze cannons. Soldiers with muskets, pikes, and crossbows were mustered on the high castles fore and aft. As the galley bore down upon them, *Alembic* courteously hove-to, dipping her colors and firing a saluting shot to leeward. The big warship made a wide circle around them before drawing up on their quarter. A plumed officer hailed through a speaking trumpet. Failing the attempted communication, he then gestured his intention to take *Alembic* under tow. There was no choice but to accept the cable, whereupon the galley's oars churned the water. As they passed the fort, another gun boomed, and up went a string of unfamiliar signal flags.

"They're too much interested in us," said Bosun. "We've been arrested."

"Or perhaps just shown a courtesy," said Steward. Absorbed in the scenery and the unfolding events, Steward felt curiously unapprehensive. They passed through a broad anchorage area sheltering hundreds of various-sized lateen-rigged craft. Among them were market boats, some with huge deck loads of vegetables and fruits, plying the waters of the city's central harbor. Laced with canals spanned by dozens of arched, ornamental bridges, the city center was dominated by magnificent, colonnaded buildings of ochre stone capped by orange tile roofs. Here and there rose golden domes.

Their destination turned out to be an inner quay, where a squad of pikemen were forming up, holding their long spears horizontally to make a fence against a gathering crowd of gawkers. The entry of the foreign vessel had been well observed.

"This much attention makes me uneasy," said Bosun, drumming the rail with nervous fingers.

"Be easy," said Steward.

The galley's oars slowed, and the tow was cast off. Pilot steered *Alembic* alongside the quay. Dock lines were passed, made fast, and Bosun and the others began putting out the fend-offs. Ordinarily, Steward would have assisted with that final chore, but overwhelmed by the proximity of the land, he stepped over the bulwark and onto the cobbled quay, where he knelt, bent low, and kissed the ground beneath him.

"Land," he said.

A moment later, he was confronted by two elaborately robed men, obviously officials, who seemed to take a particular interest in him. When Flags approached in his role of ship's ambassador, the officials ignored him and continued their efforts to communicate exclusively with Steward. They seemed preoccupied by something having to do with his clothing.

"They're interested in what you're wearing," said Flags. "What does it mean?" For their encounter with the shore, all of *Alembic*'s company had scrubbed themselves as best they could under the washdeck pump before donning their most presentable clothing. Steward had chosen the purple tunic he had last worn at their ceremonial departure. But for the fine weave of its fabric and its rare dye, however, there was little to distinguish it from similar garments seen among the onlookers. The people on the quay wore every manner of costume, from the breechcloths of beggars to the robes, doublets, and cloaks of better-heeled citizens. Here and there were turbans. Against such an eclectic array, the only remarkable thing about Steward's tunic appeared to be the interest and respect it commanded.

The puzzle was solved a few minutes later when the line of pikemen parted to admit a white-haired, plainly dressed, perky man who spoke briefly with the officials and then turned to the newcomers. Regarding them with friendly blue eyes, he addressed them in their own tongue. "Are you truly of the Port whose flag you fly?"

Assured they were, he hurriedly introduced himself as an expatriate countryman, previously first mate aboard one of the ships from the ill-fated exploratory squadron of the previous generation. His carrack's voyage had ended here, where he had dwelled ever since. As soon as *Alembic*'s flag had been identified, he had been summoned to translate.

"Call me Mate," he said. "We've much to talk of, but it'll have to wait. First off, they've told me to question you, sir," he said to Steward. "The most important thing to them is you're wearing the Royal purple, and it's worth your life to do that here unless you're of Royal blood. Right off, they want to know if you are." He seemed very apprehensive about it until Steward assured him as to his family's entitlement to Royalty's color. It was well documented in his many letters of introduction.

Mate looked tremendously relieved. "Oh, that's good, sir . . . I mean, Your Lordship. I'm o'course aware of your family, but these people will be wanting your papers. First, they must write down your full name and all your titles."

Steward had not for many years used his formal name—actually twenty-nine names—much less his titles, but with the benefit of pauses for Mate to translate and a penman to scratch it down, he was able to recollect most of his pedigree. When he had finished with the impressive recitation, the officials bowed and withdrew to examine *Alembic.* A moment later, a pair of lackeys appeared with a chair, respectfully placing it behind Steward.

"Beggin' your pardon, Your Lordship," said Mate, "but you should have a seat. There may be a bit of a wait now while they find a Royal of their own to receive you. It's not fitting for any Royal to be questioned by common officials. Y'see, you've taken 'em by surprise." He explained that state visits from foreign nobility were always arranged a long time in advance, and usually, there was some preset reason for such a visit. "Your reason for coming will be one of the first things they'll want to know when they've found somebody who ranks big enough to talk to you. What should I tell 'em, Your Lordship?"

"Sir will do," said Steward. "Tell 'em we're partners on a voyage of discovery and scientific exploration and trade—we hope." This brought immediate wrinkles to Mate's brow.

"Your pardon, sir, but being as new to this place as you are, you might want to think some about what words you use." According to Mate, it would be unwise here for a Royal personage to be in a partnership with anyone lesser. "Unless your mates are entitled, too, they'll be seen here as your servants, sir." He also felt it would be better to leave out the scientific thing because it would most likely be misunderstood, and he emphatically advised Steward against any suggestion of

*Alembic*'s having "discovered" the Southern Empire—a vast corporation of ancient kingdoms spreading over all the subcontinent and throughout a far-ranging maze of archipelagos. "They'll see it as *their* discovering *you,* sir, so best let 'em, if you see what I mean, sir." Last, he cautioned them about their reference to trade, which was something considered too common for aristocracy to pursue. "They do it, o'course, but never in person; always through somebody else." Any violation of these forms might see Steward's credentials impeached, in Mate's view, and such a thing would entail consequences too grave to bear thinking about.

"What can we tell them that they want to hear?" asked Flags, who had been listening closely.

"That my shipmates are now my servants, for starters," said Steward, vastly amused, "and I would say that's fair enough after all the meals I've cooked you and all your pots that I've scrubbed in cold seawater."

Mate went pale at his words. "If they ever hear ye say it, sir, they'll have ye discredited and dangling by your thumbs," he said. "You've been direct with me, and I'll return it. You're in shoal water here, sirs, and myself maybe, too, by association. If there's a fairway through it, believe me, it's to follow the channel they've cut for themselves and not bump up against their pride, and to praise their wine. I believe you're best off calling yourself a yachtsman, sir."

"But that is entirely what I am," said Steward. "We all are. We are gentlemen adventurers, challenging the elements to come and see this fantastic place. Will that serve?"

"It's the best tack to take," agreed Mate.

And so *Alembic* was named a yacht on the customs documents proffered by the waiting officials to Mate, who immediately busied himself with their many questions. Steward sat back to await events, since that seemed to be what was expected of him. He found the requirement to do nothing as agreeable as the surprise restoration of his aristocracy after many months of galley duty. He was mindful of Mate's cautions but unalarmed by them. He thought it really was turning into quite a marvelous day.

"Mate," he said, interrupting his conversation with the officials, "ask those fellows to send for some fruit for us–and a jug of fresh water," he added.

"Wouldn't wine be more aristocratic, sire?" suggested Flags.

"Tell 'em to send for both," said Steward.

T HE PROCESS OF alerting the Imperial Family to the unexpected arrival by yacht of a prince from a foreign land made an unusual diversion for an ascending hierarchy of personages, none of whom wanted the responsibility of a Royal stranger. The laws of hospitality to nobility were immutable: Royalty was honored as Royalty, whatever its language. Yet if an Imperial guest were discredited for whatever political, personal, or other reasons, his fortunes could abruptly turn, perhaps along with those of his sponsor. There was no protocol to cover the current situation; meanwhile, a presumed Royal visitor was being kept waiting. In a remarkably short time, the matter was brought to the attention of the Seventh Duke, the short title for the individual who was seventh in the line of succession to the Imperial throne. He was located in the gardens of the Little Palace, where he was playing an increasingly tedious game of bowls with an Earl, a Viscount, two Barons and Baronesses, a Marquis, a Marquise, a Marchioness, two adolescent nieces, and the Count Montressor. The arrival of the message brought a welcome interruption.

"Darlings," said the Seventh Duke, "duty calls me, and it is an adventure! A strange vessel has just been arrested and brought into harbor. It has made an extraordinary voyage of some kind, it seems, but the interesting part is its owner, who is a Prince from quite far away, or so says he. In any case, it's my lot to receive him. We could send for him, but let us go and see him on his yacht. We can make an expedition of it. If he's who he says he is, perhaps we'll have some diversion."

"And if he's not?" asked the Earl.

"Ah, that would be even more diverting," said the Duke, activating a general flurry as three carriages with drivers, footmen, and other attendants were hastily assembled, along with the Royal Party itself, augmented for the occasion by the elderly Dowager Duchess, incognito, attended by a Lady in Waiting with two pet dogs. Within a few minutes, all were on their way to the waterfront, with horsemen riding ahead to clear their road.

Steward witnessed the arrival of the Imperial Party as he was finishing a small melon, his third, accompanied by a most agreeable light white wine. As he pondered whether or not to request a fourth melon, he heard shouts, hooves, and the crowd parted before the Royal carriages. They rumbled to a halt; liveried retainers scurried, and the Royal Party began to debark, chattering like magpies. They seemed to Steward like an extravagantly costumed theater troupe mimicking the affectations of all the mannered aristocrats he had ever known. He could almost hear his father's voice in his ear saying, "There you have a piffle of peacocks, my boy." The thought made his grin widen. As he rose to meet them, he had the dreamlike impression of having known them always, and too well to fear anything about them. His comrades gathered behind him, and Mate moved to his side, again looking apprehensive.

"That's the Seventh Duke, the one they call the Spider Prince," said Mate, indicating a barrel-chested but spindly limbed man whose fingers fluttered like antennae.

"He does resemble a spider," Steward remarked.

"Aye, sir, and in more ways than looks, so they say. By reputation, he's a bad one. Please be careful, sir, on your life. Here he comes." But Steward could not repress his grin, and that was what greeted the Duke's eye as he approached, followed by his entourage and a herald who announced the introductions, reading Steward's from the parchment he had been handed.

"Welcome to our humble yacht," said Steward, making a bow. This was returned by the Duke, as was the smile, after a fashion.

"We are so very pleased to welcome you," he said, and when those words had been translated: "I trust you have had a pleasant voyage?"

"Very pleasant, Your Grace, but for one or two trifling inconveniences."

"I'm sure you are being very modest. I am informed your own kingdom is distant. We have had no prior communication, saving for one ship from your land that entered Imperial waters without permission."

"That is precisely what we have come to rectify," said Steward, "for the greatness of this domain has spread in legend to the ends of the farthest seas. It seemed a worthy challenge to cross them in order to make a link with you. I regret there was no way of informing you in advance of our arrival, and it is most courteous of you to receive us so generously on short notice."

"The generosity would seem to be yours, for affording us the opportunity to receive you, ah . . . appropriately. Who are these others with you?"

"Let me present my company," said Steward. "These gentlemen are the Knights of my court, with the rank of Mariner Companions Nonequerry. They are: Sir Bosun, Sir Pilot, Sir Flags, and Sir Crew." Each, in turn, made an uneasy bow. "They are noble companions and adventurers errant, and all are under my personal recognizance." The Duke nodded in response to their bows.

As all of this was going on, the gentlemen of his retinue moved to observe the strange yacht, leaving the ladies to view more closely its company of tanned, athletic young foreign yachtsmen, led by the tall Prince.

"He's like a tree," said the first Baroness behind her fan.

"More cheerful, though, and better looking," said the second Baroness.

"He looks too good to be true," said one of the nieces.

"He's true enough," said the wizened Dowager. "He has the bearing. But my young dears, do not neglect his squires, most particularly the one in red."

"Ah yes," said the Marchioness, who had spotted Flags right away. "He's my choice. If it comes to his being sold, I'll be the first to bid on that one."

"Don't count on it," said the Dowager, and her caution was borne out. A few minutes later, the Duke concluded his interview with the foreign Prince, bowed his good-byes, gave some instructions to the translator and the officials, and then swept his party back toward their carriages. "Darlings," he said, "he's a Seventh. He's a Seventh, and I'm a Seventh. Don't you think it a frightfully auspicious coincidence?"

"I suspect we'll be seeing more of him," said the Dowager, aside, as the carriages bore them away.

The departure of the Royal Party left *Alembic*'s company free for the first time to converse with their translator at the privacy of the galley table. Their countryman had much to tell them, beginning with his considerable relief at how well all had gone so far. He told them a barge had been summoned to tow *Alembic* to the Royal yacht basin, a well-sheltered and guarded haven where she would be secure, and where a coach would be sent to collect their whole company for supper with the Duke.

"Excellent," said Steward .

"Excellent you may well say, sir," said Mate, "compared to how it went for most of my mates when *our* ship was brought in." He proceeded to relate how his storm-damaged carrack had been towed to the same quay to be immediately impounded for the violation of various laws, beginning with entering Imperial waters without the required permission. That they were strangers made no difference, nor did their desperate condition. After a short proceeding conducted in a language nobody in their company could either speak or understand, they had been forced to watch their captain's public decapitation on the quay. "They done it to him right about where you were sitting today, sir," he told Steward, "right after they towed you in the same way they towed us."

Following the execution, the crew had been taken away in irons and sold into slavery. Mate and the other subordinate officers had avoided that fate only because of their rank and the need for their help in repairing the ship for its new owners. Thereafter, they had been permitted to make their new lives as best they could. With no way to return home, Mate had eventually married, become a coastal pilot, and raised a family. His children were now grown, and he was a widower. His continuing services as translator for Steward had been commandeered by the Duke, although he told them he was happy to be able to be of help in any case.

"Your help's more than valuable, and we'll see you're well paid for it," said Steward.

"You're very generous, sir, but as far as they're concerned, I'm *their* man. Right off, they've ordered me to collect all your ship's documents to deliver them up for examination."

"Let 'em examine away," Steward shrugged. "Our certificates are in good order. How could anything be disproved in any case?"

"Sir, they'll do as they please. It's a fact you're off to a lot better start than I'd dared to hope for, but I wouldn't drop your guard for a second sir, beggin' your pardon, and I wouldn't figure on sailing off again right soon."

"We've just arrived," said Steward.

"It's true there's much to be done while we're here," Bosun said, "and it will take time enough, no doubt, but I dislike the notion we're under arrest."

"Bosun," said Steward, "your stomach's grumbling because it wants a good supper, and I daresay we'll get one where we're going." He tried to imagine the table that awaited their first run ashore.

No imagining could have anticipated the events of that evening or what was to follow. Later, Steward remembered little more than a whirl of impressions. At the sequestered yacht basin, *Alembic* was secured, and her company was led away by servants to be bathed, barbered, and redressed in marked contrast to their previous toilette under the washdeck pump. Memorable was the look on Pilot's face as he was briskly toweled by female slaves and, too, Crew's expression as he was dressed in a new tunic of watered silk.

"What if I spill something?" he asked, fingering its fabric in awe.

"Don't worry about it," said Steward, selecting for himself a robe of purple edged in gold. Next, there was a coach whisking them off to a palace with a fountain outside and a sea of guests within, jeweled and coiffed, their faces all looking up at him as he stood through yet another reading of his name and titles. Again, Steward could not help smiling at the easy familiarity he felt with these gentry, and everywhere he saw his smile returned. His easy acceptance did not surprise him. He had never doubted it.

During supper, Steward was placed to the right of the Seventh Duke at the head of a low, U-shaped table nearly as big as the room; around its perimeter, guests reclined on cushions. Next to Steward was Mate, who was kept busy translating the usual social chatter, along with questions that posed little challenge. Yes, he had learned to sail as a boy. Yes, he had found his adventurous voyage rewarding thus far, particularly at this moment. During the translations, he had long moments in which to savor the courses and accompanying wines. Later, when Steward felt himself becoming logy with everything he had consumed and was wondering how he could politely gather his friends and retire, he learned that his host wished for them all to remain at the Palace as guests. It was unthinkable that any of their party should be forced to endure the cramped quarters of a small boat when they were under Imperial hospitality.

He awoke the following morning to the music of the fountains beneath the balcony and the presence of silent slaves attending him. Choosing fresh garments from a selection, Steward felt quite ready for whatever was on the menu this glorious new day ashore. He was therefore surprised to find his companions looking a bit peaked and Bosun fussing about getting back to the boat–a notion that was at once discouraged by Mate, pointing out that departure would be an unthinkable breach of hospitality.

So it was luncheon *al fresco* with the Seventh Duke and the Baroness of whatever and the Count of this and the Earl of that–and lobsters in a memorable hot-sweet sauce followed by a coach tour of the capital's scenic areas, after which there were the orange-marble baths of the Third Duke during the heat of the day prior to a return by canal boat to the Palace for an evening banquet.

Again, Steward heard his father's voice in his ear: "Remember, it's always the same play, son." And it went on–for another day and then another, until the fourth evening brought the surprise of a real play, and in Steward's honor. The Duke had engaged professional librettists, musicians, thespians, prop-makers, costume designers, seamstresses, makeup artists, and others to work around the clock for three days preparing a half-hour presentation entitled "The Perilous Voyage of a Noble Prince and His Knights." As soloists and chorus sang to the music of harps, Steward watched himself and his shipmates fighting villainous pirates, pushing through painted wooden icebergs, then suffering their long ordeal by calm under a gilt papier-mâché sun hanging overhead. Although, to those who were being represented, the whole thing seemed beyond irony, they obviously were being portrayed as sportsmen of great daring and courage who were noble and modest for all of that, and elegant in their lack of affectation. At the finale, the Prince stepped ashore and kissed the ground of the Empire of the Sun as he was welcomed by the Seventh Duke and a septet of trumpeters blowing the closing fanfare.

The play was received with great applause by not only the Seventh Duke but the Eighth, Sixth, Third, and even the First Duke as well. Delighted, Steward applauded harder than anyone as the actors repeatedly bowed, the candle footlights making the undersurfaces of their faces glow. Steward was called on to take a bow as well, which he did, laughing, summoning his Knights to do the same. Crew tripped over a footlight but was saved from falling by Bosun, and Flags's bow drew a great wave of applause, causing the lead trumpeter to play another flourish.

AFTER HIS GUESTS had departed, the Seventh Duke made a point of encountering the Dowager Duchess. "Aren't they marvelous?" he asked her.

"You mean the actors?" she asked with a small smile. "Yes, they were very clever, I thought."

"I mean our new guests, Grandmamma, as you well know."

"Yes. Perhaps it's the same."

"If this Prince has an act, it has passed me by," said the Duke.

"If he has an act, it has passed him by as well," said the old woman. "Perhaps it's the source of his power. We shall see."

"Everybody thinks he's marvelous."

"Yes, and that could perhaps be useful in some way, but I would caution you not to let your eldest brother get hold of him if you can help it. He'll want your guest's celebrity for himself. As you well know, he's resourceful."

"That would be the end of our Prince," sighed the Seventh Duke.

"Yes," agreed the Dowager Duchess. "In one way or another, it would indeed."

"How shall I protect him, Granny? As you know, I've no choice but to leave for Elysium in three days' time."

"There's your answer," said the Dowager. "Take him along with you. See that he's kept incommunicado until your departure. That shouldn't be too hard, considering the language problem. And separate him from his friends."

ON THE FOLLOWING morning, a message was delivered to *Alembic*'s company in their chambers. It arrived while they were making their selections from among the garments offered for their fifth day ashore.

"Our day's itinerary?" asked Flags as Mate broke the seal. Flags was trying on a red burnoose, striking a pose before a full-length mirror. "How do you think this looks on me?" he asked nobody in particular.

"Bloody odd," said Bosun. Bosun was as glad as any of them for their good reception, but he had begun to pine for his plain, honest sailcloth tunic again, and to be back aboard *Alembic* tending to the chores. "I don't know how much more of this I can stand. I feel incarcerated."

"If this is incarceration, who wants to rush out of it?" asked Steward. "I'm ready for more."

"You're both in luck," said Mate, looking up from the message he had been reading. "According to this, you, sir, are invited to accompany our host to Elysium, his principality. That's a long way from here, sir, but to decline would be offering offense. I'm afraid we're going to be gone for a while. I'm to come with you. As for the rest of you, sirs, you now have your own place. There's a small villa ready for you on the grounds at the yacht basin, and a coach is waiting to take you there whenever you're ready to go."

"I'll visit with you there tomorrow," said Steward.

But not until the evening before the departure for Elysium was Steward able to extricate himself from social events in order to meet with his comrades in their new quarters. These were only a few minutes' ride from the Palace, but he had found some difficulty in arranging for the visit. He finally declared to his host that he could not think of going off anywhere without making his good-byes to his shipmates. Only then did the Duke relinquish his guest. Steward was assigned a detachment of lancers as escort, so his arrival was heralded by clattering hooves and snapping pennants that brought some amusement to his friends, who were relieved to see him.

"I've had the devil of a time getting away," he told them, looking around. The villa was a wide, thick-walled structure, one of several set among shade-trees on grounds overlooking the yacht basin. There, *Alembic* floated happily among a cluster of ceremonial barges. The entire park was severed from the city's traffic by a well-guarded curtain wall. "I understood this was to be a *small* villa," said Steward.

"By their standards, it *is* small," said Pilot. "Come in and have a look." Steward's tour of the rooms led finally into a cloistered central patio, where they seated themselves round a table. At first, they exchanged only amenities while the ubiquitous slaves brought them wines and fruits.

"We're careful," said Bosun when they were quite alone, "because we know from Mate there are at least a few of Mate's old crew in this city who know our tongue. In fact, one of 'em is working for us after-noons, teaching us enough of their language to get by. Mate put us onto him. Where is Mate, by the way?"

"Packing my wardrobe. Our patron, the Seventh Duke, made him my servant without consulting either one of us about it. Accepting that any rejection would mean giving offense, I think Mate's looking forward to our journey as much as I am. He said to tell you if you're mindful of all the things he's warned us about, he might have a fair chance of seeing you when we get back in three or four months," Stew-ard sighed. "I suppose it's good enough advice, though I must say I find his views sometimes unduly dark."

"Caution's important," insisted Bosun.

"I think so, too," said Pilot. All were uneasy about Steward's im-pending separation.

"Yes," he agreed, cutting a slice of guava fruit. "Caution's good, but it's also good to be at ease. It takes a balance between them," he added, munching. "Are you indeed being as well cared for as it appears?"

"Yes, as you see," said Pilot. "It's all a bit overdone, perhaps, but your Knights count themselves fortunate to be under your wing."

Steward laughed. "We're partners forever. We all come in useful to each other in our own ways, by accident or design. In this case, my help's as accidental as my own birth. I'm glad you're all comfortable. How's our ship?"

*Alembic*'s most pressing need was to be careened–laid over on her beam-ends on first one side and then the other in order for her bottom to be cleaned, greaved, and retallowed with a toxic lime against worms and weed. This was to begin within a day or two, by slaves working under Bosun's supervision. But many other tasks and scores of things were required to make *Alembic* ready for sea again. Not only were their victuals expended but also their reserves of sailcloth, marline, lamp oil, and countless other small but indispensable items that would have to be located and obtained one by one. Bosun would organize all that. Pilot's priority was somehow to find and copy any available charts and sailing directions to the unknown ocean they had gotten themselves into. Flags would cultivate the best possible relationship with the officials who had their documents in an effort to retrieve them, and he would also promote their interests wherever opportunity afforded. He had already begun to deal with an accumulating pile of competing social invitations from persons whom he did not know but whom he knew were not to be offended. He also wanted to find someone able to repair his cracked lute.

"That's all well enough," said Bosun, "but besides refitting our boat, repairing our lute, going to parties, and adding to our girth, what do we aim to accomplish here? If well-being depends on our role, but that role is too exalted to permit our entering into trade, what profit is here to justify our investment in this voyage?"

Steward shrugged. "Something," he said, "but we haven't been here long enough to find out."

"Where and how do we seek it?"

"You can't," said Steward. "Or rather, you can, but it doesn't work; you usually find trouble. The trick's in waiting for what you want to come to you and noticing when it does."

Bosun was dubious and said so.

"All right, now, lookee here," said Steward, putting down what he was eating to give emphasis to his words. "This is the wealthiest place any of us have ever seen. Maybe it's the wealthiest place anywhere in the world, and the people who are our hosts are obviously among the wealthiest people in it. Within my direct experience, such rich soil will yield richly of its own accord if it's not disturbed. Just wait for the fruition."

"From my own experience," Flags agreed, "Steward's right."

"I'm not sure I trust that," said Bosun, "and it's for sure I don't trust any of this whole overdressed, overfed crowd, when you get right down to it."

"As to trust," Steward replied, "you should put it away. It's just no good; that's something these people know better than you, my friend. They have something to teach you."

Bosun paled. "Do you not trust *me,* then? Are you saying I cannot trust *you*?"

"I trust Bosun to be Bosun. You may trust Steward to be Steward, but why burden a friend with any other trust, unless you expect him to behave the way *you* think he should behave rather than as who he is? Where's friendship in that? As to our hosts here, I know them better than I can tell you. Believe me, they're not so much different from the gentry I've had to deal with all my life, just more overblown. In fact, I know them well enough to trust them completely as a group, to be overweening, arrogant, greedy, cruel, prideful, and potentially dangerous if they were not total slaves to their own forms and customs. As long as you understand all of that, without judgment, and avoid the taboos, you can float over their little foibles as though in a boat and everybody will say you're the perfect guests. There's a knack to it, I daresay. I've had the benefit of my father's observations as well as my own experiences. Try to see it as theater, and don't forget to applaud." He grinned. "You can trust me about that."

**B**EYOND THE WEALTH and squalor of the capital, the Imperial Highway to the south was a ribbon of stone winding through the fertile bottomlands of a great delta cultivated by legions of slaves whose black, near-naked bodies glistened with sweat and whose ribs stood out sharply. "Here's the richest farmland I've ever seen, and those poor wretches are underfed," Steward commented to Mate. The traveling coach in which they rode was passing close to a particularly emaciated group toiling under the watchful eyes of armed overseers with leashed dogs. "Those fellows and their dogs aren't suffering from undernourishment, however," he added.

"Aye, sir," said Mate, "but, beggin' your pardon, sir, I'll not translate that remark."

"I had not meant it for any ears but your own," said Steward. In their situation, the aristocrat and the translator had found an easy comradeship. They were seated together in the Seventh Duke's traveling coach, watching the landscape go past at the walking speed maintained by their caravan.

"What does he say?" asked their host. The Seventh Duke was lounging among cushions on the commodious seat facing them, receiving a foot massage from a fair young slave girl. Again and again, Steward had to tear his eyes from her.

"His Grace," Mate told the Duke, "comments with approval on the great fertility of the land, Your Grace."

"Yes," replied the Duke, "and it's worth an annual fortune to my First Brother. It's in his principality. Along with so much else. You had better warn my new friend that Elysium's not only at the ends of the earth from the capital, but it's also the smallest, poorest principality in the Empire. But then, he'll understand what it's like, being a Seventh. There's not a lot left over for us Sevenths, eh? Translate." Mate did so. Steward expressed his empathy.

"It's so good to have somebody to talk to who hasn't seen anything here before," said the Duke, shifting position slightly as the slave commenced on his other foot. Steward couldn't help noticing the movements of her body beneath her tunic. "There really is quite a lot to see along the way," the Duke continued, "though it's a bit of a bore after you've made the trip as many times as I have–most of us have." He made a vague gesture toward the score of other traveling coaches rolling along behind them. These were filled with provincial aristocrats from the various duchies, earldoms, baronies, and protectorates through which the convoy passed on its long land voyage. Behind the coaches snaked an even longer line of baggage and cook wagons. A company of dragoons led the caravan; another brought up the rear; and a cohort of harquebusiers marched in the center of the column. The Elysium caravan–only one of the many others like it serving all the lands of the Empire–was a quarterly event providing safe convoy for gentry traveling to and from the capital.

"It's been truly spoken," said the Duke, "that all roads lead to the capital, but," he sighed, "they unfortunately also lead away from it." The Duke made no secret of his preference for the city life or his annoyance at having to leave it periodically. "Elysium's taxes are collected while I'm not there, and the revenues come in from the mines, but by a miracle, so much of it vanishes. Everybody I've left in charge becomes greedy, or they get lazy, they scheme for power, and sometimes they betray. So I go back, I root out the worst of them, I make an example of those by having the most astonishingly painful things done to them with as many people watching as possible, and then I can return to civilization for a few blessed months before having to do the whole thing all over again. In a perfect world, I wouldn't have to go to Elysium at all. . . . You can have her if you want her." The last remark had been prompted by Steward's rapt gaze on the young masseuse. "Her name's Zubaida, and she really can do the most remarkable things to you," he added. "Her mother's a perfect harridan. I don't know how she produced her. Anyway, I'll have the girl sent to you when we stop for the night."

"I've been long at sea, it's true," smiled Steward. If Zubaida had any reaction to having heard herself discussed like a morsel of food, Steward saw no sign of it. "My distraction did not prevent my hearing all that you were telling me, and it would give me great pleasure to hear more of Elysium if you do not find the subject too tiring." The Duke did not find it at all tiring, and as the convoy threaded its way through the steamy landscape, he advanced Steward's education. At some point, the massage ended and Zubaida vanished.

"Now that there's room for a guest, who might a sailor like to meet?" asked the Duke with a conspiratorial look. "Perhaps the Contessa of Marmalad. She's been a perfect pest about meeting you, and she might take your fancy." The column's sedate pace allowed an easy coming and going of passengers between coaches. The Duke held up a jeweled finger, just high enough so that the gesture could be seen by his constant shadow, the Count of Montressor, riding just behind the Royal coach. Between themselves, Steward and Mate called him Whisper because that was how he usually communicated with his master, the Duke. Seeing the signal, the Count spurred forward. "Ask the Contessa if she would care to join us," said the Duke, "and see if some refreshment can be found."

The objects of both requests soon appeared–crayfish boiled in herbs, served with drawn butter, and a stylish woman who took great interest in Steward, asking him all over again the questions he had been asked a hundred times since his arrival. He reflected that she might be considered comely, but her painted face seemed grotesque by comparison with the natural beauty of the slave girl. After a while, the Duke put an end to the Contessa's futile chatter by suggesting a diversion, a bit of falconry, so the rest of the afternoon was given to the predations of a peregrine and two kestrels, until it was time to halt and set up the tent city for the night.

After supper, Steward retired to his tent with Mate for their customary private reprise of the day's happenings. Before they had concluded, the tent flap parted and Zubaida entered, bowing to Steward and standing before him with eyes cast down. Steward was again dazzled by her.

"I'll be leaving then, sir," said Mate.

"Hold fast. Ask her why she's here."

"Sir, beggin' your pardon, she's . . . uh . . . "

"Yes. Ask her anyway."

"Sir," said Mate when the question had been put and answered, "she says she's here because she was sent, o'course. A gift for the evening, like."

"Well," said Steward, "tell her she's the most tempting gift I can imagine, but I'm troubled that she's not the giver of it. At least, not of her own accord. Tell her she's excused from this assignment."

As Mate translated, she looked up with apparent consternation. "She says if you send her away, it'll look bad for her, sir. Also, sir, if you don't mind my saying it, your not accepting could give offense. She begs you to at least let her stay and give you a good rub, sir."

"A good rub. Very well, since it's her own request."

"Now I'll be on my way, sir."

THE ROAD LED at last out of the bottomlands and into hills carpeted with thick, blue-green grass, where countless cattle grazed. Skilled horsemen tended the great herds and protected them from predators. An overnight stop was made at a nobleman's plantation, where, after the usual sumptuous meal, Steward stood on a moonlit portico and listened to the singing of hundreds of slaves.

"They work better if you let 'em sing," said their local host.

"They'll work better yet if you feed them," said Steward, a remark that went untranslated.

The plains rose to a height of land beyond which were mountains with a pass high enough to cool the air. At its top, the pass was guarded by a gaunt castle decorated on its outside with horns, tusks, hooves, racks of antlers, beaks, and jawbones. Inside, a Lord showed Steward his collection of heads, all cleverly treated to appear alive. The collection covered every surface of wall and included, according to their host, a specimen of every kind of known beast in the Empire–as well as the heads of slaves who had been let run and then hunted down.

From the high pass, the road descended steeply into a vast, dense forest, threading a humid tunnel hewn through the vines and trees. Thousands of monkeys moved overhead, making a chattering racket, and Steward observed all manner of colorful birds, insects, and huge butterflies. Several times, reptiles were knocked from low limbs by the coach's passage. They fell onto the roof to be immediately brushed away by a slave whose dangerous job it was to keep the coaches free of snakes through that area. Where the sunlight penetrated the dank tangle of vegetation above them, long shafts of light slanted down through the twilight forest, dappling its rotting floor with brilliant bursts, illuminating heavy-scented, colorful flowers. Steward remarked he had never seen anything like it.

"Be grateful there's not much more of it to see before we come to the river," said the Duke, sucking on a lychee nut. Steward had learned that the next leg of their journey was to be by boat. "Being a sailor, you should find it pleasurable to be on water again. By the way, did you not find our Zubaida pleasing? You've not asked for her again."

"I would not presume upon your hospitality," said Steward.

"No presumption at all," the Duke assured him with a wave. "I'll see that she returns to you."

The journey by carriage ended at the bank of a wide river upon which the Royal Party embarked in large, flat-bottomed dhows. In the after part of these vessels, the passengers were protected from the sun by awnings; the decks were carpeted, and cushions were arranged for lounging. The ships set large, light, lateen sails, but they were also rowed from their forward halves, where the rowers were regularly hosed down to diminish their odor. The great river flowed sluggish and brown between walls of drooping greenery and mudbanks where hippopotamuses basked. The whole place, all the land, seemed to Steward to exude a fecundity beyond anything he had ever known, spawning infinite layers of life and death. One day, they watched a bird snatch a fish from the water an instant before a huge mouth full of teeth emerged and snatched the surprised bird. As it was dragged down, the bird was still swallowing the fish.

"Everything eats everything else," the Seventh Duke observed laconically. The following evening, a graphic example was provided when the flotilla anchored in a spur off the river's main channel, a breeding area for crocodiles, as Steward soon learned. While there was yet light, a skinny bullock was prodded into the water. The animal began to swim for the shore but was attacked by crocodiles converging on it from all directions. Within minutes, the whole area was a churn of twisting, gnashing reptiles, frenziedly snapping at any flesh within reach. The spectacle had a dual purpose, as an appetizer to the slave-run—in this case, a swim—scheduled for the following morning and also to draw as many crocodiles as possible to the already crowded area.

The run to be conducted here was an eagerly anticipated tradition of the journey, and there was much betting. Steward learned that slave-runs were common sporting events, although some were more spectacular than others. All involved the release of a slave into a perilous situation, which, if he made his way safely through it, became his road to freedom. In the present instance, the peril was the hundred yards of muddy water between the ducal dhow and the nearest mudflat.

While the last of the bets were being placed, a young male slave, hardly more than fifteen, was given the traditional payment for the ordeal he was to endure–a knife, a gold piece, and a document recording his freedom sealed in a bamboo tube hung around his neck. Trembling with fear but determined, the boy slid into the water and made for the shore. He forced himself to use an unhurried breast stroke in order to make as little disturbance to the water as possible and in this way swam most of the distance before his presence was detected by the crocodiles. Within only a few strokes of the nearest mudbank, however, the swimmer's head vanished in the same boil of water that had marked the end of the bullock.

"He's actually lucky it happened in the water," the Seventh Duke commented casually as he collected his winnings. "He probably drowned before experiencing too much of the sensation of being torn apart. That's what the crocs do. By twisting and turning. They can't chew, y'see, and they have to reduce him to pieces they can swallow whole. It takes a bit of time. It's still happening, actually, but you can't see much except the splashing. If he'd got ashore, they would have caught him there, and you would have watched something even more spectacular."

"It's the most barbarous entertainment I've ever seen," said Steward, struggling to keep a pleasant demeanor as he gazed with horror at the faces of those still watching.

"His Grace says it is most diverting entertainment, Your Grace," Mate told the Duke.

"Yes, it's all good sport," smiled their host, stacking the gold coins he had won. "Except, in this spot, you'll always win if you bet on the crocs, right, Montressor?"

"That is true, Your Grace," agreed Whisper. "It's a bullock and slave well spent." The Duke nodded. "It does make a bit of diversion in an otherwise tedious trip. Ah, here's breakfast."

For once, Steward did not dine. Many times since his arrival in this land, he had been reminded of a childhood incident that had remained always with him. While taking a meal one evening with his father, he had seen one of the manor's house cats catching a mouse. The cat immediately crippled the hapless rodent, preventing its escape, but allowing its struggles–actually encouraging them by toying with it. Steward had wanted to interfere on behalf of the victim, but his father had stopped him. "Leave them alone, lad. They are animals, and they do not live or die by your rules. Not having created them, how can you presume to interfere in their destinies?"

"It is cruel," Steward had said.

"It is nature. If it seems cruel to you, that is by your own definition. What would you do? Would you keep the damaged mouse in a box, thereby condemning it to an even slower death than it is now suffering? Or would you punish the cat? Would you be angry with the cat for being a cat? This is a good moment for you to stop trying to remake the world. Let it be. And please rearrange your face into something more pleasant to look at." A short while later, the cat had eaten the mouse noisily, directly under Steward's chair, with small smackings and a crunching of tiny bones. Steward had found the experience profoundly distasteful, but under his father's watchful eye, he had forced himself to listen with an impassive face as he pretended to continue his meal. He felt much the same now. "Some cats wear coronets," he said to himself.

A T THE END of the river passage was another city, where many coaches departed the convoy. Then came another forest, and finally, a last range of mountains–natural palisades that defended the Principality of Elysium from the lands to the north and east. An ancient emirate before its incorporation into the fringe of Empire, Elysium was a wide peninsula jutting into the Southern

Ocean, looking like a curled finger on the aquatint map produced by the Duke. When the reduced caravan reached the top of the pass, Steward viewed their destination from an elevation that revealed hills and forests, farmlands and rivers, villages and hamlets, all fading into purplish haze. His immediate impression was of a rich, accommodating land of great expanse.

"It is beautiful, seen from here," he said to his host.

"It's good one of us can enjoy it," said the Duke. "To me, the best part about it is that we can soon be out of this coach."

On the following morning, the Seventh Duke and his Royal guest, attended by Count Montressor and the translator, rode off ahead with an escort of dragoons, leaving the vehicles to catch up with them at the ducal Palace. Seen from the back of a cantering horse, Steward's world flew past, a world where black bison pulled plows and cattle grazed, where an increasing road traffic included camels, yaks, and other dray animals. Drovers moved to the side of the road to give the ducal party plenty of room. Again, Steward saw infinite separation between the upper and lower classes, with the inevitable slaves being somewhere below bottom. The impoverished free people seemed hardly better off than the slaves, aside from appearing less emaciated. They wore bright, cheap clothing. Their children played naked in the dirt of the road, but the natural fertility of the land permitted them existence. Weeds and parasite vines burgeoned from between the stones of foundations and walls. Everywhere Steward looked, he saw thick buildings crumbling under the assault of foliage and moisture. Even the ducal Palace showed bare stone where chunks of stucco had fallen from its surface, giving it a homey look to Steward's eye as their horses rode at last through its gates. The Palace was a low, sprawling series of structures interconnected by arched breezeways opening onto gardens. It was all whitewashed, or originally had been, and now needed a new coat. Squat, crenellated towers guarded the four corners of a central structure from the middle of which rose three gilded domes.

"It's beautiful," said Steward.

"You are as usual being generous," said the Duke. "As you see, it's a miserable country headquarters and little more. But we shall endeavor to see you're as comfortable as possible."

Steward saw little of the Duke during the first few days after their arrival. After a month with him in a coach, however, and the prospect of another month returning, his absence represented sweet freedom. Steward delighted in his quarters–light, airy chambers connected by arches, overlooking a shaded portico. There was a small adjoining apartment for Mate, who was even more relieved than Steward to be free of the Duke.

They were both well looked after by slaves, whose names Steward quickly learned. There was also the mistress and ruler of all household slaves and the mother of Zubaida, the dread Alwilda, whom the Duke had called a harridan. She was a small, wiry woman of middle years, very businesslike. Steward liked her at once, although she kept her eyes carefully downcast, as required of any slave addressing Royalty. Steward noted that her authority was genuine, beyond role, no doubt the source of the Duke's complaints.

On the night after his arrival, Steward was visited by Zubaida in his chambers, just as she had come to him every third night of their journey by direction of her owner. Having excused her from such duty at the outset, and then acceded to her own wishes, Steward had come to look forward to her visits with increasing anticipation. Their encounters were conducted in silence. He had tried to communicate, first by sign talk and later by words, after he had begun to learn a few. She refused even to look at him. After a while, he troubled her no more, simply removing his tunic, stretching himself on the bed, and letting his thoughts and his flesh dissolve under her knowing hands.

Steward found himself spending his mornings with Mate, pacing the garden, continuing each other's education. Every afternoon brought a social invitation from some member of the local aristocracy. Steward took advantage of these excursions to practice his language lessons. He found his hosts a great help, always responsive to his questions not only about the tongue but also about the place where they lived. In this way, he collected a wealth of information about Elysium– the taboos, customs, economics, and politics of the place. To this, Mate now began to add some lower-deck gossip, gleaned from the servants, with whom he could consort as another servant. Neither Steward nor Mate had any idea of what use any of the information might be, but both were of one mind that it was best to know everything they could learn about their situation.

During their first week in Elysium, it became increasingly obvious that things were not going well for the Duke. At the welcoming banquet the night after their arrival, there was a pervasive, subdued atmosphere, and the Duke was far from his usual garrulous self. Everyone seemed relieved to have the new Prince to focus on, and Steward's popularity was at once established, even more wholeheartedly than in the capital.

"You're the one bright spot in my life," the Duke had said to him at the end of one evening.

Steward excused himself from several invitations to witness public executions that his host recommended as exhibitions of great artistry. "You couldn't find a better seat, and they're going to do three at the same time tomorrow," said the Duke. "It starts at noon and should take at least a half hour. It's particularly interesting to me because I once knew all three subjects." If these events brought any cheer to Steward's host, however, it was not apparent.

"Everybody is terrified of him," Mate told Steward, "and he's been in a rage ever since he got here. The scuttlebutt has it there was no money waiting for him and he's got a lot of little problems with his Barons and a couple of big problems on the northern border."

"I daresay our host's his own worst problem," Steward replied.

In confirmation of the gossip, the Duke prepared to depart for the north with a thousand soldiers in order to "spank some naughty children who have made their teacher cross," he told Steward before leaving. "I would take you with me, but I doubt you'd find it that amusing. Besides, I'll feel better about things if I can leave you in charge. There really won't be anything you need to do, except be me for a week or two until I get back."

Steward was caught by surprise. "In charge? Surely you have a working government of deputies, proxies, ministers, counselors . . . . ?"

"Oh, yes, many, although not as many as last week, and those who remain are thieves. It is ironic that you, a foreigner, are the only nonthief here," said the Duke, starting to pace. "They're like mosquitoes drinking my blood, and there are so many I can't swat 'em all. Not yet.

You're perfectly welcome to swat some for me if you'd like. I'm leaving you four guard companies, though I doubt you'll need 'em. My precious ministers should be sufficiently terrified to do all the things they're supposed to do for the time being, and that witch Alwilda runs the Palace well enough. So I trust that being left in charge won't be too big a fly in your soup. I'd take it as a great favor. It carries no responsibility but settles an issue that will be unresolved otherwise."

Steward agreed but cautioned his host he knew nothing of Elysium's affairs. This elicited a wry chuckle from the Duke. "That would seem to make two of us," he growled, signaling a slave to strap on his greaves.

Far from being a fly in Steward's soup, the unexpected stewardship of the entire domain provided him with the kitchen keys to cook up whatever he wished, in his view.

Mate felt emphatically otherwise. "Oh, sir, there's nothing but danger in your actually *doing* anything while he's gone." The ducal dust had barely settled after the army's departure when Steward requested the presence of each Privy Council minister individually, in order of rank, for a private chat. "If you go swimmin' around in their waters they'll likely pull you under, sir," Mate warned.

"I have every intention of remaining afloat," Steward reassured him.

"I know you know the risk, sir, but if you'll allow the question, to what gain?"

"There's not as much risk as you think. From what we've both seen, we're among great confusion. We won't become part of it as long as there's no confusion with us. We're ideally situated to find out what's going on here without becoming involved. We have no baggage, and whatever we carry away will be of our own choosing. You'll see. Now, if you'll be so kind as to pass the word for my Privy Councillors."

While Mate was off on his errand, Steward sat down to appreciate his breakfast, the fragrance of the morning, and the beauty of the surrounding garden. The only disturbing ingredient was a group of skeletal-looking slaves rebuilding a wall at the other end of the terrace. Mate was soon back, accompanied by Alwilda.

"It's done, sir," he reported with resignation. "The first of them's due in a few minutes. Alwilda wants to know what room you want to use for your meetings, and do you have any special requirements?"

"I believe I'll receive them right here," said Steward. "We'll need only the usual refreshments. Except . . . " Steward's eye went to the work party. "I want to see those slaves over there fed. I want to see them eat." As this was translated, Steward saw surprise in Alwilda's eyes before she said something in response.

"She says feeding any of the outside slaves is beyond her normal authority, sir, but if you wish it, she'll do it, o'course. Did you mean right now, sir?"

"Yes. Right now. I want to see the food go into them."

"She says she'll do it right away. She says you're wise, sir, because they'll give more work if they're better fed."

"I don't care about that, but it's offensive to see hunger in the midst of such plenty." When this was translated, Alwilda lifted her gaze and looked directly into Steward's eyes.

"At last, we meet," he said, smiling at her.

The first of a nervous succession of Privy Councilors arrived a few minutes later–a pink, portly, balding pasha who was introduced as First Councilor. Steward greeted him cordially, asking Mate to put the man at ease and explain that there was nothing official about their meeting; its purpose was largely social, but he did have one question he would appreciate help with–namely, what could they do together to make things work better during the Duke's absence? "Wouldn't it be good to do something while he's gone that would make his return a pleasant surprise?"

The First Councillor did indeed think that would be a good thing, as did the Second, Third, Fourth, and Seventh Councillors in turn over the course of the day. It was explained to Steward that there was no Fifth or Sixth Councillor at the moment, those individuals just recently having ceased to exist. Still, the interviews extended well past suppertime.

"A long day, eh, Mate?" said Steward as the last of them departed.

"A long day, indeed, sir," said Mate, "and as sorry a pack of troubles as I've ever heard, if I may say so, sir."

Steward chuckled. "You may well say so. The whole thing's fundamentally corrupt. Corrupt to a fault, and it's nobody's fault. Or rather, it's always everybody else's. Given that, I've heard few problems here that can't be sorted out by a more humane form of authority than our host's."

"I've no doubt you're right, sir. You've set 'em on a better course and given 'em a bit of wind in their sails, to be sure, but it's my hope that's the end of it."

"Nothing of the sort," said Steward. "For instance, I'm interested in this mine where a new vein of gold was discovered but yields less now than before its discovery. In the morning, I want to talk to whoever knows most about that, and then there are some other people I'd like to meet. At breakfast, we'll make up a list. Remind me also to make a list of people we want to invite to supper, now that it's part of the job. Oh, yes, and cancel any more executions until I can review the situation."

"Aye, sir," said Mate, his face set. "Is that all, then, sir?"

"Almost. Let me have a word with Alwilda now."

Steward's final piece of business for the day was not one he was looking forward to. "Mother of Zubaida," he addressed her, "tell your daughter this: now that I'm acting as her master, I remove her from whatever obligation to attend me that the Duke imposed upon her."

When Mate had translated this, Alwilda had a response. "She asks if you no longer want Zubaida's visits," said Mate.

"Not unless she wishes them," Steward said, and saw behind Alwilda's eyes for the second time.

It had been an extraordinarily amusing day, he reflected later, alone in his chambers. The best yet. It had left him both tired and excited. Ordinarily, Steward was untroubled by sleeplessness in any form, but on that night, he could not release his thoughts. As though having sensed his restlessness, Zubaida came to him then, entering his sleeping chamber so silently he was unaware of her until he felt her warmth. Then there was the smell of her, releasing a whole new array of thoughts and feelings, all of which were dissolved by the magic of her massage.

STONISHING," SAID the Seventh Duke, wearing a look of amazed pleasure, "just astonishing."

"We were hoping you would be pleased," said Steward. Even the Duke's Privy Councilors seemed caught up in the general cheer their report had inspired. The Duke had not returned in a week or two as he had predicted. After a month, another thousand troops marched to join him, and word had arrived of the closure of the northern passes, effectually isolating the principality for the further three months during which the Duke had felt obliged to lead his forces. Only after sitting on a large, painful splinter that had to be removed surgically did the Duke decide to leave the campaign to his generals and return to the Palace. His arrival in a coach especially rigged with a sling for the comfort of the ducal behind had not boded well, but his councillors' reports had greatly improved his disposition.

"I am pleased with you all, and that should be sufficiently unusual to be your reward," he said, dismissing the councillors with a movement of his fingers. He then turned to Steward. "My dear friend, when I left here, it was in the hope you would find something with which to amuse yourself. I see you have. Indeed, you have." The Duke picked up the stack of parchments on which the councilors had recorded their reports.

"Here I'm holding the first detailed accounting of my money that I've ever been able to get in this place. Amazing. No doubt it's largely a pack of lies, but its mere existence, dear fellow, is as miraculous as the missing revenues that have so mysteriously reappeared during my absence. Not to mention the new revenues." Before him was empirical evidence—several chests of gold coin accompanied by a stack of ingots bearing the stamp of Elysium. "It is not ungratifying to learn that my mines are producing again, and with double the yield. How did you do this? Everybody's taking credit for it, of course, but they all concede you're the instigator." The Duke regarded Steward with a quizzical smile.

"It is exactly the sort of thing for which I was trained by my father," Steward answered honestly, "and I've had a good deal of practice at problems not so dissimilar to Elysium's, though on a lesser scale."

"And this," said the Duke, still leafing through the parchments. "The Baron of Mocha is no longer at war with the Count of Marmalad. How did you get old Marmalad to stop attacking Mocha?"

"I spoke to the Contessa of Marmalad," said Steward.

"And you've got all the wall repairs done to the Palace. That job's been going on for years. What did you do, put more slaves onto it?"

"No. In fact, there were more than enough, but they were too underfed to work properly. Feeding them was no additional expense, by the way, because you were being charged for their food all along, but the money was going elsewhere."

"Where?" asked the Duke.

"Into a hole that has been closed, I trust," said Steward. "It was only one of many."

"I hope you closed some holes with impalement stakes," rasped the Duke.

"Not actually," said Steward. "It's true enough, what you said about being surrounded by thieves, but so were the thieves. Big fish eat little fish. That is to say, any official whose pay is stolen by those above him then steals from those below him in order to have an income. My aim has been to break that chain and establish accountability. In fact, I've taken the liberty of releasing some prisoners."

"You released prisoners?" said the Duke, looking up aghast.

"I think you'll find they're of more profit to you alive. It's all in those reports."

The Duke shook his head in amazement. "I must say, dear Prinny, you have novel methods: releasing prisoners, feeding slaves, putting my executioners out of practice . . . Still, here's the proof of your pudding," said the Duke, scooping up a handful of coins and letting them fall from his fingers in a golden cascade. "What is your reward to be? Name it, my friend."

"I claim no reward," said Steward. "I'm your guest. If I was able to help while you were preoccupied, I'm glad."

"Your saying that increases my obligation," said the Duke, eyeing him. "You won't let me off the hook so easily, eh? Since your reward's to be left to me, then, let me ponder it while we feast. It's been a hard campaign. As you see, I'm wounded, alas. It's healing now, you'll be glad to hear, but a saddle became quite out of the question. Nasty campaign. I don't mind telling you the only good highlander's a dead one, and the more of 'em that way, the better. There's more to do, but I've opened the main passes again, and the lowland cattle are safe enough from the raids for a time. Let's go and eat something while we talk. I'll tell you what our neighbors in the north are up to and what I'm doing to them, and then you can be the one to give me the Palace gossip. Do we not make a fair pair of Sevenths? Let's dine alone so that we can talk freely. Which reminds me, I congratulate you on your command of our language. You barely use this interpreter now. Is he still required?" Steward emphatically assured the Duke that Mate was indispensable.

Whatever satisfaction Mate might have taken from that testimonial was interrupted by errands even before the first course as Steward was admitted into the deepest ducal intimacies regarding the workings of Elysium. Of what was said, he heard only fragments, however. Before Mate had listened long, he was sent off to find some maps, and when that was done, there was a message for him to deliver, and so it went until a late hour. Toward the end of the evening, he heard more than one matter apparently resolved.

"That's your reward, then," the Duke said. He was in as mellow a mood as Mate had ever seen him. "Your reward is Elysium itself, in a manner of speaking. As soon as I can organize a convoy, I'll return to the capital and try to get the northern mess resolved at court, which is where I'm best anyway. All my friends are there. Except for you, of course, but you will be here being me while I'm there." He paused. "If you send me twenty-five thousand, quarterly, in coin and bar, and another ten thousand for the Empress, whatever is left over is yours. How's that? Considering your talents, I should think you'll soon have more money than you can spend."

"I agree with your sentiments, but not your terms," said Steward to Mate's momentary horror as the smile froze on the Seventh Duke's face.

Steward only laughed. "I accept your proposal with three qualifications. First, I'll send you a quarterly *fifty thousand* plus *twenty thousand* for the Empress, keeping whatever surplus. Also, anytime the arrangement no longer pleases you, you may terminate it without notice. Either of us can."

"Done," said the Duke, his good humor more than restored. "It's a new thing to me to bargain with one who bargains upward, but since you are inclined to bargain, I insist on your taking two thousand in settlement of past accounts. It's a fraction of what you recovered for me, and I won't hear any argument about it. What's your next qualification?"

"Just a request, having to do with my Knights. They expected my return months ago. With another month before the caravan can arrive with news from me, they'll be concerned. I ask especially that my messages reach them without delay and that there will be a coach for them in the next return caravan. I'm inviting them to come, and I presume they all will."

"Easily done. Montressor will attend to it. And your third qualification?"

"The slave Zubaida. Will you give her to me?"

"But Prinny, I have already. You've full use of her. Is she displeasing you in some way?"

"On the contrary. Is it too much to ask you to assign her ownership to me? If I transgress, please consider the request as never having been spoken."

"If she gives you pleasure, nothing gives me greater pleasure than to give her to you. She's yours from this moment. I'll order a document signing her over to you. Be mindful of her mother."

"Thank you," said Steward.

"Now that's all settled," said the Duke, raising his goblet. "Here's to us two, then, to our joint ventures and to whatever fortune put us together. We do work rather well together, wouldn't you say?"

"Increase and prosperity to all," said Steward.

S TEWARD'S MESSAGE to his shipmates arrived several weeks later, having been delayed at the Little Palace after the Elysium caravan's arrival in the capital. The message was enclosed in a sealed money chest containing one thousand tightly packed gold pieces, each weighing a twelfth of a pound. The Duke had less interest in the gold than in what message his proxy was sending his Knights, for which reason the seals had been expertly removed by the talented Whisper. To the Duke's surprise, the letter was not in the foreign writing of the yachtsmen but in the Imperial language so that no translator was needed in order to read it.

"I see nothing in it of alarm," he said, handing the letter to the Dowager Duchess to read.

The old lady scanned its contents. "He's full of praises for Elysium," she commented.

"Yes. I think he actually likes it there."

"So it would seem. That's fortunate, considering all he's doing for us. There are some personal notes to his men. They seem innocuous enough. I trust you've searched the chest for any hidden messages? Good. He tells his friends the money's theirs to be shared equally, which seems rather excessively generous. He has sent them . . . I fear my eyes are not what they once were . . . citrus? He sent them fruit? How did it keep?"

"I recall no fruit. As you see, he's urging them to come and join him, and I cannot judge the consequences of letting them go. They may be easily enough detained on some pretext, of course. Or there are road hazards. There are so many possibilities. But it costs little enough to keep them. I'm told no difficulties have arisen from their being here, and the one who acts and sings is quite the darling of just about everybody. Where's the balance to it, Grandmamma? What would you do?"

"Nothing extreme. In fact, nothing at all as far as your amazing new Minister Regent is concerned. Or his friends. If you rock their boat, you might rock your own. Watch them, of course, but let them be until there comes some cause to rethink things."

The following day, the chest was delivered to the villa at the yacht basin by a company of halberdiers under the command of a florid

sergeant who insisted on having all four signatures on his receipt before releasing it. Steward's assumption that a chest of gold would im-
press his comrades was correct. When Pilot broke the seals and
opened the box, Bosun let out a low whistle.

"Here's a lot more money than all we've spent on our whole venture. What does he say in the letter?" Pilot glanced at the seal. Finding
it intact, he broke it and read, having to translate for Crew, the only
one of their company who had not yet gained a functional use of the
new language during the half-year they had been there.

"There are two hundred of these for each of us," Pilot told him.
"Steward has quite literally found a gold mine, and he is administrating Elysium while the Duke is back here. He hopes we're enjoying our
sojourn as much as he is. He hopes being the toast of the continent has
not spoiled you, Crew; he hopes Bosun's not getting lazy; he says he
trusts us to lock Flags up if necessary to protect him from the girls;
and he hopes I am not getting as fat as he is. Mate's well and sends regards. Steward says he would feel better if we were where he could
keep a closer eye on us, and he wants us all to come to Elysium in the
next caravan, which the Duke will arrange for us. Then there's a paragraph telling us how much we'll enjoy it, and he's sending us a small
quantity of citrus."

"Fruit?" said Bosun, puzzled. "There was no fruit. How would fruit
have kept?"

"A small enough quantity of citrus might be found *on* its basket
rather than *in* it," said Pilot, holding the letter over a candle flame. As
the parchment warmed, the characters written in lemon juice turned
brown, making visible the secret message in their own language:

> I suggest we postpone departure until we have enough gold
> with which to replace *Alembic*'s ballast. Our fortunes are
> made here. Have patience, Bosun. I'll see you all in Elysium.

But Steward was not alone in having found engaging interests; the
Empire of the Sun's cornucopia had yielded fruits for each of them. For
once, even Bosun was in no hurry to be off. Assisted by Crew, he had restored *Alembic* to fitness within weeks, thereafter accepting a commis-

sion from the Third Duke to supervise construction of a yacht much like their own, incorporating some changes for local conditions. The reconstruction was now partially in frame at the Imperial dockyard, where Bosun and Crew spent most of their days. Bosun had struck up a friendship with the dockmaster's daughter–which facilitated the work. Crew had grown attached to Oblivia the laundress, a full figured, brown-haired girl who, like himself, was considered boring. But in each other they had discovered the mutual miracle of somebody of the opposite sex whom they understood with no words, as though they were male and female of the same stuff. Sitting and holding hands after their day's work, they could watch the little dramas around them, sharing the same reactions in unison. They had no wish to be parted.

Flags was disinclined to make the long trip to Elysium just then because he was writing the libretto for an expanded and improved theatrical presentation of their voyage. The first performance was soon to be staged at the Grand Palace. Flags's career as a raconteur and performer was cometlike across the capital's firmament, and he had avoided the usual entanglements of multiple girlfriends, having established a monogamous intimacy with the beauteous widowed Dame Hydrangea. His senior by ten years, she had become his patroness in artistic circles. Together, they had hosted several social outings aboard *Alembic,* now a yacht in fact as well as name.

Pilot's great find was the Imperial Archives and Athenaeum, an inconceivably vast library containing tomes, tablets, manuscripts, scrolls, pamphlets, tractates, dissertations (bound and unbound), albums, glyphic impressions, papyri, boxed documents, illuminated parchments, encyclopedias, thesauri, incunabula, a whole roomful of stacked runestones, and ordinary volumes in scores of thousands, many of them decaying, others attacked by worms. There were new works and ancient, in many languages and pictographia, and on every imaginable subject. Pilot's initial quest for navigational information on the Southern Ocean proceeded slowly at first because of the total lack of any indexes, catalogues, or bibliographical lists. The traditional interest of the Imperial Archives was more in the accumulation of texts than in their content, he discovered.

After much rummaging, he had located enough information to

guide him to the Southern Ocean's boundaries. Pleased as he was with his finds, they were eclipsed in his view by a fascinating collection of alchemical works that included two pymanders, seven lengthy cabalistic manuscripts, several treatises on the philosophers' stone, a mercurorium, an assortment of sutras, dozens of related works less easily categorized, and the complete theorems of Pythagoras. It was a treasure trove from which he had no desire to be parted too soon.

Hence, the next caravan to Elysium bore only a packet of letters from *Alembic,* some with a touch of lemon juice, but there was little enough for any of them to hide. Each had found honorable occupation. They realized that their lives were fortunately insulated from the commonality of the capital, and even Bosun was forced to admit their good luck.

Three months later came Steward's next message, accompanied by a platoon of guards bearing a chest exactly similar to the earlier one. The letter within was a repetition of his invitation to all or any of them to come, by sea or land. There were anecdotes illustrating how very well indeed all was going in Elysium. Bosun had been concerned over the security of their first chest, finally having buried it secretly under a patio stone outside the window by his bed. Now, he felt compelled to build a proper vault, cunningly hidden and rigged with noisemakers to ring an alarm if the guardian stone was tampered with.

ONE DAY, WHILE Pilot was making painful progress through a tract on homunculi, a tall, swarthy man with an extravagant hat appeared among the stacks, rummaging in the same material that interested Pilot. He introduced himself as Melquiades, a

Gypsy, who had traveled an immense distance to visit these archives. He was delighted to find in Pilot a fellow seeker.

"Ah!" said Melquiades at their first meeting, "we meet as two miners working the same vein of ore." He was very jovial.

"I beg your pardon?" said Pilot, annoyed at having his study interrupted.

"We both pursue the purest gold, neh?"

"I pursue pure knowledge," responded taciturn Pilot with the beginning of a chill.

"Ah, but what is pure knowledge if not the purest gold?" asked Melquiades. Improbably, the garrulous Gypsy and the reclusive scholar soon became fast friends. Pilot found Melquiades amusing, full of passion, and capable of the wildest kinds of myth in the same breath with genuine insights. For instance, Melquiades claimed to have lived for one hundred and six years, although he appeared little older than Pilot, and he also claimed to have another two hundred and twenty-seven years to go before his death, according to his maternal grandmother, who was a *bruja*.

"It is the time allowed me in which to attain truth," he said, leaving Pilot unsure as to whether his new friend believed what he was saying—he appeared to—or was just having him on. It was part of Melquiades's charm that he could keep Pilot guessing.

"Yet there's something beyond truth," Pilot mused. "Or maybe between truths. I've only glimpsed it, but it makes *definitions* of truth two-dimensional."

"True," Melquiades responded, "there's one-and-one-half-fold truth on top of that and then twofold truth beyond. Some truths are quite obviously greater than others."

"By definition, that makes the lesser truths into partial truths, which is to say lies."

"True, if you choose to define it like that, but the final truth would be pure, would it not? If we do not think so, what are we both doing here among these arcane documents? A cockfight would be more entertaining."

Melquiades looked closely at Pilot. "My friend, I see without needing to be told that you have experienced the great desolation and come through it, as have I. Like yourself, I believe nothing, but I do perceive as best I can through the illusions in which I still swim."

Sometime later, while Melquiades was standing on Pilot's shoulders to get at the top of some stacks too high to reach otherwise, Pilot pursued the question. "What do you reckon to be the nature of your 'final truth'?" he asked.

"Ah," said Melquiades, "the answer to that's the grail we seek. Perhaps the answer's in the hundred thousand distillations of base matter prescribed by the Boschian alchemists. Paracelsus told me he thought they might be onto something, but their exact formula's been lost, and the process takes ten years." At this moment, a cataract of dust fell into Pilot's upturned face as Melquiades shifted a heavy bundle of wax tablets to get at whatever was beneath. "If we can dig out those secrets in this place, I for one will sequester myself in a laboratory and probe the physics and metaphysics of it."

"How can you put the two so glibly together?" asked Pilot.

"How can you so glibly separate them?" Melquiades retorted. "In theory, the physical distillations–done properly–induce a synchronistic purification of the alchemist's mind over a period of time. It must be a tremendously boring process, all those distillations. Perhaps I'll take up knitting."

"Where along the sequence is gold supposed to be produced from lead?" asked Pilot.

"Supposedly, it happens simultaneously with the transmutation of the alchemist's mind, confusion turning to illumination. Perhaps the event is allegorical, perhaps not. I frankly find my mind more confusing than things I can touch, taste, see, smell, and hear. Phewww," he added, having just found among the papers the corpse of a very dead mouse.

Some of Melquiades's most interesting observations were other than philosophical. For instance, one day while studying a *tractus philosophicus,* Pilot glanced up and found the Gypsy's dark eyes examining him narrowly. "How do you make yourself invisible?" asked Melquiades in a conversational way.

"Invisible?" asked Pilot, genuinely puzzled.

"Yes. A moment ago, when I looked up to speak to you, I could not see you although I had not heard you go anywhere. Now, I see you again although I did not hear you come back from wherever you did not go, and there you are."

"Odd," said Pilot. "One of mind's tricks."

Later, Melquiades commented, "There *is* magic, I trust you're aware."

"Do some," said Pilot. "I'd like to see."

"It is a spontaneous thing," said Melquiades, "self-existing and not something that one *does*. My maternal grandmother would tell you that magic is something that does *you*. She would also tell you that those who try to invoke magic–the real magic–tread a dangerous path. I think it behooves us to remember her words, most particularly in our line of work." Pilot would remember this for the rest of his life.

At about the time the ninth of Steward's quarterly chests arrived from Elysium, Pilot stumbled on a cuneiform manuscript, which he handed over to Melquiades, cuneiform being one of the forty-two kinds of writing with which the Gypsy was conversant. He was tremendously excited by it, suspecting it contained the basic formulas from which the Boschian alchemists had proceeded. He set about translating it at once, with Pilot making a copy for himself.

When the work was completed months later, Melquiades felt he had in hand the essence of what he had come for. His trunks of books and Gypsy trinkets were loaded aboard a baghla that would carry him on the first leg of his long journey to his homeland. There, he intended to commence the decade of seclusion to which he felt committed. He urged Pilot toward the same pursuit, "so that, when we meet again, we will have new information for each other. More and more, I am persuaded the whole thing's a study of patterns, neh? There seem so many, but perhaps they reduce to fewer. We shall see." Their hands locked, and then Melquiades was gone, his broad hat flapping as the wind filled the baghla's sails.

Without him, Pilot found the Archives a mouldering mausoleum, and he began to gather the remaining notes he wanted to take away when *Alembic* sailed. When that sailing was to be had been a matter for discussion ever since Bosun's recent completion of the Third Duke's yacht. That project had grown as whole areas were remade in order to accommodate his patron's whim. The Third Duke had been pleased with the result, but the changes and lavish decorations had destroyed the vessel's efficiency, and he was glad to be done with it. No payment had been offered or demanded.

At the same time, Flags's remarkable submission to monogamy had begun to weaken under a steady barrage of fragrances from other sources than the Dame Hydrangea, a proud and powerful woman of profound intolerance, as he had come to learn. There were other dangers, he was well aware, in this land where killing over the honor of women was commonplace. Flags had begun to think in terms of the sea again when, three years to the day from the time of their arrival, the tenth chest of gold was delivered by a detachment of cuirassiers.

"That's the last of Steward's gold there's room for in our vault," said Bosun as Pilot broke the seals, "and I say it's far more than we need to justify our venture. Let's sail to Elysium and get His Nibs and take him home."

"I'll second that," said Flags, "though we've never recovered our papers, and we'll have to finesse our departure."

"I'm for it, too," said Crew, who had never been easy about Steward's separation from the rest of them. He would miss his Oblivia as much as he knew she would miss him, but their parting had always been foreseen. Their great present to each other had been the discovery of comfort with somebody of the other sex, followed by the eventual revelation that such a thickness of comfort permitted no spark. He would leave her in far better circumstances than those in which he had found her.

"That makes three of us for it," said Bosun, "Where do you stand, Pilot?"

"Squarely with you," said Pilot, reading the accompanying note, "but Steward makes the point moot. He says, 'If you will not come to me, then I must come to you. I shall arrive by the next caravan. We have much to talk about.'" He held the paper over a flame, but no writing appeared. "That's all. Nothing further."

"Perfect," said Bosun, rubbing his hands. "That'll give us time to outfit and victual for departure without drawing attention to our intent. No flurry of activity. Steward says nothing about leaving, so he must mean it to be kept secret. Let's honor that, but be ready to sail. I can taste the sea."

All heartily agreed.

H AVING CONCLUDED an agreeable ministerial review of the principality's affairs with his councillors on the eve of his departure for the capital, Steward had time to enjoy a leisurely bath before dining with the real powers of the land. As he floated among the mosaic patterns of the tiled pool, he reflected with satisfaction on an Elysium that was now tidily taking care of itself, although there was still much to be done. His thoughts were pleasantly interrupted by Zubaida entering the chamber, disrobing, and joining him in the pool. He smiled into her eyes, remembering the first time she had returned his gaze on the magical night following his bestowal of her freedom. Now, though she returned his smile, he saw that her eyes were tearful.

"What is this?" he asked her.

"I can't help it. I'll miss you and worry about you."

"Only for the time it takes me to travel to the capital, fetch my friends, and return. Say, ten weeks."

"It makes me uneasy that you are summoned before the Empress."

"Be easy," said Steward, giving her an underwater tickle to change the subject and getting a wet smack of her hand on his stomach by way of response.

"You strike at my biggest target," laughed Steward.

Steward's supper with his closest confidential advisers took the form of an informal family affair. Mate, now titled and looking ten years younger, had become coordinator of most ministerial activities. He and Alwilde and Zubaida were the only ones privy to Steward's full confidence. Alwilde had received her freedom soon after her daughter, by Steward's special petition to the Seventh Duke, but had remained at her station, zealously expanding it to incorporate a vast intelligence network of slaves. Through their combined access to the comings, goings, thinkings and secrets of Elysium, she had been able to provide Steward with all the information he needed to take action only where success had been certain. She loved him as intensely as she had hated the Duke, although her manner was as leathery as always.

"It's not here there'll be any problem while you're gone," Alwilde told him. "The Barons are fat and happy; the people have greater prosperity than they've ever known; and your decree of regulations for the care and feeding of the slaves has got you their loyalty. They sing about you."

Zubaida was amused. "Your slave-runs are the only ones where the slave always gets away." The humor of it made her forget her apprehensions for the moment, and her laughter was for Steward a musical note in the warmth of the evening. Through her, he knew love's definition, and through all of them, he had seen the seeds of his own generosity burst and flourish.

"In short," said Alwilde, "*here* you've got friends from the top of society to its bottom–"

"Except for some retired tax-collectors, satraps, executioners, and accountants," Steward smiled.

"It's not *here* we fear for your safety," Alwilde persisted. "It's beyond Elysium's borders."

"And all's not totally secure even here," said Mate, who was at least as nervous about Steward's departure as the others. "As soon as word gets out that you're gone, there'll be pranks, and the northern highlands still aren't subjugated."

"Nor should they be," said Steward, thumping the table. "To subjugate the highlanders, you'd have to kill them, and what a waste. I, for one, like their spirit. Besides, there's got to be the seed of rebellion in a land or where's freedom?"

"Then you'll always have a menace there," said Mate.

"What we've got there is the most efficient force of light infantry I've ever seen. Nobody can fight like those people, and they're now more my friends than my enemies. That alliance–when I can think of a way to stop the highlanders from stealing everybody's cattle–will unite Elysium militarily and secure our borders. With a handful of properly rigged warships off our coasts, and the highlanders at the passes, no enemy could force entrance into Elysium." Steward drummed his fingers, looking perplexed for a moment. "D'you know,

I think the thing to do is just *give* the highlanders the damned cattle, till they break the habit of stealing 'em. We can certainly buy a lot of cattle for what it costs to keep an army to protect them. You might look into that while I'm gone."

Mate shook his head. "Of course, I will, sir, but all that you say about your control here *is* the worrisome part." In Mate's emphatic view, the Duke could not help but know that Elysium had now become a true power, and Steward was its source. While the letters that arrived from the capital were sugary, there was no telling the Duke's real mind. Mate thought it most likely to have taken a jealous, suspicious turn, in which case the capital would be a dangerous place for his master. Worse, he had been summoned to an audience with the Empress, with unknown portent. "I'll ask it of you again, sir. Let me go in your stead. You can use the border troubles as an excuse for staying home. I'll be safe enough as your emissary in the capital, and you'll be safe here. I'll fetch your friends back with me or get them to bring me back aboard *Alembic,* as you wish. I'd feel better about that job than being left in charge while you're gone." Zubaida and Alwilde firmly endorsed Mate's words.

Steward plucked a grape and popped it into his mouth. "Between yourselves and the administrators under you, you *are* all running the place now. You'll make a good regent, Mate. I've no worries for any of us. As to my safety, I'm touched by your concern, but I think you're inventing imaginary dangers." Steward held up his finger and reminded Mate that Elysium was now providing the Duke ten times as much gold as before. A vast sum was going in the same caravan that would take him. "Do you think they want to trifle with the keeper of their golden sow?"

Steward held up a second finger, making the point that if anything happened to the Duke's administrator, he would again have to take on the problems of a principality that hated him as cordially as he hated it. Steward's third point was his own manifest innocence. "Although he may know I've consolidated power here, his spies will have brought him no whiff of a threat because there isn't one. No conspiracies exist. Fourth, the Empress. My meeting with her is long overdue. If I were her, I would want to meet me, too, and I want the meeting as much as she does. Elysium must stay open to the world if our prosperity is to increase, and this personal contact is a necessary link."

Steward smiled reassuringly. "If she's uneasy about me, I'll put her mind to rest. Fifth . . ."–Steward held up all five fingers, the lamplight reflecting on their rings–"the question of my shipmates. They are the true reason for my journey. My letters have not persuaded them from the occupations that have taken their fancy, but if I can *talk* with them, I can bring them back. Here, they'll have everything, and they'll bring spice to our lives. With them, Elysium will be complete."

WITH THE ARRIVAL of the heavily guarded caravan from Elysium, the Seventh Duke was expecting Steward's presence, but to his irritation, his guest sent a note saying he would be there when he had escorted the five chests he wished to see delivered to his comrades.

"I want him followed," said the Duke to Whisper, "and his friends are to be watched closely as long as he's here." The Count of Montressor nodded and vanished, leaving the Duke to make his way to the apartments of the Dowager, who received him while browsing among her vast collection of tropical birds.

"Again, he attacks my pride," said the Duke, concluding his report to his lifelong adviser. He was agitated, alternately seating himself, nibbling at the gold chains around his neck, then getting up to pace.

"What is that compared to the quarter million he just has brought you?" asked the Dowager.

The Duke stiffened. "I put no price on my pride," he said.

"That's the difference between you and the Empress, who puts no pride on her price. Perhaps you'll learn it someday."

"I don't need riddles right now, Granny. The man's usurped my principality. He's made me look bad, I know, whatever my spies report. Who trusts them? Who trusts him? How can I tell what he's really up to?"

"Not by assuming his mind works as yours works."

"Works?" growled the Duke. "Montressor's got something that

works. It's a slow concoction of a kind that doesn't give you a purple tongue or any other indication as to the cause of death. One digestive cycle does the trick. Who does he think he *is,* making *me* wait for *him*?"

"I doubt he intended it that way," she said, feeding dates to the mynahs. "All his behavior, from everything we've seen, leads me to suspect he is an innocent, in greater and lesser ways. Perhaps such phenomena are bred more elsewhere than here. In any case, he's made you wealthier than most of your brothers are. Nor is the Empress inclined to be displeased with him. As you value your life, take no step to make yourself the object of Imperial displeasure. You've done enough of that, if I may say so. Your Prince is your savior at this moment."

"There is the no small matter of my pride," the Duke reminded her.

"If there must be a blood sacrifice, let it be his Knights, but not while he's here, and arrange to make it seem they sailed away and were lost at sea–a common occurrence, I believe–which would probably cause him appreciable pain."

"They could try to leave at any time. Their boat's in readiness."

"*Nobody leaves.* Behold my golden cockatoo. Is he not a magnificent bird? See how he puffs up!"

S TEWARD'S SECOND VISIT to the villa of his comrades was announced in the same way as his first, by a clatter of cavalry hooves that brought *Alembic*'s crew out on the run to meet him.

"At last," he called to them, dismounting from his destrier with the assistance of a groom. Then, he was hugging them, as best he could with his great girth. "I can no longer embrace you all at once as I used to," he observed.

"Nor any one of us you," said Pilot.

"Prosperity has made you ever so much more the man," agreed Flags.

"You need a strong horse," said Bosun, ever practical.

"It's the food in Elysium, which is but one of the delights I have to tell you about. Where do you want these put?" he asked as the five chests were brought forward.

"Five this time!" Bosun exclaimed. "Into the house for the moment," he said, leading the way. When they were settled in the courtyard, Steward raised his hand to end the banter. "We have much to say to one another, but our amusements must wait. I've little time. I've come directly to you, rather than to the palace, and if I'm here long, I risk giving offense. I've many things to tell you, but the long and short of it is this: we've our own kingdom." He paused. Seeing only stunned looks, he elaborated, repeating many of the things he had told them by letter in praise of Elysium. "It's all ours. I'm running it and, for various reasons I'll explain later, I can give you every assurance that I'm going to continue running it. We will together, if you'd like. Elysium offers you all of the homes, friends, wealth, and comforts you could ever desire and the occupation of your choosing. The gold you've had from me is a fraction of what's there for us; I've been sending it only to emphasize my words and to make my invitations more persuasive, but they've all missed their mark. Now, I've come to fetch you."

"We were expecting to leave when you arrived," said Bosun. "We're ready to sail."

"I reckoned you would be," grinned Steward. "Can you navigate us to Elysium, Pilot? I've brought you some charts. I must say, I shan't mind a touch of sea air myself."

"You misunderstand," said Bosun. "Home's where we want to go. Thanks to your generosity, we've near half a ton of gold now, to stack on the ballast."

"Scores of times our investment and more," said Pilot, "and in truth, it seems sufficient."

"But it's not enough yet to replace our leaden ballast," said Steward, "which is what I promised you. In Elysium, I'll make good that promise, if that's what you still want when you've been there for a bit. Another idea's also occurred to me—the building of a galleon to navigate back to the Port. Think of what that would carry in gold! We have every resource necessary to do it, to go back and forth, and to found another kingdom on the seas. I cannot adequately emphasize the resources at my disposal. *Our* disposal. Everything you can think of, and it's all mine. *Ours.*" As he spoke, he saw their expressions pass from surprise to dismay.

When the most persuasive things he could think of to say to them had left them unmoved, it was his own turn to be dismayed. "You're all fixed on sailing for home?" he asked, hardly believing.

"With the first fair breeze," said Bosun with a set face, "but we're incomplete without you." All chimed in trying to persuade Steward to return with them.

"Ah, yes. You'll need a cook again."

"I'll cook if you'll just come," said Crew. "Let's none of us decide anything right now until we can all sleep on it."

"You're right," said Steward, rising. "Let's sleep on it. I've pressing obligations in any case, including an interview with the Empress tomorrow morning. I'll give her your regards."

"Even better, try to retrieve *Alembic*'s documents and get us our clearance so we don't have to sneak out," Flags said. "I've been unable to get our papers back for some reason. Maybe you'll be able to do better. We'll need them whatever's to happen." Promising to do what he could, Steward took his departure, leaving his distressed comrades to discuss the new play of events.

"He's not the Steward who sailed in here with us," said Bosun with sadness. "They've got him covered with jewels and stuffed like a goose."

"He is heavy," agreed Pilot.

"Heavy enough to get sunk in the muck of this place, it seems," Flags observed glumly. Crew sighed.

S UPPER WITH THE Duke had an icing of cordiality spread thickly enough to conceal the cake of suspicion beneath it, but Steward caught its flavor. The Seventh Duke's jovial banter was too familiar, painfully forced, and laced with sly questions. They went on until a late hour, with the Duke insisting on round after round of drinks. The evening ended messily, with the host yielding to the cumulative effects of the alcohol and flashing the guest an incautious look of black hatred before falling face forward into a bowl of fruit yogurt. For once, Steward found no amusement in it. All that he had heard and seen had been deeply disturbing. He was grateful to be able to retire to his chambers, although sleep evaded him there. Fuzzy though his mind felt, it was alive with the thoughts generated by a day that had ended just about as badly as possible. Also, the night was uncomfortably hot, and the sunrise brought no breeze with it. A morning bath was restorative prior to his audience with the Empress of the Sun.

The Empress was so massively fat that she required a special throne. Tables laden with food were set to either hand within her reach. According to one of the Duke's tidbits of gossip the previous evening, the Empress's throne was especially constructed to contain a toilet so her massive personage need not be shifted in order to void. Observing the Imperial presence and her seat, Steward could not tell if it was true. The monarch was enveloped by a loose burnoose that covered everything. Also in attendance was an old lady he dimly recalled having once met.

"I believe you've met the Dowager Duchess?" said the Empress.

"I'm very pleased to see you again," said Steward, bowing.

"And I you," said the Dowager. "We hear so much of you but see so little."

"He's been busy, m'dear" said the Empress. Then, to Steward: "You *have* been busy, haven't you? You've made a very prosperous principality out of a place that used to be a profitless backwater. Under your stewardship, Elysium's the only state within the Empire to over-pay its taxes, and by increasing sums." She gazed speculatively at Steward. "I trust you're amply rewarding yourself, too?"

Steward smiled. "Yes, Your Majesty, although my needs are not so extensive."

"If not profit, what is your goal?"

"Improvement, Your Majesty. There's still much to be done. It is my passion."

"Your talent for administration is undeniable," said the Empress, nibbling from a bowl of eels in brine. "We're told you've had some previous experience?"

"Yes, Your Majesty, administrating my father's lands and holdings. He was a good teacher to me."

"You must miss him. You must miss all of your family and people. Will you take one of these eels? They're quite delicious."

"Thank you, Your Majesty, but my stomach's unsettled from travel. I do indeed miss both my parents, as well as the rest of my family, and I will send a letter to them with my Knights, who will soon sail for home, I regret to say, if they can recover our ship's documents from your port authorities."

"Documents? If there's a problem, it's probably with the damned petty officialdom, as usual. They're simply impossible." The slightest movement of the Imperial finger brought a silent satrap with poised pen.

"Whatever documents belong to the Administrator of Elysium's yacht are to be located and returned, along with whatever clearances they need. This is to be done on–When do you return to Elysium?" she asked Steward.

"The return caravan departs the day after tomorrow, Your Majesty. I've little time here."

"Ah. Your friends will doubtless want to see you off. So let us date the clearances for the day following, to permit their withdrawal a seemly space behind their master's." Another finger twitch dismissed the satrap. "How else can I be of service to you?"

"I have nothing else, Your Majesty, and I'm in your debt as it is."

"Do you hear all of this, my dear Duchess? We have here a Seventh Prince of quite a different stripe from some other Seventh Princes we know, eh? A loyal son who respects and listens to his parents, who also keeps honest accountings, whose only request for a favor is on behalf of his friends who have disappointed him, yet who knows how to run a kingdom better than most Kings." She glanced back at Steward. "Tell me, young man, what's to stop you from claiming Elysium as your own if you took the whim? And what could we do about it if you did?"

"Your Majesty has a long and powerful arm. As things stand, the only change I want is for continued improvement. That depends in great measure upon keeping Elysium open and peaceful, with expanded commerce. For instance, with the right kind of ships, a sea route can be opened with the capital." The Empress regarded him with narrow eyes, slits enfolded with pouches of flesh. From deep in her began something like a roll of distant thunder; at the same time, her jowls began to shake. Steward realized the Empress was laughing.

"*As things stand.* Very good. Well, well. Then let's *let* things stand. If you won't have a bite with us, I must insist on your taking a drop of wine so that we can drink to things as they stand. This vintage is noted for its bouquet." The rest of the interview was given to a discussion of the wines of Elysium, until Steward was graciously permitted to withdraw.

"Oh, he's good. I like him," said the Empress to the Duchess after he had left. "Yes, he could be dangerous, but he's forthright, too, and controllable thereby. There are so many uses for him. Perhaps he can do for some other principalities what he's done for Elysium. In any case, there he'll be until I decide otherwise, and you may tell your problem grandson that I want things kept . . . as they stand."

"I fear his pride's been pricked in this process."

"It's no small target."

"He wants revenge, and you know him. I think he'll be appeased if given his Administrator's four sailors to dispose of."

Again, the Empress's eyes narrowed, this time with displeasure. "Take him this message from me: I hold him personally responsible that nothing, *nothing,* happens to deprive us of this new talent, his only credit, and if he makes any mistake here, it'll be his last. Principalities are birthrights that may be taken away. The same is true of heads. I suppose there's no harm in letting our Spider Prince do something nasty to the four sailors if that'll keep him in rein. They've given offense to their master in any case, it seems. But let it be after he's gone and in a way that doesn't leave tracks."

"My thinking, too," said the Dowager. "I'll tell him what you've said when I see him."

$S$ TEWARD EMERGED from the cool marble corridors of the Grand Palace into the swelter of another unseasonably hot day. Again, he had been unsettled, although this time he could not put his finger on the source of it. His administration of Elysium had now the Imperial seal of approval. What matter if the fat Empress and the sepulchral old woman had left a sour taste in his mouth? He'd been well received, and his comrades' problems had been dealt with, although he was by no means reconciled to their departure, and they were his next order of business.

Thinking to dispel the sluggishness he felt, Steward decided to walk to the yacht basin through the city streets, so his equerry escort was dismissed and he strolled with a bodyguard of foot janissaries preceding him and others bringing up the rear. Lost in a clash of problems, he did not notice his guards brushing a group of beggars from his path, bodily shifting a legless boy out of their way. He walked on, trying to think of something to say to his comrades that would be more persuasive than anything he had told them previously. Nothing came to mind, and halfway to the basin, he decided to return to the Little Palace and try instead to capture the sleep that had evaded him the previous night. Abruptly, he turned and walked back in the direction from which they had come, to the surprise of his rear guards, who nearly piled into one another with the change of course. The legless beggar saw them returning and managed to drag himself out of their way with his arms.

Then, there was the subsurface animosity of his host, certainly something that would have to be examined and treated with finesse. As luck had it, Steward's thoughts of the Duke coincided with the passage of his troop through a stinking meat market, past rows of plucked fowls and hanging sides of venison, ham, whole pigs, quarters of beef, shoulders of mutton, and other less identifiable pieces of meat, along with all of the flyblown buckets of brains, kidneys, hearts, livers, tongues, testicles, and other edible bits, plus tubs of bloody bones. Shoppers bartered with gory butchers; still-extant cattle lowed in their pens; steaming tumbrels rattled along; here and there, a dog was chased away; Steward saw one that was too slow on its feet caught by a butcher's wife.

"Bad luck for you," he said under his breath.

He arrived in his quarters oozing perspiration and went directly into the pool, strewing his clothing behind him. He floated in the water, willing each of his body's parts in turn into a state of relaxation, as Zubaida had taught him. The thought of her helped, and after a while, Steward felt he could sleep.

The satin sheets of his couch were cool to his naked body after the bath, and sleep soon did come, although it was restless. At some point, he half awoke, sensing a presence near him, but he saw nothing when he opened his eyes and was soon snoring again. He remembered dreaming of the Empress offering him a bowl of something delicious, something he was trying to eat. He discovered his mouth had extended itself outward from his face until it was at the end of a long, thin stalk. The mouth went easily and conveniently into the dish, but the thinness of its tube would not permit the passage of any satisfying quantity of the food, and all that came through were a few tantalizing drops of gravy. It was maddening. He seemed to have become all stomach, but he was prevented from feeding it by his inadequate mouth. Suddenly, he looked into the bowl and found it filled with live worms.

He was startled into full wakefulness by the dream's vividness. It was late afternoon. The heat was undiminished, and his mouth felt thick. At his bedside was a carafe of persimmon juice, chilled by ice from the mountains. It was delicious, and he drank down a cup of it, then half of another, and lay back to recapture his sleep.

Whisper watched him from behind a spy slit and calculated the approximate time. His activities had kept him from reporting to the Seventh Duke yet that day, and he now slipped out the way he had come, quietly removing the carafe of persimmon juice on his way.

Steward was shortly reawakened by a long scream rising from the enclosed courtyard below his windows. He groaned. His host's torturers were having sport with some poor wretch down in the courtyard. Another scream rose, became shrill, started to fade in a slow glissando, and then was renewed again, piercingly. There was no guessing how long it would last. Grimly, Steward reckoned the average duration of these events to be less than a half hour, but the strength of the screams promised endurance, and there was no telling. He pulled all the cushions within reach around his head to diminish the sound, but it only half worked. Feeling unable to breathe, he emerged and sat up just as a huge, amber pelican came waddling into his chamber from the porch, where it had landed. Its beak pouch sagged to the floor with the weight of a large fish, and as Steward watched, the bird stretched its neck upward, threw back its head, and tried to swallow the fish. It failed. A tremendous shriek from below seemed to inspire it to a renewed effort; gathering itself, the pelican made another gulp, this time working its throat muscles until the fish slid past and into the bird. It then squatted heavily and regarded Steward with a filmy eye while the sounds from the courtyard changed to a series of hideous burblings.

Abruptly, Steward vomited convulsively onto the floor, then sat bent forward with his head between his knees. The last sounds from outside must have indicated a mortal stroke of some kind, for merciful silence followed. After a few minutes, he began feeling somewhat less terrible and headed for the bath, on the way glimpsing himself in a tall mirror. He stopped to regard his reflection. For the first time, he saw his naked body as a disgusting thing, obese, with a stomach that made him resemble the creature of his bad dream. Caught in a space between thought, he experienced revulsion and was forced to regard himself eye to eye. The sun dipped below the nearby rooftops. He was aware of the movements of slaves entering the chamber, lighting lamps, freshening the bathwater, and cleaning the mess he'd left by his bed, but his stunned meditation was not interrupted until he was approached by a diffident squire asking him if he intended to take supper in his rooms.

"Nothing," said Steward, heading for the bath, "but I'll have my plain purple tunic laid out, if you please. It's the oldest one." While soaking, he removed the various rings from his fingers, all but the one he had been given by his father bearing the crest of their noble family and its motto: "In Nothingness Is All." He looked at it again for the first time in many years and was just able to see the incised characters in the fading twilight.

Emerging from the tub, he felt like a man who had survived a tree's falling on him, and he viewed the world with the eyes of a newborn child. He called for his writing kit and a lamp and, dipping his quill, commenced a letter to Mate:

> The gods willing, when you read this, I will be at sea, bound home. I am torn from you not by choice but by a turn of circumstances. I now know that if I return to Elysium as I intended, war will follow me as surely as my shadow. I know no language in which I can tell you of my sadness at this farewell.
>
> I leave you in an interesting position. By a warrant that now has the Imperial Seal on it, my actions as Elysium's Administrator are confirmed, including your appointment as my proxy. When you learn I have been kidnapped and taken away aboard *Alembic*, all power devolves upon yourself, to do with as you will. Since my departure will be held blameless, you'll likely be confirmed in the role. I doubt the Duke wants to return. If he does, you may choose to fight. If you do, you may say you are acting in my name if you wish. You'll have an in-

stant alliance with the highland lords in any quarrel with the Duke, and with highlanders at the passes, Elysium is safe. More to fear is treachery from within, but Alwilde will hear of it before it's even hatched, as you know. You have rare power.

Alternatively, you may take an honorable retirement to any one of the havens available to you. Some are far from Elysium. You will find attached your warrant to the Treasurer assigning you full disposal of my considerable personal holdings. It is my wish that they be divided equally between yourself, Zubaida, and Alwilde. With these resources, you all have your freedom to do as you will. I will yearn in future years to know how all of you are faring. If it is ever in my power, I vow to send a ship to trade with Elysium and make a communication between us again. Until then, and always, your devoted friend.

Steward fixed it with the seal of Elysium. Drawing a fresh sheet of parchment, he penned a similar message to Alwilda and, finally, to Zubaida, vowing to send a ship for her or return himself when *Alembic* had found the route. When finished, he summoned the Captain of his own company of mounted archers, a trusted and devoted officer who had escorted his caravan to the capital.

"With your life," he said, handing over the packet of letters to the young officer, "see these delivered safe in Elysium. Take the whole troop as escort. Saddle up as for a local errand. I'll meet you below. We'll depart here in company, but thence you're to Elysium by the fastest way you can devise."

There was a last note left to write, to his host. The first paragraph was devoted to a greeting in proper form. The second read:

Although I've been feeling poorly, I think a touch of sea air will restore me. Hence, I will sail today around the bay with my comrades by way of saying farewell to them, and nothing would give me greater pleasure than your joining us, should you care to. My Knights are threatening to kidnap me, I've learned, although I trust it's a joke. Anyway, if you're with us, they won't dare. I'll invite some others, too. Noon departure.

Liking the inspiration to invite the Duke for a sail at an hour when he hoped to be well at sea, he wrote out two similar invitations, all with the joke about his abduction, to spread the word further. When they were finished, he gave instructions for their delivery in the morning, donned a plain cloak, and departed without a backward glance.

Steward's third visit to his comrades' villa was far less conspicuous than the first two. This time, while still at a distance from the yacht basin, he sent his horse with his mounted escort and walked the rest of the way. His late-night knock at the door took all within by surprise.

"Who's there?" called Bosun.

"The fattest shipmate you've got," said Steward. "Open up." Then he was within, telling his friends of his decision to rejoin *Alembic* for the voyage home. "But," he said, "we leave now–that is, early in the morning. There's a fair wind out of the harbor, and we mustn't waste it."

"We've got no port clearances," said Flags.

"We can't afford to wait for 'em. We must sail. From the moment our intentions are known, we'll all be fugitives, and the consequences if we fail to get clear do not bear thinking about. You're taking me on a yachting sail, y'see, and kidnapping me." He explained the steps he had taken to protect friends who could be tainted by association when he gave such great offense as to leave unbidden. "All's attended. I'm done here, and *Alembic* had better be as ready for sea as you told me she was. How are provisions?" There was sufficient to last them to a distant archipelago where they could safely refit and revictual for another long passage to the Western Isles on their way home.

"It's straightforward enough once we're at sea," said Pilot, "but what's your plan for clearing this place? That war galley's been tied up close by *Alembic* since yesterday, and there's been unusual activity. We think we might be being watched."

Steward's plan had the advantage of great simplicity. During breakfast, they would stroll to *Alembic* in a leisurely way and begin to prepare her for a yachting sail with guests. Festive buntings would be run up, an awning would be rigged, her sail gaskets would be loosed, and she would be casually warped to the end of the quay. There, they would mention to anyone interested that they were going to check sails and rigging and return for the guests. "Then, you kidnap me, and we sail away," he concluded. "I hadn't reckoned on the galley, however."

"Leave the galley to me," said Bosun, "I've a plan for dealing with her."

"Then, what's left to do but load those?" asked Steward, pointing to the chests of gold.

"This is the only thing we couldn't load without drawing too much attention," Bosun explained. Steward looked at the chests and sighed.

"Ah, my friends, if I could only tell you what a tiny sum this was to me yesterday and how grateful I am to have a fifth part of it today." All agreed, for it was a great fortune.

"If they don't want to see us go," said Bosun, "they'll certainly not want to see *that* go, so we'd best take it aboard when the moon is down." Accordingly, the lamps were doused. An hour later, five dark and silent figures emerged, each bearing a chest to *Alembic*. When, after the third foray, the figures did not appear again, a black shadow detached itself from a mass of bushes and vanished in the direction of the Little Palace. This happened moments before Bosun reemerged and went back to the yacht harbor. (He returned a half hour later, wet.)

Sunrise found a yachting party emerging from the villa and straggling down to the wharf with baskets, as though for a picnic. This early in the day the grounds were empty, but the crew of the galley was moving around on her decks. As *Alembic*'s crew approached, they were met by the warship's Captain, followed by a detachment of marines with their officer.

"Here's trouble," said Bosun. "There are a lot more of them than there are of us."

"Be easy," said Steward, "and carry on with preparations. I'll deal with this."

"Order arms!" called the marine sergeant; pike butts descended smartly to the wharf's flagstones. The Captain bowed to Steward with a flourish and introduced himself.

"A most pleasant morning, Your Grace."

"Indeed," said Steward, "and greatly enhanced by the presence of yourself and your fine ship."

"Your Grace is too kind. I hope I will not be considered presumptuous in asking if your sailors are making preparations to depart?"

"Depart?" asked Steward with mild surprise. "Why, no, unless you mean depart for a trip around the bay with the Seventh Duke and my other guests this noon. It's for that event my men are preparing now. Why do you ask?"

"Alas, it is my duty, Your Grace. I've orders under Imperial Seal to detain any undocumented vessel from leaving the harbor, and I'm given to understand your men have no clearances."

Steward smiled. "Clearances for a yachting party with Royal guests? How amusing. I doubt that's what your orders meant, Captain."

The galley Captain's brow furrowed with a hint of uncertainty. "I . . . know nothing of a yachting party."

"No, I expect you would not get in a lot of yachting, being a professional, but it's great fun, I can assure you." Steward permitted his eye to drift to *Alembic,* where he saw gaskets being removed and halliard falls being cleared from their pins. "So many ropes, eh? Your ship, on the other hand, makes its own wind. How many sweeps does she pull?" he asked, starting a technical conversation regarding the merits of oar versus sail that occupied some time. When preparations were complete, Flags approached to announce they were ready to shift their vessel to the end of the dock, where lines and sails could be better checked, bows on to the breeze.

"Excellent," said Steward. "Perhaps the Captain here will let us borrow two or three of his marines to help warp around? Would that be asking too much of you, sir?" The plumed officer hesitated only for a moment. His orders to detain the foreign yacht were clear, but he had not anticipated the presence of the Administrator of Elysium. In any case, the yacht could not escape his fast warship, and he saw no harm in humoring its powerful owner. Within a few minutes, *Alembic* was being warped to her new position by the Imperial marines. Just as things were looking most promising, however, a rumble of hooves was heard, heralding the rapid approach of a half-troop of cavalry, black hussars, with none other than Whisper, the Count of Montressor, preceding the detachment with its sergeant.

"That ship goes nowhere!" cried the Count even before he had reined to a halt.

With his attention fixed on *Alembic* and her crew, he did not recognize the cloaked, hooded figure standing aside with the galley Captain. "That vessel's detained, and on it is stolen gold," he called, dismounting. "Sergeant, search the boat and arrest its crew."

"Hold fast, Montressor," said Steward, pulling the hood from his head.

"You?" Whisper's face went pale at the sight of a man who should have been on his deathbed. He caught himself. "Your Grace? Ah, good morning. I . . . had not expected to find you here."

"Apparently not. My men are preparing to take out a yachting party to which your master is invited. If you detain them, you detain us all. Whatever's in your mind?" Steward fixed him with a steely stare. Whisper was caught off guard by the situation as much as Steward, but he was a cool veteran at the unexpected.

"Your Grace, while I know nothing of any yachting party, you may count my arrival here lucky, for I've information that your crew has smuggled aboard that ship some fifteen thousand in gold, all that you've sent from Elysium. Unless *you're* planning to depart, Your Grace"–Whisper cocked an eye at him–"then we must conclude they're attempting to make off with it."

"Ah," said Steward, suddenly breaking into a smile. "Now, I see your alarm. Your trip's been unnecessary, however, for the money's been put aboard by my own orders for transportation by sea to Elysium. It was, of course, loaded by night, not to draw attention. I thank you for your concern, but I'm afraid you've just exposed our secret. It's no matter, however, for it's well enough guarded now, and I'm sure the Captain here will regard what he's heard as confidential, won't you, Captain?"

More than anyone, the galley Captain looked confused by the situation. "Your Grace, I've no orders regarding any gold," he said uneasily, "but it is irregular. In any case, my orders to detain this ship in harbor are firm." Bosun, Pilot, Flags, and Crew had come trotting to find out what the commotion was about, arriving just in time to hear the Captain's words.

"My instructions from the Seventh Duke are the same, Your Grace," said Whisper.

"Here's trouble," said Bosun in their own tongue.

Steward turned to him and responded in the Imperial language. "The duty of these officers is to detain *Alembic* from making any voyage until the ship has proper clearance, as is respectful, and those are my own orders, too, d'you understand?" Going along with whatever Steward was up to, they all nodded. "Good," he said, turning back to the officers with a smile. "Gentlemen, we're all in agreement. By the way, while I was lunching with the Empress yesterday, she promised *Alembic*'s papers would be put aboard her by tomorrow. I trust that will then serve to free my ship."

"When she's rightly documented, I've no warrant to hold her," said the Captain. "Until then . . . "

"Good," Steward interrupted him. "Now that we're in perfect agreement, perhaps we can get on with our preparations to take the Duke sailing. I believe my men wanted to shake out the sails first and make one or two adjustments. Right, men?" Steward's face brightened further. "Montressor, I've a splendid idea. You must come along with us! I'll show you around our ship. She really is the most marvelous little thing. You can see how her sails work. The Duke's not due until noon, and we've plenty of time." He held out his arm to sweep Whisper along with him toward *Alembic,* but Whisper did not sweep so easily.

"Your Grace, I was unaware of my master's intention to go yachting today. Perhaps he did not receive your invitation. I shall send word of this to him at once." So saying, he turned to dispatch a rider.

"We're caught," said Bosun, again in their own tongue. This time, Steward answered in kind. "So it seems, but there's another card to play. It's an expensive one, however. What if it costs us everything but our ship to get clear of this place? Are you for it? Or would you rather stay?"

"There's no price on freedom," said Bosun, feeling the claustrophobia of captivity closing around him. All agreed. When the messenger had galloped away, Whisper returned. "I should think the Duke will join us here shortly, Your Grace, although whether he'll wish to go sailing remains to be seen. Nor do I think he's aware of Your Grace's movement of such a sum of money."

This made Steward's eyebrows lift. "Gentlemen, it's easy to dispose of your concerns regarding my money." He turned to his comrades. "Let's have those money chests up here on the dock without delay. Between the marines and the hussars, I've no fear for its safety." Both the galley Captain and Whisper were startled by the bizarre tack events had taken, and before they could fathom it, the first of the chests was being swung down onto the dock. Steward bent and opened its lid, revealing its neatly stacked rolls of heavy gold pieces. Withdrawing one coin, he proffered it for his listeners to look at, as though they might be somehow suspicious of it. Both men recoiled from seeming so, and the Captain quickly closed the lid again as two more chests arrived.

"Your Grace, please forgive me, but such a thing left open's a temptation to all the world."

"Under your care, and with Montressor's cavalry, I'd say the temptations will be minimal. Come along, Montressor. We've never gotten to know each other. Welcome to my ship. I insist you come aboard. Not to accept would give me offense now." This time, Whisper had no choice but to be swept along. "She has two masts, you see," said Steward, gesticulating toward the rigging, bustling Whisper over the rail. Then, to his friends in their tongue: "Handle the last chest so it bursts open when you drop it on the dock; stand by to slip the lines at the same time. Then all aboard, lively."

"Aye aye," said Bosun.

"My apologies for speaking a language you cannot understand," he addressed the Count. "It is boat talk, you see. Oops, I believe they've dropped a box." He called out: "Captain, would you see that tidied up for me? I need my crew now. Come aboard, you men, and let's show the Count we know our ropes." Beset by distractions, the galley Captain gave orders to the dazzled troops. Their attention was transfixed on the fortune spilled at their feet. "We'll pick it up again a half hour hence!" called Steward as *Alembic* slowly drifted away from the wharf.

Whisper started for the rail with an alarmed look but was detained by Steward. "You'll find this most amusing, I assure you. We'll have made our preparations by the time the Duke arrives. It's only an evolution or two my men must do. I caution you, the space to the dock's too wide now, and I wouldn't try to jump it. Calm yourself. All's going well. Come and join me for a bit of refreshment while we watch them try the sails. Oh, dear, I'm afraid nobody's put out anything to sup on yet. Well, well. Let's not disturb the lads while they're setting that mainsail." Released from its brails, the big sail fell open, luffing.

"Jib halliards, heave," said Bosun. Under backed jib, the vessel fell away from the wind on a port tack and was then trimmed to a diagonal course to the harbor entrance, not directly toward it. Showing no undue signs of hurry, *Alembic*'s crew loosed the topsail and then the mizzen.

"Ah, how she leaps forward, eh, Montressor? See how far we've come in no time." That was exactly what an unsettled Whisper was looking at. The soldiers on the wharf were already beyond hailing range, and they were getting smaller by the moment. To his comrades, Steward said, "Let's gybe, and take the opposite diagonal for the entrance, as though we're doing evolutions. Every inch we can gain now, we'll need. We've got to get clear of the forts before any alarm's given. On the next leg, we'll be far enough from shore for you to subdue our passenger if you're neat about it. Now, we can leave a witness to my kidnapping, so don't hurt him any more than necessary." Reverting to the common language, Steward said, "I fear during my long absence they've become too independent-minded and need a bit of instruction. Well, I say give 'em their freedom, eh? I'm happy in Elysium, and they want to go home after I've left. Have you sailed before, Montressor? No? Ah, what a treat for you, then. See how well the craft does on this new tack. Look back along our wake–Whoops!"

Bosun felled Whisper from behind with a sharp rap from a belaying pin, and Pilot caught him, lowering his inert form into a sitting position and propping him there, a figure in semirepose. Bosun cautioned he would come around soon enough.

"Then I'd best go below," said Steward. "Tie him to something that floats, ready to chuck him over when we pass between the forts. You can lock *me* in the galley. Let me know when he comes round, and I'll yell and pound. Tell him you've kidnapped me. The charade's to protect my friends in Elysium."

Bosun was suddenly alerted to something else: "I believe the war galley's getting under way," he said, peering at the shore. Though now distant, the big ship could just be seen being thrust from the dock; out came her banks of oars churning the water, and simultaneously, one of her large lateen sails popped out, at once catching the wind. Within moments, the galley was charging through the water.

"I should think about . . . now," said Bosun, and a moment later, oars seemed to fly in all directions as the big ship took a sickening lurch. As they watched, its sail billowed and collapsed.

"That's his lot," said Bosun, who, the night before, had fastened a sufficient length of underwater rope between the wharf and the galley's rudder to tear it off if the ship had good way on when the bite came. That had happened, and Bosun had gotten a mast into the bargain. Shortly thereafter, the Count of Montressor obligingly regained consciousness, with a headache that did not prevent him from hearing the indignant bellowings and thumpings of the kidnapped Administrator of Elysium.

"We mean to fetch him home," said Flags, jerking his thumb toward the closed hatch, "for the reward his family will pay us, but we don't want you." With that, Flags and Bosun dropped Whisper over the side with a keg to keep him afloat while awaiting rescue; Steward's last glimpse of him was as the smaller of two diminishing black dots bobbing in their wake. The forts were behind them when they heard signal guns, and by the time the gunners could muster and fire a salvo, *Alembic* was out of range with a fair wind behind her.

Although they were safely away, there was little elation. All of them thought of the fortune on the dock, and Steward had left behind more than that. He brooded by the taffrail, staring back as the continent behind them grew hazy on the horizon. They left him to his solitude until the first watch change, when Flags said, "I reckon you've left some good friends behind?"

"Yes," he nodded. "I have. I'll tell you about them sometime."

"This morning when we arose," said Bosun, "we had fifteen thousand of your gold to call ours; now we've no piece of it left to justify the four years and more that we've been gone."

"Not true," said Steward. Digging in the deep pockets of his old purple tunic, he brought forth the coin he had held when the galley Captain had slammed the lid on the chest. Holding it now to the light, he examined both sides, one bearing a profile of the fat Empress, the other the Imperial symbol, a pelican with open beak. Steward closed his fingers on the coin, feeling its heft for a moment, and then threw it high in the air. It winked yellow at the peak of its arc and then made a tiny splash in their wake.

"Now, it's true," he said.

# IX  At the Western Isles

THE SUN HAD SWOLLEN as it dipped into the sea ahead, its gold modulating to orange and finally to crimson as its last remnant vanished into the horizon. An astonishing flash of pure turquoise marked its moment of surrender to the awakening fires of the night–a nascent moon, the stars, and a fall of meteors, space voyagers sparkling brightly in the last moments of their lives.

Flags basked in the sheer beauty of it as he held the helm. Feeling the thrust of the tiller against his hip, he intuitively anticipated the easy surge. A perfect quartering breeze blew, and the ship rose and fell, lifting her stern to each overtaking sea, riding for a moment the rush of its crest before settling into the trough as the wave hurried past with a long hiss and a sigh; then, the ship was picked up in turn by the next wave moving up astern, its velvet loom marked by the boiling phosphorescence of *Alembic*'s wake.

"Up and down, up and down, up and down–my life's story played to me in endless repetition, but ah, what a glorious theater we have tonight," Flags said to nobody in particular. It was just the kind of night sailors must remember as old men, he thought, when more turbulent memories faded. He wondered if he would remember this night into the infinite future of his own old age.

A warm glow of lamplight forward from the open galley scuttle reflected on the figures of Bosun and Crew, off watch, having a jar of grog with Steward, whose profile had lessened appreciably during the months since their escape from the Southern Continent. Pilot was pacing the deck, thinking whatever thoughts Pilot thought when he paced. For an instant, Flags had the vivid illusion that his figure was a hole in the sky; then, Pilot's path took him into the light from the galley, making him again visible. Flags felt infinitely secure with Pilot's pacing. He had brought them through island groups and archipelagos with consummate skill, finding remote ports of call in waters for which his charts were cursory at best. Flags had no idea how he had done it. Whatever the unfathomable mechanisms of Pilot's mind, he had now safely navigated *Alembic* to the last island group recorded on any of the Imperial charts. Somewhere ahead, they would seek a safe anchorage in which they could careen and refit a last time before tending again north through the treacherous, uncharted area between the Southern Ocean and the Northern.

A part of Flags was already home. To him, his meteoric career in the Imperial capital was the pinnacle of this voyage, for no sophisticated culture or civilization would be found in any port of call here. Indeed, there were no known ports at all. That was just as well, for *Alembic*'s money box was nearly depleted, leaving as their only assets the beads, knives, cloth, and trinkets remaining from the original cargo. Fortunately, these things were proving as useful in trade with the islanders as they had with the caribou people, so *Alembic*'s basic needs had been secured in the places they had touched. Flags was resigned to their returning home with little more than the glory of their accomplishment. The loss of the gold they had once taken for granted had been a hard blow, softened now by time and gales and new islands. They had wondered whether they might yet find any cargo to make the voyage profitable. Flags mused about what, if anything, desirable existed in this most remote of the world's backwaters. Then, he grinned to himself.

It would be very satisfactory to dally without complication with some savage maiden, perhaps an island orchid who would open by moonlight. He tried not to think of all the desirable–very desirable–women he had let pass during his disciplined three-year fidelity to one woman. Out of that, he had gotten nothing but disillusionment, and it was an experiment he did not contemplate repeating anytime soon. Ironically, all the women he had seen since escaping Hydrangea's tether had been grotesque creatures, with teeth stained reddish black from a nut they chewed and with pendulous breasts. Some had worn a bone in the lower lip, which pulled it down to the chin.

He glanced at the binnacle, found he had come off course by half a point, and gave the tiller just the touch needed to correct. Perhaps the Western Isles would offer better fare, an uncomplex creature from whom his departure would be less hectic. He had left the Imperial capital in the nick of time to avoid the inevitable consequences that his mere existence seemed always to generate. Flags could not understand how this embarrassing pattern could play again and again, although it seemed obvious that his own *desirability* (there was no other word) was somehow at the root. He accurately saw himself as a consummately amiable person who was intelligent, talented, physically beautiful–thrice-blessed by all the greater and lesser gods. Whence, then, this inevitable twist that made every situation something to be escaped? Why did it always happen?

Here came Pilot, pacing aft.

"Pilot, do you ever see things in terms of patterns?" Flags asked.

Pilot approached with a slight smile. "Patterns? Yes, since you ask. Why do you ask?"

Flags shrugged, not having formed his thoughts. "I don't know. I suppose from some feeling of being caught in one."

"Only one? You may be in luck. I feel caught in an infinity of them." Pilot made a sweeping gesture toward the sky. "Behold the stars and planets all making their grand patterns above while the waves beneath play others; then there are the patterns in and between the patterns. Are they all in some way synchronistic? The astrologers would have us believe that destiny can be read in the patterns of the heavens, and for the same purpose, the ancients disemboweled animals to read the patterns formed by their spilled entrails. I have seen an old woman casting bones to read the future from their patterns and then seen her predictions come true, making a mockery of all science. Do you remember the patterns of the Oracle's sticks? What patterns are these? Are they all interwoven in some curious way? Can such a thing as *one* pattern be distilled from them all? If so, perhaps you've found it, my friend." Pilot sighed and continued: "To me, the patterns seem harmonic *and* chaotic, in mind as in matter. Perhaps alchemy offers an explanation."

Flags did not understand what Pilot had said, but he liked it. He could put those words to rhyme. He had often borrowed Pilot's offhand profundities for his own poetry, thereby enriching it with a kind of cosmic touch despite–maybe because of–their obscurity. "What patterns *are* these?" he repeated in his mind; then, experimenting with the accented word: "What patterns are *these*?" With a sonorous delivery, it would be good. He almost said it aloud to Pilot and then checked himself. Although Pilot had shown unusual signs of warmth in the past year or so, Flags had been pricked too many times by his wry wit to be other than wary around him. From childhood days, Flags had seen Pilot as the only completely unseduceable person he knew. Though flinty, he did have a lively sense of humor that came out unexpectedly, never when Flags was trying to induce it. Nothing contrived worked with Pilot. And yet, even Pilot seemed bemused by the magic of this fantastic night. As one, the two silent opposites by the binnacle swayed together to the movement of the ship, watching the black silhouettes of the sails wheeling against the moon, listening to the long sighs of the waves.

"Now I've a question for *you*," Pilot said a while later, after Bosun had climbed to the crosstrees and Steward had gone below to clean the galley. "What do you think about when you're making love to a girl?"

The question was uncharacteristically personal for Pilot, and it caught Flags by surprise. He pondered it. "It depends somewhat upon the girl. They're, of course, so very different. But the thing I most think about while making love to a girl is the same thing that's always on my mind at any time I'm with her, if I'm awake, which is what I can do to please her. Any woman will reward that, I find. But it can be work."

"What reward do you take from it?" asked Pilot.

Flags shrugged. "Just that. Her love."

"To what end?"

"Ah, Pilot, you've gone straight for the heart of the matter. I have a greater talent for getting what I want than for knowing what to do with it after I've gotten it. Anyway, I have no better answer for your question than you had for mine earlier. Are you asking me this to stab me or on your own account?"

"Mine," said Pilot. "You see, I've no experience with anything having to do with girls, nor much predilection for affairs of the heart, and I know no better source to ask about it than you who have made a specialty of love. What is it? What does it feel like to you? How would you define it to one who's never felt it?"

Flags considered. "It's a warming thing, all around, but beyond that, it's indescribable even for a poet. I can't say how far it goes. The things I love are little and personal—the way this one tosses her mane like an angry horse or the way that one sings to herself or the way another laughs; all those things and many others I've loved, and maybe there's no greater love than the sum of those small parts. I don't know. I've sometimes had the feeling I've spent my whole life on love's surface, and there's a depth I haven't found. It's certain I've not met my true mate, nor do I know there is such a thing. Alas, for every quality I find to love in a woman, time invariably reveals something equal and opposite that's irritating."

Pilot laughed. "I've never experienced anything like that, and your description makes it sound even more confusing than I've been led to think. I thank you for it, however."

Flags was pleased to have gotten a laugh from Pilot. How fond he was of Pilot, and most particularly on this night. All of them. What a cast of characters his shipmates were. One by one on this voyage he had watched each driven to near insanity, each in his own way, and each in turn had come through apparently all the better for the experience. Flags had the distinct impression of having watched them all grow up—in fact, felt somewhat motherly toward them.

Like a punctuation mark to his thought, the unmistakable sound of Crew's laugh came loudly out of the open scuttle. Flags and Pilot smiled at each other. While Crew had discovered how to laugh, it happened rarely enough to be something of an event whenever it did. Bosun called down to them from the crosstrees: "Start the bugger laughing and you can't get him to stop. What did you say to him, Steward?" Steward's head appeared at once in the hatch.

"I told him the scuttlebutt, that the Dame Hydrangea never let Flags get away from her even one time in three years. Her leash was very, very short." Crew's head appeared next to him.

Crew was hiccuping with laughter. "You never . . . told any of us . . . that, Flags."

"No, I daresay he hasn't," said Steward, "but the sources for this scuttlebutt are reliable. Very, very reliable."

"Impossible," Bosun called down from the crosstrees. "No steel or leather could ever hold back our Flags in call, and I won't hear my brother reviled in this way."

"While technically possible," offered Pilot, reasonably, "the odds against restraining Flags are mathematically incalculable."

Hugely pleased by their attention, the object of all their humor gathered himself in dignity. "Ahem. Gentlemen. Since it pleases our cook to serve up this helping of scuttlebutt he's held in reserve until now, I'll affirm at least a part of it." Flags assumed a look of considerable modesty: "Brethren, I did indeed remain faithful to the Dame Hydrangea for the period of time you mention–"

"Impossible," said Bosun.

"Unlikely," agreed Pilot.

"You have my word on it," said Flags.

"By all that's holy, she *did* put the leash to him!" yelled Bosun as he slid down to the deck on a halliard. "And it's our fault for letting him out of our sight."

"She put the leash to him hard," agreed Steward with great sadness, "and a sorry thing to behold it was, so they say."

"Ah, but gentlemen, you are suffering the delusion that Hydrangea needed a leash." Flags's tone became more confidential. "And so she did. But my friends, it was *not* made of leather or steel." He paused, dropping his voice. "It was velvet. Velvet of the softest kind, I can assure you. Tickly velvet." His voice had become so low at the final words, Steward had to come up out of the galley and walk aft to hear what he was saying, and Crew was right behind him.

"So in the end, you may speak of my leash if you like to amuse your-selves with frivolous banter, but gentlemen, it was a leash I wouldn't mind having the feel of right now. Ahhh." He sighed blissfully, then abruptly changed the subject. "What else can we talk about?"

"Oh, no you don't," said Steward. "You got us, and now you're going to have to give us the story."

"I'm afraid that's impossible," Flags said, affecting indignation. "Why, in order to make you understand, I would have to tell you the most intimate details about the lady. I would have to describe the very taste of her lips, the sensation to my nose of her nether curls, and I would have to describe the undescribable fleshiness of the insides of her thighs, her breasts, her tricks with butterflies, brushes, and unbe-lievable lotions. These are no light matters. I would have to somehow take you into her character in depth, just as I have interviewed her, at full length. If I were to tell of these things, you would surely repeat them at some time or other, and if word ever got back, she would be dishonored by the gossip."

"Oh, come on, Flags," said Steward, seating himself on the hen coop. "You never talk about your women, and this one's far behind us. Let's hear the best you've got about the Dame. She *was* extraordi-narily beautiful."

Flags reflected for a moment on the real Hydrangea and decided to create a more composite creature for their fancy. "Beautiful? Yes. Her face you've seen, and the look of her in a gown, but it may surprise you to learn what she sometimes wore beneath that gown. . . ." As he spun them a story, he had more than ever the feeling of being a naughty Mother Goose telling her boys a bedtime tale. Keeping them easily spellbound long enough to be sure of having consigned them to several nights of randy dreams, Mother Flags was beginning to seek for a con-clusion to the fantasy when nature provided it. Facing forward, with the helm, he was the first to notice a red glow ahead, dim and distant in the darkness. As soon as he had seen it, the thing brightened, and then all beheld it. Something about it gave Flags a stir of uneasiness.

"Another volcano," said Pilot. Somewhere well over the horizon ahead, the earth was spewing forth some of her deep fires. Volcanoes were not unusual in these seas; several times, they had seen smoke plumes, always at a great distance, although *Alembic*'s course had taken them past a number of islands that had been cast up as molten debris. The entire area was volcanic.

"There's our end to the story," said Flags, "for my words are starting fires in the night. The one ahead lies on our course. What danger, Pilot?"

"It's very distant. Perhaps we'll find our island before we get that far. If not, we can give the thing a good offing. I doubt there's much danger unless one erupts right under you, and the odds of that happening seem remote."

All watched the phenomenon for a few minutes, until Steward rose, stretched, growled, and remarked, "Flags, I'd say you've had your revenge for my scuttlebutt and then some." He went back to finish the galley chores, and the audience dispersed.

Flags felt even more exhilarated than ever, watching the rubescent glow, seeing its complimentary color in the emerald churn of *Alembic*'s wake. He felt the warm trade wind on his neck. It really was quite the most glorious night. For the first time in years, he thought of a long-forgotten quatrain:

> Swiftly, swiftly flew the ship,
> Yet she sail'ed softly, too:
> Sweetly, sweetly blew the breeze–
> On me alone it blew.

As *Vessle* CAME IN through the gentle surf and nosed the sand, Flags, Crew, and Bosun jumped out, grabbed the gunwales of their little tender, and ran her onto the beach, up above the surf line, where her painter could be tied to a palm tree.

"That's our last load landed," said Crew, "and I want a coconut." Close off the beach, *Alembic* floated securely at anchor on the azure waters of the lagoon, now lightened of all empty casks, perishable stores, and personal gear wanted for a camp ashore.

"I'll join you," said Flags, beginning to browse the ground looking for fallen coconuts. Bosun's view was upward, at the bunches hanging high overhead. He had watched a native run up one of those trees using a simple bight of line, a trick he planned to learn, although there were sufficient fallen ones here. He was soon opening them with his cutlass. This he had strapped on three days earlier when *Alembic* had come sniffing into the lagoon to be approached by a whole fleet of pirogues with grass-mat sails. The only reason he still wore the cutlass now, however, was as a coconut-opener. The cheerful islanders had laughed with innocent delight at the ship's foreign presence, eagerly guiding them to this sheltered, deepwater anchorage across the lagoon from their village. Then, they had swarmed aboard–men, women, and children–with no invitation and little clothing, examining every feature of *Alembic* with childlike curiosity. Golden-skinned, black-haired girls had hung flower chains around their necks until their heads were nearly smothered in blossoms.

"Ahhhh," said Flags, taking a deep drink of coconut milk and lying back in the sand. Crew and Bosun flopped down next to him. Even Bosun had been thoroughly seduced by the earthly paradise they had found. All around rose the sheltering escarpments of an extinct volcano, leagues in circumference, lushly wooded. Above each craggy peak floated its own cloud, and everywhere were waterfalls and springs. Under the trees, there was a wonderful freshness, with none of the bloat or decay of the Southern Continent. The contrast was marked. Fallen palm fronds carpeted the forest floor, smothering extensive undergrowth so the cool breeze played between the trees. Steward had been delighted at the local fare. Fruits and vegetables grew wild; goats grazed the mountain meadows; small pigs ran through the woods; and great turtles deposited delicious eggs in the warm sands.

Also in marked contrast to the intrigues of the Empire was the natural hospitality of the islanders. Here, it was without artifice, imposing no restrictions and knowing none. On their first night ashore, *Alembic*'s crew had been treated to a feast. Festooned with flowers, they had eaten roast pig and pineapple with native bread, washing it down with cool-tasting coconut liquor, which soon had them dancing by torchlight to the drums and bamboo flutes. Afterward, all of them, even Pilot, had been captured by dark-haired girls who seemed to compete for their company. Pilot's brittle but determined efforts to dance caused a good deal of mirth, and when a lithe beauty in a grass skirt gyrated up to him and started bumping him playfully with her hip to put him into the motion, there was a good laugh all around. Later, she had led him off somewhere to make boom-boom, as it was called. So open were the seductions, and so good-humored, Flags could find no trace whatever here of any kind of sexual inhibition or jealousy.

The following morning, the five sailors began preparations to careen by moving ashore, into an unused grass-mat house facing the lagoon. This had one large room covered by coconut-frond thatching. When Flags managed to communicate the question as to who owned the place, the unmistakable answer from the villagers was nobody. The place was just there. The thatching required some minor attention, as did some holes in the floor and walls, but the repairs had been easy enough. They had slung their hammocks and set up housekeeping. Behind the structure was a spring from which to drink and to fill their water casks to keep them soaked and tight during the time they would remain there.

How long that was to be was an open question, Flags reflected with pleasure, digging his toes into the warm sand. With any luck, Bosun's customary restlessness to be on the move would be checked long enough for them all to enjoy the place. There would be the careening, which they would have to do by themselves this time. That could take weeks, and there was an infinity of other things to be done.

Steward would have to reprovision. Pilot had no idea how long it would take him to discover what he needed to know of the waters beyond here. He thought he would need to learn a bit of the language in order to obtain that information. At the thought of Pilot, Flags laughed. In fact, their navigator's absence at this moment was probably because of his "language lessons," as he referred to them—somewhat aloofly. His shipmates frequently reminded him that his language instructress was also his dance teacher, and they irreverently asked him about the other instructions he was receiving. Her name was Alea, and she gleefully joined in the onslaught on Pilot's besieged dignity. She seemed to be very fond of him, and Flags reckoned there would be no immediate pressure from Pilot for a departure. Nor would there be from Crew, nor Steward, who was always readier to stay ashore than put to sea, and who was loving the simplicity of Island life. He, too, had found a wahine (as the Island maids were called), whom he said reminded him a bit of the girl he had left behind in Elysium. No, Flags thought comfortably, there would be no hasty departure from here. Nor was there any need here to limit himself to only one flower at a time. He had asked for an orchid and found himself garlanded with them.

A smell of cooking wafted across the beach from the outdoor kitchen where Steward was brewing up a turtle stew. At the same time, Steward exercised the seignorial rights of the cook—to press into service the friends for whom he's cooking. "Come on, you lot. Crew, let's have some of those coconuts up here; Bosun, I need tubers and prickly pears from the hillside; Flags, how about fetching down a couple of buckets of spring water."

"When Royalty speaks . . . ," said Flags, getting to his feet. Lugging an empty breaker, he followed the small path they had beaten through the ferns and flowers for a few hundred feet to a deep, clear pool fed by a small waterfall. It was the lowest of several that bubbled down the steep hillside over a series of ledges. At the near edge of the pool, where the path intersected it, the water was still and mirrorlike. Flags paused to gaze with satisfaction at his own reflection against the backdrop of dark trees and bright flowers. Something moved, catching his eye, and then his breath was taken away by the mirrored vision of a goddess. Looking up, he found that the vision was real. Standing in the falls on a ledge above him was the most astonishingly beautiful girl he had ever seen in his life–except that description was inadequate. Completely inadequate. Under a crown of flowers, she regarded him. Flags realized he had let his mouth hang open and closed it with a snap. Collecting himself, he rendered her his most winning smile. Abruptly, she ran nimbly up the rocks, vanishing among the foliage. Flags was after her as fast as he could climb, which was not very fast, as it turned out, because he slipped several times on the rocks. By the time he arrived at the spot where she had stood, she was gone.

The next morning, *Alembic* was worked into a carefully selected moorage with deep water right up to the beach. There she was secured by warps and springs to trees; her heavy ballast pigs were laboriously swung up from the bilge one by one, loaded on a log float, and rafted to the nearby beach. A few islanders who had paddled over to their camp to watch cheerfully lent a hand for a while, but even so the job took the rest of the day, and it was warm work. Several times, Flags ignored the water butt on the beach to stroll to the spring, but his vision did not reappear.

The following morning began the actual process of careenage. With all her hatches and scuttles sealed, *Alembic* was slowly levered over onto her starboard side by means of a six-part tackle rigged between the mast doubling and the base of a palm tree. After much heaving, the mast was brought down sufficiently to lay the boat onto her beam ends, exposing her keel. This done, breaming and scraping began to clear her of the accumulated weed and barnacles. For the breaming, torches made from dried grass were lit and held against the hull; the flames loosened the coating of old pitch, tallow, sulfur, and lye, along with all the remaining weeds and barnacles. These were clustered most thickly in a belt around the waterline, but every inch below it had to be laboriously burned and scraped, and by the end of each workday, everybody was filmed with sweat, smoke, and dirt. After bathing in the lagoon, Flags always returned to the forest pool, finding nobody.

The side of the hull was eventually clean enough to pay with a fresh mixture of tree gum and lime, after which the boat was ready to be righted. *Alembic* floated again on an even keel. The islanders applauded, telling the sailors to join them in the village that evening for a celebration. The islanders celebrated just about anything, it seemed to the visitors, who were more than happy to join in. Again, there was a community meal, with most of the village's inhabitants on hand. Again, the meal was followed with music and dancing by torchlight.

Alea got Pilot up and prancing, like the rest of them–all but Flags. Ordinarily, he would have been first up. Girls were everywhere but not the one he sought. After a while, he allowed himself to be pulled to his feet by a wahine he had met previously. Then, a moment later, he saw his goddess. She was among a group of old women and younger girls, playing a game with the children and hopping around on one leg. It was unmistakably her. Moving to the edge of the torchlight, he dropped out of the dancing and stood nearby, watching her play with the children, at one with them, giggling, silly as an adolescent, although he reckoned she must be closer to his own age. There was something endearing about it.

After he had watched her for seemingly quite a long time, he finally caught her attention. Her eyes met his. He smiled. She smiled back, then returned to the game. Flags knew better than to linger, awaiting her pleasure. The counterploy was to leave, so he returned to his comrades. He found Pilot panting but happy from his recent exertions, lying with his head in Alea's lap. Pilot was so far the only one of them to have learned enough of the language to be able to phrase Flags's question about the girl. He pointed her out to Alea, who knew her at once.

"Her name is Dakine," Pilot translated, pronouncing it "Dah-kee-nee." Alea made a gesture to her head and momentarily crossed her eyes. "She says the girl's simple in her head," Pilot added.

Flags was stunned. A disabled mind had no part in his vision, nor could he believe of it. He sipped at his coconut liquor, watching Dakine until he saw her leave the gathering and walk away down a moonlit path toward the water. Unhesitatingly, he followed, catching up with her where the path opened onto the beach. Hearing his approach, she stopped and regarded him. The moon was behind her, over the water, and he could not see her face in the darkness, but she had the same dignity of bearing that had captured him at the waterfall. How could it belong to someone deranged? He reached out with his hand toward her almost without willing it.

She took it, gave it a jerk, and pulled him along with her across the beach and into the sea, with hardly a pause to drop her grass skirt onto the sand before pulling Flags into the water, fully clothed, behind her. The next thing he knew, she had him standing in chest-deep water and was embracing him, nakedly, deliciously, frustratingly. How could he get out of his clothes without breaking their embrace? He was wondering this when a surf rose up and gave him a head-over-heels tumble. By the time he regained his footing, Dakine had retrieved her skirt and was running back into the trees. He followed her, but she was gone.

"How did you get all wet?" asked Crew, when Flags rejoined his comrades a few minutes later. Alea again touched her finger to her head with the cross-eyed look.

The following morning, *Alembic*'s position was changed end-for-end, so the whole breaming and scraping process could be repeated to her port side. The work went slowly, partly because everybody was feeling an aftermath of the night before and partly because they could not communicate answers to the islanders' questions.

"Why do you work so hard?" and, "What is your hurry?" they were asked.

The questions took time to be understood and more time to try to answer. Flags tried, and Bosun and Pilot were seduced into this genial distraction, while Steward abandoned the job completely in favor of a nap in the shade. When Dakine unexpectedly appeared in a pirogue with two small children, Crew was the last breamer still working.

Flags saw Dakine at once, and before his visitor had dragged her canoe out of the surf line, he was there to help her with it. That done, the children ran over to watch Crew applying the flaming torches to the strange boat. Flags stood smiling at her. How could this magnificent creature be a simpleton? Feeling suddenly self-conscious just to be standing there, he reached out to her as he had the night before. At the same instant, she turned to pick something from the canoe, and he found himself reaching into thin air; when she turned to face him again, his hand stuck out, awkward and empty, so she put a guava fruit in it. Taking another guava for herself, Dakine plumped down into the sand, keeping an eye on the children. Flags sat down next to her.

He could not learn from her by sign language whose children she had brought, but it was easy to establish they were not her own. He struggled with other questions having to do with her age, where she lived, who was in her family, and such like, until the difficulty of getting anything across began to make him feel dazed. She seemed distracted and not much interested in working at communication. After a while, he gave it up. With a deep sigh, he lay back, his elbows in the sand. The moment he did this, Dakine turned and smiled at him.

Next, the children were back again, and for the next hour, Dakine directed the burial of Flags under a mountain of sand, until only his head stuck out. Then she left, forcing him to come bursting out of his mound in order to help her drag her canoe back into the water. She said something to him that he could not understand, gave him a wave, and went paddling off.

That evening at supper, he had more questions for Alea, who had moved in with Pilot. "Ask her why she said Dakine's not right in the head. What did she mean?"

Flags by now had enough words in the islanders' tongue to need no translation for the short answer: "She is crazy."

Through Pilot, Alea was able to elaborate. According to her, Dakine's craziness was well-known. She had been deranged by the tragic death of both her parents when she was a small child. After that, she spoke to no one for years and continued to play with the small children while her peers grew up. She was thought to have become permanently mute until, one day in her twelfth year, she had unexpectedly opened her mouth and announced in a clear voice that she was a daughter of the Sun God and was there to help them all. It had not occurred to the islanders that they needed any help, so most agreed she was still crazy even though she could talk again.

When, shortly thereafter, she bloomed into her legendary beauty, men had voyaged from other islands just to behold her. Some fell immediately in love with her whatever her problems, but her lack of interest in uninvited suitors eventually drove them all away, reinforcing convictions that she was a half-wit. She was seldom away from the very old and very young people whose company she seemed to prefer. She looked after any number of them, living with this family or that, wherever she seemed most wanted. In this way, she had indeed become very helpful to a great many people on the island.

"But she is quite mad," Alea concluded. "You will find out if you become one of her suitors." Flags resolved to make no judgment about Dakine's wits until he could learn enough of her language to talk to her.

Dakine arrived in her canoe again the next day, bringing as passenger an ancient woman, wrinkled like a prune, who was delighted to be lifted out of the boat by Flags. After a while, when Dakine seemed to be more interested in explaining to her aged companion what the men were doing to the boat, Flags left them and returned to work. He hoped she might approach him, but she did not, and later, when he saw them preparing to depart, he lifted the old lady back into the canoe and waved good-bye.

These were the first of a succession of daily visits by Dakine to the work site, always with elderly or very young companions. Sometimes, she helped Flags in learning words, but she showed no great interest in language exercises. Since she seemed to prefer silence, he obliged her, taking his language lessons from others and watching for things that might amuse her. His greatest success occurred by accident one day when he pointed out to her a cloud in the distinct shape of a seated man with upright phallus. She laughed with apparent delight and called it to the attention of the two grandmothers who were her wards for the afternoon.

Flags began to feel desperate. Surely, Dakine must remember their moonlit kiss? He patiently watched for an opening that might take things back in that direction. At the same time, he resolved he would not be the one to take advantage of any girl whose wits were scrambled. To be sure, she was childish, but so delightfully, and her eyes seemed to miss nothing . . . except himself.

"Why do you come to see me?" he asked her one day, exercising his increasing vocabulary. The question came out after he had sat with her during so long a silence he couldn't be sure she remembered he was there. The gist of her answer seemed, disappointingly, to be that their new boatworks and all of their activity were so entertaining to her various wards. He reluctantly had to concede that there was something wrong with her, or so it seemed, and he considered dropping her, but it was disconcerting not having her to drop. He resolved to take up again with some other wahine, but he did not, and when the long job on *Alembic*'s hull was done and the ballast was being restored, he was troubled at the thought of life without her visits.

"Will you still come to see me after this work is finished?" he asked her.

"Why?" she asked. The same response from any other woman he had ever known would have been an artifice, but with Dakine, he was unsure. Her eyes were huge and clear.

"To see me," he smiled.

"But I *do* see you," she said.

"May *I* come to see *you,* then?" he asked, plunging down the risky trail of a suitor.

"You see me now," she said.

"I would like to be with you again . . . more."

"I have many people to care for," she said, drawing squiggles in the sand with her toe.

"Do you have room for one more?" Flags asked, as compellingly as he could. She regarded him at length, then shrugged, and walked away as though she had forgotten him. Almost as an afterthought, she stopped and turned. "Very well. Since you ask," she said, then departed. Irritating as it was, Flags did see an ironical humor in it. Simply put, he, Flags, the sophisticated lover, darling of three civilizations, had found his greatest challenge in a creature who was imbecilic even by primitive standards. He took the more comforting view–that all this was a mere exercise in passing, his attempt to help a creature to whom his heart went out in compassion. Given an opportunity, he thought he might be able to penetrate her child mind enough to help her a bit during the time he had to spend there. He wished that he could visit her as she visited him, but she lived with different families, an awkward situation. He reminded himself to be patient, and his patience was rewarded.

As good as her word, Dakine did return after the boatworks' closure, and on the day after *Alembic* was refloated, he saw her approaching in her canoe, apparently alone. He waded into the water to meet her and looked inside the pirogue to see if there were any children hiding in it.

"You have nobody to look after today?"

"I have *you* to look after now, for a little while. Since you need special attention," she added. He did, indeed. He suggested showing her the boat, and she was delighted with *Alembic*'s wonders. She rang the ship's bell, was fascinated with Pilot's sand glasses, and then wanted to climb to the masthead. When they descended, he showed her their cabin below, where she immediately scrambled into his bunk, stretched out deliciously, and closed her eyes. Then she was up and away, full of questions about everything until she left.

The same pattern of visits replayed itself every day for another week. Dakine's canoe would appear in midafternoon, then they would have an hour or two together. She gave him lessons in paddling a pirogue and took him rock-fish spearing on the reef; Flags rigged a spare halliard from an overhanging tree to make a long swing out over the lagoon, dropping its rider into the water with a splash at the end of its arc. Dakine swam and played naked with no trace of self-consciousness. He tried to do the same, although it frequently happened that he had to stay in the water longer than she did, lest his body betray his state of mind before he wanted it revealed. Once or twice, he had made a game of pursuing her in the water, but she swam like a fish, and he soon gave it up. At all costs, he wanted to avoid any appearance of pursuit.

One day, she took him to the site of an ancient battle in which the islanders had, after ages of warfare, conclusively defeated their legendary enemies the Lizard Men. The site was on a high plateau, covered with crimson flowers.

"These are the blood flowers," she explained. "Because true warriors are gods, whenever one dies, the blood flower always grows in that spot. You cannot kill the flower even if you put a rock on top of it, because when the rock is worn away, the flower will grow again." In the field of the fallen warriors, Flags learned that the Islands had known no real wars since that one, except for the Wars of Pigs, so-called because the only disputes that had arisen since olden times had to do with the ownership of pigs. Dakine described in great detail the feathered helmets and capes the warriors would don for the ceremonial warfare.

"They are so beautiful in all their feathers, and they are such wonderful big men. Very big men," she said, comically taking a warrior stance, and pretending to hold a huge phallus in her hand. "Then, they dance around each other like this," she went on, doing an imitation of two men with war clubs circling each other. "Then, one of them will land a blow"–she went through these motions–"and then, the battle is over. Afterward, there is a big feast to celebrate that this has happened, and the pig is roasted for it, and everybody eats it."

As they walked down from the mountain, he took her hand in his. "Are there not wars over women?" Flags asked.

Dakine looked surprised at the question. "Why would there be?"

"*I* would fight for *you*," said Flags, "but not for a pig, I think."

Dakine was tremendously amused, telling him he had it backward. "If you must fight, isn't it more sensible to do it for something you can own?" she asked.

Flags pondered this as Dakine led him on a trail to a clear pool, naturally heated by the earth's deep fires, and they stopped to bathe. "Patience," Flags cautioned himself. After they had both lolled in the hot water at opposite sides of the pool, Dakine emerged and stood at its edge, arching, stretching her limbs.

"You are a goddess," he said to her.

"Yes," she replied offhandedly, wringing the water out of her hair.

"The first time I saw you, I thought you were a goddess," he said truthfully, "but I don't yet know what kind. Are you a goddess of love?"

"Only as a means. First, I am a messenger goddess sent by my father the Sun to bring the truth of the gods to my people. And maybe to you, since you are here. We shall see." Flags was reminded of her delusions; all was as Alea had said. And yet, she did look every inch a goddess, standing there, condescending to him as though *he* were the retarded child.

"If you are its bringer, truth must be a very popular thing here," he said.

"Oh, no. Most people prefer make-believe to truth." The ends of her long hair just grazed the dimples over her buttocks as she swished it back and forth. "Sometimes, I have to be very patient with my children. Like with you," she said, turning to face him.

"You treat me as you would treat a child," observed Flags.

Dakine giggled. "You treat *me* as you would treat a child," she said.

Ah, by the gods, this was getting unbearable, Flags thought. In her simpleness, she obviously did not know the effect she was having on him. Or maybe she did.

He saw the sparkle of the droplets on her body, and his endurance broke. "I, too, am a messenger of truth," he said, striding out of the water.

She laughed, clapping her hands in applause. "Yes," she said pointing, "there is a big hard truth right there! Do you think I can stand so much truth all at once?" She reclined and beckoned him. "Come and let us find out."

A ND SO, FLAGS fell in love. Beyond in love. Love on a level he had never suspected. Love that held for him a profound sense of responsibility for his role in what was, after all, the seduction of a girl whose mind had been arrested in its childhood. On the other hand, he felt his actions were justified by his love for her and by his determination to be true and kind to her for the rest of the time they would have together. He was determined to do what he could to awaken her intelligence while delighting in the rest of her.

The latter was easier than the former, as it turned out. Although her daily visits continued, Flags could not induce her to spend the night with him because of the obligation she felt toward her various wards, and his time with her seemed far too limited. Most of it seemed given to lovemaking. That she enjoyed this as much as he did he ascribed to his considerable expertise.

"Do you remember when we first embraced?" he asked her one day during a moment of rest. She nodded. "Why did you wait so long to come to me again?" he asked her.

"I came to you every day, and you wanted to play children. So since I was giving you special attention, I humored you. Now you're *really* getting special attention."

Only one thing troubled him. While she had given him her body, he felt she had not yet learned to surrender her mind, and he felt he must have that in order to help her. Cute as her delusionary role of child-goddess was, he felt he had indulged her enough in that regard. He would be gentle about it, of course, but he determined to humor her fantasies no more, even if it meant no physical lovemaking for a visit or two. He reckoned that if he could talk some sense into her, that would be the greatest gift he could leave her. He even found himself toying with the idea of taking her home with him, or at least considering it, depending on what progress she made. He resolved to start on the following day.

To his surprise, however, the usual time for her visit came and went with no sign of Dakine's pirogue on the lagoon, leaving him with an unwanted emptiness. He passed the time by helping Bosun move his personal things back aboard *Alembic,* where he was establishing residency with his newly acquired full-time wahine, a strong girl and a good worker, like himself. The house had become overly crowded, with Pilot living with Alea in a section they had partitioned with grass mats hung from the rafters. Another wahine had attached herself to Crew, and Steward had two live-in kitchen helpers. With all of the goings and comings of the girls and their cheerful relatives, there was a great bustle around the place that only added to Flags's restlessness. He found Pilot getting an advanced language lesson from Alea.

*"Oooo, ow, ouw, oh, ooh, wow; wi, wee, whee, ee,"* Pilot was saying

when Flags found him. "Oh, hullo, Flags. Do you realize this language contains well over a hundred vowels but only twenty consonants? Listen to these: *y, ey, eye, ye, ee, yeh, uyu, yueee, uyuyueeoa.* If you say the last one right, it's only one sound. Where's Dakine?" Flags shrugged and changed the subject, asking Pilot what he had learned so far about the waters to the north.

"Nothing yet," said Pilot, "but by tomorrow or the next day, perhaps I'll be judged handy enough with the language to talk to the old navigators. Right, Alea?"

"Yes," she said, "but you must say *uyueeoah,* not *oyueeoa,* if you want to be understood. Flags says it better than you do. Now try."

"*Uyueeoah,*" said Pilot, obediently.

Wandering elsewhere, Flags found Steward on the porch, showing one of his two helpers how to peel the last of *Alembic*'s potatoes, while the other one pounded breadfruit. Nearby, Crew was tending his own new girlfriend's older child as the mother nursed the other.

"Very domestic," was Flags's comment.

"What more could a man ever ask?" asked Steward with an expansive gesture. "Babies, coconuts, good company, and nobody owning any of it. Where's Dakine?"

"I don't follow her around," said Flags.

Nor did she come the next day, which left him doubly agitated—first, at her continued absence; second, at his own agitation. He wasn't used to it and did not like it. What had become of her? Was she looking after someone ill? Could she be ill herself? He resolved that if she did not come on the following day, he would go the village and find her. After supper, however, he changed his mind and decided to see if he could locate Dakine that very evening. Perhaps someplace might be found where they could spend the night together in the village. Borrowing Alea's pirogue, he set sail for the other side of the lagoon.

Flags managed to find the family with which Dakine had most recently been staying, but from them, he learned she had gone to a place near the next village. He also learned it could be reached in an hour's walk over an easy path. Finding the grassy route well lit by the full moon, he started out. It felt wonderful to be taking some initiative for a change, and it was a perfect night. As he walked, he weighed the pros and cons of actually taking Dakine home with him. When the thought had first come to him, it had seemed far-fetched, but lately, it seemed distinctly less so. Room could be found for her on *Alembic;* they could create a space in the cargo hold where they could sling a hammock for two. Dakine could help in the galley. Steward was always glad for help. Once he got her back home, there would be so much to teach her, but the idea of taking on the mentor's role with her seemed delightful. And his mother would help. It would be great fun dressing her properly. He smiled at the thought of the effect she would create at any, *any,* social gathering at home. Of course, so much depended upon her ability to understand the things he had yet to teach her.

His destination had been described to him as the first grouping of houses he would find on the trail. He found them easily, with their thatched roofs reflecting geometric patterns of moonlight among the trees. He saw nobody about, although the throaty sound of a lone bamboo flute drifted over the compound. Approaching, he saw in two or three windows the dull reflection of low-burning lamps, but he could see no figures inside. He stood undecided as to how to proceed. He knew nothing about the people who lived here. Were they abed for the night? No, there was the flute. In which of the low grass houses was Dakine? Was this the right place at all? Seeing the momentary movement of a shadow in the structure farthest removed, Flags went toward the window in which it had appeared. As he drew nearer, it seemed the music was coming from there. Also, a girl's laugh. Dakine's? He edged up to the large window and gazed into the room.

Thoroughly adjusted to darkness, his eyes fell directly on the lamp, then needed a moment to adjust. The first figure he saw was that of the flute player, a naked man seated on a mat by the light, swaying to the music and to the beat of—he heard the rhythmic sounds of lovemaking at the same time he saw shadowy movements at the edge of the lamplight only a few feet away.

He saw the shape of a broad back tightly embraced by a pair of legs, unquestionably female. His heart constricted at the momentary illusion that the legs were Dakine's, but he quickly rejected that notion. The flautist increased the tempo and the drive of the music. Before Flags's fascinated gaze, muscles tensed, and the rockings quickened.

He couldn't help but smile. What an amazing thing to behold, he thought; how extraordinarily erotic. With sighs and gasps and a final convulsion, the movements ceased. The legs lowered themselves. So did the man's head, so that his partner's face was for the first time visible to the voyeur's gaze. Flags's heart went back to where it had been before and beyond. The girl *was* Dakine. Galvanized, he was unable to flee or attack. A moment, later Dakine opened her eyes and looked directly at him. She smiled, extending her arm toward him, and made a beckoning motion with her fingers.

Flags fled. Later, he remembered little of his headlong escape from that place, except for crashing hard into a tree on his way back toward the road. Somehow, he arrived back at the village, got into Alea's canoe, and paddled for home. He did recollect letting the canoe drift for a while in the middle of the darkened waters of the lagoon as he howled at the night sky like a stricken animal.

The next morning found him haggard. It went without saying that he was finished with Dakine. Obviously, her wits were more scrambled than he had realized. While it had been apparent from the first that she was no virgin, he had assumed that was because she had been taken advantage of by some lover. But now, who could know what legions she was entertaining? Who could have guessed how vulnerable she was to her own lusts? How could he ever have given his love to such a wanton creature?

When the sun rose out of the eastern sea, he resolved to make this the first day of a more sane existence. How he had been dazzled! He rose, went down the beach, and bathed, feeling better for it and for his new direction, away from her. Free again, he put her from his mind once and for all, went back to the house, and began making up breakfast for the household, something he had never before done. He wondered if Dakine would come at her usual time that afternoon. Probably not, he thought, but in case she did, he did not want to be anywhere around. He considered other places to be and other things to do.

But somehow, he was on the beach where she customarily landed, and he was racked by a wave of conflicting emotions when he saw her pirogue heading toward him across the lagoon. He prepared for her penitence, but she waved to him cheerfully, then laughed as she beached her boat. He stood facing her grimly. This was not something she was going to charm her way out of. It was good-bye. To say farewell was his sole reason for being there.

"You are amused," he stated, woodenly, causing her to double over laughing as she stepped out of the canoe.

Then she went quite rigid, assuming his own posture, and glowered back at him with a perfect imitation of himself. "You look like a post that's trying to have a baby," she told him.

"Last night," he said. Nothing else.

"Yes, how did you find me, and what made you run away?" she asked, with every appearance of innocence.

He blinked. Even allowing for the islanders' promiscuity, surely she must see that this was too much. "You were in the arms of a lover. And there was the flute player. Was he another lover?" he asked, acidly.

"Yes, of course," said Dakine, puzzled at his ill humor. "They are both musicians. They were taking turns making music. We were having a wonderful time, and you would have liked them. Didn't you have a nice time watching us make boom-boom?"

"Watching?" Flags could hardly believe this.

"Yes. What you saw. Did it not make you want to make boom-boom, too? I would like to have watched him with me. I am very pretty. He is very handsome. It must have been fun to watch, but then you ran away." Flags felt every thought in his head collide with some equal and opposite thought, all simultaneously; at the same time, he felt inexplicably excited. He was speechless. "Do you want me to go away?" she asked him.

"No," he heard himself say, "but *no* more lovers. I can't stand your making boom-boom with somebody else." He wanted to say he would forgive her if she would promise that—but there was no Island word for *forgive*, nor for *jealous*. "I want you for myself," he said lamely.

"I think you must want a pig, then," said Dakine, regarding him seriously.

"I . . . love you," he said to her for the first time, reaching toward her.

She took his hand. "That's good," she said, "because I don't know if it would be possible to teach you anything at all if you did not. You need so much more special attention than anybody, my word. Very well. Since you ask it, I will not make boom-boom with anybody but you for a little while, and we will see how that works. Do you want to make boom-boom now?" she asked brightly.

So Dakine was forgiven on the grounds that she did not understand the seriousness of her promiscuity but was willing to curtail it. When, sometime later, they returned to the canoe, Flags impulsively gave her his ruby ring. After admiring its red brilliance this way and that in the light, she withdrew from the bottom of the boat the small basket that contained all of her worldly possessions. Adding the ring to its jumbled contents, she rummaged until she found a return gift to give him. This was a pink pearl.

Thereafter, her visits continued in an unbroken succession of idyllic encounters. Realizing that her education would have to be a long-term thing, Flags largely let it go and allowed himself to enjoy her as she was, including her fantasies.

"Are you the only goddess on the Island?" he asked her one day.

"I don't know," she said with a shrug. "Maybe there are others of different kinds, ones who either do not know it or do not say. I did not know I was one until I was nearly twelve."

"How can you be a goddess and not know *everything*?" he asked.

"I will explain," she said. "A long time ago, and ever after, the gods–maybe being bored with being gods and the holders of all truth–decided to amuse themselves with a game. They took crumbs from themselves and made them into islanders. At the same time, it was amusing to make the islanders forget the truth. It was done by first of all making the illusion of a seductive place to live, so the islanders could look around and say, '*I* am standing here looking at *that* coconut tree.' So right away, the islanders forgot they *were* the coconut tree, too, and there were all kinds of other things to be separate from as well. They were all illusions, but they seemed so real. Then, it was noticed that some of the coconut trees were better than other ones. Some were so runty they did not even grow coconuts, so the islanders began to see the trees as good ones or bad ones. Well, of course, everybody then had a lot of names to make up and other things to think about, like who had the best trees and why. Things like that. Well, by then, the islanders' minds were so busy with their thoughts, and their illusions were so dense, they had become *completely* confused and forgot that it was all just a big joke they were playing on themselves anyway. And that was the game."

"What was that?" asked Flags. Something she said had caught him even though he could make no sense of it.

"The game is for the islanders to remember they *are* the gods and not whatever they made up along with coconut trees. There are different kinds of messengers. I am a girl one. That is my work. Do you understand?"

"I perceive your girlness," he said, "and that you are a goddess, and that we belong together, you and I."

"Are we not together now?" she asked. "What does it mean, this *belong*?"

"It means"–he nuzzled the nape of her neck and began to stroke her–"that you are mine, and I am yours, and together we are in paradise." And so they were, it seemed, as the last of the ship's refit went reluctantly forward.

Steward and the others took an immediate interest in Dakine's pearl when Flags showed it to them, for if they could trade for pearls here, they might yet justify their voyage commercially. Steward asked to borrow the pearl to show people what they were looking for, but Flags would not let it leave him. For him, paradise would not be completely gained until he could induce Dakine to live with him, pending which he wanted whatever fragment of her he could carry. Repeatedly, he had asked her to move in with him, always being refused.

"Why not?" he asked her at first.

"There are no *whys* for the gods," she said, apparently feeling that it was the core definition of deity. "If you need a reason, it's that my children and old people need me more than you do at night. But you should learn, as long as you have the 'whys,' you'll never be a god."

"Why not?" he teased.

"Yes. Why, why not. They are the same. Maybe you will learn something yet if you continue to listen," she said, rapping him on the head with a bunch of flowers.

"If it were not for your wards, would you come and live with me?"
Dakine gave him a stern look and began flogging him with the flowers. "First 'whys' and now 'ifs.' Illusions! No 'whys,' no 'ifs.'" A rain of petals settled on his hair and shoulders.

He was reminded of a dream in which Dakine was laughing at him from behind a translucent but unbreachable wall as he stood helplessly before it, waving a sword. Behind him was an army with siege engines, but no force could win those battlements under Dakine's rules of engagement. Yet she was always sneaking out like a raiding party to play some prank on him when he wasn't looking. She loved to catch him with a surprise splash of cold spring water whenever she could or put land crabs into his bedding or hand him a morsel of food containing a secret hot pepper.

In another dream, she appeared to him with reddened skin, wearing unusual garments and a necklace of tiny skulls with others hanging from her waistband; she did a wrathful dance before him, thrusting at him from time to time with a spear she carried in one hand and swinging at him with a vicious-looking hooked knife that she carried in the other. Her unpredictable thrusts and slashes were ever so playful, but it seemed to him any one of them could have killed him, and he had awakened in a sweat. He had many other dreams about her, including some that were so erotic as to arouse him in his sleep even though he had exhausted himself with her only hours earlier. Her lovemaking was endlessly playful and spontaneous, at last making him see his own performance as a mere repertory of memorized tricks.

He realized he was beyond in love with her. Only now did he see that everything he had ever called love previously paled before the awesome reality of the thing itself. A well and truly smitten Flags was something his comrades had never seen before. Between Dakine's visits, he sat with them as of old, but sometimes, they had only his corporeal self.

"Has anybody seen Flags lately?" asked Pilot one evening at supper. Flags was seated right with them but staring at some distant point in the cosmos.

"He was here earlier," remarked Steward, looking around.

Even Crew fell in with it. "He's not under the table," he said, looking there.

Not until the subject of a sailing date for *Alembic* arose could they capture his attention, and then he spoke against it. "What's our hurry?" he wanted to know, pointing out their success at trading the remaining cargo for pearls. "We have Dakine to thank for putting us on to that," he added.

"We've got all the pearls that were on hand here," said Bosun, "and it's a slow process, diving for more. Besides, we've run out of things to trade. I grant it's pleasant enough here, but what more can we accomplish by staying? *Alembic* will soon be starting to foul, and who wants to careen again?" Bosun's points were compelling, all agreed, even Steward, who was also reluctant to leave. Pilot was of Bosun's view, making the point that the winds would favor them only if they left soon, before the typhoon season.

"There's nothing more to be learned on this or any neighboring island about the waters we must cross. The islanders quite simply don't voyage north. They say it's dangerous. It will be less dangerous if we've a fair wind for our attack on it. I love it here as much as any of you, but we've done what we came here to do . . . and more," he added a bit wistfully. "But to remain longer is off our purpose, indulgent, and dangerous."

"Indulgent," Steward repeated. "Ye gods, everything that's good carries indulgence like rot spore in living wood." He sighed. "You're right, Pilot, as usual."

"Well, let's go home, then," said Crew, who shared all their views and who had recently gotten more experience in caring for very small infants than he had bargained for. All looked at Flags, who sat with his head in his hands, more eloquent in silence than in anything he could say. In fact, there was nothing he could say, for he realized too well that his shipmates were right and certainly unshakable in their resolve. They had never seen him look so miserable.

"Bring Dakine along," said Steward. "She'll make a useful sixth hand. If she wants to come," he added. Flags shook his head.

"That's the rub. She doesn't. She's not coming. Believe me, I've done everything I can to persuade her." They believed him, and they were sad for his anguish, but it was obviously time to start loading the water butts, casking the salt pork, and preparing the ship.

The initial decision was to leave for home in three days, when most of the village would pack up anyway and sail for a neighboring island, where a great annual gathering and feast were to be held. When the plan was put to Alea and the other wahines of the household, however, the sailors were persuaded to sail in company with the pirogues to the feast, there to make a celebration of their good-byes. It would take them only a day's sail off their course.

"Are you not happy to be sailing home?" asked Dakine when Flags told her of *Alembic*'s planned departure.

"Not without you," he said. "If you'll come with me, I'll love you forever, and with all my heart I promise you."

"You are going to do that anyway," she said.

"You would like my friends at home, and they would adore you."

"Your friends would say you have taken up with a crazy girl. They even say it here."

"Then they'd have to say the same about me, because whatever your craziness is, I've caught it." He brooded for a moment. "I can't bear the thought of leaving you. If I stay, will you promise–"

"No ifs and no promises," she said. "Haven't you learned anything I've taught you?"

"Apparently not," he sighed, "so I'd better stay until I do. Without conditions."

FLAGS'S DECISION to remain among the islanders was far easier for him to tell Dakine than his comrades. He felt torn from them, but the alternative opened gales of anguish that he could not see weathering. He had survived more than one sleepless night letting his mind tack between his options: abandoning everything of his former life (and his bereft mother), probably forever, or nevermore seeing Dakine when he left her paradise. When he considered the latter, he started to feel like a condemned man given a few hours of festivity prior to his execution. It was too painful to be borne.

The news was glumly received by his comrades, although it was not entirely unexpected. They had watched the whole evolution of his catastrophic preoccupation with Dakine but had been helpless to prevent it. Friendly counseling had fallen on deaf ears, and his intention to remain behind when they made their good-byes at the gathering could not be shaken. Sadly, a replacement would have to be chosen from among the many eager adventurers who had begged to sail with *Alembic*.

The time of the gathering came. The whole village was in a cheerful uproar, with families piling into their laden pirogues with whatever possessions they wanted for the journey, along with children, old folks, and pets. Less festively, *Alembic* was undergoing her own drama of departure as the last of the barrels were stowed in her hold and chickens were battened into the quarterdeck coops. There were no women aboard for the first short leg of their passage, a situation not of their own choosing. All would like to have had the company of their wahines, but the gathering was traditionally a family event demanding the presence of all, including daughters. Although without a family of her own, Dakine had more than ever to do attending all the orphaned young and the elderly who needed her help. During the chaos of the embarkation, she did find time to pay a hurried visit to Flags, bringing him a blood flower.

"I'm bringing this to you because you are a warrior now," she said, smiling at him. She put the flower in his hair and then paddled away.

"I'll see you tomorrow," he waved.

She paused in her paddling. "Yes," she said.

By midmorning, most of the fleet was under way more or less in a group, followed by a few stragglers who had been delayed by having left something or other behind. *Alembic* got off to a head start, stretching her sails and running out through the pass, then trimming to a beam reach. It was a studding-sail breeze, and *Alembic* made good speed, but her deep-draft hull was no match in these conditions for the big outrigger pirogues skimming the wavetops under their crab-claw sails. During the afternoon, they sailed past in clusters, waving cheerfully, making motions for *Alembic* to sail faster. It was a magnificent yachting holiday for all the islanders and would have been aboard *Alembic* as well, but for the knowledge of Flags's impending departure.

Watching the flotilla sail past provided diversion, picking out friends. Alea's pirogue sailed close by, then darted in front of them so she and her sisters could strew orchid petals in their path while singing them a song. Dakine's pirogue, identifiable by its reddish-brown sail, was one of the last stragglers, but it passed at too great a distance for Flags to be able to make out which of the distant waving figures was Dakine. He waved back. He would see her soon enough.

He made some jocular attempt to recall the more humorous events he and his lifelong friends had experienced together, but his effort did not have the cheerful effect he had intended, and he left off. There was some discussion about the young islander who would be taken aboard at the gathering. He was a good sailor, well met, and very eager for the adventure that he knew might take him away forever. Otherwise, there seemed little else to talk about. Pilot went below to recommence his interminable navigational notes; Steward vanished into the galley; and Bosun ran aloft leaving Crew at the helm. Off watch, Flags walked forward and took a seat. Draping himself by the rail, he eased the ache he felt for his friends, who seemed already gone. He watched the distant red sail of Dakine's craft. It was far ahead of them at twilight, when Flags succumbed to the effects of too many sleepless nights. Resting his head on the caprail, he closed his eyes and was soon asleep.

At some time after moonrise, he dreamed again of Dakine, a strange and troubling dream in which she gave him everything he had ever wanted. They were standing in the moonlit surf, with warm water swirling around their legs. He took her by the shoulders and held her, looking into her eyes, communicating to her the depth of his love, at the same time telling her with a newfound authority that she *must* come with him on their ship. "Very well," she said, and looked at him with infinite sadness. His relief was tremendous, but then he saw for the first time tears in her eyes. "I will come with you, then, since that is what you want," she said, and as he took her into his arms, she changed into a poor, sad-eyed, pink, curly-tailed piglet, which he knew he must keep by him for all time, for he had somehow imprisoned Dakine the goddess in the pig. It was the saddest thing that had ever happened, and he sobbed for what he had done to her.

He did not know whether he was awakened by the sound of his actual sobbing or the eight bells marking the end of the second dog-watch. They erupted into his consciousness simultaneously, and he realized his face was drenched with tears, his nose running. Clearing his head with a sharp outbreath, he reached into the galley for a rag, blew his nose, and put himself in order. On the deck where he had been sleeping, he found the blood flower Dakine had given him and held it, thinking of what she had told him when she had stuck it in his hair. How did a warrior behave? He was standing looking at the flower when Pilot came up from below.

"This is the place where we would turn north for home if we weren't going west to the gathering," the navigator remarked to Crew and Bosun.

Flags turned to them and spoke without willing it. "Home!" he heard himself say. "Let's turn home."

"What?" said Steward, sticking his head out of the galley.

"Let's go home," Flags repeated, feeling tears starting to well again. "But if you want me to come, let's turn now. I swear, if you take me to that Island, you'll never see me again. Take us away from here now. No good-byes!" He turned and walked back to the bow. The others all looked at one another.

"No good-byes," said Steward. "I like it. I'm for it."

Pilot thought of sweet Alea and his own impending sad farewell. "I'm for it, too," he said, and Bosun and Crew were in agreement. "Very well, then. Sheets and braces! Flags has called a weather course; we'll come up to north by west." Down went the helm, and *Alembic* turned to claw to windward, taking them away from their late destination at a wide angle.

Just after midnight, the horizon to port was abruptly illuminated by a swelling, brilliant red glow. Flags saw it instantly, for it came from the place where he had been staring, in the direction where he had last glimpsed the sail of Dakine's pirogue. From somewhere in that area, a corridor into the molten center of the earth had opened and was vomiting flame. Moments after the light, there arrived a tremendous detonation, and then another and another, bringing up the watch below at a run. They all watched in awe.

"That is close," said Pilot, "and we could get wind off it. Let go the sheets. Lively." Moments later, a hot wind roared past, making all the blocks rattle, and soon after the wind there was a wave like a black mountain, followed by others, all successively smaller in size, until the ocean was placid again but for the bloodred light.

"Is that not somewhere near where we would be had we continued on our original course?" asked Steward. Pilot nodded. They watched the fiery sky in silence. In it, Dakine's face appeared very vividly to Flags, and she was no longer sad, but laughing at him again, her hair washed in flames. This is how he remembered her until the moment of his death.

# X  The Barrier

THE SHIP WAS hove to in wind and mist, her staysail backed,
her mainsail alternately filling and then spilling as the two
sails competed with each other, both luffing alternately. Thus,
she rode perfectly balanced, poised to take flight on either tack. Until
that moment of decision arrived, she shouldered slowly through the
night and the driving mist, dozing, awaiting the whim of her masters,
resting while they rested little. Back and forth paced Pilot, seven paces
each way from the break of the quarterdeck to the mizzen bitts.
Forward, Bosun paced, though more irregularly, with an occasional
abrupt climb to the masthead to see if it might have poked out above
the night mist. It had not. Only the crack of warm light from the galley
scuttle and the smaller glow from the binnacle lamp relieved the
darkness.

*Alembic* was in uncertain circumstances somewhere along the
southwest-facing arc of the immense midocean maze of reefs and
shoals that the islanders called, simply, the barrier. Again, Pilot re-

flected that but for his initial decision to challenge the northern passage, they would have encountered this monumental obstacle some six years earlier, and from the other side. His last view of the barrier had been the previous afternoon, before the mist had enclosed them. At least, they were in an area where some of the obstructions were visible above the waves. The ocean here was studded with sharp fingers of black rock, barren and jagged, resembling an entire horizon of witches' claws. Pilot knew that there were other claws just beneath the water's surface, for they had brushed one earlier. It was just a nudge, with no apparent damage, but the sickening grind of wood against rock had ended any further exploration there.

Helm lashed, they were hove to on this night as they had been every night since they had first sighted the barrier six weeks before. They had immediately learned the folly of sailing blindly near it, for the obstructions sometimes put out tentacles of tortuous shallows. It had taken three days to beat around the largest of them. Endless sandbanks had been their first view of the barrier, spreading before them in vast patterns, the highest just awash.

After a week of prowling the treacherous edge of the banks, they had finally come upon a possible opening. They had edged north into it, sailing for days as the banks thickened around them, until finally, painfully, it had become apparent they were in a cul-de-sac, and they were forced to turn and beat out again. There had been other such seductive blind leads, all of them dangerous. Thrice they had been forced to kedge, having grounded firmly, and Pilot had since stopped counting the times *Alembic*'s keel had tasted sand. Subsequently, they had skirted forests of treacherous coral. Still later, there was more sand, seemingly unbroken but for huge, blind lagoons that had taken hours each to sail into and out of. Now, there were these witches' rocks.

The baffling surprises of the barrier seemed endless. At times, they sailed in perpetual shallows, at other times in water where the sounding lead would find bottom only if it struck the peak of a vertical rock sliver. Nor was there any regularity to the changes of weather or wind, although there was an increasing tendency toward fogs and mists as they crept northwest. Pilot glanced first into the binnacle, then at the run of the sand in the glass, calculating their rate of drift, continuing to keep as close a record of their position as possible under the circumstances. He had hoped to create a chart of the barrier in passing, but its complexities had precluded anything but the record of an ill-defined, obstacle-studded edge. He turned the sand glass and rang the watch change.

"You'd better get some sleep, Bosun," he said to his fellow pacer of the decks.

"Aye," said Bosun. "Nasty business, this. I'll bring a blanket above and sleep here."

Here came Crew, deck watch, to take a sounding. Pilot heard the splash of the lead but could barely make out Crew's form at the chain plates, hauling in line.

"No bottom."

It meant nothing, Pilot reflected, and was probably wasted work. Crew finished coiling down the line and came aft. "No change," Pilot told him. "I reckon we've made a league or so of southing since we hove to."

"Well," said Crew, looking at the bright side of things, "it's a good thing we've clear water on that side of us, anyway."

That was, of course, the thing. If the barrier did in fact turn out to be impenetrable, they could make a clear run back to the Islands in safe waters. He was aware they might be left with no choice. They had consumed six weeks' worth of provisions and drunk six weeks' worth of water. There was still plenty of each aboard–indeed, they could keep the sea for many months until pressed to the extreme limit of hardship–but they knew that a voyage of at least three months awaited them on the other side of the barrier, which they were no closer to penetrating than they had been upon first sighting it. Their time was being quickly used up.

"You should sleep also, Crew," said Pilot. "We're safe enough for the moment. The helm's lashed, and there's nothing to see anyway." Crew nodded, fetching a blanket for protection against the damp. He curled up against the starboard bitt forward, where his dim form balanced that of Bosun, against the port side bitt. All aboard were fatigued, and none more than Pilot. Now, as the others slept, he thought again of the many similarities between their current situation and their first near-disastrous boyhood expedition in *Vessle*. After a while, he stopped his pacing and seated himself wearily on the companionway hatch. He distinctly remembered doing that and listening to the sounds of the ship, the wind, and the seas slapping against the hull. He did not remember going to sleep, although later he was forced to conclude that he must have dozed off. A dream was the only explanation he could think of for the astonishing thing that happened.

As he rested, a voice came out of the night. "*Ahoi!*" it said, a startling illusion. Pilot knew well the hallucinations of fog, which could be audial as well as visual. Usually, one heard such things as breaking seas where none existed. Once, Pilot had thought he had heard music but never before a voice.

"*Ahoi!*" came the voice again, nearer and unmistakable this time. It brought Pilot to his feet in amazement. Something was emerging from the darkness close alongside . . . a splash . . . oars . . . a point of darkness less dense. Astoundingly, he made out the form of a small skiff bearing a solitary rower, close aboard.

"*Ahoi! Goeden avond!*" The figure, a man wearing a broad-brimmed hat with one edge cocked, shipped his oars and grabbed onto the chain plates. Although Pilot did not speak the man's language, he recognized it as one from their own part of the Northern Ocean. Amazing.

"Identify yourself," said Pilot, in his own tongue.

"Captain Vanderdecken, at your service," said the individual, speaking Pilot's language with a softly guttural accent. "My ship's hove-to to leeward. I heard your bell; I thought I would make a visit. Here's my line," he said, flipping his painter over the rail and following it himself with the sure movements of an expert seaman. Pilot took the line and then automatically payed it out to allow the skiff to tow clear. Turning to face his visitor, he saw by the dim light of the binnacle a bearded and weathered face peering at him. It belonged to a sensibly cloaked seaman of late middle years. Apparently, he saw nothing remarkable about his being there.

Pilot opened his mouth to call out and rouse his shipmates, but Vanderdecken put a finger to his lips. "No need to awaken your friends. I cannot remain with you for very long. Just long enough for a pipe," he said, producing a cased clay pipe, "and maybe– You wouldn't by any chance have any Genever, would you? No? Rum?"

"We've a bit of rum left," said Pilot, "but–"

"Very kind of you to offer. I'll mind the deck while you fetch it. And if you have any shag tobacco . . . I have some myself," he said, rummaging in his pockets, then producing a soggy leather bag, "but it's wet, y'see. It's the mist. Gets into everything. And if you got a coal from your galley fire, I would be very obliged to you." Something in the mariner's manner compelled Pilot to do as he had been asked. When he returned, Vanderdecken had seated himself comfortably aft and was digging at the pipe's bowl with his knife. "Thank you," he said.

"Who are you? What are you doing out here?" asked Pilot.

"As you see," said the Captain out of the side of his mouth; he was lighting the pipe by holding the coal to it on the knife blade.

"Please identify your ship," persisted Pilot, determined to get a better answer. "If you please–"

He was interrupted by an impatient gesture. "Let's not waste our time," said the Captain. "You're out here in the dark and with not much idea where you are, trying to figure a way through yon reefs and shoals. Would you say that is correct?"

Pilot nodded. "Do you have navigational information for these waters?" he asked.

"*Ja*, a little, but no sea chart, and I do not know if I can tell you anything to help you."

"Is there a passage?"

"*Ja*, so they say."

"You've not been through it?"

"I feel like I've been through every pass in the world," said the Captain wearily; "I can't even remember."

"That's not much help to me," said Pilot. "Do you or do you not know anything about these waters?"

"I know 'em well enough to be out on 'em in a skiff at night and to find *you*."

Pilot slowly sat down across from this apparition, studying him. He tried a new tack. "What can you tell me that will help us to navigate this vessel through the barrier?" he asked.

The Captain studied him back for a moment, puffing on his pipe. "Well," he said, after a while, "you got to let go."

"I beg your pardon?"

"You got to let go," repeated Vanderdecken. Seeing the baffled look on his listener's face, he elaborated. "You been sailing along this barrier for some time now? Probably following every *verdomde* blind lead that looks like it might go through? Probably going aground and bouncing off rocks, getting nowhere?"

Pilot nodded. "That's right," he allowed.

"And is it right to say you are a good navigator, but your books and instruments you are finding of little use to you here?"

"Yes," said Pilot. "Pray continue."

His visitor shrugged. "I just told you. You got to let go."

"Can you please clarify?" asked Pilot.

The Captain retamped his pipe bowl with a leathery thumb. "*Ja*, I will try. You don't have the time to go exploring everything that looks like a hole in that barrier. If you do, you are going to get drowned or run out of water and victuals. What can you do? Well, you got to *sniff* for it. You grab the seat of your pants, like this–" he said, reaching down and demonstrating–"and you sniff, sniff, sniff." He held his nose prominently forward. "Then when you come to a real passage, if you do, you know it."

"That is completely unscientific," said Pilot.

"*Ja*," the Captain agreed, sipping his rum, "but it's all you got."

"This works for you?" asked Pilot.

"*Ja*, it works if you notice what you're looking for before you go thinking about it." The Captain tapped ashes over the side, replaced the pipe in its case, put the case back in his pocket, finished off his rum, and stood up.

"That's what I come to tell you. Now, I go back to my ship," he said, freeing the painter to his dinghy and bringing it alongside.

"So your advice to me is to throw away all of my training, everything I ever learned, and . . . you say *sniff* for a way though?" Pilot summarized.

"*Ja*, you got to sniff, but you don't throw anything away. You're going to need everything you learned before. Then, you just–"

"Let go," Pilot finished his sentence for him.

"*Ja*," he nodded. "Would you keep a turn with this line while I get aboard my skiff?" Pilot took the line and held it for him while he judged his timing, stepped into the diminutive skiff on the lift of a wave, and took up his oars.

"What you suggest sounds mightily dangerous," said Pilot, throwing the line into the boat so that his visitor could push away.

"*Ja*, maybe. Nobody would blame you for being worried. It's the safest thing for you to just head her back the way you came. The Islands are safe, and with the westerly wind we get tomorrow, you can run back. Thanks for the rum. *Goeden avond; veel geluk.*" So saying, he vanished into the night and mist.

The following morning, the wind did go into the west, clearing the mist away, revealing the dire rocks just visible on the northern horizon. Skirting them meant another dreary slog to weather. Downwind, an easy run to the Islands beckoned. Unhesitatingly, Pilot put the ship's nose back toward the barrier. He could not help thinking about his strange and vivid dream. He remembered its entire dialectic, although he could not remember awakening. He did find himself examining the deck around where Captain Vanderdecken had sat. He half feared he would find tobacco crumbs there, but there were none.

Pilot saw the impossibility of pursuing their previous detailed examination of the barrier's vast, hostile fringe. Now, he sailed to skirt the obstacle, clear of outlying dangers with a good offing, permitting much faster progress along it. During the next fortnight, he passed a number of possible gaps for no apparent reason, to the astonishment of his mates.

"This looks like a good place to poke into," said Bosun one day as they sailed across a wide, inviting bay extending beyond their view to the north. They had all been studying it as they nudged in toward it.

"Not here," said Pilot at last. "Come back to west."

"Why not here?" Bosun had wanted to know.

"I don't know," Pilot said. "It doesn't smell right." The rest of them wondered what had come over him.

On the first day of their third month at sea, as they skirted an apparently impenetrable area of breakers, Pilot suddenly commanded the helm up and plunged the ship into the turbulent water, with Bosun, Flags, and Steward frantically adjusting sheets and braces, and Crew working the lead as fast as he could cast it and reel it back in. Pilot followed a zigzag course through the boil and into a clear channel beyond. It had been a breathless moment, and it was the first of many, for the course they followed was torturous, narrow, and strewn with hazards. By night, they anchored; by day, they edged cautiously through waters where, as Bosun put it, "no sane man should go."

On one wind-torn afternoon, Pilot held the tiller as *Alembic* was blown down a long stretch of channel between banks with horrendous seas crashing on the shallows to either hand, churning the sand from the bottom until the whole ocean boiled yellow. Under storm sails, they careened along helplessly on the huge swells that hove under them, following a narrow passage between the breakers. There was no room to maneuver or anchor. Their only choice was to drive before the gale with their hearts in their mouths. Before their horrified eyes, the channel ahead appeared to close, blocked by more breakers; their destruction seemed assured until, at the last moment, there opened on the port bow a previously invisible side channel that they scooted into, hardly believing they were still alive.

A week after they had entered the shoals, their channel broadened into an expansive gulf, where soundings indicated a deepening slope. As their view of the barrier diminished to the south, and no new obstructions appeared on the opposite horizon, they realized that they were in clear water again–in the same ocean in which their voyage had begun.

"How did you figure your way through?" Bosun asked Pilot.

"I didn't," was Pilot's terse response.

# XI  The Return

LTHOUGH *Alembic* had edged back onto Pilot's master charts of the known seas, many thousands of hard-sailing miles still lay ahead and week after week of ocean as the ship drove from autumn in the Southern Hemisphere into a northern spring. At first, there were the subequatorial trade winds, then doldrums, then the trades again, with Pilot's course following a roundabout route to take advantage of the known wind and current patterns. Distant cloud masses often indicated the presence of land beyond the horizon, but the ship was not diverted from her course. With every league that passed under the keel bringing them closer to the end of the voyage, home became increasingly the favorite topic of conversation.

They wondered what changes they would find when they arrived and what they would do when they got there. All agreed their voyage would be a much-celebrated event even without Steward's chests of gold. They thought the sale of the pearls would perhaps repay their original investment, leaving the boat itself to show for profit. While this would be a modest commercial success at best, it was at least on the profit side of the balance rather than the other, as Bosun pointed out. Similarly, while the clockwise circumnavigation of their own continent and beyond had turned up no easy access route to the Southern Continent or the Western Isles, in finding them, their company had accomplished an amazing piece of seamanship. Pilot now had at least partial charts of seas previously unknown, and all agreed *Alembic*'s return would immortalize him.

"Pilot, you're going to be famous," observed Bosun one evening. The topic had been reopened because that afternoon *Alembic* had fetched at last the latitude line of their home Port, and she was now running down it. With no way of establishing their longitude, they did not know how much more ocean separated them from their destination, but it was somewhere dead ahead, and they were close enough to feel the excitement of it. When the first dogwatch was rung, all were on deck, lounging aft while the ship bubbled along on a reach, largely steering herself.

"I'm a little jealous," Bosun continued, "because you're going to make a handy sum by selling your charts and sailing directions."

"I've a better idea for you, Pilot," said Steward, bringing up a pet scheme he had mentioned before without results: "When we get back, and after we've had a chance to get sorted out, I'll work out a way to obtain a proper ship, a galleon, to open a trading route direct to Elysium. We'll have our gold back yet if we do that. I propose a financial partnership. We can all be in on it, but we'll need *you* to find the right route."

Pilot was unenthusiastic, pointing out difficulties. "Of the two routes we know, we now see only too well that the northern one's unworkable. As for the southern passage, we've still no more knowledge of a truly navigable pass through the barrier than before. We only made it though . . . by a nose. Even if I'd had time to plot it properly, it's too dangerous."

"There must be other passes—better ones," Steward said. "If anyone can find them, you can. You're a born explorer. What better opportunity to practice your passion?"

But Pilot shook his head. "My next exploring will be in a laboratory, not on a ship," he said, thinking for a moment of Melquiades, wondering what progress his friend was making. Equipped with all his notes and preparatory study, Pilot had already organized in his mind the materials he would need to make a sequestered, methodical assault on the mysteries of alchemy. He had every intention of sorting its fact from its fiction.

"But your idea's a good one," he encouraged Steward, "and you can find somebody else. You'll certainly have my charts and notes, and I'll invest whatever money I can. There are other navigators."

"Not like you," sighed Steward. He saw the scheme as the brightest point in the life he would soon resume, which would probably pick up where he had left it off–helping his father with the estate and listening to everybody else's squabbles. He did look forward to telling his father all about his adventures. He wondered how the old lion was.

"If you ever do find a way to send a ship in that direction again," said Flags, "I trust you'll charge your Captain to touch at the Island for whatever news can be got from there."

Steward nodded. Flags alone carried any hope of their friends' surviving the cataclysm that *Alembic* had avoided only because of his last-minute change of mind. He fingered the little leather pouch suspended over his breast, feeling inside it the form of Dakine's pearl. He intended to have it set at the first opportunity, perhaps in a pendant. He was as undecided about that as the direction of the rest of his life. He felt he had experienced a rebirth of some kind, but such a singularly painful one as to have left him stunned. The hard work of running the ship and the passage of time had helped ease the pain over Dakine, but not the groundlessness that she had left as a legacy. Home felt like a lifeline, especially now that it was so close. Even his mother's love would be welcome. He knew the celebration of *Alembic*'s return would spread; he would translate *The Adventurous Voyage* into their own language, at the same time completing it. That cheered him a bit.

Even Crew was enthusiastic about getting back at last, though it would inevitably mean the dispersal of his friends again. Perhaps Steward would indeed get together another expedition, or perhaps

Crew would work with Bosun, who favored a continuing partnership of another kind.

Bosun thought good money could be made by sailing *Alembic* as a coastwise packet. He had proposed running her in that capacity to provide continuing employment for her and himself and whomever else, with profits divided equitably. All had agreed it was a good idea, and it looked as though Bosun was destined at last to become *Alembic*'s Captain. He was confident that her impending fame would draw all the passengers and small cargo she could carry along routes he was already plotting. He looked up at the weathered rigging. All of her running lines were gray and stretched, and her sails were mosaics of patchwork. The tropics had been hard on her, opening deep weather checks in all her spars. *Alembic* was still strong and able, but she was no longer the gleaming jewel that had sailed forth nearly seven years before. Her original varnish had long since flaked away and been painted over, and her paint was scarred and stained; her decks were shagged; rust streaks descended her sides from the chain plates. Frowning, Bosun knew that he really should do a few things right now to spruce her up a bit for her grand entry, but he decided to remain where he was, sitting with his shipmates.

Pilot followed Bosun's gaze, read his thoughts, and decided to twit his comrade. "Bosun, don't you think you should be getting the ship in better order for our reception?" he asked.

"Absolutely," said Bosun, not moving, "but Steward's taught me how to relax, y'see, and I'm no good anymore."

Flags started to sing: "*He's no bloody good for anything; he's no bloody good at allll . . .*" All joined in for a verse or two, Bosun included.

"Thirty-three–almost thirty-four–years old, and he's all played out," sighed Steward when they had left off singing. "Look at the man, a mere remnant of his former self."

"The same can be said of you," came the automatic riposte. "You're the only one among us who can lose six stone without vanishing, and as for the rest of you lot–any of whom I'll race up the rigging anytime– you all look like you've come through a war."

It was true. After months at sea under a four-hours-on, four-hours-off watch schedule, *Alembic*'s sailors were as weathered as their ship. All wore patches over patches; all had deep lines etched around their eyes; and Pilot's beard had begun to whiten, giving him an even frostier appearance than ever. They would mark their thirty-fourth birthday in two days.

"With any luck, we could be home for our birthday," said Flags. "In any case, I think it's time for haircuts during the forenoon watch tomorrow," he judged, eyeing his shipmates. "Starting with you, Crew. You're beginning to look like a bear, and they might shoot you." So the barbershop opened for business on the main hatch at four bells in the forenoon watch under a morning sun shining down from a clear, blue northern sky. After the haircuts, the washdeck pump was rigged, and everybody had a bath. The afternoon watch witnessed drying laundry strung up in the lower rigging, and before supper, Steward heated shaving water for anybody who wanted it. He was quite comfortable himself with his beard, though Flags had trimmed it considerably.

Just before dark, Steward announced he smelled land. There was no sign of it from the masthead, and the lead as yet found no bottom, but sail was shortened. There was a sense of land in the air. It was at the end of the middle watch, in the darkest part of the night, just before dawn, that Bosun, in the crosstrees, saw a pinprick of light in the blackness before them, right on their course. He immediately alerted Pilot, on the helm, and within a moment, everybody was on deck and then into the rigging, for the light was as yet too distant to be seen from the deck. For that reason, Pilot thought it to be a light of considerable power, and quite possibly the Port's great lighthouse–the very one that had guided them home as boys in *Vessle*. Soon, the light was swallowed by the sun rising in the same spot, and the dawn revealed the unmistakable profile of their own headland just to port. A mighty cheer went up from *Alembic,* with everybody pounding Pilot on his back, full of congratulations for having brought them home with such precision. Bosun shook his head in awe at the feat: "When I first saw the light, the bowsprit was on it like a needle," he told them.

"Home for a birthday dinner," said Steward, rubbing his hands. They had been on plain rations for weeks.

"I should think earlier," said Pilot. "Hullo, what's this? Sail ho, dead ahead. Two sails. What are you doing down on deck, Bosun?" Bosun swarmed up the ratlines on the double, followed by all but the helmsman.

"There's four . . . no, five . . . ships, just hull up now," Bosun called. "They're in single file. Warships, by God. They're headed right toward us." All of *Alembic*'s colors were run up. On an opposing course, they were soon passing the battle line, dipping the jack to a big two-decker in the van and then to each of the frigates behind, in turn. None bothered to return the courtesy.

"They're on business," observed Pilot. "Is it war? We'll soon know."

Pilot's question was answered even sooner than anticipated when *Alembic* was intercepted off the headland by a naval cutter with guns run out. A swivel gun boomed to windward, signaling them to heave to, and within a few minutes, a boat bearing a Lieutenant and an armed boarding party of seamen pulled alongside. The officer came over the rail, curtly demanded the ship's Captain, was told there wasn't one, scowled, and demanded their papers. When told these had been lost, his scowl deepened. Flags tried to explain who they were and what they had done, but it fell on deaf ears.

"You've no clearances, no letters, no passports, and it's wartime. This ship is seized."

"Why you idiot–" Bosun blurted before catching himself and choking off anything further. It took Flags and Pilot a quarter-hour to cool the Lieutenant and persuade him to send a gig ashore to verify their identity. So the rest of the birthday morning was spent hove-to on the starboard tack, and much of the afternoon was passed on the port tack. During this frustrating wait for the gig's return, they were guarded by a master's mate and five men who eyed their every move, fingering cutlasses. From these men, they learned of a great naval battle between the forces of the Port and its allies against a rival coalition of other sea powers off the outer banks. The action had been bloody but indecisive, and the entire coast was fully mobilized for further conflict. The war had just begun.

Not until eight bells in the afternoon did the shore boat return, having encountered some difficulty in establishing *Alembic*'s identity. Eventually, somebody had been located to clear them, for they were summarily released.

"Well, at least we'll still be in and ashore by suppertime," said Steward, as they filled away again for the harbor entrance, "and perhaps now that somebody knows we're coming, we'll be met."

"I'll load up the guns," said Bosun, "and we'll give the south castle a good salute as we come 'round the breakwater. That should catch some attention." As they passed the lighthouse, Bosun inserted a quill of priming powder into the gun's vent, adjusted the match in his linstock, and then applied it to the priming. He had loaded with a double charge and expected a good roar, but nothing happened.

"The priming won't ignite," he said, grinding the match into the vent bowl without results.

"It's got too damp," Pilot observed, as the castle slid past unsaluted.

"Well, at least nobody noticed the foul-up," said Flags.

In fact, nobody paid any attention to them at all. Proceeding under shortened sail, they found both outer and inner harbors packed with shipping, more than they had ever seen there before. There were merchantmen awaiting convoy as well as warships, and everywhere was a bustling traffic of harbor craft, all going about their business with no notice of ragamuffin *Alembic* loafing along under her patches. Locating a satisfactory spot in which to drop the anchor took time, and then an hour was needed to secure the ship, draw the charges from the guns, and bundle up whatever possessions they wished to carry ashore. There was an air of unreality to their being again in this familiar place, doing these matter-of-fact things.

"Here comes somebody to see us!" said Bosun, spotting a lug-rigged quay punt heading for them. All but Crew prepared to go ashore. *Alembic* could not be left untended, and Crew had volunteered to stand watch. "You all have parents to go to, and I don't," was his simple response to Steward's insistence that straws be drawn for that dreary duty. As it happened, however, the quay punt brought no loved ones or friends but a puffy customs officer who wanted to inspect them. He was as nonplussed as the naval Lieutenant had been by their lack of documents, but Steward's name was their passport, and he left after looking at their empty hold.

The supper hour was on them by the time it became apparent that they were going to have to get themselves ashore, either by rigging the hoist to launch *Vessle* or by engaging a wherry. The latter being the more expedient, they hailed a passing craft rowed by a boy who was delighted at the opportunity to make a few pennies. So the shore party clambered into his boat, and he pulled for the central docks, plying the heavy oars with all the strength in his skinny frame until Bosun stood up and changed seats with him. With Bosun pulling, they were soon out of Crew's sight among the clustered shipping. By agreement, all would rendezvous aboard *Alembic* the following morning, to find a permanent berth where she could be duly stripped, cleaned, and prepared for her next service. Crew would help Bosun with that. Then, he supposed he would stay with the ship.

He leaned on the rail for a while, looking at the old Port, picking out well-remembered landmarks and seeing some not so familiar. He noticed that the dock where *Vessle* used to lie was now extended, with spurs jutting out from it where none had been. The kirk tower now had a cap on it, and there appeared to be two harbors for the fishing boats instead of one. One of the oldest stone quays had been renovated, making an area of white stone against the black. He saw some new buildings. The whole city looked both grayer and smaller than he had recollected. The familiar skyline with its wall was unchanged, but everything seemed somehow different.

A small boatload of women and children passed by, no doubt some naval officer's family returning from a visit to papa's ship. Crew waved to them, and the smallest child, a wee thing with a mob of golden curls, waved vigorously back at him until subdued by one of the women. Then, when nobody was looking, the child made another little secret wave to him with just her fingers. He waggled his own back at her. He thought about children and families for a while, until his attention was taken by a passing lighter with a bronze cannon barrel slung to its deck. It was an exceptionally large gun–he judged it to be a twenty-four pounder–and he followed its progress out to a big two-decker. There, some time elapsed while the lighter was positioned carefully alongside the warship at a point where the gun could be seized and hoisted by tackles, then taken in through one of the gunports, cascabel first, by a system of transverse tackles. The whole process took about an hour. It occurred to Crew that Bosun would have been interested to see how that was done, although he would probably know how to do it already.

Crew sighed, reflecting for the thousandth time on the wondrous qualities of his four friends, his family. Long gone was whatever ache or feeling of deprivation he had once felt for having none of those qualities himself; his sigh was purely because he was going to miss his family so much. That thought had come to him with increasing frequency lately. Feeling no urge to nourish it, he simply let it go and returned to his observations of the world around him, the strange, cheerful, sad world of his childhood. Over by the docks, he saw a training group loading ballast stone into a botter. There was a market smack with what looked like fresh produce being warped along, too far away to hail. Steward would have hailed it anyway, probably. Feeling now hungry enough to brave the last of *Alembic*'s stores, Crew went into the galley. He emerged a few minutes later with some hard bread, boucanned meat, and a fragment of dried coconut. It was the moment of sunset. As he sat down, the naval ships in the anchorage began firing their traditional evening guns, as though talking to one another:

*Boom. Good night.*

*Boom. Thank you very much; good night yourself.*

Crew watched their flags come fluttering down and had just managed to gnaw through one corner of the leathery boucan when a surprise voice came from the gathering gloom behind him.

"Ahoy, *Alembic*!" It was Steward, standing in the sternsheets of a wherry, holding the old picnic basket they had used as boys, now bulging again with food. "I've got things here you'll like better for your birthday supper, Crew. Throw that garbage away and take this." He handed Crew the basket, plus a sack of bottles.

"You're back!" Crew exclaimed.

Steward gave the wherryman a coin and clambered aboard. "Yes. Look, here's your favorite sausage, plus breads, cheeses, apples–all kinds of things. Let's make a table on the chicken coop. Ah, and here's a roast pheasant." Busily, Steward laid it all out. "Eat, eat, eat."

Crew tore off a pheasant leg. "How come you're back so soon?" he asked. "How are your parents? How's the family? What news from the Manor?"

"First the food," said Steward. "Will you have ale, porter, scrumpy, or . . . ah, claret, I believe. And there's rum and cake for dessert. I'll light us a lantern. You start."

Not until Crew could eat no more would Steward provide any news. He had not wanted to spoil his friend's meal. "Do you want the good news first, or the bad? Very well, the good: I've seen a few of our friends—some cousins you know and a handful of the old household gang. You'll be glad to hear old Nanny's still got firm control of the nursery and told me to tell you to come and see her right away because she wants to give you a good scolding for staying away so long. Everybody thought we were dead. I've already had my scolding, and she's in good form. That Nan's holding down her corner of the universe—and my finding the old picnic basket in the same place—are the two best pieces of news I've got." Steward paused, uncorked the rum, and poured a tumblerful for both of them.

"Now. The Master. I'm told my father at some point began to lose his mind and then did lose it entirely a year or so ago. He's run off and is living in a cave somewhere and won't talk to anybody. I'll have to try to find him as soon as the boat business is settled."

"Your mother?" Crew asked.

"Dead. The flux." He took a good swig of rum. "My fourth and second brothers killed each other in a duel. Simultaneous thrusts. Number Six I saw, but he did not know me, being drunk. Let's drink to him. Number Five is presumed well, having gone on an extended hunting trip right after the war broke out, leaving Number Three more or less to run everything as best he can under the authority of Number One, who is as we remember him but worse. Much worse. The head cook's quit; Major Domo's down with gout; there was a fire in the south tower; the whole place looks run-down, and the kitchens smell of rancid grease. I think there are some other things I'm forgetting, but with any luck, I won't remember them until tomorrow. Here's to a more cheerful reception for the rest of us."

"Ahoy, *Alembic!*" Another call out of the night. Flags in a borrowed pram with more food and drink for Crew.

"Brother Flags," said Steward, his face brightening. "You've come just as we were taking a bit of rum. What brings *you* back tonight?" he added, suddenly fearful of further calamity. "How could you have gotten away from your mother so soon? Is she all right?"

Flags nodded. "She's out for the evening." There was a bit more Flags could have added, but he chose not to. He had gone up the hill to his mother's house with, for once, a yearning for her. At last, he understood her consuming love for him. He now knew the feel of it, the wrenching helplessness, and for the first time, he felt prepared to accept it from his mother. He had no other gift for her but this, which he reckoned was the greatest gift he could bring her.

A stunned maid had admitted him to the house, then rushed off to find his mother, who he learned was dressing in costume for a masked ball somewhere. While waiting, he looked into the familiar rooms leading off the entryway, finding all of them completely redecorated. From another maid, he learned that his mother had remarried the year before, and while he was digesting this, she appeared at the head of the stairs in a red brocade gown, looking younger than he remembered her, radiant even, far from the frumpy mummy he had anticipated.

"Mother!" his voice had come out startled.

"Is it really you? Darling! Oh, I knew you'd come home to me someday." She had rushed down the stairs as Flags went up, meeting her on the middle landing for hugs and kisses. Then, she held him at arm's length to admire him, beaming at him.

"I'm yours for the evening," he told her, holding her hands, but he learned she was committed as a cohostess of the party of the season, to which he was certainly invited but he had no costume and she was rather in a hurry because her hair needed fixing and she was going to be late meeting Flags's new stepfather, whom she knew he was going to love and would meet tomorrow when they could also have a chance to tell each other all about themselves when he showed up for luncheon at noon.

Then, she was gone, leaving him to make his hellos to the kitchen staff and answer their questions as best he could as he ate the meal they served him. Afterward, they made up a package of food for him to take back to Crew.

"I'll see my mother tomorrow," sighed Flags, turning the subject to Steward. "How are things at the Manor?"

Steward was spared answering by the sound of yet another hail: "*Alembic* ahoy!" This time, it was Bosun. "I've brought you a late supper, Crew. Oh, hullo. What are you two doing here?"

Unlike his comrades, Bosun had found both his parents in good fettle but working like demons at the tavern. A harbor crowded with wartime shipping meant a tavern full of sailors, so many that Bosun had trouble penetrating the densely packed mass of drinkers and diners within. When he did, he found his father wrestling a full barrel of beer up from the cellar and was immediately pressed into service. "Thundering ghosts!" roared his father. "We thought you were dead! Good to see ye, lad! I'd give ye a hug, but this barrel's between us. Ye'd better give me a hand with it. Unhhh," he grunted, lifting. "I'll bet ye've got some tales. Have ye seen y'r mum yet? No? She's directing the kitchen. P'raps ye'd best go let 'er know y'r back while I tap this keg. There's a pile of thirsty customers waiting for it, as y'see." Bosun's mother, supervising a half dozen perspiring women, was sweatier and more florid than any of them. When he walked into the crowded kitchen, she stuck a mop in his hand before she even realized who he was. Like her husband, she was overjoyed to see their prodigal back, but in the circumstances, neither of his parents could give him any attention just then. Having eaten, he had stayed around helping out until he'd tired of breathing the heavy smoke and had returned to *Alembic* with a supper for Crew.

"I'll manage a visit with my parents tomorrow," he said, then paused to consider the tavern's hours and his own probable work schedule. "Or perhaps the day after. But what brings you two back? We're only missing Pilot."

"Not so," said Pilot's voice. And there he was, standing next to them at the edge of the lamplight, having rowed out and somehow come aboard without being seen or heard. He, too, had a parcel of food and a bottle for Crew. He added these things to the pile of previous offerings.

"We're provisioning for another trip," said Steward, "and from your grim look, you're as ready to go as we are. Here's a bit of rum for you. What news?" Pilot accepted the glass, sat down on deck, and told them of his homecoming. Most of his time ashore had been spent holding the hand of his mother, who had suffered a stroke that had left her unable to recognize him or anyone else. She was well looked after by his aunts, with whom she now stayed and from whom Pilot learned of his father. Made Vice Admiral, he had been cut in half by a cannonball at the recent Battle of the Outer Banks. There had been a state funeral for him only a fortnight earlier. The house was being tended by the old housekeeper, who had prepared a meal for Pilot, another for the waif whose boat they had hired, and another for Crew.

"I thought my news was worse than anybody else's could be," said Steward, "but I was wrong."

Pilot sighed. "Everything's transient," he said. "By the way, when we were thought dead by all others, my father held us safe and well. Will you join me in a toast to his memory?" There was a slight delay while glasses were filled, then: "My father, friend and teacher to all of us, who died a hero's death on his quarterdeck: Here's to the Captain!"

"The Captain!" came the echo.

Pilot, saddened but phlegmatic, asked Steward the meaning of his own remark, and Steward told them all of his glum reception.

"Let's go back to sea," said Bosun. All growled their approval.

"Except, where's left to go?" asked Pilot, inducing a silence.

Thus, *Alembic*'s crew was spontaneously rejoined on her quarter-deck for a moment of shared emptiness.

In the space, Crew raised his glass: "To all of us! At least *we're* not dead, and we haven't lost our minds."

"I'll drink to that," said Flags, doing so, "but I think you're wrong about not having lost our minds. We've all gone round the bend; you just don't see it because you've got used to it gradually. But have you looked at *this* place? Do you see how changed it is? I don't mean the new wharves and buildings, or the people. It's the same place we left, despite the war and all that's happened, *but it's not the same.* It seems crazy. Ergo, *we* are crazy, no?" All immediately agreed, a meeting of minds that coincided with the end of the second bottle of rum. Fortunately, other bottles had arrived with all the recent supplies, so there was plenty with which to toast all the world's crazy people and then all the sane ones and then others more specific: Alea, Oblivia, the Zubaida that none but Steward had met, Mate, Uyuruk, Melquiades, and others. Pilot whimsically toasted the Flying Dutchman; wives of the Reindeer Clan were drunk to; a glass was raised to the lost fifteen chests of gold; and that was followed by a fresh round of toasts to Dakine, their benefactress, the giver of the pearl that had seeded the supply that would finance a fresh start in their lives.

At some point, Flags found his lute, and there were several rounds of improvisational verses of a birthday song to themselves until yells came from across the water telling them to pipe down. This so irritated Flags that he was inspired to fire a cannon in the direction of the criticism; he started forward toward the gunner's stores, lurching slightly, with every intention of commencing a cannonade, but was reminded of the wet priming powder.

He satisfied himself instead with having a powerful piss in the direction of his target. "Take that," he said.

He returned to the quarterdeck just in time to help restrain Bosun, who, having become convinced that they were going back to sea, had first started to cast off the sail gaskets and then tried to cut their anchor line. By then, there were four empty rum bottles distributed around the deck, although one of these had been more spilled than drunk, having been knocked over during the brief scuffle to subdue Bosun.

"Nev' mind." said Steward, "There's more."

At some point, Pilot stood to make what he heralded as an important announcement. Steadying himself against the binnacle, he held up a commanding finger, regarded them all with great, round owl's eyes, and said: "We have made a huge . . . wheel. Y'see? A circle. The whirlpool omen. An' we're right back where we . . . where we . . . started." So saying, he slid to the deck, although he revived briefly later, roused by Crew's laugh, to join in on a few more bars of song.

The comrades' shaky but heartfelt harmonies rang over the dark waters of the Port, their own human realm of home, as foreign a place as ever they had been.

T HE FOLLOWING MORNING, the task of decommissioning *Alembic* got off to a slow start. The young waif with the wherry was again retained so the ravaged sailors would have two boats at their disposal for errands, the first and most urgent of which was fetching a butt of fresh water. The ship's remaining supply was thick in the cask; nobody had thought to bring water the previous evening, and everyone awoke with a pressing thirst. After it was quenched, better progress was made. By noon, relatives and friends who had learned of their return began to show up, and more came the next day, everyone greeting them as though they had returned from the dead. On the third day, *Alembic* was shifted to a dockside berth, where her unloading and repair could commence, allowing more time for personal errands.

Having obtained directions to the cave where his father was dwelling, Steward went there as soon as he could depart, expecting the worst. According to what he had been told, after his mother's death, the Master had shown decreasing inclination to deal with his interests until his unusual behavior had become a real source of concern. Then, one day he had simply vanished. There had been a great flap and search involving his entire numerous family, their friends, all the estate's many servants and tenants, the Port's entire guards batallion, the city fencibles, foresters for miles around, fire wardens, and everybody else who wanted to join in–comprising an army in their own right because of the huge reward offered for the great man's return.

Some weeks later, he was accidentally discovered by some children in a cave a half-day's ride from the Manor. Nothing would induce him to leave or even respond to any of those who tried to reason with him. Apparently, he wielded all of his fearful authority of old when he wanted to, although he was described as quite peaceable if left to himself. To the intense mortification of his family, he was found to have been spending his afternoons with a begging bowl at a public crossroads nearby, where many a search party had passed him by without recognizing him. An arrangement had been made to deliver subsistence to him in order to keep him from public charity, and an armed guard was established near the cavern to protect him from miscreants. He was so revered by the many people whose lives he had enriched that he was constantly brought offerings of food.

Nearing his destination, Steward encountered the guard, a sergeant with two men-at-arms, who pointed out the direction in which the Master could be found. The cave site was still a good distance away.

"'E won't let us get any closer, or 'e t'rows dung at us, y'see, sir," explained the sergeant, "an' we hadda move a ways away. " 'E t'rows turds at ever'body what approaches 'im except chil'run. Beggin' y'r pardon, sir, but 'e'll prob'ly t'row at you, too, an' 'e *can* t'row, so's ye'd better be keerful, sir." Steward approached warily, but nothing was thrown at him. The cave opened onto a hillside ledge overlooking the forest below, and in its entrance sat his father, cross-legged, doing nothing at all, apparently.

When he saw Steward, his face lit up with a tremendous smile. "Dear boy," he said, holding out his arms.

"Father," said Steward, going to him and embracing him. In order to do it, he had to sit down also, for the Master did not rise. When they had hugged, they regarded each other, the old man beaming, Steward smiling back at him perplexedly. He saw no madness in his father's cheerful face and little more age in it than he remembered. His hair and beard were longer, but he seemed to be in good enough health, and his clothing—a woolen shepherd's frock—was adequate and fairly clean. Rolled up under him was a heavy cloak, doing service as a ground cushion, for the day was a warm one. Sunlight fell through the trees, making mottled patches on the sward.

"I *knew* you were well," said the Master. "How was your voyage?"

"We made a circumnavigation of our entire continent and much else, too. It's a long story. Father . . . what has happened to you?"

"As you see."

"What I see is you sitting in front of a cave doing nothing noticeable." The Master nodded happily. "Well," said Steward, arranging himself facing him, "I'm not moving from this spot until I learn what you're doing here."

"In that case, I'd better tell you right away, because I think you're soon going to want to move. In point of fact, when you arrived, I was watching the activity around the anthill you're now sitting on." Steward looked under himself, felt a first bite, then leaped to his feet brushing scores of ants from his legs and bottom while his father rocked back and forth laughing.

Steward chose a new seat a few paces removed. "They bit me," he said.

"You sat on their world," said the old man. "It's taken them several weeks to build what you erased in a moment."

Steward considered what he had said. "Yes," he responded; "and *you* seem to have abandoned a world that you and our ancestors have built over centuries. From what I've been able to glean in the short time I've been back, all that work's now coming undone. Has my mother's death done this to you?" Steward waited for a response, but none came. His father closed his eyes as though resting them.

"There's been great disorganization without you," Steward pressed. "The family's power is on the wane, along with our many interests. And now war. I don't yet know the details, but I fear for what I'm finding." His father nodded, not opening his eyes. "Do you not care?" A shrug. Steward tried another tack. "Everybody thinks you've gone mad. Is it true?" Another shrug. "But they also say you'll speak to nobody, and you're speaking to me, and they say you throw shit at everybody, but you threw none at me."

The Master smiled, still with his eyes closed. "You're neither nobody nor everybody," he commented.

"Father!" Steward pleaded. At first, he had been encouraged by his father's apparent lucidity and good humor, but now his anguish was returning, fueled by frustration. "*Please* tell me you're all right."

"I'm all right."

"And not crazy," he added.

His father opened one eye. "Am I crazy for having thrown shit at soldiers? Haven't you ever wanted to?" he chuckled. "How many sane people do you think there are who get to do it?"

"But *why*? Why *all* of this?"

The Master opened his other eye as well, regarded his agitated son, and growled with a well-remembered authority. "Have I not taught you never to make explanations? Do you think I should now refute my own teachings?"

"Yes, I do in this instance," said Steward. "What you've done . . . what you're doing seems contrary to everything you've taught me."

"How's that?"

"Think of your people, those you've cared for so well," said Steward, probing for his father's great generosity. "How can you now abandon them? Things really are going to hell with my eldest brother, whom you know better than I, acting as Regent–or rather, *not* acting as Regent–while you're here watching ants. And when you die, he's heir to all. If there's anything left. Why have you abandoned us?"

"Abandoned," the old man repeated, seeming to ruminate upon the word. "I think it's better to say I've left you all on your own, which is where you are anyway, with or without me, or anybody else. Any other notion's a dangerous illusion."

"Father, it seems ungenerous to me. You've been the best provider and protector any of us have ever known."

"What would you do," asked the Master, "if you discovered you were protecting everybody from being on their own, so thoroughly as to make them defenseless? And here's another question for you: since your eldest brother is fated to succeed me, would you rather he ascend to an exalted position, with great power over people, or to one so weakened he's unable to do much damage? Believe me, my withdrawal hasn't left people in as big a pickle as you think. As you point out, my successor *is* the pickle everybody finds on their plate, and he's better swallowed gradually, don't you think?"

Steward shook his head sadly. "So easily you discuss the fall of a great house," said Steward, "a house you've helped build."

"These things happen," his father shrugged. "If you look at the history of the family, you'll see it's had its ups and downs all along. Its survival seems amazing, but still it's here somehow. Perhaps it will survive the down that is inexorably now beginning, as you have witnessed. In fact, the spore of this down was active at the top of the up and probably there at its conception. I don't think you can stop the process. Kings are really such helpless creatures," he added.

"I've been a king, or something very much like that, since last I was with you," Steward said, proud to be able to tell this to his father.

"Well, I knew you had it in you. I've always thought it ironical that my seventh boy was the only king in the lot." The Master smiled, closing his eyes again.

"Would you like to hear about the fantastic things that have happened to us?" asked Steward, primed to tell him.

"Yes, that would be nice," said the Master. "Perhaps on your next visit. Will you come to see me again?"

"Of course"–was this a dismissal?–"but . . . I've pressing things to ask you now that I'm here, finding you saner than those who call you crazy. I'll put everybody right about that when I get back–and I want to see you better looked after."

"You'll do no such thing. You'll tell 'em I'm mad as a hatter, and as long as nobody but you comes to bother me, and as long as I don't have to see those guards, I'll be quite all right. People bring me food all the time. They bring me so much it feeds all the guards, too, not to mention some animals and birds and a few children who've taken to coming around, whose parents apparently don't feed them enough." The Master threw up his arms. "The whole process follows me, y'see! In any case, if you go back and say I'm *not* crazy, they'll have to get up a tremendous investigation and send people to try to talk to me again, and I'm telling you right now, I'll throw shit at the first one who comes up the path. So spare us both all the fuss. I order it."

Steward blinked. "Yes, sire, but I hope you'll let me do whatever I can to make you more comfortable. Since you've chosen to become a hermit, certainly a cabin can be found or–"

His father raised his hand. "I've what I want here. I'd prefer not sharing the hill with the guards, but I suppose they're necessary to let the world know I'm alive, which keeps some kind of check on the heir."

"What are your other commands for me, sire? I'm at your service."

"None."

"But . . . regarding the family's affairs, the estate, the ships . . . If you desire it, I'll bring everything I've learned to bear on working out the problems. I've had a considerable experience now with administration by proxy, and I daresay my brother might be susceptible to some similar manipulation. Perhaps this downward plunge of our family's fortunes may be checked and reversed."

The old man rearranged himself to stick his legs out in front of him, into a puddle of sunlight. "Perhaps checked, but not reversed, I think. The pattern's inexorable."

"What's your advice, then?" Steward asked.

His father laughed, rocking backward so the light illuminated his hair, making it glow. "How can I give you any advice?" he asked. "I would say, if you take on such a project, be prepared for a task similar to single-handedly stopping a heavy wagon from going downhill once it's started to roll. I saved you from that before by sending you away. Now, you're on your own."

"Perhaps it's as you say," said Steward, "but what else is there to do?"

"In my own case, nothing," his father responded.

"Don't you find it . . . terribly boring?"

"Absolutely. My life now's like a very bland soup base in which more surprising ingredients are better tasted."

"What ingredients?" asked Steward, unsure as to what his father had meant.

"You'd have to try the soup," said the Master. "You're certainly welcome to join me here in the cave. You'd have to get used to living among ashes, I'm afraid, and it is a bit primitive, but it's not so uncomfortable as you might think, and you'd be amazed at the activity always going on. So many entertainments."

"Where?"

"Everywhere," his father gestured expansively. "You've met the red ants, but not the black ones, nor the spiders, moths, sparrows, raccoons, owls, serpents, turtles–"

"Perhaps I may yet," said Steward. "You really have become a renunciate, haven't you?"

"Only in the sense of having emptied the contents of an old pot. Now, you mustn't let me detain you. I'm glad you've come, but I suspect you've other things you want to do, and I have to gather sticks for my fire before it gets any later. No, I don't want help with it, dear boy; it's part of my little day. Do come back in a week or two, however, and let's chat again or perhaps just sit together. It's far less exhausting."

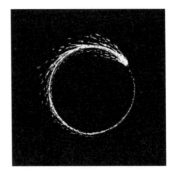

PILOT ALSO HAD a particular personal errand, although he was unable to attend to it immediately because of other things more pressing. First, there was the settlement of his father's estate as well as the establishment of a new regimen for a household of three: the old housekeeper, himself, and the adolescent waif–named Waif–whose services he had retained ever since *Alembic*'s arrival. The orphan's battered old boat was his all; by day, he had eked out his living in it, and by night, he had slept in it, curling up under a tarpaulin. He had no other home. He was a perky, bright lad, however, who had proved reliable for errands and chores, so Pilot had given him a room off the kitchen and set him to work cleaning, painting, and preparing the garret as an alchemical laboratory.

For the laboratory's assembly, all kinds of glass and copper vessels and tubes were needed, most of them having to be especially fabricated. Pilot put that work under commission without delay. Then, he had to prepare the inevitable long written report of *Alembic*'s voyage to the Board of Admiralty and to submit it along with a request for permission to publish the charts and rutters he had made. The Lords Commissioner wanted to examine all of his notes, and he spent weeks answering the endless questions of the examiners.

A month passed before he was able to find a day in which to make his way one final time into the labyrinth with its abyssal black hole. Ever since his dark dreams among the Arctic ice–dreams that had seemed to somehow leak out from that hole and into himself–he had resolved to replace the stone lid that had been too heavy for a boy to lift.

"Aha!" he exclaimed when he found among his childhood possessions (all carefully boxed and saved by his mother) not only his original maps of the labyrinth but his censer, torches, staff, and even his old soft-soled boots, which had so aided his footing in the dark passageways.

"Did you call?" asked Waif, sticking his head into the room. He was holding a mop.

"You know I did not," said Pilot. "I said, 'Aha,' which is hardly a summons. Back to work with you, and here, find some tallow to soften up these old boots. They haven't been worn in twenty years."

"What's *that*?" asked the boy, pointing to the censer Pilot was dangling. "And what are those? Maps? Can I see? What are they for?" He was looking at the schematic diagrams of the labyrinth spread out all over the floor. Although Pilot found himself incessantly pestered with Waif's questions, he liked the boy's irrepressible curiosity and had undertaken to educate him, as time and patience allowed. Waif reminded Pilot somewhat of himself at that age; there was even a physical resemblance. From the first, there had been a sense of connection between the weathered scholar and the illiterate boy.

"It's *may* I see, not *can* I," said Pilot. "They're maps of a pattern of tunnels."

"Tunnels! Where are they? Is that what you have those torches for? Are you going inside? What's in them? Can I come?"

"It's *may* I come. *May* I."

"May I?"

"Better. But you may not. Now, I want you to finish with the floors, oil the boots, and clean all the new retorts and beakers by suppertime. And if you break one, I'll skin you."

"I'll do everything, an' I'll be careful, but then please can't I come? *Please*?"

"Out."

But the following morning, Pilot relented under a barrage of renewed pleadings, conditionally. "The place I'm taking you is a secret," he said, "and you're to do precisely what I tell you, with no argument about it at all. Do you understand? And you're never to go back there afterward. I want your promise to all of that." Waif emphatically promised. "Very well. We'll see how you do. Here, you can carry the satchel."

As they climbed the hill toward Steward's estate, Pilot wondered if the entrance to the labyrinth would still be there. Among the changes wrought on the Port by the current war were some partial renovations of the wall to make it militarily serviceable again. Whole sections had been restored. He was relieved, therefore, to find the area around the old entrance apparently unaltered, looking very much as he remembered it, except a great tangle of vines and brush now smothered the base of the wall. After much probing, Pilot found the heavy planks covering the old entrance. They were now quite rotten. When he seized one to pull it aside, it crumbled in his hand, revealing the threshold of darkness behind.

"Ooooooh!" said Waif, peering into it.

*Drip . . . drip . . . drip . . .* came the sound of distant droplets from somewhere inside. Pilot opened the satchel and removed the things they would carry in with them, explaining to Waif the various ways in which he had to be careful. "And no talking," he concluded. "If you must say something, whisper."

"Is there something dangerous in there?" whispered Waif, as he nervously eyed the entrance.

"I don't think so, but you never know what you might find. Do you want to go home?"

Waif shook his head. "No, but can I stay close to you?"

"You *may*, you can, and in fact, you must. Here, tie this to your belt."

Pilot handed him the other end of a short rope that he had fastened to his own belt, then lit a lantern and entered the darkness with the wide-eyed boy close at his heels. Almost immediately, Pilot realized he had lost much of his old sense of the dark maze, and he was forced to pick his way carefully through stretches where once he had been able to run in total darkness. Now, the corridors of sweaty stone all seemed unfamiliar to him, and he was forced frequently to stop to consult his map.

"What are we looking for?" whispered Waif. Pilot's answer was a finger to his lips, and they moved on. Several times, he encountered chalk marks he had made two decades earlier, and he recognized enough places that he did remember–such as the central chamber with a dozen different tunnels leading off from it–to confirm his route. Deeper and deeper into the labyrinth they went until at last they stood before the rocks he had piled over the crypt of the black pit.

"Now, you can remove your rope," he told Waif, "and let's shift these rocks." The ancient coverlid was soon exposed.

"Where does that go?" whispered the boy.

"Down," said Pilot, removing the lid, feeling the exhalation of air from the chamber below. The lantern light did little to penetrate its gloom. "Come along," he said, "and mind your footing on the steps. They're steep." Descending, he saw his light dimly touch the cylindrical form of the well casing in the middle of the room. Placing the lantern on a flagstone, he lit both torches. At once, the whole crypt with its vaulting was illuminated by dancing torchlight, and again, he beheld the circular casing of the unfathomable black hole. It was just as he had left it–open, with the stone cap leaning against it.

"What's that," Waif asked, following his gaze.

"As you see," said Pilot. The boy went to it and held his torch so that he could look into it.

"It's a well, " he announced.

"I think not," said Pilot.

"I can't see any water," Waif admitted. Picking up a piece of broken mortar, he dropped it in and listened for the end of its fall.

"I didn't hear it hit, did you?" he asked.

"No."

"How deep is it, do you know?" Pilot shook his head. "I know how we can find out," Waif said.

"How?"

"By dropping in one of our torches. Can I?"

"*May* I. Yes. Why not," said Pilot. The boy held out the torch, then let it go. Down it fell, its light becoming smaller and smaller and then vanishing into the dark digestion of the pit. Waif made a low whistle. "That's *really* deep. Where did they put the dirt when they dug it? How far down does it go?"

"I can't answer those questions," said Pilot.

"We need a long, long line," Waif said, "one that's long enough to get all the way down. We could tie several together if we needed to. It can't *not* have a bottom."

"I would say that's a physical impossibility," Pilot agreed.

"Who made it? Whatever use is is it?"

"As to the first, I have no idea. As to the second, all that comes to mind is as a symbol of mind. My own, at least."

"What does that mean?"

"If it means anything other than nothing, it escapes me," Pilot answered.

"Please can't we have a try at finding bottom?"

"Why?" asked Pilot.

"Why not?" asked Waif.

"Good lad." Pilot smiled at his promising new protégé's perfect riposte.

"Oh, *please*?" Waif was doing a little dance of frustration.

"Let it go, lad. We've more interesting business." Pilot levered the capstone until the heavy wafer stood upright against the case wall. "Here, give me a hand; we'll hoist it up and over the rim, then slide it back in place."

"Did you take it off?" asked Waif, grunting with the effort of the lift. Pilot nodded.

"Well, if there's nothing down there, why do we need to cover it up again?"

"Respectful to leave things as you found them." Pilot slid the stone back into position over the pit. "There's that," he said, dusting his hands.

## XII  A Birthday Celebration

OSUN CHECKED the list of the many things that had needed doing prior to his departure, and having done them all, he kissed his wife good-bye, gave his little boy a playful cuff, got one in return, took up his old forest green boat cloak and a change of clothing, and headed out the door bound for the waterfront, noting with satisfaction that the wind had a northerly slant from a sky that portended continuing fair weather. Barring unforeseen anomalies.

He walked briskly, wanting to get there a bit early in case Crew needed a hand with any last-minute chore before the arrival of the other guests. Well, of course, they weren't guests at all. They were *Alembic*'s original crew, her real crew and her owning partners still, although it had been so long since they had all stood together on her decks, they seemed like guests. He felt like a guest himself, having relinquished her command some seven years ago, after three successful years as her Captain. Bosun's mind blew through a summary of his career, his marriage, his children, all the details of his very active and successful (so far) operations. Breezes of his thought played through current concerns: the high price of flax, the difficulty of finding efficient workers these days and all the difficulties of dealing with them when he had them, which was true of all employees, which reminded him of the rebellious apprentices. Catching his thoughts, he abruptly deflected them to his present business, which was no business at all, but the pleasure of a birthday celebration on board *Alembic* with all of her original crew, their first complete reunion in ten years. Also, there was an ingredient of mystery on top of the anticipation. He quickened his step.

Rounding the corner onto the street of wharves, he saw *Alembic* flying all of her flags except the one he carried in the bag over his shoulder. There was Crew, working the washdeck pump. When Bosun had relinquished command, Crew had become Captain. Ever since, he'd been running the little ship very profitably and efficiently, crediting his success to the lessons he'd learned from the rest of them and also to his wife, Gretchen, known to the harbor community as Gretchen the Fierce. Bosun wondered how Crew had managed to persuade her to move ashore for three days.

"Yay, Crew!" hailed Bosun, as of old.

"Mornin', Captain, and good birthday." Bosun let his eye take in the tidy, familiar decks and their furnishings. Little *Vessle* was secured in her chocks; the brass cannons were polished; the scarred deck planking was holystoned; the rigging looked in order, although a couple of halliards were beginning to want replacement. Everywhere he saw fresh paint and other signs of recent work on their little ship. She did look little to him—hardly more than deck cargo for some of the other ships in which he had acquired interest in recent years.

"I hope she passes your inspection," said Crew.

"I'd better have a look." Bosun came aboard and put an arm around his old friend. "I see you've got all her flags flying but the one you didn't have. Here it is." He produced a parcel from his kit bag. Unrolling it, Crew held out their original house flag, with its five vertical bars of blue, green, white, amber, and red. These hues were much faded, for the old standard had seen hard service and had many repairs. Bosun had taken it with him for safekeeping when he had turned over *Alembic*'s command. Up went the old flag, fluttering to the main peak.

"Now, our ship's as she was again," Bosun noted, belaying the flag halliard. Crew agreed that was nearly so. The years of *Alembic*'s coastal travels as a packet boat in war and peace had seen some inevitable alterations. The chicken coops had been removed to make more room for deck cargo, and the main hatch had sensibly been widened for her new work.

"I made the crew and the training lads put her back to the way we knew her best," Crew told him, "at least as much as possible." Bosun knew Crew had been supervising a training group lately. The lads had obviously augmented the labors of *Alembic*'s small crew in the recent renovation.

"She's lovely," said Bosun. "Any changes below?"

"Not since your time. Have a look. I'll finish what I was doing."

The aftercabin was as Bosun had partitioned it during his tenure, with two small passenger cabins and a larger master's cabin, still with Pilot's old chart table and locker. That was now bulging with other things, although Pilot's sand glasses and some of his navigational tools were still in their racks and apparently doing good service. Pilot. What memories he evoked. Bosun carried his inspection of the belowdeck areas forward. The hold had a small crew's compartment built into it. He was glad to find the galley and his old locker under the forepeak unchanged. The latter was as permeated as ever with the nostalgic perfume of pine tar.

The sound of horse's hooves and voices on the dock told him of an arrival, and he went above. It was Steward, with a pair of house carls from the Manor plus a tumbrel containing a couple of small kegs, some covered baskets, a box of bottles packed in straw, another of fruit, two or three sacks, and a big earthenware pot, which one of the minions almost dropped when he tried to unload it.

"Careful there, it's still hot," said Steward, stepping aboard. "That's a good stew, and with any luck, it'll still be warm for our first meal; it's one less I'll have to cook. I'm out of practice, but I've brought some special stores for us. Good birthday, by the by. Careful there, handling those bottles."

As the last of the tumbrel's contents was passed down, Flags appeared, all smiles, full of greetings, with his old seabag over his shoulder, thinly packed.

"This bag has less in it than ever before," Steward commented when it was handed down to him from the dock.

"Yes," Flags agreed. "If it had been my mother packing it for a three-day trip, we wouldn't be able to lift it between the two of us." Flags's mother, having now survived her third husband, had sewn them a new replacement flag for the ragged old original, which she had also sewn. He presented it with a flourish as soon as he had climbed aboard, quoting a few appropriate lines from his now famous play *The Adventurous Voyage*. An immediate triumph, that production had assured the fortune of his meteoric theatrical troupe, sending it on to other ventures.

"I always told everybody you were going to be famous," his mother reminded him every chance she got. She had a private box at his theater and was usually in it, often joined by Flags's childhood sweetheart, Rosemaryn, to whom he was now betrothed.

"Where's Pilot?" he asked

Pilot was, of course, the big question. While the rest of them had kept good contact, Pilot had vanished from their lives years ago. After their return, the astonishing portfolio of charts and rutters that he had amassed during their voyage had been confiscated by the Lords Commissioners, who honored him with a glowing letter of thanks for his services to the government. The government saw no immediate commercial possibilities from Pilot's discoveries, but it was deemed prudent to keep his information out of anybody else's hands.

At the time, Pilot had just shrugged it off, saying that he had expected nothing else anyway (which was apparently true because he had kept duplicates, including a set for Steward) and that he was more interested in his alchemical studies. So saying, he had sequestered himself in his laboratory and seldom emerged. On the rare occasions when he had been persuaded out by his old friends, he had seemed as glad for their company as they had been for his, but he had carried a preoccupation, as though a part of his mind had remained among the bubbling bottles and mystical paraphernalia that had been described to them by Waif. Pilot's assistant and student knew nothing of his master's purposes, however, and when Pilot was questioned about his activities, his answers had been either evasive or incomprehensible.

"I'll explain better what I'm doing when I understand it better myself," he had said. His absorption had increased until, five years ago, he had announced that he was leaving on a trip of undetermined duration, bound nobody knew where. "I'd gladly tell you where I'm going, except I'm not sure," he had told them, saying his good-byes, promising to communicate if possible. Prior to this departure, he had dismantled his laboratory. Burying some of it and throwing all the rest away, he had put his property and affairs into the hands of Waif and the housekeeper and had vanished. Nobody had heard from him since–until a fortnight ago, when Waif had received from a messenger a note signed by Pilot and addressed to them all:

> I trust this finds you all in good health. I'm bound home and plan to be with you for our forty-fourth birthday. Let us celebrate. Best would be a yachting holiday aboard *Alembic* of three days' duration. Can this be done? Otherwise, elsewhere, your choice, but let it be just the five of us. We've matters to discuss. Instruct Waif regarding arrangements.
>
> Pilot.

This had caused a flurry of consultations and replannings of busy lives, culminating in their all being where they now stood, aboard their ship again, ready to sail, awaiting only their mysterious friend.

"What are these *matters* he wants to discuss, d'you suppose?" asked Bosun. "His message doesn't tell much, meaning he's up to something, if I know him."

"What?" asked Crew.

"For sure, a little voyage out of our everyday lives," offered Steward, "and I'm ready." His father's prediction of the overloaded wagon was a good analogy for his youngest son's situation since he had undertaken the management of his family's interests. For this birthday event, Steward had put a rock under the wagon's wheel, leaving it and its entire load of problems parked pending his return. The rock was his good wife Elna, a very capable mother and keeper of the castle. Except she was pregnant again, which had to be taken into consideration.

Bosun was empathetic: "I'm ready, too, for a small vacation, but I don't want to get too relaxed until I know more about why Pilot's called us all together again now. Remember, the *last* time he called a rendezvous like this, it took us away nearly for good."

"Be easy," said Steward. "Where could he take us in three days?"

"We'll see," said Bosun, watching the glass. "He's about due."

Flags wanted to know about how Steward's father, the old Master, was enjoying his recent reemergence into the world. He was finally established in a cottage where he could better direct the distribution to needy people of the amazing quantities of food brought to him by pilgrims from far and wide. During his decade of solitude, he had come to be regarded as more a saint than a madman. Steward visited with him often, never with business questions.

Steward had effectively taken over the father's role, but with a flair of his own. For instance, when learning that the Ancient Mariner was still alive and more emaciated than ever, Steward had immediately hired him to ply his story for the rest of his days in the Manor's biggest dining hall. There, the ageless penitent was well provided for, and he in return kept the place scoured of all the sponging in-laws, plus the habitual slackers, shirkers, clergymen, buskers, and scrimshanders. The Manor's food consumption was cut nearly in half.

Again, Bosun looked at the sand glass. It had nearly run out. "Do you suppose something might have happened to Pilot?" he fretted. "I visited his house last evening, but Waif said he hadn't yet arrived. Perhaps he's had some delay on the road."

"He'll be here," said Steward, "although it wouldn't surprise me if he appeared in a puff of smoke."

"Pilot never needed smoke to appear or disappear," Flags noted.

But this time, Pilot's approach was seen. Just as the watch bells began to ring on the nearby ships, an unmistakable, gangly, gray, monklike figure hove into view around the corner at the end of the dock, waving to the comrades gathered on the little ship's quarterdeck.

"Ahoy, *Alembic!*" Then, he was there among them, cheerful, pale and skinny as ever but apparently healthy, getting hugs and poundings from all, returning them. His facial angles seemed sharper, and his eyebrows were prematurely white, making him look more than ever like a hollow-cheeked, round-eyed snowy owl.

"Where have you been?" they all wanted to know.

"That I'll answer over a rum," Pilot said. "I see we've our old flag flying and a new replacement waiting. Let's put it up. A new flag for a new voyage, what do you say?"

Bosun obligingly went to the halliard and began lowering the old flag. "As you wish, although wherever it is we're going will be something less grand than a voyage. We have just the three days you suggested in your note. Where do you intend on taking us, Pilot?"

"Out," said Pilot, with a wave toward the ocean. The new flag fluttered up to the truck and gave a snap. "Are we ready to get under way?" asked Pilot. "Are you still Captain, Crew?"

"I was until you all arrived," said Crew, "but everybody's Captain in this company."

*Alembic*'s sailors brought all the lines aboard but a bow warp, at the same time setting the mizzen so that her stern drifted out; the running bight of the bow line was lengthened so the long bowsprit cleared the dock pilings as the boat came around to point into the wind. The mainsail was freed of its brails, then up the rigging ran Bosun, followed by Flags, who was notably slower. Out along the topsail yard they went, casting off the gaskets so that when the bunt and clew lines were slacked, the sail fell free, backwinding. The running bight was slipped and brought aboard, loosing *Alembic* from the shore, to make sternway.

"Jib halliards," called Bosun, coming down a backstay.

"Backwind the heads'l to starboard," said Pilot, at the helm, judging distances within the crowded anchorage. Up went the jib, down went the helm, and *Alembic* payed off the wind. Her sternway was checked, and then the ship began to move forward.

"Topsail lift," called Bosun, as Flags and Crew jumped to the fall to help hoist the yard. "Make her squeak. Now sheet home!" Edgeways to the wind, the square sail undulated. "Now braces," came the final command in the sequence. With all plain sail drawing, *Alembic* bubbled happily forward on a reach toward the old fort at the end of the seawall.

"Are the gunner's stores where they belong?" Bosun asked Crew. They were. Bosun ducked below and was soon back, loading one of the brass three-pounders with a saluting charge. As their ship cleared the harbor, the gun boomed out, startling the lone sentry on the battlements. There had been peace for eight years past, and he had been having a morning nap.

"What's our heading?" asked Bosun.

"I'll put us on a westerly course if nobody objects," said Pilot.

"The ocean's empty in that direction," observed Steward.

"Yes," said Pilot. "Open sea. We've the dust of the land to wash away." So the sails were trimmed to a westerly course, and everybody went to work coiling down the sheets and halliard falls. By the time that was done and the braces were flaked on deck, and the dock lines were properly stowed, Flags and Steward were sweat-soaked.

"Seen from the dock," panted Steward, "*Alembic* has seemed smaller and smaller to me as the years have gone by, but now she seems twice as big as I remember. I've been as long out of practice in ship handling as in cookery, I fear."

Flags agreed. "The same here. I reckon Crew's the only one of us who's still got good sea legs."

"Speak for yourself," said Bosun. "I'll still give odds to anybody here who wants to race me through the rigging, and a handicap, too. How about you, Pilot?"

Pilot smiled. "You've no takers, Bosun. I'd be no more match for you. My travels have taken me by land, not sea this time."

"To where?" Crew wanted to know.

"There's a story that will take longer than we've got for this holiday," the navigator answered, "although I'll make a start to it. But first, I want to know the news of all of you. And what of the ship you sent to Elysium, Steward–any word?"

Faithful to his promise, Steward had dispatched a vessel by the southern route. "But that was before you left yourself, and she's vanished. Posted missing." There was nothing more to be said about that, but lots of other news for Pilot. Over the course of the afternoon, they all replayed to him their lives from the time he'd left, while the sounds of the sea made musical accompaniment. *Alembic* chuckled along through the summer sea in a breeze that held all afternoon but veered north, putting the wind on their beam and the land below their horizon by suppertime.

By the time all their stories were told and discussed, the watch had changed; supper had been served and finished; and the sun was dipping into a cloudbank on the western horizon as the moon rose on the other. A watch schedule was set as of old, the square topsail was taken in, and *Alembic* was hove-to for the night. With the helm lashed, their position was secure enough to permit a continuation to their discussions below, around the lamplit galley table. Every few minutes, Bosun stuck his head above decks, just to check on things.

"To summarize everything," Flags told Pilot, "all of our lives have become . . . what word to use . . . *ordinary.* Very ordinary, compared to before. We've all seen freedom's tail-feathers, and all of us but Crew have swallowed the anchor. We each have our little dramas ongoing, but on the whole, we have become extraordinarily ordinary, as you see."

"Good," said Pilot, nodding.

"Why do you say, 'Good'?" asked Flags, who did not always see it that way.

"It's good ground. Useful for what's to follow."

"Follow?" Bosun pricked up his ears. "Have you become a seer, Pilot? Before you tell us what's to follow, let's hear your own story. It's time for that. When last seen, you were breaking up a bunch of odd-looking bottles and jugs and carrying out the glass. What came of all your secret experiments, and where did you go afterward?"

"My experiments, as you rightly call them, came neither to nothing nor not to nothing."

"In other words, your alchemy did not work?" asked Bosun.

"I've found two kinds of alchemy. The first is concerned primarily with the reactions of chemical ingredients that are manipulated in order to alter them. Nature's patterns are examined and combined according to other patterns—movements of the celestial bodies, the geometry of a squared circle, or combinations of the four elemental energies in various juxtapositions. (Actually, there are five, although most western alchemists have not known that, I find.) In any case, the search is for purification, essence, by altering physical matter."

Steward belched.

"Precisely," said Pilot. "You couldn't have put my own reaction to it more eloquently, although it took me five years in a laboratory to get to that conclusion."

"You seem to be telling us that whatever you were doing did not work," Bosun pressed. "You discovered nothing, then? No gold?"

"No physical gold, but one discovers things always," said Pilot. "A bit of chemistry and science, for instance."

"Then, science has been your reward?"

"No. It's ever astonishing, of course, but of limited usefulness in the end, always creating as much illusion as it attempts to dispel, the greatest illusion of all being that there's any salvation in it. It is ever a two-edged sword."

"But you mentioned a second kind of alchemy," Bosun reminded him.

"Indeed," said Pilot. "Even more dangerous but a lot more promising." Just as he said this, there came a rumble of thunder so distant as to be hardly audible, more felt.

"Thunder?" said Bosun, sticking his head out of the hatch for a look. "There's a summer bank of heat clouds out there somewhere, to the west, not coming this way. Proceed, Pilot. The second way?"

"In it, the principle's the same, but the base matter's the stuff of mind, beyond physics."

"Mind?"

"Yes. Which is to say magic," Pilot added.

Bosun whistled. "So you *can* do magic?"

"In the immortal words of Melquiades, you don't do magic–it does you."

"Then you're *not* a magician?" Bosun persisted.

"Not yet entirely. For that, I need the rest of me, which is all of *you*, as it turns out."

"That's what I've said from the beginning," Crew noted.

"Let's keep the conversation on course," said Bosun. "Back to your story, Pilot. So you spent your five sequestered years here cooking up something that made you break up your bottles and bury them. Last time I saw you, you'd just done that. Then, you vanished. Where to? And what did you find there?"

"My search was for nothing, as it turned out, although at the time it seemed like something. Indeed, it was–and still is, for that matter. In fact, you could say that nothing is everything, all in all." This got groans and protests from everybody around the table but Steward, who viewed Pilot with a startled look, fingering his ring.

"You're talking in tongues, Pilot," said Flags.

"Please forgive me. I did get a bit ahead of myself there," Pilot conceded. "I was discussing the final distillation. It's only glimpsed as yet, although Steward seems to have an inkling of it. I think you all do. It's only a question of recognition."

"Get on with it, man," said Bosun. "You're talking about some kind of magic, and what's that got to do with us?"

"Magic happens," Pilot allowed, with a wave of his hand. "Like gold, it's incidental to the quest but is not the goal."

"What *is* this goal?" Bosun persisted.

"Nothing," said Pilot. "For the moment, the quest *is* the goal. Or you could say it the other way 'round."

Flags threw up his hands in despair, but Bosun was caught by something. "There's some merit in what you say . . . ," he mused. "Within my own experience, I've never found a reward more rewarding than the process."

"Why don't I understand what you're talking about?" asked Flags. "Can you give us an example? What's *nothing* got to do with anything?"

"What else is left when all illusion's been peeled away?" asked Pilot. Suddenly, Flags was struck by the similarity between Dakine's view of deity and Pilot's words.

"All is mind, and there's the magic, and that's our work," Pilot added.

Bosun corrected him: "You mean *your* work."

"Yours, too, mate, whether you know it or not, but only by a final forging of our unbroken circle. It will take great balance, and there's certainly risk in it, but when have any of you been puny in the face of a worthy challenge? So it turns out our quest is far from over. It seemed finished to all of us when we returned, but here we are, hove-to, all together, ready to trim our sails on a new course. My brothers, I propose we take up our voyage again. Although our destination's no clearer than it was before, this time I've better sailing directions."

Steward spoke for all of them: "You can't be serious about this, Pilot. We've all felt nostalgia for our old times, to be sure. More often than I can remember, I've yearned to be as far away from here as I could go; to be young again; to be with all of you again, adventuring. But I'm captive now to my family and my obligations." He sighed. "So many obligations. But I've made them, and I'll stand by them. It's the same with all here." All growled agreement.

Pilot leaned forward on the table, putting his fingertips together. "Our new adventure's bigger than before, and there's room in it for whatever's in your lives. I've heard nothing from any of you that's not of good use. Since nothing's the goal and there's nowhere to go, everything's useful, including all obligations. These things I can promise you. Also, the taste of magic, the real magic. How many sailors do you reckon get to sail those waters?"

"If I hear you correctly," said Bosun, "you are proposing an allegorical voyage. That sounds manageable perhaps within our lives as they are, and safe enough, but where's the adventure in it?"

Pilot skewered them all with his look. "I warned you there are risks. If you pursue the magic, I promise you as many shoals, fogs, gales, delights, and traps as anything you've known. It's nothing to be taken lightly, and I wouldn't suggest it to anybody except yourselves. Ourselves. All together."

Steward was the first to respond. "Pilot, we've all shown a talent for putting ourselves in harm's way and then getting out of it, but none of us more than you. For better or worse, it's always been interesting, and I must say the past ten years have opened a new emptiness in me. I'm with you."

"I thought I had put adventure behind me," said Flags. "But I'll follow where you navigate, Pilot." He felt the prickle of gooseflesh as he said it.

"Me, too," Crew nodded.

"Very well," said Bosun. "Under the conditions you've described, let's continue, but you've evaded telling us what you've been up to these five years past: where have you been, and where are you taking us, Pilot?"

"I'll start now," said Pilot. "We've three days to make a beginning out here. Bosun, make your check of what's going on above, and we'll commence." Bosun poked his head up out of the scuttle. His attention was immediately taken by a flickering of distant light. He watched it for a few moments, sniffing the night wind, then rejoined the company.

"There's heat lightning in the west," he reported, "but all seems well enough. Proceed, Pilot."

Above, unseen, the whole horizon to seaward came alive with the white glow of the summer lightning, making a black silhouette of *Alembic* hove to. Thus, she hung in balance, poised, rising and falling, the golden warmth of her cabin lights making a dance of reflected patterns on the dark seas passing under her.